REAVERBANE

THE MELDERBLOOD CHRONICLES
BOOK 4

E.A. WINTERS

DRAGONLEAFPRESS

To my science teacher mom, who does not kick me out of the family when I call her up and ask questions like whether or not the information I've gathered on building a homemade bomb with medieval-accessible materials is realistic.

SOCIAL MEDIA

Connect with me on social media! [1]

- Website and newsletter: eawinters.com
- Facebook: facebook.com/eawintersnovels
- TikTok: @eawinters
- Instagram: @e.a.winters

---

1. Warning: connecting on social media may lead to exclusive content, behind the scenes snapshots, and joining a community that is way more fun than your daily to-do list. Engage with caution.

1

Market day hit like confetti made of glass shards.

Aviama reached to twist the sapphire ring on her finger, wincing as she wrenched the slender skin stretched thin around the bone instead. Her mother was dead, and the last shreds of the tender comfort she'd dared to imagine from her mother's ring had turned to ghosts. The slavers had stripped her of all but the clothes on her back, exchanging her rings for dirt stains, the memory of the queen's perfume for human excrement.

No ring, no mother, no rescuer.

Old straw in the bowels of the ship offered pungent odors but a softer cushion than the meager fresh straw the sailors had thrown on top that dug and itched its way into her skin like needles. At least the sensation reminded her that she was alive.

Beside her in the straw, Sai breathed long and deep. Sleep had been hard to come by on the voyage. In the corner on the other side of the room, one woman's labored, rattled breathing had chased any hope Aviama had of unconsciousness far away. Darkness filled their lives from sunup to sundown, with only dim pricks of light trickling in through the slats of the boards overhead. The hatch at the top of the stairs opened three times a day: twice for gruel, and once for stale bread. The light was blinding when the hatch opened, and responses among the women ranged from desperate snatching and brawling to lethargic apathy. Skeletons daring to desire life. Fish in a barrel, mouths opened wide for the hope of a morsel, pushing and shoving to be the lucky one to score the largest piece of bread—or any bread at all, if the big fish had it their way.

And they often did.

Across from her, Durga slept too, curled into a ball at the base of the stairs where she'd staked out a prime position for the next bread toss. Silhouettes of fifty other women packed like sardines into the hull of *Raisa's Revenge,* the slave ship the dirty scoundrel Onkar Dhoka had sold them to after surviving Ghosts' Gorge. Most of the women were either in the throes of fitful sleep or occupied by staring listlessly into the nothingness of their cramped confinement. As for the men—Chenzira, Umed, and Manan—Aviama hadn't seen them since the day they'd been captured.

She didn't know how long it had been. Aviama had tried to keep count of the days at first, but as days turned into weeks, and weeks may or may not have turned into months, she lost track. Her fingers ran along the dirty material of her trousers, where the hidden pocket concealed a little whittled wooden moth and a scrap of paper. She pursed her lips, glanced up at the half-conscious women around her, and shifted her position against the hull of the ship. Someone's head lolled over her stretched-out ankle. Aviama's leg had long since fallen asleep, and the movement as she shifted sent needle-like tingling up and down the limb.

Based on the calls of the sailors earlier, it was morning, but bread wasn't the only thing seeping down to them in leftover scraps. The sun fell on the ship four decks up, but not in the cargo deck. Only rats and refuse lived down here. Aviama figured that in Captain Abasi's eyes, she now belonged to the latter category.

Why had Onkar sold them to Abasi? Did he really get that much extra cash from the trade? Was he that heartless, to take her money, break their deal, and then sell her for more and wash his hands of her fate?

Something didn't add up. Onkar might be a slippery swindler and a shrewd businessman, but neither explained the cryptic note in her pocket. She dug it out, unfolded the slip of parchment, and squinted down at it, tilting it against the dim light.

> *When the time is right, be Raisa.*
> *—GF*

Aviama pursed her lips. If Chenzira was right, and he seemed to be, then Onkar Dhoka's real initials were GF. Onkar had gotten a fistful of Aviama's braid and yanked her near him for the handoff to Abasi, the captain of the slave ship. He absolutely could have slipped the note into her pocket without her noticing. He was a thief.

But why should she care about the instructions of a traitorous thief? And even if she did care, what did it mean to *be* Raisa? Raisa was a historical figure, a melderblood from the time of The Crumbling—one of the four melders responsible for the death of magic six hundred years ago. Or supposed death, since it returned three years ago, reappearing in long-dormant bloodlines. Was she supposed to end magic? Or was it a play on the name of the ship, *Raisa's Revenge*?

Heavy boots ran across the planks overhead, raining dirt

down through the cracks from the sailors' berth. Aviama snapped her head up—and stared straight into Durga's flint expression. Her eyes had always been as hard and sharp as her nose, and even the masked humility in the pretense of her role as Aviama's maidservant had fallen away pretty quickly, as it became clearer that the girl was little more than the queen's lackey. And when opportunity arose to align herself with a stronger authority, Durga abandoned the queen in favor of Prince Shiva.

It was only a matter of time before Durga found a new master to serve. And when she did, she'd sell secrets for a pretty penny. Durga knew Chenzira was really the outcast runaway prince of Keket, missing for four years. She knew Aviama was princess of Jannemar. She knew their entire party were melders, and which elemental powers they possessed.

To her credit, Durga hadn't been stupid enough to reveal their power as windcallers to the slavers. Yet.

Based on Onkar's warning, which Chenzira had confirmed, nothing would land a knife across their throats faster than disclosing their abilities. And without any idea where they were in the ocean, or how far from land, it would be impossible to procure both food and protection for as long as they'd need them without being slaughtered in their sleep on the way.

That's one thing Onkar's cryptic note was right about. The timing had to be right.

Particles of caked mud landed on Sai's face, and she flinched. Aviama ripped her gaze from Durga's unblinking glare and brushed the dirt from Sai's face as she stirred. Aviama turned her back to Durga, pretending to fuss over the straw stuck in Sai's matted hair.

Aviama crinkled the tiny paper into a ball, placed it in her mouth, and choked it down her dry throat. The message was weird enough to remember, and whatever it meant, she probably shouldn't be caught carrying it. Especially not with Durga around.

Shouts rang out from the decks above, and the shells of women in the cramped space shifted and groaned in response. Durga tensed, feet underneath her, hands taut on the floor, as she glanced up the staircase toward the hatch. The sight of her languid figure, alert and on edge, reminded Aviama of a cat. But was she expecting to evade a predator or pounce on a mouse?

Durga's powers were strong, if uncontrolled and chaotic. Aviama had the rare advantage of formal training in her powers by the only remaining expert in tabeun abilities, but even so, Durga remained a worthy adversary.

The hatch at the top of the stairs opened, and light poured down into the filth of the women's cell. Aviama blanched, holding a hand up against the light as a heavyset sailor clunked his way down the steps. The wood creaked under his weight. He scrunched up his nose in disgust.

"Everyone out. It's time to clean up."

Aviama's empty stomach dropped to her toes as she scrambled to her feet. This was it. The day everything would change.

Was Chenzira already on the upper deck, waiting for her? Should she blast everyone backward with her windcalling abilities the moment they reached land or look for opportunities with fewer people around? She didn't have eyes on the back of her head, and knives and arrows could still take her down if she wasn't on her game.

Aviama pulled Sai to her feet and reached for another young girl beside her. The girl was younger than Aviama, maybe only sixteen, with dark-brown eyes that swam with the weight of the world. A child between the ages of two and three gripped the girl's tunic at the shoulder, stuffing her own fist in her mouth. She hadn't seen any other children on the ship, and though she'd seen this little girl on the voyage, she'd made no sound since Aviama first boarded. Aviama tried to wrangle up an encouraging smile, but she was pretty sure it looked more like a sickly grimace.

"Hurry up! What's wrong with you?"

Aviama whirled toward the sailor, a biting retort burning in her throat, but the sailor wasn't looking at her. He was looking past Durga to two women huddled in the straw in the corner. One had streaked gray hair and wrinkles across a drawn face, eyes still closed. The other's facial features showed what the older woman must have looked like thirty years prior.

Aviama recognized her as Teja. She'd said she was from Radha, and that Radha had sold some of their own to displace people in the north who'd been involved in riots. The younger woman shook the older gently. "Please, we have to go. Get up."

The sailor wrinkled his nose again as he descended three more steps down into the refuse pit of the women's room. "Get her up. Captain said he wants you on deck *now*. I won't ask again."

Teja held up an apologetic hand. "She's been sick. She just needs a moment, please." Teja shook her mother hard, then pulled on her arm. No response.

Aviama glanced down at the older woman's hands. Her nail beds and fingertips were gray enough to match her hair. She slumped awkwardly against the hull of the ship. Aviama's heart stopped. How long had it been since she'd heard the rattled breathing in the corner? She hadn't noticed it stop. But now that she thought about it, it had been several minutes since she'd last heard it.

The sailor shook his head and stomped the rest of the way down, shoving through the women to get to the pair in the corner. He reached for the curved sword at his belt, the sickle-like weapon the other women had called a khopesh. Aviama's heart lurched to her throat. She shoved forward through the women, but they were already shoulder to shoulder. She could barely move.

The man gripped the handle of his khopesh and lifted it over his head. Teja screamed and threw herself over her mother's body.

"Stop!"

Aviama surged forward through the bodies of breathing, staring corpses. Statues, every one of them—not a single one lifting a finger to intervene.

Four more rows of people stood between her and the sailor as the khopesh swung. Aviama thrust her palm forward, hidden by the bodies of the women. Wind whisked down through the hatch to respond to her summons, a current of air in a long snake-like tendril wrapping around his foot and tugging sideways. Durga dove between the man and the mother-daughter pair in the corner, hands up toward the sailor's face in defense.

The sailor stumbled as Aviama's air current caught his foot, and the blade jerked midair, nicking Durga's ear and embedding in the hull of the ship. The man cursed, ripped the blade free, and struck Durga across the face. She fell back, but her eyes burned with blazing fire. Durga lifted her chin and leveled the sailor with a cool stare, looking down her sharp nose at him as if he were a petulant child and she the authority between them.

"She's coming. Start with the others."

The sailor's lip curled. His knuckles whitened on the handle of his blade, but he dipped his head. "See that she does. That was a warning. I won't miss twice."

Yes, you totally missed on purpose. What a dramatic intimidation gesture.

Durga's jaw clenched, but to her credit, she said nothing.

The sailor started to turn away, then spun back to examine the older woman. He pursed his lips. "I'll send someone to deal with the body. Don't try to bring her. It'll only slow us down. Anyone who stays behind with the dead will be buried with her."

The hairs on the back of Aviama's neck stood on end at the callous cruelty of his tone. The woman's mother had just died. But then, what would a slaver care about that? If she was that close to death, she wouldn't have achieved a good price ...

The sailor seized another woman by the elbow and threw her toward the stairs. "Up! Now!"

The women dutifully shuffled toward the stairs. Aviama steeled herself to move forward. She exchanged a glance with Sai. *Did that just happen?* But the older woman was already dead. What could they do now?

Straw snapped underfoot. Grimy hands slid along the rough wood of the ship's side for stability. Above deck, running feet and shouting men docked the ship. Below, only shallow breathing and the soft sobs of a bereaved daughter interrupted their progress toward the stairs.

Durga took Teja by the elbow and pulled her up. Aviama pushed to Teja's side and took her other elbow, pulling her along between them. She cast a glance backward to check on the teenager with the toddler. The toddler's dirt-caked fingernails still curled into her mother's garment. She blinked back at Aviama, but made no sound, no sign of outward distress.

No joy, no sorrow. Only flat, empty acceptance of a pallid existence.

How long had these women been on the ship before

Raisa's Revenge met them on the opposite end of Ghosts' Gorge?

Sai put a hand on the teenager's shoulder and guided her up the steps behind Aviama and Durga. Teja leaned heavily on Aviama and Durga's arms, weeping bitterly.

Durga's face was set. She glared up at the sailor at the top of the stairs and hissed under her breath to Aviama. "When are you going to stop pretending to be a nobody and *do* something?"

Aviama swallowed. "When we find Chenzira and the others and aren't on a ship. And when I find my horn."

"Don't waste time on trinkets. We've got to get out of here."

"It's not a trinket. We might need it."

Makana, the siren Aviama had befriended, along with her father, the chieftain of the Iolani, had given the battle horn to Aviama as a gift. They'd said it could be heard from far away, and if she blew it, help would come. She hadn't even had it a single night before Onkar sold her to Abasi, and Abasi took it.

Aviama bit her lip. She was far from home, and Radha still planned on destroying Jannemar. Her family, specifically. The few that were left. And the sea was the fastest way to get from Keket to Jannemar.

Women pressed around her on every side. Sailors busied themselves with this or that, striding from one end of the ship to the other. But as Aviama reached the upper deck, she saw they'd already docked. The ship rocked, but only as it always did in the water. The lines were already secured, *Raisa's Revenge* resting from her voyage at last.

The wharf spread out before them, alive with activity. The *Revenge* was the largest vessel in the harbor, towering over a few smaller ships and a litany of skiffs and fishing boats. A whitewashed fortress stood sentry close to the shore, cannons protruding from lookout points along its walls. Beyond it, adobe buildings lined the shore and filled the island as far as the eye could see, broken up by modest courtyards, wheat and barley fields, dirt roads, and a small river weaving through them all.

Morning light sparkled across crystal-blue waters, washing up on pearl-white beaches. Tamarisk and acacia trees dotted the land, interrupting the warm sandy neutrals of wheat and dust. The people themselves seemed uniform, all draped in some form of white as they made their way to work or to market. Were some of them headed to the same market Abasi was taking them to?

Aviama tried to imagine a father kissing his wife and children goodbye for the day and thinking through a to-do list: go to that business meeting, buy materials to fix the leaky roof, assess a possible real estate purchase, and buy a human person. The usual. She shuddered.

Abasi rapped his knuckles on the railing, calling her attention back to the ship. Aviama's gut wrenched. The Iolani battle horn glittered at his belt. He jerked his head to Masud, his slave driver. Masud spoke to the sailors in a language Aviama did not know, and the men began to tie the wrists of each of the fifty women and loop them through one long rope connecting them all together.

Durga leaned in to Aviama. "Now?"

Aviama swallowed. "I don't see Chenzira. Or Umed or Manan. Where are they?"

Sai pressed closer to hear their conversation. "Maybe they're still below deck. We'll be sold at the same market, won't we?"

Aviama's mouth went dry. What if … no, she couldn't think it. But the more she thought about it, a burning set into her chest until the words spilled out. "What if they've already been sold?"

Sai pursed her lips and shook her head. "It's morning. We just arrived."

"Yes, but it's not early morning." Durga squinted up at the sun as it climbed higher and higher into the eastern sky. "It's closer to mid-morning. They had time to take the men off the ship. Maybe they used the separation to threaten the men into submission. Maybe several of them were taken captive with wives or other relatives they care about."

Mid-morning might have been an exaggeration, but if the men had been removed in the gray hazy hours before sunrise, they could have been gone for a couple of hours by now. Unless they were still in cargo, and Abasi planned to keep them there until the women were safely removed.

A shadow fell across the women, and Aviama looked up into the face of a tall, muscular sailor with the expression she imagined a person would have if they never ate breakfast, suffered from severe indigestion, and mutilated baby animals in their spare time. She offered him a halfhearted smile as he seized her wrists and secured them in such a way that he must have expected they'd float away without a hundred pounds of force crushing them together. *Biscuits*, what a face.

Aviama took a deep breath. "Where are the men?"

Masud glowered down at her and threaded the long rope through her wrists. He said nothing, his brief eye contact serving as the only indication he'd heard her. The line began to move, and the other women's weight pulled Aviama's hands forward as they went.

Her chest caved in as she stumbled after the women, Teja pulled along behind her as Masud moved on to add Durga and Sai to the line. Knots tightened her stomach as the first of the women up ahead stepped off the *Revenge* onto dry land.

How was she supposed to be Raisa? Why had Chenzira told her not to let anyone know who she was or what she could do? And if she chose to ignore him, how could she use her windcalling without hitting the wrong person, with her hands tied and yanked in every direction as they walked?

A new thought hit her, and her mouth went dry. Was Abasi's crew melderblood? What would they do if they found out *she* was melderblood before Chenzira even knew where she was?

Aviama cleared her throat and tried again. "Where are the men?"

The corner of Masud's mouth twitched.

"Ladies first."

2

Aviama had longed for market day. Just to do something *different*. To have the opportunity to escape this forsaken vessel. But as much as she'd longed for it, she'd also dreaded it, because her nightmares of what-ifs could come true. Until now, she had semi-successfully sequestered the swirling dark thoughts away to the nights, reminding herself they weren't real.

Yet.

But now, as aquamarine greens and blues kissed white-sand beaches, clear water lulling the ship and washing up in a consistent rhythm on the shore, every midnight nightmare flooded back to haunt her. The quiet of the morning, the bustle of normalcy on the island—it was all a ruse.

Aviama shuffled after the other women, eyeing the Iolani battle horn at Abasi's side as she passed. Makana's horn. *Her* horn.

A testament that sirens and humans could coexist and even be friends. She was going to need as many of those as she could get.

The women ahead in the line disembarked, pulling each

other over as this one or that one lost their balance. Aviama's feet hit the wood planks of the dock, and her knees nearly buckled at the strange stillness of land. She shot a burst of air from her palms on instinct to push her back upright, and Durga gripped her elbow to steady her. Sai sucked in a breath as Teja's eyes widened. The poor girl's jaw dropped.

Aviama grimaced. Now would be a great time to know why Chenzira hadn't wanted anyone to know she was melderblood. Did he mean *anyone,* or only the slave drivers? Would it drive up her price, or make her a liability to dispatch? And if she wasn't supposed to let anyone know she was melderblood, what did Onkar's note mean—to be Raisa?

Masud leaped over the rail to the dock as the last of the fifty women in line made it off the ship. The man brushed past them to the head of the line, and two dozen armed men fell in around them. Aviama scanned the dock. If Abasi had crest-breakers, any move by the water could be a bad call. But with an island this size, where could they run?

Raisa's Revenge towered over the rest of the ships in the harbor. Three men in white tunics looked up from their work on the skiff opposite the *Revenge.* One drank in the sight of the women, letting an ogling gaze linger on each one. His eyes landed on Aviama, and he licked his lips. Her skin crawled like a thousand spiders had been let loose in her tunic, but she snapped her head forward and took one step at a time down the dock and away from him. Next to the skiff, a pair of fish-ermen sorted their catch, too focused on their work to care about the destroyed lives passing by—the human beings reduced to property for profit.

Masud led the women off the deck, onto the sand, and down to the water where another group of fishermen repaired nets and separated fish. He reached into his waistband and tossed a few bars of soap at the women, then jerked his head toward the water.

"Clean up. You'll not fetch a good price smelling like latrine rats."

Aviama's bare feet squished in the sand as the women shuffled to the water, the cool of the crystal water a balm to her feet. A hermit crab scuttled out of the way of her toes, its sunset-orange and buttercup-yellow shell contrasted with a scallop shell splashed with rings of lavender deepening in shade with each layer.

Lavender. Lilac. Shiva.

Aviama's chest tightened. She stared at the purple shell, her throat constricting. The girl in front of her tugged forward, pulling her along. Aviama crushed the purple shell with her heel as she went, shoving it deep down into the sand.

Is that what she'd done to Shiva, when she'd blasted him over the railing of the *Wraithweaver* and left him at the mercy of the Iolani? She'd left him to his death, or worse. Radha had imprisoned Makana in the menagerie for years. What would they do to him in return?

She could feel the memories before they hit, like the moment before an inevitable yawn takes over the body. Suddenly, Shiva was there, lifting her hand to his lips when they'd first met. The eyes she'd wished would be only for her. The ridiculous song she'd written for him, and sang only to herself, after she found him twined in Marija's arms before she'd learned the truth.

How naïve she'd been. How stupid. And then his eyes *were* only for her. Controlling her, smothering her, threatening her. His arms at her waist, his mouth crushing hers. *Convince me ...*

Aviama shuddered as the words came back to her.

If you do not convince me that I am your greatest dream, that

*you are obsessively, head over heels in love with me ... I'll kill one of
the women attending you.*

His love had been a lie, but his threats never were. Bhumi's
head landed on a platter, just like he promised, on the
Wraithweaver.

Again she saw him, plucking a lilac sprig from the bush
and tucking it behind her ear with as much care as if she'd
been made of porcelain. What had he said, at the end, in
Ghosts' Gorge?

*Am I so evil? To not want to be used, to not want to be someone
else's pawn? To create a future for my kingdom?*

He'd been a victim, too, hadn't he? Used by his parents, by
the court, by opposing kingdoms. Radha had fallen prey to the
lure of tabeun magic before, and it had led to The Crumbling
all those years ago. Maybe he really believed he had to do
whatever it took to stop melderbloods from destroying his
homeland once again.

But wasn't he responsible for his actions too? Wasn't it
right that justice finally rain down on his cocky head?
Wouldn't he have killed them all if she'd left him on the ship?
Wouldn't he—

"Aviama!"

She snapped her head up just in time to get a mouthful of
ocean as Durga splashed her with icy water. Aviama gasped as
the cold water doused her tunic, and it clung to her skin.
Beyond Durga, Masud was glaring at her with the same indi-
gestion-afflicted look he'd worn before.

"Stop stewing. You're going to get us killed."

Aviama spit out the salt water and nodded. "Right, okay.
Sorry."

Durga rolled her eyes. "Don't be sorry. Be smart. You'll
have plenty of time to sulk when you're dead."

Sai ran a hand through her wet hair and eyed the armed

men watching from every side. "This is the worst place to make a scene."

Aviama coughed up the rest of the water she'd choked on when Durga splashed her, and she followed suit of the other women. She took the soap bar from Durga and let the clear water wash away the grime—and smell—of their long voyage. The salt still burned her throat as she ran the soap along her skin and rinsed it off in the sea.

Burn. Burning.

Shiva had sworn that every Shamaran would burn. How long had they traveled? Had Radha already invaded Jannemar? Had anyone survived? If they'd taken the Horon Mines, had they already formed the wyronite into housing artifacts for tabeun powers?

Splashhh.

Aviama coughed and sputtered at the second onslaught, and this time sent a cascading wall of water back at Durga. "All right, all right!"

Durga glared at her and arched an eyebrow. *Get your head on straight, Aviama.*

Masud waded into the water toward Aviama, Teja, Durga, and Sai at the back of the line, his khopesh raised in his hand. "That's enough! Let's go!"

Teja cleared her throat. "Who are you people?" Her hushed voice wavered as she looked from Aviama to Durga to Sai.

"No one of consequence."

"Who talks like that?"

Aviama pursed her lips. Durga smirked. Sai groaned.

But as much as Aviama hated to admit it, Durga was right. It was time to think about the here and now. It was time to consider when to be a chameleon ... and when to be Raisa.

Masud seized Aviama by the arm and shoved her toward

the sand. She resisted the urge to knock him flat on his back with a wall of wind, but twisted to check on Sai at the back as the line between their hands went taut and yanked them out of the shallows and up onto the beach.

Sai slipped once, and Durga caught her elbow. Masud strode up ahead but glanced back at them no less than four times in the next sixty seconds. He tapped two guards on the shoulder and jerked his head toward the rear of the line, and they wordlessly moved to obey his command.

Aviama caught Sai and Durga's gaze and lifted her chin to indicate the additional guards coming toward the rear. "We've gotten Masud's special attention. Keep your heads down. Follow my lead."

Sai dropped her head down and stared at her feet, dejected and hopeless as any of the rest. "Plan?"

Aviama dipped her head as the guards passed. "Maybe."

Teja's face paled. Twice she opened her mouth as if to speak, but then thought better of it and clamped it shut. Up ahead, the baby in the arms of the young mother blinked back at Aviama, eyes round but apathetic. The hollow shells of defeated women moved step after step from one nightmare to the next.

A fresh round of shouts rocked the air with some new commotion from the docks. Aviama tilted her head sideways, letting her wet hair hang like a curtain in front of her bowed head, casting a sideways glance back toward *Raisa's Revenge.* Her heart pinched, and a yawning chasm opened in her chest.

Chenzira.

His beard was longer than she remembered, and scruffy, not the perfectly manicured features she was used to. His tunic was several shades darker than she remembered it, but she imagined her own clothes had taken on quite a few layers of grime over the weeks or months of travel they'd endured.

Abasi struck him across the face, and he spun against the railing—harder, she thought, than the blow would have required.

In the space of that moment, Chenzira's gaze locked onto hers, and the breath left her body. He gripped the railing with one hand but dropped the other out of view. The sands beneath her feet shifted. She stumbled, and the sand itself locked around her ankles and propelled her forward before releasing her in an upright position on the beach. The last of the ocean's reaching waves washed the sand from her toes as she left the water behind.

Aviama reached up and pulled her long blonde tresses away from her face, angling her palm just so as she did. Wind whipped about her face, blowing her hair back behind her as a long tendril of air current flew from her hand and up over the expanse of sand and across the dock, ruffling Chenzira's hair in a gentle whisper.

She could almost feel him smile at their silent exchange.

Tally.

The guard quickened his pace and rapped Aviama on the shoulder with the end of his khopesh. "Get moving. We've got a long walk."

Aviama nodded and shuffled forward, head still down, shoulders slightly slumped, the picture of acquiescence. Warmth flooded her chest just as a volcano of molten lava threatened to break her apart from the inside. Chenzira was safe.

Well, maybe not safe. But alive. And he knew where she was, and she knew where he was, even though neither could reach the other.

What would Abasi do if he knew he'd imprisoned his prince and planned to sell him like cattle to the highest bidder? What would the royal family of Keket do? Abasi should fear for his life! He should beg for forgiveness before showering them with riches and bribes, the last-ditch effort of a dying man to incur the favor of the son of the king.

How well do you know him?

The thought caught her off guard. An utterly ridiculous question. She knew him plenty well. He was the man who'd teased her when she was lost in the House of the Blessing Sun —that horrific palace with more curses than blessings, more darkness than sun. He was the light of hope pouring into the gloom, the promise of survival, the strength she needed when her own had failed.

I won't let you marry him.

Chenzira had seen her when no one else did, had cared about *her* rather than an agenda.

I will find you.

His words had carried her through more than one pit of darkest black, when her soul was crushed on all sides by a weight yet unknown to her nineteen years of life. Or was it twenty? Had her birthday passed?

Yet she'd also met him when they both broke into King Dahnuk's private study. He was a spy, a thief. He'd run from home and embroiled himself with criminals like Darsh and swindlers like Onkar Dhoka.

Was he really the sort of man she could rely on? Why would Chenzira's family betray him? Why would he not be safe in his own country?

White sands shifted into dusty roads as Masud directed the line of fifty female products—that's all they were, wasn't it? —out of sight of the docks and away from the men. Aquamarine blue shone at the horizon against the adobe houses, light sands, and white-draped people, deepening to a pure azure blue as the cloudless sky stretched over them.

What if Chenzira's family wanted him killed, and that's

why he had to leave Keket? Or what if they were waiting to accept him back home with open arms, and once he made it home, he wouldn't need her anymore?

How many men had she seen corrupted by power? Azi, her uncle, had died by it. The entire monarchy of Belvidore had been crushed in the name of ambition. Even her sister had almost succumbed to its allure.

What if Chenzira came to power and became just like Shiva? Power made good men evil, but without power, Chenzira would have no means of defense against those already twisted by its grip.

Aviama shook her head to clear it and shoved one foot in front of the other. The women in front of her kicked up dust on her feet and ankles, as her own bare feet passed on the experience to Teja behind her, and Durga and Sai behind her.

Without Chenzira, Aviama would be dead. And without Aviama, Chenzira would be dead. The two of them took care of each other. It was as simple as that.

But as the cavernous emptiness in her chest deepened, the sun beating down on her, every step carrying her further from Chenzira and closer to a market where she'd be sold to who knows who and separated from the few people she had left, her stomach dropped like a sack of rotten tomatoes. What if it wasn't enough?

A small lump in the hidden compartment of her waistband bumped against her arm as she walked, reminding her of the second part of Onkar Dhoka's parting gift. Along with the note to be Raisa, he'd included a little wooden carving of a moth wielding a sword. From the weak, something mighty. From the invisible, something unexpected.

She could only pray that when the time came, she would know what it meant to be Raisa.

3

Grit and sand caked Aviama's feet and ankles. The sun was hot against her back, drying her wet clothes and hair. The rope around her wrists chaffed. She could already see red marks forming at the edges where the coarse chords shifted along her skin.

Tamarisk and acacia trees interrupted the landscape at intervals as they passed modest homes, courtyards, and wheat and barley fields. But the further they walked, the taller everything got, from the land itself rising upward, to stately trees prouder of the island's center than its outskirts, and white-washed houses taller, grander, and brighter than any along its fringes.

At their shuffling pace, it had taken them an hour or so to reach the stretch of road they now walked. Dirt and dust still reigned supreme as the island's primary street construction, though intricate seashell mosaic designs did line the way from the road to the finest houses.

Aviama's back ached from sleeping in ninety-seven horrible positions between hard wood and scratchy straw night after night. Her legs burned and her stomach grumbled.

Wouldn't they be worth more well fed and less sour-faced? Maybe she should mention it to Masud. His business acumen could use some improvement. But so could his people skills, and she was not about to make him hate her more than he already did.

A swirl of seashells cut across the road and zigzagged back and forth along it, the dirt transitioning into a packed-down terracotta. Aviama followed the pattern, more and more seashells gathering toward the white alabaster statue of a woman towering four meters high over a public square. Men and women alike parted to allow them passage, cheering and leering at them as they passed. An older man reached out and pinched her arm. She flinched away from him, his cackling laugh filling her ears as he moved on to reach out for Sai.

Small children giggled and chased each other around the statue, its base shimmering in rings of mother-of-pearl. The stone-faced woman looked down on them, stern and unmoved by their joviality in the face of the thriving slave trade being celebrated under her nose. In one arm she clutched a book, inscribed with letters Aviama could not read, and with the other she extended her palm outward. A puff of curling, swirling air flew from her hand into an oval shield before her, both the shield and the air made of glass or crystal, twinkling in the sun.

Aviama gaped up at her. She was a windcaller. Could it be Raisa, one of the four infamous melderbloods who had brought an end to magic six hundred years ago? Was Onkar somehow hinting about this statue in his note—would she need a shield of her own?

Masud swung his thick arm through the crowds, pushing them back to make way as he angled toward a wide wooden platform stretching the length of the square on one end. A buxom woman half-falling out of her white-linen dress crushed three bystanders to weasel her way close enough to grip and feel the bony arms of two of the bound women as they were paraded by.

One of the guards smacked her hand away and let out a string of words in a foreign language Aviama did not recognize.

Teja translated under her breath. "You touch it, you buy it, he says. Hands off the merchandise."

Aviama winced at the phrasing. "You speak Keket?"

"Keketi. Yes."

Masud led the women up the stairs of the platform and strode to the center. He spread his hands and cracked a smile Aviama would not have believed he was capable of if she hadn't seen it with her own eyes.

One of the guards worked his way down the women, working them free of the long rope connecting them all, but leaving their wrists tied. Durga and Sai huddled close to Teja and Aviama at the back of the group as Teja translated Masud's speech in hushed tones.

"Has Captain Abasi ever failed you?"

Laughter, cheers. Masud clapped his hands together and rubbed them back and forth as if he had the juiciest of tales to tell.

"We bring you only the best of the best, and this time is no exception! Many of you have waited months for this day. And now, at last, it has arrived!"

Whoops and hollers from the crowd. One man pointed a long finger at the women and raised his voice. Teja cleared her throat. "He says the shipment is smaller than usual. He has a business to run, and he hopes there are more men coming than the meager supply of women."

Masud wagged a finger, his crooked grin widening. "Not so! We always bring the same quality! In the past, we've made up for standard quality by higher quantity, but today, we bring you premium stock. Each is worth twice as much as last year's haul, but for you, we offer only the best prices."

Bile shot up the back of Aviama's throat, burning at the back of her mouth. The emptiness inside her stretched wider, but as it did, the volcano in her chest raged hotter and hotter to fill it. A blaze set inside her bones as her gaze swept over the faces of eager buyers. Some were skeptical of Masud's sales pitch. Others were already examining the merchandise, hunger in their eyes.

What did they need slave labor for? Household duties? Working the fields?

A stout older man with a scar across his nose raked his gaze over her body, head to toe. He grinned as he took in every curve, exposing two missing teeth. Aviama's lip curled before she could stop it, and she stepped back into the safety of the crowd, dipping behind a taller woman on the platform to shield herself from the man's ogling. A chill ran down her spine. Maybe menial labor wasn't all the people of the island wanted women for.

She glanced up at the statue again. *When the time is right, be Raisa.*

Biscuits. The time was only ripening with every passing moment. Aviama curled her hands into fists. If she focused and used both hands in the same direction, she could use her melder powers while bound. Just as she had sent the curl of wind toward Chenzira on the ship. But could she fight off a mob when they were an hour from the water, had no shoes, money, or resources, and no horse or boat?

Teja was still translating, though Aviama had forgotten to listen until now. A man handed Masud a stack of wooden signs with rope around them and beckoned to the first woman. She stepped forward, eyes blank and listless, and

Masud stood her on a raised block and looped the sign over her head so that the wood rested against her chest. He waggled a writing utensil between his fingers.

"The men are on their way, but as is our custom, we'll start with the ladies. Here, we have noted the minimum starting bid. Who sees something they like? Who wants an easier life, starting today?"

Aviama clenched her fists tighter, her knuckles whitening as her nails dug into her palms. This was wrong. And she was going to end it.

How could she free herself and doom all the others to slavery? If she got away—*when* she got away—she'd bring down the whole establishment. But she had to wait for Chenzira.

Her gaze went again to the statue, then dropped toward its pearly base. A man leaned against the statue there, but he didn't fit in with the crowd of white-and-sandy neutral clothing. He didn't haggle or crane his neck. He only stared. At her.

Dark eyes rimmed with kohl pierced her through from beneath the rim of a black hat with a red feather wisping in the breeze. The man's face was tanned by many days in the sun, his dark jacket faded at the shoulders. Gold glittered at his ears and on his fingers, and a loose white tunic exposed the curve of his well-muscled chest.

Aviama snapped her head back to Masud, pretending to understand or care what he was saying. Why had the man looked at her like that? Why was he dressed differently? What did he want?

She tried to keep her eyes fixed forward but couldn't help but chance a glance back toward the statue a moment later. Was he still staring? Would he make a bid for her? Had she done something out of the ordinary that he looked at her neither with hunger nor curiosity, but with suspicion?

But he was gone. Feather and all, though she searched the square, there was no sign of the man in the dark hat.

Woman after woman was sold. Aviama's gut wrenched. She glanced toward the back of the square in the direction of the docks. Where were the men? What if the women were all sold by the time Chenzira, Manan, and Umed came?

Masud pulled another woman out of their ranks and set her on the raised block. Another wooden sign around another neck, to write another agreed-upon price for another buyer. Shouts, haggling, bid after bid—and then it was over, and the woman was shuffled off to the side as the next product was put on display.

A gentle breeze wafted through the air, playing with the ends of her hair. Aviama shifted her weight. She stuck out too much with her blonde hair and light eyes. The women from Radha, Keket, and surrounding areas all had darker hair, rich, deep eyes, and naturally sun-kissed skin in a range of beautiful shades from almond to bronze to acacia. She imagined her own would soon look more lobster than anything else, and theirs would remain as intended.

But the difference made her a sore thumb. And today, being unique was not an advantage. How could she hide from peering eyes, or sneak windcalling, or do anything surreptitious with the constant attention of the crowd?

The time for being a chameleon was nearing its end. Not because she was unwilling, but because it was getting more and more impossible to blend in. And because there was no way Aviama was going to let Sai and Teja get sold and separated without doing something about it.

Biscuits, even Durga. And the teenager with the baby. The doe-eyed girl standing on the block now, tremors of terror rocking her body. How could she abandon them?

Aviama balanced on one foot to scratch at her ankle with

the other, where coarse, crusted sand agitated her skin. How long should she wait for the men?

It no longer mattered that Onkar and even Chenzira had warned her against showing her powers. She didn't have to tell everyone she was Princess Aviama of Jannemar. Her identity could stay hidden. But melderbloods were cropping up everywhere, and it was time to show this insane island just what she was made of.

What if they're all melders?

The thought infiltrated her mind like a missile crashing through a barrier. She grimaced, then clenched her jaw. She'd just have to take that chance.

If not now, then when?

She glanced up at the current sale. Masud grinned at a new buyer and marked the wooden sign around the woman's neck. *Sold.* One of Masud's men shuffled the woman off to the side, and Masud picked out a new victim for the block—the girl with the baby.

The little girl locked eyes with Aviama, and in the space of that moment, the expanse within Aviama's chest imploded. Where once there was a chasm, a dam broke. Searing, boiling water whistled through the barrier and filled her body with liquid flame.

That girl wasn't going anywhere.

Aviama stared at her feet and willed the wind to come to her. Slow and steady. Soft and sure. The breeze wafting through her hair halted its course at her command, spinning in the other direction in a sharp current change back to Aviama.

Durga stiffened. Teja whimpered. Sai straightened.

Power tasted sweet.

Aviama looked up. A young boy flashed a mischievous grin at her from the fringes of the crowd. A flame danced on the edge of one fingertip. She tilted her head as she examined him, when another sight caught the corner of her eye.

Across the square, beyond the statue, Abasi led a line of men with their arms bound behind their backs. Abasi offered a nauseating smile to the crowd as he moved, his guards pressing the people back from the parade of human wares. His attire was jasmine-white, though of higher quality than the rest of the islanders. He strode in with the confidence of a king, waving like a conqueror on the crest of his latest victory. The sun glinted off the gold on his forearms and the gem-studded collar upon his bare chest as he turned this way and that to take in the adoring crowd.

And there, looped through Abasi's belt and nestled against his hip, was Aviama's battle horn. There could be no mistaking it. She'd never seen anything like the gift the Iolani had given her—a large conch shell expertly carved in patterns of shells and waves, with two Iolani depicted protecting sea life. Rubies glittered all along its edges, and the carved figures shimmered with mother-of-pearl.

Abasi turned to the side, leading the men around the perimeter of the square toward the platform. The line of men wound behind him, prodded along by Abasi's goons. Aviama's heart stopped, the gathering wind swirling in impatient eddies around her hands, pressing in around her as it begged to be set free.

Chenzira led the procession, arms tied behind him, threadbare tunic doing little to hide the lines of his muscled chest. His sleeves were rolled to the elbow, and a brazen woman from the crowd reached out to touch the cords of his forearms. He ignored her, eyes locked on Aviama as he walked.

Her lips parted. Her chest tightened. He was safe. He was here.

She'd dreamed of little else than seeing him again. Her nightmares had been filled with images of Jannemar ablaze, Shamaran Castle burning, dead dragons, and the decapitated heads of all her loved ones delivered to her door one after the other. But her *dreams*—her dreams of light, when she'd dared to have them, had been of Chenzira.

What if they were different together when they were free? What if they escaped, and his view of her changed when they had time alone together? What if they'd only seen each other through honeyed crystal, and landing in Keket would knock the crystal askew—

"Laqad bat!"

Masud pumped his fist in the air and pointed at a tall, gangly shrew of a woman with beaded hair, twice as much kohl around her eyes as any other woman in the crowd, and a sharp gaze that looked as if it could cut glass.

Aviama leaned in toward Teja. "What did he say?"

"Sold." Teja shifted her weight. "They've agreed upon a price. He's said it after every sale."

Masud seized the young girl by the arm as she clutched the child tight against her chest, pulled her off the platform, and shoved her into the arms of a guard on the far side. The shrew gave a winsome grin that sent bile up the back of Aviama's throat and edged her way to the edge of the crowd to collect.

Fewer women stood to the side than Aviama remembered. Her gut wrenched. Not all the buyers were staying to see all the slaves. They took their latest purchase and left. If the woman took the teenager and the baby, they'd disappear, never to be seen again.

Aviama shot a glance back at the base of the statue. The fireblood boy was gone. The man with the black hat and the red feather was gone. The shrew was already disappearing around the side of the platform as the teenager and the little girl were shuffled off the stage.

She shifted behind Sai. Maybe she could get to the back of the remaining women and hop down behind the stage. Maybe she could intervene without causing as big of a scene. Maybe—

Iron fingers wrapped around her upper arm and yanked her center stage. The wind she'd gathered dissipated in a soft *whoosh.* Masud half shoved, half lifted Aviama up onto the block as every eye descended on her small frame.

Masud whistled and grinned at the crowd. He said something in Keketi, and several of the men snickered. Aviama swallowed. She was too exposed, too vulnerable. As if she stood naked before a flame, its harsh fire licking at her tender flesh.

She searched for Chenzira and found him behind Abasi, at the base of the platform to her left. A muscle in his jaw twitched. He looked up at her. Islanders began to haggle with Masud over her price.

Terror rippled through her, a cold chill creeping up her spine and standing the hairs on end at the nape of her neck.

Umed and Manan, loyal melders she'd met on the *Wraith-weaver,* stood in place behind Chenzira in a group of maybe forty male slaves for purchase. Behind her and to the left, Sai, Durga, and Teja awaited their fates with the remaining women. To her right, the shrew counted out coins for the teenager and baby.

She was going to be sick. But just as a wave of horror rocked her body, the boiling sensation overtook her again. White-hot fury enveloped her horror and swallowed her in blazing energy. She hadn't left Jannemar and been held hostage in Radha, escaped the palace and been dumped onto a ship, and survived Ghosts' Gorge, only to be shuffled off to a slave ship and sold to a nowheresville island to live out her days under the thumb of yet another form of tyranny—while Radha invaded her home and Jannemar fell.

And that baby wasn't going anywhere.

Wind rushed to her palms. Chenzira glanced at her hands and back up to her eyes. He shook his head.

When the time comes, be Raisa.

Aviama bit her lip. She hoped he would forgive her. But she couldn't let the girl disappear.

She threw her bound wrists in a wide arc over the square and released the gale at her fingertips.

The market was over.

4

Whistling wind sliced through the air.

CRACKKKK.

The glass swirl of the statue melder's wind shattered in an explosion of sparkling shards. Screams ripped through the square as men, women, and children alike ducked for cover—mostly behind each other. Masud lifted a hand toward her, and Aviama lunged forward before she could think. She ripped the khopesh from his belt and blasted him off the platform with a powerful gust.

Aviama tossed the khopesh to Sai, who caught it and began to cut through Durga's bonds as Aviama dove for the teen and the shrew. Maybe it wasn't the time to be Raisa, but it was too late now to be anything else. The woman gaped at Aviama, eyes bulging as if she'd seen a ghost. She didn't protest when Aviama took hold of the young girl with the baby and steered her behind the platform. She didn't say a word. Only stared.

Chaos broke out like hornets from a raided hive. Steel glinted in Aviama's peripheral vision from the platform above and to her right, the floor built at eye level to those standing on the ground. Sai's khopesh cut through the last of Durga's bonds, and she lurched for the man. His neck cracked, and his body toppled sideways.

They were going to get hit. Aviama ran forward, pulling the girl out of the way, but she wasn't fast enough. The heavy corpse smashed into the teen, knocking her to the ground. The girl half-cushioned the baby's fall, but the momentum dumped the little girl out of safe arms and onto the shell-mosaic ground under the creaking boards of the platform.

The baby screamed then, the first time Aviama had heard her cry. Aviama yanked the corpse off the teenager, and the young woman plunged under the platform after the child.

The ground shifted beneath Aviama's feet. Her heart lodged in her throat as she reached a trembling hand up, as if wind could stop an earthquake.

"Stop!"

Was it Chenzira? Or another quakemaker? It didn't matter. No one could hear her, but she was a magnet, and every human in the area seemed to throw themselves at the magnetic pull she didn't want to give off.

Three men jumped down from the back of the platform, sickle blades in hand. Aviama darted around the corner, dodging blood spatter in the dust, and came face to face with Masud. He half-crouched behind the structure and lifted a hand, a fireball doubling in size between his palms as he set his flint gaze upon her face.

Whooooosh.

Aviama threw both hands into a mighty gust that swept two men off their feet as they ran up behind her, the gale catching Masud up into the air over the platform. His body shook as it floated there. Her arms strained in the exertion. He was heavy, and the wind wanted to be free. It took focus to keep him aloft. But where was the baby? Where was Chenzira? Was Sai okay?

Masud began to plummet, then Aviama felt the strain on her lift, and Masud's position stabilized. Aviama glanced to the platform and saw Sai had gotten free of her restraints and was pouring her own windcalling abilities out to assist Aviama, though her hands stayed subtly by her sides as she huddled behind two fallen bodies, eyeing the man in the air.

Bless her, Sai was a saint.

The ground shifted again, and Aviama stumbled. The wind left her as her hands flew to steady herself as she fell. The platform shook and splintered. A baby cried.

Masud fell.

A short bull of a man, shorter than Aviama but twice her size in solid muscle, tossed an opponent to the ground just in time to steal the man's sickle and thrust it upward into Masud's falling body. Umed. He glanced back at her and moved to rip the sickle free of Masud's abdomen, but the man had fallen face down. Umed kicked the corpse over, seized the trapped blade handle in both hands, and jerked it free with a nauseating squelch as the weapon tore through decimated organs.

Twenty paces off, Abasi's face flushed red as he barked orders in Keketi. His forty male slaves had erupted from hopeless servitude into rebellious fighters. Beyond the *Revenge* slavers and hostages turned combatants, the crowd was a mass of wide eyes, open mouths, furrowed brows, and shielded eyes. More than one looked up reverently at the broken statue of the melderblood set up in their central square.

Someone shouted her name.

Aviama looked up. A knife soared through the air toward

her throat. With a flick of her wrist, Aviama spun it around and sailed the handle into her palm. She tucked the blade into her waistband and rotated toward the sound of the crying baby.

Her wrists were still bound. She hadn't had time to rectify that particular situation. But with the help of the wind, she could still save the teen and the baby before the stage structure broke apart and crushed everyone and everything underneath it. The wood creaked again.

A crackling orange glow called her attention to the far corner. It was ablaze. Aviama's mouth went dry. When had that happened?

Crickkkkk—snap.

The platform collapsed.

"Nooo!"

Aviama threw herself between the falling slats and rolled to a crouch under the stage. Heat flew beneath the boards, thick black smoke billowing from the far end. A section of platform had snagged halfway into its descent, leaving a pocket of tenuous safety barely fitting Aviama's small body and the upper half of the teen.

The girl lay on her side, a splintered board driving into the back of her neck, pinning her to the ground. Her eyes were misted over with the haze of death, staring through the gathering smoke like a phantom, the memory of mothers stripped away too soon.

Aviama's gaze darted left and right. Where was the baby?

Debris fell, and Aviama flinched away from the raining splinters of wood. Sweat broke out on her brow. She sucked in quick, shallow breaths, but her lungs burned with each contaminated pull of smoke. Her eyes stung. Her stomach churned.

Where was the baby?

Aviama reached out to the girl, brushing her dusty

knuckles along the girl's young, innocent face. Blood spread out from the place where the board had impaled her at the back of the neck, reaching like spider veins in all directions as if searching for its next victim.

Another cry. The baby was alive. She spun.

"Aviama!"

The voice came like a shadow in the night. She had to find the baby.

"Aviama! Get out of there!"

"There's a baby! I have to get the baby!"

How many of the words she managed to get out through her coughs, she didn't know. She didn't care. She just had to—

There. Beyond the young girl, in another pocket of air, quickly filling with smoke. Embers glowed in the breaking boards over the child's head, backlighting her graceful curls in tiger-lily orange and blood red. Tears cut rivers down dusty cheeks, and coughs racked frail shoulders, interrupting the little one's screams.

A splintering ripple over Aviama's head sent a shiver down her spine, chasing the sweat drip sinking down her back. But her hands were bound, and she was less effective with the wind than usual. She couldn't protect them both. Could she?

Aviama threw up a barrier of air over the little girl, the light hitting the barrier so that the air seemed to move and wave when she looked at it. Flaming wood broke apart and hit the air shield Aviama had tossed up, floating there above the girl's head, sending a shower of embers in all directions on impact.

She had to get to the baby without dropping her hands. Without breaking the barrier shield. Aviama scooted past the dead teen, ducking as another board broke through the platform and sank its sharp splinters into the ground. It was a marvel the thing had managed to stay up so long, with the tremors in the ground shaking its foundation. The remaining structure would come tumbling around their ears at any moment.

A silver blade caked with blood and dirt bit into the shifting ground and broken shells beside her. Aviama recoiled with a yelp, the yelp sending her into a coughing fit. Her hands shook. The barrier over the child wavered.

A man was connected to the blade, gipping the khopesh with crimson-crusted knuckles. An arm looped around her waist and tugged her against his side. He smelled of ash and salvation.

But she wasn't the one who needed it most. She shook her head.

"I can save her!"

"I know you can."

Chenzira worked the blade between the singed fibers of the rope still tied around her wrists and cut her free. "You're going to need your hands. We're all getting out."

Aviama nodded. Tears stung her eyes. But that was all the time they had for sentimentality. With Aviama's hands free, she expanded the barrier to cover them and the child as the platform crumbled around them. With one arm, Chenzira held Aviama close, and with the other, he commanded the ground. Shells broke and dirt rose, breaking apart and rear-ranging, carrying them forward on the crest of a rolling wave. Wood cracked, splintered, and plunged to the ground on every side, like spears cutting through the water at fish in a barrel.

The baby coughed and looked up at the glowing firewood floating over her head. She reached up to touch it, distracted by the light.

Aviama launched herself forward, and Chenzira sent them skidding around the little girl to keep hold of Aviama as she moved. Aviama scooped up the baby and cradled her against her chest, keeping one arm free to maintain the barrier overhead.

With a splintering crash, their one remaining exit, a one-meter gap several paces off, disintegrated into dust and smoke. Chenzira jerked them back from more falling debris and shoved the ground upward instead. Aviama caught her breath. They were going up through the hole in the platform over the place where the baby had been.

As the blazing boards fell away, Aviama added a punch to their ascent with a gust of air propelling them up and out of the inferno down below. Chenzira's long legs hit the corner of the platform first, kicking off the edge and sending them down into the dirt. Two walls of wind Aviama had not ordered stabilized them in the air and landed them with a *thud* on their feet before the charred remains of the stage turned to kindling.

Chenzira began to let go, then stiffened, his arm tightening closer around her waist.

"No one but you has outed themselves as a melder. Let's keep it that way."

"Masud was one."

"Did he let the people see?"

Aviama hesitated. He'd had his back to the people, and the stage blocking him on one side. But why?

She adjusted the little girl in her arms. The little thing was breathing and seemed to have returned to the silent state she'd worn throughout the voyage. But her large eyes took in the crowd with unblinking interest. Aviama straightened and followed her gaze.

The throng gawked at her. To a man, the Keketi islanders stared in eerie silent expectation, their ogling replaced with open awe.

Aviama shifted her weight, adjusting the child in her arms. The motherless child. Orphaned and alone. The little girl seized a fistful of Aviama's golden waves and stared up at her with eyes made of innocence and stolen dreams. Something about that gaze grounded her. Who did the baby have in that moment but Aviama?

Chenzira tugged her forward, and the people parted before them without a word. Umed materialized next to them, a sickle in his hand, bleeding from his temple. Manan wriggled out from under the bodies of two guards and joined them, a khopesh sheathed on a new belt around his waist.

Aviama eyed the crowd on either side and kept her voice low. "Good to have you both back in one piece."

Umed dipped his head. "A little blood spatter now and then keeps the soul alive, Commander."

"As you say," Manan agreed. "And same to you."

Aviama twisted to see Durga and Sai. Beyond them, nearly a hundred freed male and female slaves fell in at their rear. Half the men held stolen weapons. Half the women looked like they'd fall over at any moment. Teja had her arms wrapped around a woman with bruises over her nose and a black eye forming on one side of her face.

What was she supposed to do with all these people? Did any of them know how to sail? How could they get a ship, and how was she supposed to get them all back to their respective homelands?

Durga faked a cough. "The battle horn."

Aviama stopped in her tracks. She turned to Chenzira. "I need it."

He set his jaw, and for a moment she feared he would tell her no. That they didn't have time. That it would only cause a scene and make things worse. But then he dipped his head, dropped his arm from her waist, and marched through the crowd toward a man still slumped on the ground at the base of the collapsed platform.

Abasi.

His foot seemed trapped under the structure, though Aviama suspected it was the ground itself swallowing his ankle under the plank laying on top. The man held a knife in one hand and protected his latest treasure in the other, a sparkling ruby-and-pearl-encrusted conch shell.

The people moved aside for Chenzira as he strode across the square with all the authority of a man who owned whatever land he walked on. Abasi yanked at his ankle, but he only succeeded in sinking further into the dirt. He lifted the knife in his hands and swung at Chenzira. Chenzira evaded the attack and stripped the blade from Abasi's hands in one smooth motion. He dropped his knee on Abasi's forearm, trapping it to the ground, decked the man across the jaw, and slipped the battle horn tether over the slaver's head and shoulder and free from his body. Chenzira turned on his heel, leaving Abasi in the dust at his feet, and threw the delicate shell high up into the air over the heads of the crowd.

Behind him, a freed slave mercilessly finished off Abasi with a stolen sickle sword.

Aviama's heart lurched to her throat. The horn would break.

She slipped the baby onto her hip and threw up one hand, catching the shell in a cushion of air and floating it softly and gently across the square and down to her waiting hand. The pair of pearl Iolani figures carved into the side of the shell shimmered in the sunlight, the rubies twinkling in pure red flashes in her palm. A ripple of whispers moved through the people in a wave and turned as one to gape at her once again, as if waiting for her to perform her next trick.

The swath of humanity before her stared up at the white alabaster statue of the windcaller in the center of their square, then down at the broken gale scattered in glass shards at the stone woman's feet. Islanders nudged each other and breathed hushed questions to their neighbors in Keketi before turning their gazes back to Aviama.

She didn't understand what they were saying, save for one word. Aviama's mouth went dry.

Raisa.

5

Aviama set the tether across her torso so the Iolani battle horn rested against her hip on one side, the little girl set upon the other. When she turned to check on Chenzira, he was marching toward her, wearing one of Abasi's gold armbands, and clutching the slaver's other armband, gem-studded collar, and knife in one hand. He winked at her.

She pursed her lips to suppress a smile. "Decided to give them a little show, did you?"

"You're the one who decided to give them a show. I only offered a finale."

Aviama winced. She'd gone against Chenzira to do it, too —and she had a feeling that the conversation wasn't over. But now wasn't the time to continue it. She started walking again, and the people moved out of the way as she went. Aviama kept her voice soft, but loud enough for Sai and Durga to hear.

"Thanks for the assist. When we landed."

Sai gave a gentle dip of the head. "Don't mention it."

Durga snorted. "No, mention it. We saved your stupid lives and made you look amazing in the process. You're welcome."

Manan glanced across the square. "We need a ship. A smaller one than *Raisa's Revenge.*"

Aviama's stomach soured. And then grumbled. How long had it been since she'd gotten meager rations of stale bread for dinner?

"How are we supposed to get a ship?"

How was she supposed to get *breakfast,* much less an entire ship stocked with supplies?

Chenzira placed a hand on the small of her back and flipped the knife in his free hand. "We're not going to the docks."

"Where are we going?"

He tilted his head toward a mountain in the distance. Aviama stifled a groan. Every eye was on her. No need to show weakness over a long walk.

"Why?"

"Trust me. We go there first, and then we lay out our plans. When we are out of earshot of everyone." He hesitated, then clenched his jaw. "We have much to discuss."

Biscuits. He *was* mad she'd used her powers. But what else was she supposed to do? Let them all get sold off as slaves and split apart to the ends of the island?

Aviama gave a short nod. She skirted the broken glass around the statue and lifted her chin as her bare feet kicked up the dirt across the square. She might have worn these clothes for months, and now they were layered with ash. A soft breeze played with the long waves of her hair. She smelled like smoke.

Still they whispered as she passed, some even dipping their heads in reverence. She'd destroyed their market and shattered their statue. Dark smoke still billowed up into the blue sky from the cinders of the platform's remains. She was a melder, but so were any number of others who'd realized their tabeun powers since the Awakening.

Why weren't they angry? Why didn't more melders fight back, and why did none of them reveal themselves? What had changed so drastically?

Aviama played with the ends of the toddler's curls, and the girl laid her head on Aviama's shoulder. An uneasy feeling spread in her stomach as they trooped out of the square and angled toward the mountain. "Teja?"

The woman extracted herself from the woman she had been comforting, patting her on the arm and hurrying up to Aviama's side. "Yes?"

Aviama cleared her throat. "What are they saying? Why is everyone looking at me?"

Durga arched an eyebrow. "You need another reason, *other* than the fact you just blasted everyone around you, saved the slaves, and ripped apart every important thing in their public square?"

Teja dipped her head, cutting an impatient look at Durga, and dropped her voice so low Aviama had to strain to hear it. "They say you are the reincarnation of Raisa, powerful wind-caller from The Crumbling. They say you are not fully human. They say you triumph over death and have come to save Jazir from the oppression of the monarchy."

Aviama glanced at Chenzira. A muscle twitched in his neck, but he said nothing. She looked back at Teja. "What is Jazir?"

Teja blinked. "The three islands in this community of Keket. Jazir."

Aviama nodded as if she had suddenly recalled information long lost—details she totally knew, and had only momentarily forgotten. For the first time, Aviama wished she'd paid better attention to geography when she was younger. She knew all the major kingdoms and locations, but not so much the smaller regions and subsections of each one.

She cast a glance back behind her, and her heart stopped. She whipped her head back around, gripping the girl in her arms close to her chest. "They're all following us."

Chenzira pursed his lips. "You made an impression."

"I shouldn't have. Melderbloods have been back for several years now. It's nothing new."

"It is here. Years ago, Keket removed the melderbloods from this portion of the kingdom. Tabeun abilities are genetic, and without them, the entire community was insulated from powers. The few outsiders who come to the island know better than to show themselves here—the few melders who've cropped up in Jazir over the last three years have been killed as soon as their powers awakened."

Aviama's lips parted. "But I thought Keket was friendly to magic."

The knife in Chenzira's hands flipped up through the air, catching the light on its blade before he snatched it back on its descent. "We're divided on that point. The Return brought the issue back to light after years of having it put to bed."

"And the slaves? Why wouldn't they free themselves if no one on the island is a melder, and the slaves come from other places where they might have powers?"

Chenzira shook his head. "Masud and others on Abasi's crew are melders, and they aren't interested in melderblood slaves. They like having all the power, but they know business in Jazir will disappear if they out themselves as melders. Jazir wants nothing to do with powers, and they revere Raisa, one of the last melderbloods from six hundred years ago, who helped to destroy magic in The Crumbling. They believe her spirit protects them, and they honor her final wishes by keeping the islands pure of tabeun influence."

His lip curled on the word *pure*. Chenzira glanced down at his hands, picking off a piece of crusted, dried blood from his knuckles. "Abasi casts a wide net, and once he has the stock he wants for his next human shipment, he kills any that demonstrate melderblood ability. None of the slaves are melders."

Teja tilted her head in the child's direction. "The young girl with the baby wasn't her mother. The mother had come on board with me in northern Radha. Her name was Bishakha, which means star. She was lovely." Teja paused, her voice thick with emotion. She cleared her throat and continued. "She knew Abasi had melders on his crew, so she hid her powers. But as the voyage progressed, she would sometimes use her powers to keep us warm at night. Until she was discovered."

Aviama almost didn't want to know. Didn't want to ask. But she did. She had to. "What happened?"

"One of the sailors saw the light. He told Masud, and Masud came for her. She heard the shout and passed the baby to the teenager for fear the baby would be killed also, since genetically she might become a melder too. They dragged her to the stairs, killed her in front of us, and dumped her body overboard. From that day on, the girl held onto the toddler and didn't let go."

The wind left Aviama's lungs in a *whoosh*. Her heart hurt, like an iron hand had plunged through her chest, seized her heart, and begun to squeeze with crushing force.

Wrong. So wrong.

How had the world come to this? Why did everyone hate with such depth? Or perhaps it was not hatred, but a frivolous disregard for human life, in which a person only held value to the extent that they provided utility to the powerful. Aviama wasn't sure which was worse.

Tears welled in her eyes. The iron hand around her heart

clenched harder, so that she almost feared it would burst. Could such evil be stopped?

She thought about Shiva, whom she had doomed to the mercy of the Iolani in Ghosts' Gorge. He'd done atrocious, horrible things. He would have kept killing, kept slaughtering melders if she hadn't stopped him. The only time he exhibited vulnerability was when he made a calculated move to weaken her defenses.

Leaving him with Ali'i Makuakan was a death sentence. The single remaining question was whether his death would be tortuous and slow after a long despairing imprisonment, or decisive and swift. Was she right to hand him over? Did it make her as bad as Shiva to leave him to death?

If she thought he deserved it, did that make her just? Or heartless? Part of her wanted to believe he could have changed, but if she believed it, her guilt needled at her like the straw in the base of the excrement pit cell in the hull of *Raisa's Revenge*. No matter how she tossed or turned, still the straw poked and prodded and needled. It was there when she fell asleep, and it remained when she woke again.

For all her decrying violence, for all her complaints to Chenzira that no one should die in the effort to stop the Tanashai family ruling Radha, she herself had turned to violence on more than one occasion. Aviama could still feel the might of her rage the day she blasted the door off her room on the *Wraithweaver*, dumped the konnolan into the sea, and turned Shiva's wall to splinters. She'd seen through a sieve of blood, red touching everything in her path as she rose on the fuming crest of her storm, up over the prow.

She'd planned to rip Shiva to pieces before someone killed her. She'd almost succeeded.

Something wet ran down her cheek, a gentle breeze kissing at the moisture as it made a trail down the dust on her face. Aviama reached up to wipe away the tear, when the little girl poked it, and it dribbled down onto the toddler's finger.

Aviama sniffled, allowing the curve of the girl's smooth cheek and softness of her large round eyes to pull all her focus.

She looked back at Teja. "Do you know ... do you know her name? Or if she has other family?"

Teja gave a sad smile, but even that broke apart halfway through. "I'm sorry. I don't know her name. Bishakha was an easy target for Abasi because she lived in the slums on the outskirts. No family, and the father didn't stick around for the baby. She spoke of it only once. She was quiet."

Aviama stared back at the baby. Chenzira sidestepped closer as they walked, his arm brushing hers with every stride —a gentle reminder of his presence. She leaned into him once in silent thanks and let them fall into rhythmic quiet as they left the square behind and cut through the town toward the mountain.

Footfalls, shuffling dust, and hushed murmurs of salvation and miracles punctuated a melancholy atmosphere. The hope in their tone, the light of their faces, the curiosity of their sharp eyes as they studied her only served to deepen the emptiness in Aviama's chest. She reached for her fingers to twist her mother's ring, an anxious habit she'd yet to break.

But though the habit remained, her mother's ring did not.

Abasi had taken them, and there was no going back now. A lump lodged in her throat. It burned like fire. The ache of death returned with a vengeance.

She stared at the girl in her arms.

Two orphan girls who had watched their mothers die.

Chenzira reached for her hand, and she clutched it until her knuckles turned white from the strain.

The opportunity to be a chameleon was gone. The time to

be Raisa had come and gone, and now hundreds of people with a practice of murdering melders followed her every move.

Chenzira had warned her not to reveal herself, but she had. She'd trusted a swindler over the man who'd supported her from the beginning. And now, not only had she not had breakfast, but the list of mouths to feed was expanding exponentially as Keketi men, women, and children joined the throng trailing their progress up the mountain.

How many of them would try to kill her? How quickly would the reverence fade into a lethal mob when she wasn't what they'd hoped for?

Her heart grew heavier with every step. Behind her, she left a pile of bodies and a burning platform. Ahead, the mountain loomed.

Change was in the air, but it smelled like rotten death.

6

The mountain grew larger and larger. The grumbling in her stomach grew louder and louder. And her eyes were playing tricks on her as they left the adobe-lined streets behind. Because twice Aviama could have sworn she'd seen the young boy from the square—the one with fire dancing on his fingertip.

But Chenzira had said there were no melders on the island. And each time she thought she saw the boy, he was gone when she looked again, swallowed by the crowd. Or, more likely, he was never there at all. She must have dreamed it. At a distance, any young kid could have made her think of the fireblood boy.

Some of the crowd had splintered off over the past couple of hours of walking, but others had come to fill the gaps. Manan estimated three hundred people had wound up following them to the mountain. Aviama stifled a gag. What was she supposed to do with three hundred people? How many of them wanted to kill her? Would the rest die of starvation, or turn back to their homes when supper came and went, and she still hadn't done anything interesting?

What did they *want*?

Aviama was out of her depth with these strange people, with their white clothes, adobe houses, and sand-dusted streets. They spoke a language she did not know and had expectations she could hardly hope to understand. Even their mountains were all wrong. Mountains were supposed to have trees. They were supposed to have cover and hide people who ran into their forests for refuge.

This one had none of those things. It stood bare against the landscape, stripped of proper foliage, and painted with stripes of terracotta, copper, and wood-fired clay. Mount Zobaat, Teja had called it.

"It means whirlwind," she'd said.

Of course it did.

The baby—the toddler girl with no name—slept against Chenzira's shoulder, her little curls bobbing with the bounce of his gait. It hadn't taken long for Aviama's arms to ache from holding her, but she'd turned down Chenzira's offer to help until the girl was asleep. Aviama would be there when the girl woke up.

She should never wake to abandonment.

Another hour passed, and they reached the base of the mountain. Chenzira pushed forward, rarely passing her, but leading nonetheless. If he wanted to make it look as though she were the one in charge of their destination, he probably should have avoided a pace that made her wheeze like a dog on its last legs.

Nothing said authoritative leadership like wheezing and doubling over to suck in desperate breaths, which Aviama desperately wanted to do. Her legs burned. Her muscles ached. The steep incline and navigation of rocky outcroppings worked her calf muscles as if she'd been walking through a sludge pit up to her knees.

Chenzira cast her a sideways glance, then slipped his free hand into hers. Two fingers paused on the inside of her wrist. He hesitated, his head dipping on the beat. He was counting.

She grimaced. Her heart pounded against her chest, betraying her.

Chenzira frowned. "You need to stop. But we need to get further up."

"I'm fine." A cough took her over as she said the last word, and she pursed her lips at her body's betrayal. "It wouldn't be so bad if I hadn't had such an eventful morning."

"Blasting people in every direction and inhaling all that smoke probably didn't help."

"Thank you. I'll try to avoid it in the future."

"You should have avoided it to begin with."

Aviama's throat tightened. She tilted her head toward the sleeping baby on his shoulder. "You think I should have left her to die?"

His eyes darkened. "No. I think you should have listened to me when I told you not to show off your powers."

Chenzira scanned the mountain ahead. He dropped her hand and made a sweeping motion in front of him in an exaggerated gesture. *This way, Highness.*

Aviama balled her hands into fists, relaxing them only with effort. *You're the one who left me alone. Did you want me sold to the highest bidder? Don't you care about all those women?*

The words flew to her tongue, a fire in her throat begging for escape. If she hadn't kept her teeth clenched, they would have escaped. She knew her accusations weren't fair. He'd been a captive too. What choice had he had?

His clipped tone was enough to tell her he wasn't in a listening mood. But he didn't have to act like she was stupid. How was she supposed to know what the consequences might have been? How did *he* know that these consequences weren't still *more* favorable than being sold and split up in different directions?

Aviama planted a foot on a crag high and to her right in the direction Chenzira had indicated and lurched toward it with nothing to support her but her failing legs' muscles and a wave of bitterness. Her foot slipped, and for a moment all she saw was blue sky and sharp rock. Her heart stopped.

Strong fingers seized her by the elbow and hauled her up. Chenzira leveled her with a look, all amusement gone from his eyes. "Take small steps."

Biscuits. Aviama straightened and pulled free of his grasp. "I'm fine."

Chenzira frowned, but said nothing, instead tossing his head in the direction of a few large rocks off to the side and offering a hand to Durga, who climbed up to the landing next. It was easy to see why Chenzira had wanted this spot. Reprieve from the sharp ascent came in a narrow plateau with a semicircle of rock soaring overhead before them, with spikes of stone jutting up at intervals along the direction from which they'd come so that only a few sensible points of entry or exit existed.

Aviama crossed to one of the rocks, shoved hard to roll it against the back wall, and sank down on it. She reached for the baby, and Chenzira passed the little girl, still sleeping, into her lap. Durga shoved another free rock over beside Aviama and perched on it.

"It's a little icy over here for an island that wants to melt my skin off, don't you think?"

Aviama pursed her lips. "What are you talking about?"

Several paces away, Chenzira helped Sai and Teja up next, followed by Umed and Manan, letting the remaining masses settle themselves wherever they saw fit on the mountain after that. Umed and Chenzira took up positions by the easiest entrances to the plateau, making it clear no one else was invited into the small space.

Durga leaned in. "You and Ch—you and him." She jerked her head at Chenzira, and Aviama squirmed in her seat. But she didn't miss Durga's avoidance of Chenzira's name. Surely, it would be unwise to use the name of a missing prince who had fallen out of favor with the royal family. At least, that's what Aviama assumed. It wasn't only Aviama's identity she was charged with keeping secret. Chenzira's name was dangerous too—perhaps more so—though she had yet to fully understand why.

Durga rolled her eyes. "I thought your lovey-dovey stuff was obnoxious, but this is worse. Show no weakness. No drama while you're on goddess status with the people, okay?"

Sai sat on the ground on Aviama's other side and leaned back against the limestone wall. "We do need to be careful about appearances."

Appearances. What a despicable reason to do anything. The word sent a chill down her spine, chasing the sweat beads running down from the nape of her neck.

Shiva had been all about appearances. He'd been nothing *but* appearances. Fake smiles, forced kisses, public shows. She wanted nothing to do with it. But the curious crowd could turn to a mob in the blink of an eye.

Aviama half-stood to see over the rock formation jutting up at the edge of their landing. People filled the mountainside, and as she came into view, a murmur swept through them like a breeze. Heads swiveled in her direction. Children craned their necks. Her mouth went dry.

She made eye contact with a middle-aged woman as her gaze roved from one side of the crowd to the other. The woman's eyes bulged, and she clambered up the mountainside and lunged for the landing, a cloth bundle clutched in her hands.

"Duqatun Elwehi! Duqatun Elwehi!"

Umed stopped the woman and shook his head firmly. The woman held out the bundle past Umed's thick torso, and one fold of the cloth fell free. Bread. Food.

Aviama's stomach grumbled as she stared at it. Her mouth watered. She glanced up at Teja, standing awkwardly behind Manan and Chenzira, and motioned her over.

"What is she saying?"

Teja inclined her head in a half-bow. Her large eyes were round with a reverent respect, but her hands wringing betrayed her anxiety. "She calls you Duchess of the Air. It is the title they call Raisa the Windcaller. The belief is spreading that you are her reincarnated spirit, sent to save them. She offers food to you in exchange for favor."

Aviama's jaw dropped. *Biscuits.* This was getting out of hand. "I can't—but I'm not—"

Durga jumped up and knelt in front of Aviama in a show of deference, then hissed in her face. "Are you insane? I'm starving. If they say you're a dancing monkey, and they want to give the monkey food, I say you give them a jig and take the bread."

Durga jabbed Teja in the ribs. "Translate for me."

Teja made a tentative sidestep toward Durga, and Durga spread her hands. A sweet smile Aviama had hardly imagined possible on the girl's condescending face lit her features, and a gentle gust of wind carried the bundle from the woman's hands, up into the air in the sight of the crowd, and down into Aviama's lap.

"I am Duqatun's highest-ranking assistant."

Of course she was. And apparently Duqatun's hands and feet and mouth too, because Aviama had not summoned the wind that brought the bread from the woman, and Aviama definitely did not agree to whatever Durga was about to spout next.

But Teja was already translating.

"We know how difficult your lives have been. And unjustly so!"

Chenzira's cheeks flushed red as his head whipped toward Durga, and a vein on his neck looked about ready to pop. He spun toward her. A knot formed in Aviama's stomach. She passed the bread and the sleeping baby to Sai and leaped to her feet, reaching Durga only a step before Chenzira did.

She couldn't let him do whatever he was about to do when he got to Durga. Not with the islanders watching. And she couldn't let Durga talk them into a hole they couldn't get out of.

Aviama laid a hand on each of their arms, and they turned toward her. The knot in her stomach tripled under the weight of the challenge in Durga's gaze and the steely glare in Chenzira's. She winced, just once, and took a deep breath.

In with the princess. Out with the fear. In with diplomacy. Out with crippling uncertainty.

She nodded at Teja and lifted her voice.

"Justice is our mission."

Cheers. Aviama drew in their approval and forged ahead.

"Oppression in all its forms is wrong, as I know you've seen in your own islands here in Jazir. Thus so, we start with the slaves from *Raisa's Revenge*. They are hereby set free, and the fees you paid for them can be found in Abasi's coffers."

Confused glances. A few outright glares. Mumbles.

"We need some time now, but we thank you for your understanding and attention. What wonderful people live here on Jazir to welcome us so well! Surely, no finer people can be found in all of Keket!"

A cheer went up again, though less enthused than the first. The air had gone stale, as if the warmth of the sun had soured.

Durga pounded a fist into the air. "For justice! Duqatun Elwehi!"

A cry went up to the sky, as fist after fist soared over the heads of the waiting masses. "Duqatun Elwehi!"

Aviama smiled and waved, and Durga and Chenzira did the same as they stood on either side of her.

Fake. Pretentious. Lies.

Durga cleared her throat and hissed low beside her. "Do something exciting. A finale."

Aviama lifted her hands, and small pebbles and dirt were caught up in the air. It wasn't pretty, but there wasn't much to work with on a bald mountain with clay and stone, surrounded by nothing but nothing. For an instant, panic welled in her chest.

Durga had suggested a finale, and in response, Aviama held aloft a cloud of dirt. Ridiculous.

But then an idea dropped into her mind, and her hands were moving up and sideways, dancing this way and that until the wind whipped the dirt and rocks into a shape—the shape of a woman. The woman formed in a haze and blew a great gust of air, and the gravel and dust of her body escaped through that gust into a heart. Just as the heart took shape, Aviama clapped her hands, and the heart exploded in a shower of falling rock and dust over the far side of the mountain.

The ground shook beneath her feet as if the clap of her hands had pulled a boom of thunder from an azure sky. Aviama's own heart surged to her throat, and she seized Chenzira's arm for support. A quakemaker must be in the crowd.

He'd come to expose her for the hack that she was. To prove that melderbloods filled the world, and Aviama was not a reincarnation of anyone, but one of many. To show she'd been tossed at the people to feed their fantasies of the deified dead—when all she really wanted was a meal and a boat to carry her as far from their horrible little island as possible.

Then she caught a glimpse of Chenzira's face. His lips cocked into half a smirk on one side, and he laid his hand over hers where her white knuckles still gripped his arm.

Relief nearly knocked her over as she steadied herself and gave a dramatic curtsy to the people. But the familiar rote motions of the curtsy brought with them images of Shiva, the man she'd killed. Adoring crowds had filled the streets of Rajaad outside the House of the Blessing Sun, too, throwing flowers at the image of a happy couple that did not exist. Everything about them had been a lie. Shiva had sold his soul to further his agendas. How far into the darkness might this new deception drag her?

Because that was the thing about appearances—they weren't real. And if they couldn't find their way off the island before the facade crashed down around them, they'd be as dead as the girl under the slave market platform.

7

The bundle of bread was more than they could have expected, but less than they needed. Umed, Manan, Chenzira, Durga, Sai, Teja, and Aviama—plus a baby—made eight. Four large slices inside meant they each got half a piece. Aviama was done with hers in four bites, and Chenzira ate his whole. She wasn't even sure he chewed.

The toddler woke, ate, and contented herself tugging on the ends of Aviama's hair. She was an odd child, not to cry or show emotion. But they were both orphans, and who looked out for the fatherless and motherless like older, more-experienced orphans?

Durga had hardly licked the crumbs off her fingers before suggesting they take up a food offering for Duqatun Elwehi. Sai pointed out that taking the people's resources would do little to earn their favor and keep the peace, and Umed recommended they look for ways to fish off the coast on the other side of the mountain. All the suggestions so far for food or escape relied on either the people's generosity toward their newfound revered goddess or going into town.

But only Chenzira and Teja spoke Keketi, and Chenzira had no interest in going to town himself.

Manan ran a hand over his face and turned to Chenzira. "You had the smarts to get Abasi's jeweled collar and gold armbands. That should get us something."

Manan sat on the plateau next to Sai, with Aviama and the other two women still on their seats against the rock wall. Umed and Chenzira stood, their gazes roving at intervals across the crowd. The people seemed to have settled in for the long haul on the slope of the mountain. Didn't they have anything better to do?

"Yes, but there aren't legitimate pawn shops here." Chenzira folded his arms. "The only place likely to buy from us would be a criminal enterprise, or maybe a jeweler. And jewelers are not exactly common on the poorer islands."

Sai leaned her head back against the rock. Her shoulders sagged. "We need cash. Coins. Something to buy a boat and supplies."

Chenzira shook his head. "Abasi's collar is only going to go so far, even if we could get coin for it."

"We have the battle horn."

Aviama snapped her head up toward Durga, her eyes lit with the excitement of a fresh scheme. Aviama's hand went to the horn at her hip. Her stomach dropped.

Chenzira set his jaw. "No, *we* don't. Aviama does. And it's not for trade."

"It might be when you get hungry enough."

"It's not for trade." Aviama shifted the horn to a new position closer to Sai than to Durga. Durga rolled her eyes. The little girl in Aviama's lap poked the horn. Aviama gave her a gentle squeeze.

Teja bit her lip. "Are you really going to overthrow the monarchy?"

All heads turned to Teja. Aviama blinked. "What?"

Teja wrung her hands and grimaced before folding her hands in her lap and pinching the ends of each finger in succession. "I know you're not Raisa." Here she glanced up at Aviama, and Aviama wondered if she was trying to convince them or herself. "You're melders. I'm Keketi, but better traveled than the Jazir. My brother married a Radhan woman, and my mother and I were visiting in northern Radha when we were taken. Abasi didn't care that we were Keketi. He's taken slaves from other areas of Keket before."

She stared down at her hands. Aviama's chest hitched. Another woman whose mother had been killed before her eyes. Sai, too, had lost parents to a monarchical regime, though she hadn't been there to see it. Was there no end to tyranny? Could peace only be bought with blood?

"The Jazir believe Raisa descended in a whirlwind on this mountain six hundred years ago. The three islands hold a festival in her honor every year. I know what melders are. But even though you aren't Raisa, you still freed the slaves from *Raisa's Revenge*. Will you free the other slaves on the island too? Do you really want justice? Could you stop the monarchy's tariffs or change the leadership? Maybe ... maybe you aren't really Raisa. But maybe you *could* be."

Aviama's lips parted.

Fake. Lies. More lies.

But she *had* freed the slaves from *Raisa's Revenge*. And there were more on the island. Was it fair to save a few, and not the rest? What would she do with the freed slaves now? Was she responsible for getting them home? Aviama couldn't even afford food for the small band of them as it was, much less seventy more.

Durga grinned. "She's thinking about it."

"I am not! I—" Aviama hesitated. She glanced at Chenzira.

Something flickered across his face. Resentment? Anger? Sadness? But by the time the thought entered her mind, the expression was gone. Aviama sighed. "I hate pretending. I've spent so much of the last months pretending. It's not right."

Teja shrugged. "Neither is one person owning another person."

The woman's gaze came to rest upon the little girl in Aviama's lap, who was busy wrapping a long tendril of Aviama's golden hair around a skinny finger. How could someone purchase another person? How could this girl, this nameless girl, be robbed of her family and future and life? Of her personhood? Someone else's daughter was on the island right now, scared and alone, treated like garbage. Could she really stand by and watch and do nothing?

Tears welled in Aviama's eyes. She blinked hard to force them back, but one escaped down her cheek anyway. She sniffed. "I think ..."

Chenzira cleared his throat. "I need to talk to Aviama alone."

Durga snorted. "Where?"

Chenzira leveled her with a cool stare. "Leave that to me. The rest of you stay here. Umed, keep watch. Send Manan to inform me if anything changes. Sai, take the kid."

He started to turn away, then paused, and turned back to Durga. "If you breathe a word to the people, I'll cut your tongue out. And Teja, if you translate a single syllable that she says, I'll have the mountain swallow your feet and we will leave you here."

Durga scowled. Teja gaped at him and nodded fervently. "Of course. I won't say a word. Forgive me."

Sai eyed Aviama, and Aviama caught her glance. The warm little body on her lap was more comforting than she'd anticipated, and she didn't want to give her up. Aviama slipped her arms around the girl's small torso and hugged her tight. "I'll be right back. I'll come back for you, okay?"

Aviama gave the little girl a kiss on the top of the head, and the toddler patted her face and went willingly into Sai's arms. Chenzira held out a hand toward Aviama, and she took it. His face was set, jaw tight. But his hold on her hand was soft.

Chenzira put a hand on the side of the rock wall at their backs. It trembled under his touch. The edge of the wall shifted with a scraping, sliding sound. Aviama threw up a barrier of air around them to muffle the sound, but she wasn't sure how much got through, or how big of a barrier to make. He dropped her hand to put both palms to use, brow furrowed in deep concentration as his hands ran along the rock. The end of the wall shoved over, and the top reformed across an opening into a small archway and dark recess into the mountain.

He reached for her hand again, and she took it, the little girl's face still in her mind's eye as Chenzira ducked under the opening. A sharp bend took them out of the light of prying eyes and into a rough, rocky hollow about two paces across.

Aviama's eyebrows soared. "Wow, nice work."

"It wore me out more than I thought, but it'll do the job."

Chenzira ran a hand over his beard, thicker and less perfectly groomed than she was accustomed to. It wasn't unattractive. She wasn't sure he could do anything to his hair or clothes that would hide the cut of his jawline, the lines of his chest and muscled arms, the handsome face and sharp, cinnamon eyes flecked with molten gold.

He looked up at her, and she realized her mouth had been open. She snapped it shut and bit her lip. They had to focus. They had to strategize. They had to—

Both spoke at once.

"She needs a name."

"You can't free all the slaves."

A beat of silence. Chenzira and Aviama stared at one another, then spoke in unison.

"What?"

Aviama shook her head, unsure what she was hearing. "I never said we would. But slavery is wrong. And if we can do something about it, shouldn't we?"

Chenzira glanced toward the entrance and swallowed. "Barrier, please. Listening ears."

Aviama pursed her lips, but raised her hands and formed a bubble around them to keep the sound in.

Chenzira gave a short nod, satisfied. "It's not about whether or not we *should*, but whether or not we *can*—and whether or not, *if* we could, it would actually help anything in the long run."

She squinted up at him. Her stomach knotted seven times over and twisted, like a rag wrung out when it was already dry. "So ... you agree that slavery is bad. And you think we should just ... think it's bad. And not do anything."

"I didn't say that. I'm saying you aren't thinking about consequences. You're impulsive. Like when I told you not to reveal your powers, and you did it anyway. I was asking you to trust me, because I didn't have time to tell you *why,* and you didn't. Now, you see a sad baby and want to give her a name and get attached, and you see slaves and you want to free them and throw the entire kingdom upside-down, when we haven't even figured out supper."

Heat flushed her cheeks. She twisted her fingers where her rings used to be and tapped at one of the rubies on the battle horn at her hip.

"I *did* do what you asked. I didn't tell anyone on the ship of my abilities, and neither did Sai or Durga. Which, considering Durga, is rather amazing, I might add. Maybe you should have thought about that before you started shooting accusations when you gave me zero details and expected me to be okay with everyone getting separated."

She crossed her arms to cover the lump in her throat, but her voice cracked when she spoke again. "I was scared I'd never see you again."

Chenzira peered down at her, and she looked away. Tears threatened to brim along her lashes, and she blinked hard to keep them at bay. *Biscuits.* Stupid emotions. She felt pathetic.

But then Chenzira ran a gentle hand down her arm, and a tingle ran along her skin in the cool of the mountain. He stepped closer. "I will always find you. If you had been sold, I would have come for you." He sighed, and his breath tickled her neck. "I need you to trust me. We're not in Jannemar. We're not in Radha. I know you're used to taking care of things. But we're in my world. And there are things about it that you don't understand."

Was she used to taking care of things? Five years ago, she was used to her parents and brother and older sister taking care of things. In that order. Now, her parents were dead, her brother was king, and her older sister was a shell of her former self. Aviama had been sent to spy on Radha and prevent an insult that could lead to invasion, but invasion was upon her homeland anyway—and if her old handservant Murin didn't reach Jannemar before the Radhan army did, Zephan would have no warning before the onslaught.

Every Shamaran will burn.

That's what Shiva had promised. And though Shiva may be dead, he'd not worked alone to get the ball rolling. The plan was in motion. Zephan, Avaya, and Aviama were the only Shamarans left. Three siblings with an appointment to die.

She'd been on her own ever since she arrived in Radha and they took her bodyguard away. Darsh had been a false ally. Onkar had turned on her in the end. Chenzira was her only constant, but trust was hard in the absence of information.

Trust was harder than it once was, in general. Being burned did that to a person. But she wanted to trust Chenzira. He'd never given her reason to doubt him.

She took a deep breath, swallowing the lump back down her esophagus into the pit in her belly. "I know we're in your world. But we haven't exactly had heart to hearts about Keket, and you've not told me anything about what really happened that caused you to run away. Not to mention why that means we can't help the slaves."

"People owning people is obscene. But do you remember what you did in the brig of the *Wraithweaver*? Shiva threatened Sona, and you were ready to sacrifice yourself to keep one man from being killed. In return, you played into his hands, and he killed Sona anyway. People aren't good, Aviama. You don't want to kill anyone, you say too much blood is spilled, but then how would you stop the slavers? Would you kill them? Do you counter slavery with blood?"

Chenzira stepped closer again, and she took a half-step back, until her back was against the rock and her hand was on his chest to keep him at bay. She had to think.

Chenzira continued. "Or do you find a long-lost fortune and buy them all? If you bought them all, you'd still be creating demand, and the slavers would happily supply it. Your bleeding heart would bleed money right into their coffers. Half the Keket economy exists on the backs of slaves. Without them, costs soar. Poor people become destitute. Businesses die. You're going to need a better answer than a nice speech and a couple of wind tricks if you want a long-term solution."

She'd gotten lucky at the market. She knew that. The

island was amazed by her powers, awed by the farce they so tightly clung to about the reincarnated Raisa. Anywhere else, a horde of other melders could have come up against her and overpowered her by sheer numbers. And even if she did free the slaves on this one island, wouldn't the slavers only continue the trade when she left? Or would the islanders go to another isle over to get their human labor?

What would she do with them once they were free? How would they get home? What would she do with the ones she'd already freed—and if she left them to their own devices, would they riot or steal for food, or be beaten back into slavery by the locals?

Her mind was spinning. She didn't give a rotten fig about Keket's economy. Not with its reliance on free labor to build it. Maybe the kingdom *needed* to be turned on its head. And if slavery really was the linchpin for the economic stability of the nation, they wouldn't give it up without a fight.

Just as Shiva would never have given up his power or removed his greedy hands from the throats of melders who might impact his ambitious aims.

He would have continued until the day he died. Wouldn't he?

He had to die.

Didn't he? Or had she played judge on a man from another nation, taking a life she had no right to take?

Aviama slipped her hand down from Chenzira's chest and placed her hands behind her at the small of her back, twisting the skin of her naked fingers away from his prying eyes. But they saw right through her. His gaze pierced her soul.

Would he think less of her if she believed something different than he thought? Already the space between them was larger than she'd imagined in her dreams of the last months. She'd done nothing but imagine what it would be

like to be together again. And now at last they were together—
but were they together?

She'd longed to see him again, terrified of being separated.
But it would be worse to be together, but not *together*—that
who she really was would be exposed and he wouldn't like it.
Or who he really was would be exposed and that she wouldn't
like it.

What if, when the dust settled, and kingdoms were not on
fire, and they had the space to breathe, he no longer cared for
her? What if he only liked an idea of her, one born in chaos,
and without chaos, they could not survive? What if their
experiences had changed her, and he did not like the
changes?

Aviama grimaced. She twisted her fingers and swallowed
and blanched. He tilted his head, and she shifted her weight.
Her breath came fast. If she didn't say it, she never would.

"What if I've changed my mind? What if I've decided
sometimes blood is required?"

The air went cold, and a chill ran down her spine. This
was it. The moment when he would reject her. The moment
when he would realize the woman he liked and the woman
she was were not the same.

Why did she have to speak without thinking? Why did she
have to spout every thought when he was near? But harboring
a secret from him would have been worse. She risked a glance
up into Chenzira's face, and his eyes were searching hers like a
ship fixed on a lighthouse. Looking for the light. Looking for
something to hold on to.

But she was a whirlwind, and she didn't always know
which way the wind would take her. It was Chenzira that was
always steady, always firm. An anchor to her wind and waves.

He slipped a hand to the small of her back and stopped
her fingers from twisting the place where her rings were miss-

ing. The warmth of his hands swallowed both of hers as his arms encircled her.

"I, too, believe there are times when freedom must be bought with blood. But the times you've acted that way have frightened me. You were a storm with wings, imploding from the inside out, and the blood you seemed intent to spill was your own. If you want a fight, I've no doubt you'll find one. They tend to follow you. But stop doing it alone."

Her mouth went dry. She thought of the murderous rage that had swept over her when she saw no way out but to kill and be killed. When everything in her world was tinted in crimson red. He'd shared his concern then. It must have looked like she'd done it again at the market.

But Chenzira was still asking her to trust without handing out all the information.

She twined her fingers through his warm ones behind her back and tilted her chin up toward him. "If we're going to do things together, you need to give me more information. A lot more. Let's start with why you ran away from home four years ago."

hump, thump, thump.

Aviama's heartbeat drummed a rhythm loud and clear. Her head pounded with the rush of it, and she half expected Chenzira to check her pulse again. But his own breathing seemed to have ticked up a notch, and his gaze, though his eyes were on her, seemed to be focused on something far away.

He'd said he wanted to save his sister. He'd asked her to come to Keket with him one day to rescue her. And that it wasn't safe for him to return. But he'd never said why.

Chenzira opened his mouth, then closed it and pulled her into his chest. She started to protest, but when his arms tightened around her and wouldn't let go, something about the urgency in his hold gave her pause. He wasn't trying to shut her up. He wanted closeness. He wanted comfort. It was hard to talk about.

They stood there for several long minutes, Aviama breathing in sweat and sea salt, Chenzira's cheek against her hair. She waited, and at last the wait was rewarded.

"I ... didn't want to become my father."

"What was he doing that you didn't want to be like?"

"Bolstering slave trade, for one. Greasing the wheels for an alliance with Radha, for two. The way he was with women. The pressures to rule the way he wanted. It was clear I had only two options: become the man he wanted, a man I could never live with myself to be, or leave."

Aviama pressed her lips together. It didn't sound good, but the specifics were still about as clear as a mud puddle on a cloudy day.

A hacking cough from the doorway ripped Aviama from their conversation, and the two of them snapped their heads up. Manan rubbed his throat as if the imaginary cough-causing malady still irked him. Once he saw he had their attention, he leaned into the dark space.

"We have company. Melderbloods, to be exact. They want to join up."

Chenzira stiffened. "Sand and sea."

Aviama blinked. She glanced between Manan and Chenzira. "Join up? Join what?"

Manan gave her a look, as though she were missing something obvious. "The revolution. They don't believe you're Raisa, but they've been hiding their abilities here on the island, and they're ready to offer their assistance."

Chenzira's warnings flooded her mind. The islanders believed she was not fully human, some reincarnation of a savior figure. Breaking that belief could cause a mob, and fueling it would only cause word of her presence and fear of her intentions to spread among the other islands and governing authorities.

Now melderbloods had called her bluff and were at the door. If she was leading a revolution, would she let strangers with their own secret motives get close to her? If she wasn't, would they destroy the fragile naivety of the islanders and plunge them all into danger as the hundreds of people on the mountainside came to see her as a traitorous pretender?

The wind left her lungs. "Biscuits."

Chenzira's hold on her tightened. "Let's focus on getting ourselves safe first, and deal with saving the world afterward, okay?"

Sounded reasonable. But all those people ... all the freed slaves ... all the men and women yet to be saved ...

Aviama sucked in a long breath. "What if we can save a few other people at the same time?"

Chenzira cleared his throat, and Aviama wondered if it covered up a stifled groan. "You've put a target on our backs. If we don't move soon, all the other islands of Keket will know about us, and I'd hoped to move about more freely. We'll help as many people as we can, but my top priority is you. Deal?"

She winced. "Deal."

He gave a nod, satisfied, and pulled her in to plant a kiss on her forehead. She leaned into him, then just as he began to pull away, she put a hand on his chest. "And the baby."

"What?"

"The baby. She comes. I won't leave her. She doesn't have anyone."

He laughed. "Okay, the baby too."

The ice in the air between them snapped like icicles slamming into spring and melting into a crystal pool. Aviama grinned. "She needs a name."

"I suppose she does."

She squealed and leaned in to peck him on the cheek as Manan disappeared around the corner. Aviama darted toward the door, chest swelling with sunshine and butterflies and broken things made new again, when an iron hold seized her by the arm. Chenzira spun her back to him with the fervor of a desert longing for rain.

Her lips parted in surprise, and his mouth crashed into hers. Strong hands cradled her face in his hands, and with the magic of his touch, every fear washed away as a tidal wave swept over them, filled with emotion and craving and answered questions.

He slid one hand to the nape of her neck, pulling her into him, his other arm drawing her body to his. Then the urgency stopped. He drew away to look at her, suddenly unsure. But his eyes were honey, and his arms were life, setting a blaze of desire and wholeness under her skin.

The realization hit her like a sledgehammer. Perhaps Chenzira had answered her question whether he still wanted her. But he still waited for her to answer his.

Silly man. There were a thousand unknowns up in the air at the moment, but this need not be one of them. Aviama's mouth twisted into a smile she couldn't help but show, and she threw both arms around his neck and pulled him to her once again. His arms encircled her waist, and his lips sealed over hers, mouth and tongue moving as if the tighter they held each other, the more the fire of that moment might keep the world and its problems at bay.

When they broke apart, both were breathless. Aviama grinned at his flustered state. He wasn't easy to fluster, but there he was, with flushed cheeks and disheveled hair, looking at her as though he'd found the only treasure that existed in all the universe.

He smiled back at her and tucked a stray hair behind her ear. She must have looked just as crazy. Hurriedly, she raked her hands through her hair to make herself a little more presentable, and leaned in again—close enough to kiss, but only brushing her lips against his, teasing him.

"You still owe me a story."

He nudged her nose with his. "As soon as possible, Tally. I promise."

She gave a nod and half-skipped out of the hollowed-out room where light had filled the dark from within and out into the sunshine of reality—and stopped in her tracks at the door.

Three Keketi men stood at the edge of the plateau. Two of them towered a full head over Umed—leaner than Umed's solid tree-trunk frame, but tall and strong. Their faces were similar, both bearded, one with long hair flowing free past his shoulders and a white tunic; the other wore his hair tied back, a white wrap over one shoulder that covered most of his chest, a dagger at his waist, and a satchel slung across his back. Both wore the same loose white trousers, billowing from the waist and gathered again at the ankle.

The third was little more than a boy, perhaps fourteen. The larger two dwarfed him and his short, slight, bony figure, and Aviama wondered if he might blow away in a breeze. He wore sand-colored trousers, an oversized V-shaped tunic, and a loose headscarf that blended almost perfectly into the sun-soaked, baked-clay hue of the mountain beneath their feet.

Only one of the three carried any weapon, but the confidence in their eyes said they didn't need it. At least, the confidence in the taller two—the boy put up a decent front, but though he puffed out his chest, his thumb hadn't stopped tapping at his thigh since Aviama first laid eyes on him.

The boy's eyes widened when he saw her, and he pulled up to his full height. Which still made him slightly shorter than Aviama. The giants stepped forward, and she realized they'd been standing on footing below the plateau rather than on it, so that when they moved toward her, they grew another few inches.

Teja wrung her hands. Durga's glare sharpened like a knife

on a whetting stone as she took in the movement. She caught Aviama's eye. Aviama pursed her lips. Teja looked far too nervous. Their new friends were unknown and dangerous. Whether Aviama was human or not, melderblood or not, she'd been painted as a revolutionary. A figure to be awed. Why would those around her crumble the instant they were challenged?

The Keketi woman shifted her weight and wrung her hands again, and Durga jabbed her in the ribs. Teja winced. But her hands stopped moving.

Durga jerked her head toward the men and arched an eyebrow at Teja. "Translate."

Teja sidestepped toward Aviama and sucked in a breath. "They say you are not who you say you are."

Chenzira's shoulders dropped into a relaxed swagger as he strode forward to appraise the newcomers. He nodded to Aviama. It was her show. In public, at least.

Aviama let her practiced diplomatic smile descend on the tense muscles of her face. She lifted her chin. "Let's see how closely they've been paying attention, then. Ask them—who do I say that I am?"

Chenzira folded his arms across his chest, feet planted a shoulder's width apart, near enough to defend but just far enough to let Aviama stand alone.

The boy glanced at Chenzira and folded his arms to mirror his position. "We speak common tongue. We aren't from the islands, so we know several heart languages as well as common tongue."

His voice was as young as his slight figure would suggest, smooth but excitable, and higher than that of a man beyond the age of maturity.

"Let's not make a spectacle of ourselves. Come sit." Aviama swept a hand behind her and turned her back on her guests to walk a measured, unhurried pace toward the rock wall and little rocky seats they'd rolled into the space when they arrived.

Her heart pounded as she turned her back, but Umed and Manan were there. Sai and Durga were there. Chenzira was there. She could afford to look gutsy in the presence of such protection.

Aviama selected the tallest of the rocks for herself and perched on its edge. The boy started toward one of the available rocks, then checked himself as he noticed his two massive shadows did not sit. He cleared his throat and cast a look this way and that, as though the wispy white clouds had eyes and the rocks had ears.

"My name is Husani. And yours is not Raisa."

Sai bounced the little girl on her knee in the archway of Chenzira's newly constructed door. Her leg halted mid-bounce, then continued as if she'd not heard a thing. Durga slipped past the three men to stand at Aviama's right hand, clearly taking seriously her self-appointed role as Duqatun's highest-ranking assistant.

It was weird having Durga take on a supporting role, even as an act. She'd been a maidservant mole serving Aviama but working for the queen in Radha and promoted herself to Shiva's lackey when opportunity arose. When Shiva was left to the Iolani, and Onkar sold her to Abasi, along with Aviama and the others, a new alliance was necessary.

And when the islanders decided Aviama was Raisa, the plan was set in stone. Durga would be Aviama's most important assistant. Aviama trusted her about as far as a mosquito trusted a spider. But for now, at least, their purposes were aligned: stay alive and get off the island.

Aviama's secret goal would also include keeping Durga's mouth shut from spouting things on her behalf that she had no business saying. Like confirming Aviama was the Duchess of the Air, for example. Or trying to fuel a frenzied awe of Aviama to get food offerings from the people.

She tilted her head at Husani, then glanced beyond him to the two men who had yet to speak before returning her focus to the boy. "Do you recall me saying my name?"

The boy hesitated, then eyed Durga. "*She* said you were Duqatun Elwehi."

Aviama arched an eyebrow. "*I* said nothing."

Husani's lips flattened in a tight line. His index finger tapped his arm. "Who are you, then?"

Aviama turned to Chenzira. "It is a strange thing to approach someone else, make accusations, and then demand personal information, don't you think?"

The corner of his mouth twitched. "I wouldn't say it encourages openness. It also begs the question of whether the boy would be so bold if not for the very large babysitters attached to him."

Husani's face turned beet red. He opened his mouth, then snapped it shut as a large hand settled on his shoulder. The one without weapons spoke first.

"My name is Osahar. This is my brother Zahur. We are friends of Husani."

Considering the resemblance, Aviama wouldn't have been surprised if they were twins. She gave a nod. "What can I do for you, Osahar?"

"The better question might be what we can do for you."

The man's accent was thick, his voice low. She strained to catch his next words.

"You are not Keketi or Radhan. You speak common tongue, but do not act common. And you know nothing of the culture. You are—how is it—over your head."

Aviama leaned against the rock wall at her back. "Suppose you found me out, and I knew nothing of the culture and was a helpless, lost little bird. Why would you help me?"

"Not common."

"Not lost."

Both replies came at once, the first from Zahur, who spoke for the first time, and the second from Osahar. Zahur held up a finger, and a flame danced on its tip. He opened his hand, and the fire grew into a small sphere, which he tossed to his brother. Osahar caught it, doubled it in size, and tossed it through the dark doorway into Chenzira's makeshift meeting room.

Sai jumped. The toddler reached for the fire. And the light went out against the stone, leaving only a small trail of smoke.

Firebloods. Chenzira caught Aviama's eye, and there was a light in it. He wanted them. They no longer had any firebloods in their party. Not since Laksh had died carrying out Aviama's instructions. On the *Wraithweaver,* he'd come to see her as his commander, risking and ultimately losing his life as reward for his loyalty.

But why would they help? And what did they want?

Chenzira nodded at the boy. "And you?"

Husani grinned, and the pebbles at their feet zigzagged across the plateau.

Chenzira shrugged. "Theirs was cooler."

The boy's face scrunched up like the coils of a riled-up viper. "Mine would be too conspicuous if I did it big! One of you is a quakemaker too. We felt it. I'm just too smart to make the same mistake."

Osahar tapped him twice on the shoulder, and the kid settled down.

Chenzira held up a hand, but he was smiling. "I'm kidding. You did fine. Okay, so you're melders. Why should we care?"

Zahur arched an eyebrow. "If they know you liar, big problem. If we help you lie, safe. Why we help you lie? You tell us. What you doing? Maybe we help."

Aviama glanced at Chenzira. His smile had faded, but his eyes sparked with interest. Still, they weren't planning on overthrowing the Keketi government. And Chenzira had just re-emphasized to her the importance of keeping their identities secret. He caught her eye. It was a daring look. The sort he had when he was about to do something stupid.

Durga inclined her head toward their guests and knelt beside Aviama. The contrast between her languid pose and pristine servant's submissiveness nearly made Aviama laugh aloud as the girl leaned in and whispered sweetly in her ear. "They're half the size of the island. Use them. If I don't eat in the next twenty-four hours, I will be positively feral. Get me off this forsaken rock."

Ah, there it was. The opportunist snob Aviama had come to know. Durga straightened, folding her hands demurely in front of her.

Aviama pursed her lips, then leaned forward and dropped her voice to just above a whisper. "You aren't happy with how things have been run in Keket. You aren't in love with the Jazir islands. Your abilities are wasted here."

All three fixed their gazes on Aviama's face. Behind them, Manan and Umed exchanged a glance. Beside her, the toddler collected pebbles and dropped them into Sai's waiting hands.

Expanding their circle was dangerous. After Darsh, Aviama knew better than to assume a person was an ally based on blood alone. Melder blood did not a friendship make. The more lies she fed them, the worse off they would be when the truth came out—and friendships turned to enemies.

But she couldn't very well continue on with hundreds of people sitting around waiting for her to do something interesting. Something incredible. Something divine.

And to Durga's point, they needed to eat. Having people in their corner whom the crowds did not recognize as part of Raisa's entourage was an advantage.

She spread her hands. "As it happens, I'm in need of fire-bloods, and could make use of a quakemaker. And we need a discreet way off the island."

Osahar swept his gaze across the people on the mountain-side. The people he'd lived among. Pawns devoted to a six-hundred-year dead melderblood human and a nonsensical objective to cleanse the island of people like him. People like her. He returned his focus to Aviama. "To Siada?"

The main island. The island where the royal family lived, and the monarchy ruled the land. A monarchy at risk of losing the favor of its people. Aviama opened her mouth, but Chenzira answered first.

"Not yet. But eventually, yes."

Husani's eyes narrowed to slits and shot a skeptical glance in Aviama's direction. "You don't look like a military leader."

Aviama smiled. "Good. The king won't think so either."

9

Food and a boat took the cake on the day's priorities. Oh, what Aviama wouldn't give for a slice of cake. Biscuits. If she was dreaming, why not make it an entire cake? Maybe a bakery ...

Her mouth watered at the thought, and her stomach growled in vehement protest of its neglect. Chenzira had given one of Abasi's gold bracelets to Husani, and the boy had wriggled through the crowd down the mountain and disappeared. The plan was for Husani to sell it to contacts he claimed to have and return with provisions. But the way his eyes had glinted as his long, skinny fingers wrapped around the ornament—well, it didn't inspire confidence in the kid's loyalty.

In the meantime, Chenzira had sent Manan, Sai, and Teja on a scouting mission down the other side of the mountain to find the best route to the beach, leaving himself, Aviama, Umed, and Durga with the baby—and the two monstrous melders they'd picked up.

Durga had volunteered to go, a motion Chenzira had shot down the instant the words left her mouth. She scowled, but didn't make a fuss. Perhaps she valued her fragile position as most important Duqatun assistant, or perhaps she knew Chenzira trusted her even less than Aviama did, and he would never send her off alone with only one other melderblood to defend himself if she attacked.

Chenzira stood with Umed off to one side, the two of them speaking in low tones as the sun made its slow descent. They each cast a glance over the small crew on the narrow plateau at least twice per minute. Durga sat on the ground and dragged a long finger in the dust, her expression as sour as spoiled milk, opposite Osahar and Zahur. The brothers sat cross-legged on the ground and amused themselves with a game involving a circle drawn on the ground and a pile of pebbles.

Teja leaned against the wall, eyes closed, but Aviama guessed she was awake and listening. She imagined Osahar and Zahur had come to a similar conclusion, considering how infrequently they spoke to one another in Keketi.

The crowd had dwindled, but two hundred or so faithfully waited for their Raisa to speak again. Which is why Aviama sat on the ground with the baby, out of sight in the shadow of Chenzira's roughhewn archway, dancing wisps of air through her curls and floating rocks up in front of her for the girl to grab.

The kid needed a name. It wasn't like Aviama didn't know other things were more pressing. But how long could a person go without personhood? The girl was already a person, but without a name, was her importance acknowledged?

Besides, if she stopped thinking about the little girl, she started thinking about what Chenzira said—that she couldn't save everyone and would need to allow slavery to continue in the region, and that she was helpless, and they might all die. Okay, so maybe that's not exactly what he said, but it was close enough.

The girl snatched a pebble out of the air and stared up at Aviama with big, round eyes. Aviama clapped and smiled. "Yay! You did it! Let's try again—oops, too slow! It moved."

She grinned at the girl and imagined the baby smiled back. She didn't, but her eyes were bright, and she threw another fistful of rocks into the air for Aviama to catch.

Aviama flipped her palm upward, enveloping the girl's offering of pebbles in a cushion of air, dancing them this way and that to avoid the child's fast fingers. Her throat constricted, and a pit in her stomach plummeted into the deep abyss she generally tried to pretend wasn't there. But it always was, and when life grew quiet, her thoughts often wandered into memories of death and despair.

"You and I have a lot in common. We both watched our mothers die. We're both orphans. We both sailed with a pig named Abasi. And, apparently, your mother was a melder." Aviama paused. "I wonder if mine was."

Aviama's mother, Sharsi, had died before The Return. So had her father. Tabeun power must have run in her family for her to have acquired it, but since magic was asleep for the entirety of her parents' lives, there was no way to know for sure which of them might have had powers, or which ability they may have wound up with had they lived long enough to find out.

Her shoulders sagged, and the pebbles dipped. The baby caught one and clapped, looking to Aviama for approval. Aviama managed a halfhearted smile.

"Did you really intend to free all the slaves?"

She glanced up. Osahar studied her.

Durga's finger stilled in the dirt. Zahur scooped up another round of pebbles from inside the dirt-drawn circle and tossed them in the air.

Aviama hesitated. *Yes. I do intend to free them all.* But Chenzira's caution rang in her mind, and she kept the words back. "I didn't free them all."

True. Tragic. Regrettable.

Zahur caught three pebbles and set them outside the circle. He didn't toss more.

"It was, what you say, smoke signal. King will know you come. Using Jazir make you fame before main island."

Osahar considered this. "You'll be legendary before you hit Siada."

Durga sniffed. "She *is* legendary."

Aviama knew better than to be flattered. Durga liked the power she got by association with Aviama. The more powerful Aviama became, the more influence Durga herself gained.

"No. *Raisa* is legendary. A dead legend." Osahar gestured at Aviama. "*She* is a nobody like us, with a few extra friends."

"She's not a nobody."

All heads swiveled to Teja. Her eyes snapped open, and she drilled the men with a cool stare. "How much change have you seen over the years? How long have you lived here, hiding your abilities, and standing by as they killed melders? Yet she freed nearly one hundred slaves within two hours of reaching shore."

Osahar's mouth flattened into a firm line. "If she's not a nobody, why hasn't she told us her name?"

Aviama's heart stopped. *Aviama Shamaran, Princess of Jannemar, daughter of the kingdom that brought back the magic that flows through your veins even now. Top of Radha's kill list. Excellent bargaining chip for Keket.* It's not like Jannemar could afford a generous ransom in the wake of their war with Belvidore to the south, and Radha on the verge of invasion to the northeast.

Not to mention her traveling companion was the missing prince of Keket, which apparently skyrocketed their chances of being murdered. Not that she understood why. He still owed her a story.

Aviama considered a haughty position, to show off a confidence she far from felt. An air of importance, funneling Durga's energy to sell the facade. But just thinking about it sucked all the energy from her body, like water from a grape until all that was left was a shriveled raisin baking in the sun. She looked back down at the rocks on the ground and floated another up into the air.

"No one is making you stay."

"If we go, you die."

Durga prickled. "By whose hand?"

Osahar shrugged. "The people. Melderblood slavers. The government, who no doubt will hear of you and come to squash rebellion. Starvation."

Aviama lifted a pebble over the girl's head. "We've made it through worse."

"What have you made it through?"

Aviama lifted her gaze to meet Osahar. "You don't trust me. I think that's reasonable of you. I don't trust you either. But if you want to know my life story, you're going to have to prove your intentions a little better than you have so far."

He held up both hands, palms out, in defense. "Fair enough."

Zahur nodded at the child. "Why you still have the baby? Will slow down. War no place for child."

Aviama stared down at the girl's dark curls and deep, endless eyes. "She's not mine. But she ... is me, in a way. I can't leave her in a place like this." Not when she might be melderblood. Not when they might enslave or kill her.

Osahar's eyes narrowed, but whatever he was about to say, he kept to himself. Instead, he picked a new topic. "How did you do your demonstration? It was ... precise."

Durga straightened. "She can open locks too."

A shocked hush fell over the group as Teja, Osahar, and Zahur absorbed the information.

Aviama shot Durga a look. Must she run her mouth at every opportunity? Durga lifted one shoulder and smirked.

Osahar turned to Aviama. "Teach us."

Chenzira glanced in her direction, and Umed mirrored him, shifting closer to the group. Beyond them, the sky blazed in hues of canary yellow and tangerine orange, casting its fading light across the sandstone mountainside. Aviama dusted off her fingers and gathered her feet to peer over the formation nearest them. The still-waiting crowd dotted the face of the rock below like lilies in their white attire.

A murmur rippled through the crowd, and she ducked back down, peering through a narrow crack instead. Down toward the city, people walked about like tiny dots to and fro among the adobe homes. Some gave up waiting for Raisa to impress them and headed home along a dirt path. Others were returning with blankets, satchels, and dry wood.

Were they really going to sleep out here on the mountain? How long would they wait before demanding something more?

A group of perhaps twenty people arranged large stones on a narrow flat strip of mountain fifty paces down from Aviama's position. It looked like a rectangular box. Or an altar. Or a pyre.

A small boy stood next to them, twirling a twig of kindling in his fingers, staring directly at her.

He grinned and held up a finger. Fire danced on its tip.

10

I f the structure was a pyre, what—or who—did they intend to burn?

Every Shamaran will burn.

Had Shiva known somehow that this would be her end? Had Onkar known it and told her to be Raisa to bring about this very moment? If Osahar and Zahur were melders, if Husani was a melder, who was to say how many on the island would sacrifice her to bring about a new era?

They would kill her and claim she blessed them all with power. That she reincarnated for this purpose, to die to divide her abilities and bring tabeun power to the island. Though whether the intent was to curse or to bless, they might debate for years to come.

The people needed a reason to wait. She needed to stall. She needed—

"Tally."

A hand settled on her shoulder, and she jumped. Aviama twisted, throwing a blast of air before she registered who it was. Chenzira flew backward. Umed and Osahar leaped after him. Each caught an elbow just before he hit the rock wall behind them. Aviama's hand flew to her mouth.

"I'm sorry. I'm sorry." She spun to look back through the crack. The boy was gone again. How did he do that?

She shoved off the ground and ran forward, but Chenzira was already waving her off. "It's fine. You didn't hear me."

"Um, no." Durga shot him a look. "You called her twice before you touched her."

Aviama bit her lip. "Guess I was lost in thought."

Durga rocked to her feet and popped a hand on her hip. "You didn't answer Osahar either."

Aviama glared at her. *Thanks for that.*

Chenzira cleared his throat. "Husani is back. He got us a bundle of preserved meat and some cash." His expression darkened as he eyed the young man. "Less change than I expected."

Husani shrugged. "Desperation is expensive, and so is paying with stolen goods."

Umed grunted. "Any chance your pockets are heavier than usual?"

Aviama didn't hear the answer. She pivoted from Umed and Husani to the rest of the plateau. "Where's the baby?"

Durga glanced up, darted into the dark hole Chenzira had made before, and reappeared. She shook her head.

Aviama's stomach dropped. How could she have lost her? She'd only looked away for a second.

Chenzira was talking, but Aviama didn't hear. She spied a narrow opening on the side of the plateau between the edge of the rock wall and the next jagged formation jutting up from the ground. She launched herself through the slight space, just wide enough for her to slip through—which meant it was wide enough for the toddler too.

The fringes of the Keketi islanders were visible from her

position, but no little girl toddled toward them. The people pushed inward to busy themselves building the structure, and Aviama ducked low and lunged up the mountain in the opposite direction. Could she have climbed far with those little legs? But if not, where had she gone?

Then she saw the boy disappearing around the side of the rock up ahead.

Aviama threw herself over a rocky ledge after the boy, her bare feet hitting the rock on the other side. Mount Zobaat rose high above her, but everything on that side was visible and empty. A small footpath wound around the side of the mountain. Aviama sprinted around the bend, and there he was—the boy, perhaps ten years old, hopping like a frog from rock to rock. His spindly little arms held the little girl tight, her curls bouncing over his shoulder as he moved.

"Stop!"

Aviama threw up a wind barrier. The boy bumped into it and stumbled backward, and she lifted both hands to funnel air around both sides of the boy as he held the toddler, cushioning the two of them from any fall as she lurched toward them. The fireblood boy turned around.

For the first time, the little girl's slender arms lifted toward her, expectation in her eyes. Aviama's heart swelled, a balm for the vines of terror squeezing the life out of her chest after losing the baby for those two agonizing minutes.

The boy stood on a narrow landing with a precipitous drop off two steps to his left as he rotated to face her. Aviama reached for the little girl, but a dark shadow fell between her and the children.

"Didn't take you for a kidnapper."

Aviama reeled backward to take stock of the intruder. Dark jacket. Kohl around the eyes. Gold on his ears and fingers. Topped with a black hat and a red feather.

He grinned. "I thought burning stuff to the ground was more your style."

The wind left her lungs. She craned her neck around his body to check on the little girl. Her round eyes stared back at Aviama. Waiting. For her.

Aviama swallowed and tried to draw herself up tall, as though she were someone to fear. "It's what happens when someone gets between me and my goal. You should probably move."

He put a hand on his chest. "I would never keep a child from its mother. But wait—is that what I would be doing?"

A chill ran down her spine. Aviama called the wind, and it answered in gusts pooling in her palms. The man held up his hands.

"None of that, missy. They're a little too close to the cliff to toss wind around, wouldn't you say?" He tossed a glance in the direction of the boy and the toddler, and the air whipping around her hands faltered.

But she had more control than most melderbloods. She could pull him toward her and leave the kids alone. Unless the boy panicked when the man fell and dropped the girl in the process. Was it the kid's father?

A memory hit her then, unbidden. Wind whistling from a victim's lungs to her hungry hands. Crushed windpipes. A swift death to any man, at her literal fingertips. She wouldn't even have to touch him.

Goosebumps fled up her arms. No. Murder was not the solution to every problem. How could she jump so quickly to it, just because she could?

Power was intoxicating. It had consumed her uncle and nearly swallowed her sister whole. Her sister had gotten caught up with housing artifacts, objects infused with sifal magic—forbidden magic. Aviama's magic was tabeun. It was natural. But still its power glittered like gold in a dark cave, whispering sweet nothings and drawing her in.

How much was too much? *Just a little bit more.*

That's what had happened to Shiva. And with each new step she took away from Shiva, the more she felt she had become him. She had blasted the man over the railing of the *Wraithweaver,* and for what? His evil clung to her like tar.

But this man in the black hat stood between her and an orphan child.

Aviama stretched out her fingers, testing the limits of her abilities. His breath came fast. She could feel it.

"You are more nervous than you look."

He shrugged. If he was surprised by her assertion, he didn't show it. "I wouldn't call it nervousness. Excited, maybe. It's not every day I encounter a goddess."

Aviama's gaze flitted to the children. The boy adjusted the little girl in his arms. Her eyes were still on Aviama's face. She glanced back up at the man. "If you see one, let me know."

He cocked his head. "Awfully eager to give up your divinity."

Where was Chenzira? Hadn't he realized she was gone? Had Osahar and Zahur stopped him? Aviama's mouth went dry. Were the brothers working with this man?

She'd been set up. She was a fool.

The man in the hat twisted a ring on his finger, reminding her of her own loss. He spread his hands, as if his empty hands would put her at ease. "You're tense. Relax. I'm not here to hurt anyone. I wanted to meet you."

"I'd say it's been a pleasure, but lying is exhausting."

"I take it you would know." His eyes narrowed. And then, like dark clouds melting into the horizon, his countenance lit, and he rubbed his hands together as if he just realized what to make for supper and all the ingredients had been dumped in his lap ready to use. "You know what's even more surprising than meeting a goddess?"

Getting framed as one, probably. But Aviama said nothing. His breath still came fast, but steady, like a hound catching the thrill of the hunt. If she could distract him long enough, perhaps the boy would move. Or if Aviama could draw the man away from the children, maybe she could get between him and the kids. She dropped her shoulders and let her head droop, sucking in a shallow breath and backing away. She tossed furtive glances this way and that, as though she were cornered and powerless—unable to drop him where he stood the moment she chose.

"A goddess who is in desperate need of my assistance. A woman is never more beguiling than when she fiercely needs me." He winked. She stifled a groan.

Rocks shifted behind her, and a stone twice the size of her fist clattered down from the direction she'd come.

"She here! Not run."

"Keep your voice down, bird brain. Do you *want* the whole island down our throats?"

Zahur skidded to a halt as he rounded the edge of the mountain, and Durga slammed into him at the sudden stop.

The man in the black hat cast a glance at the towering man behind Aviama and the sharp-nosed woman beyond him. He looked back at Aviama. "You need a ticket off the island."

Another voice came from Aviama's left. "Whatever vessel she takes, we intend to be on it."

Osahar.

Behind her, Zahur and Durga closed in. To her left, Osahar bounded over the rocks, Chenzira close behind. Ahead and just to her right, the boy held the toddler girl. His slender arms tired, and Aviama's heart surged to her throat as the boy plopped her down on the ground three short steps from death off the cliff.

Four paces in front of her, the man with the black hat set his hands on his hips and watched with no small amusement as the observation gallery to their little meeting expanded.

Osahar's hand clenched into a fist. A vein bulged on his neck as he debated whether to show his powers, after holding them at bay so long on the island. Chenzira's eyes swept over the situation, and Aviama held up a hand, moving only her eyes to indicate the children on the cliff's edge.

Chenzira followed her gaze. She hoped he understood her. *An earthquake could kill the kids.*

The man laughed. "You hold them all in your pretty little hand, don't you?"

Aviama sent a rivulet of air over the man's shoulder, the ends of his hair moving in the breeze as the wind snaked around him into a barrier on the cliff side of the children. He arched an eyebrow in her direction, and she leveled him with as unconcerned a look as she could muster. "If I did, and you threatened me, how would that go for you?"

He stuffed his hand into a pocket. Chenzira stiffened, but the man produced only a handful of something that looked to be dusted with sugar. The scent of ginger wafted in her direction as he popped one into his mouth. "Oh, I think you're the one doing all the threatening. I only said I wanted to meet you. And that I could solve your problem."

Chenzira crossed not toward Aviama, but toward the man's back, until he was twenty paces away and in line with the children.

The man in the black hat took a step away from Aviama and back toward the boulder, blocking the path and cutting off Chenzira's approach. He popped another candied ginger in his mouth.

"I see you've taken on some new henchmen since you landed. I'm not the henchman type, but I'm no friend of the king myself. And I've got a ship."

Chenzira's hand twitched. He caught Aviama's eye, then cleared his throat to draw the man's attention to himself. "Where does it make berth?"

The man looked Chenzira up and down, and for the first time, he hesitated. "Next port is Siada. But we pass an island or two on the way, and I could be convinced to make a stop if that's not your destination."

"We aren't headed to Siada. We go to Anhiraf."

Interest sparked the man's face. "What is your business there?"

Chenzira's mouth twitched. "If it were your business, you would know."

Was he mocking him? Or enjoying the exchange?

The man seemed as unsure of Chenzira's intentions as Aviama. He waved Chenzira off as if he and his claims were about as significant as a gnat.

"My business was with the lady." He turned to Aviama. "What is your destination?"

Aviama had no idea what Anhiraf was. It could be an island. Or a city on an island. Or a legendary old hermit living in a hovel, busied only with keeping visitors off his grass. But this was Chenzira's world, and she hadn't heard the rest of Chenzira's story.

And he'd asked her to trust him.

She swallowed. "Anhiraf."

The man inclined his head with a smirk. "Anhiraf it is. Shall we make ready?"

Aviama opened her mouth, but words failed her. Was he kidding? He would take her and her entire party on his ship, and deliver them where she wanted to go without question or incident?

Chenzira filled the silence. "Can your vessel be here by nightfall?"

The man turned to Chenzira, and Aviama shot him a glare behind the black-hatted man's back.

"As sure as I'm standing before you. All I'll need is payment, and we'll be on our way the moment the sun is down." He grinned.

Behind him, the young boy scuffed his toe in the dirt, bored with the adult talk. Beside him, the toddler stuck a hand out over the ledge. The man flinched, one hand instinctively reaching in her direction. The little girl's hand bumped into Aviama's barrier, and his brows shot up.

Aviama clenched her jaw. She'd boarded two ships in the last months. Neither of them had been voluntary, and neither had been pleasant experiences. But she was anxious for the exchange to be over, and perhaps after they left the man, she could remind Chenzira how insane it would be to take the stranger up on his offer. "What do you charge?"

The man bobbed his head from one side to the other as if haggling with himself over a price he'd yet to determine. "I still have the boy to think about. Mouths to feed, you know. Can't be all about charity, no matter how good the cause." He licked the ginger off his fingers and flashed a pearly smile. "I think a jeweled collar and two golden armbands would do it."

Everything Chenzira had taken from Abasi. The man with the black hat may have disappeared from the base of the statue in the square, but he'd been watching the whole time.

But one of the armbands had been given to Husani to sell for food.

Aviama exchanged a glance with Chenzira. Chenzira ran a

hand through his beard and tapped his neck twice. Aviama looked back at the stranger.

"Jeweled collar or nothing."

"Didn't know you were in a position to haggle. But if you plan on overthrowing the government, I can give you a discount. Jeweled collar it is." He gestured to the boy behind him. The kid picked up the little girl under the arms and scuffled forward with her. The girl lifted a hand toward Aviama, and Aviama scooped her up into her arms.

You're safe now. It's okay.

Her hair smelled of salt and clay and dust, but her little arms sliding around Aviama's neck felt like arriving home after a night in back-alley streets riddled with robbers. Aviama wrapped her own arms around the girl, as if locking the door to the home. As if by sheer will, no one could break in and steal whatever she held onto tight enough.

"Pleasure doing business." The man scanned Aviama with the toddler, then turned to the entourage standing around them and flashed a grin. "It just so happens that my ship is anchored nearby. I'll take a few of you men with me to make preparations, and we can be off as soon as night falls."

Durga looked him up and down as if she could steal any overlooked ginger just by gawking. "And whose ship will we be taking?"

He inclined his head. "Mine, naturally."

Osahar crossed his arms. "Give us your name."

The man tipped his hat and bowed. "I'll tell you mine when the lady tells me hers."

11

Osahar and Zahur turned toward her as one. Durga shot her a look and mouthed *Raisa,* an option Aviama immediately dismissed. The man in the black hat was under no delusions that she was a real goddess, and there was little reason to insult him before they boarded his ship. Using any Jannemari name was out of the question. Aviama had no intentions of giving the man hints on where she was from. But she also didn't know many names from this region.

The little girl tugged on her golden hair as it cascaded over her shoulder. Aviama shifted her weight and raised her eyes to the stranger.

"Bishakha."

"Interesting choice." He tilted his head at her. "Was it the blonde hair or the pale skin that made you think to claim Keket as your origin?"

Aviama blanched. No matter the color, she was grateful her hair was long. She looked down at the toddler in her arms, and it fell like a curtain to hide the heat flushing her cheeks beet red. When she looked up a moment later, the man was still looking at her.

He pursed his lips, a twinkle in his eye, then gave a satisfied nod. "Took you longer to come up with than it should have, but not so long as I expected."

She frowned. "And yours?"

"Florian."

Durga snorted. Chenzira scoffed. Aviama's gut twisted, and the heat in her face worsened.

A Curion name. Which *Florian*, with his Keketi accent and rich, ruddy skin tone, most assuredly was not.

Fine. The Jannemari girl would call herself Bishakha, and the Keketi man would call himself Florian. At least they all had something to call each other, even if no one believed the names were true.

"Commander."

Florian's head snapped up at the title. Aviama's head swiveled to see Manan standing to her left, just beyond a boulder at their rear. She hadn't noticed him join them. How long had he been standing there?

"Yes?"

"The people are restless. Several approached the landing to look for you. You weren't there. Umed is trying to talk to them through Teja, but they're not listening. They're pressing in on the plateau, trying to see into the doorway. Soon they will come around the mountain."

Florian eyed Manan and took a step closer to Aviama. His voice was quiet. "*Commander* Bishakha, is it?" Mocking or merely amused, she could not tell. But his gaze lit with a mischievous curiosity. The thrill of a chase. "A woman who rejects goddess status and will not use other titles she is awarded. But responds readily to the respect of your associates. You are odd, Commander. And you do not look military to me."

Aviama shifted the child to her hip, leaving one hand free, and squared her shoulders as she drilled Florian with a cool stare. "You're very preoccupied with appearances." Her gaze drifted to the red feather billowing in the wind from the top of his black hat. "I'm not impressed by them myself."

"Be interested enough to get the people under control. The last time a man betrayed them, they burned him in the public square. And if the people follow you when you come, I'll leave you behind. No need to add meat for their bonfires." He turned to the boy, signaled something to him, and the kid dashed off down the mountain with the agility and expert footing of a young goat. He turned back to Aviama. "Give them something to do. Redirect their focus."

From the looks of the stone pyre they were setting up, the people might burn their deities too. Aviama didn't trust Florian, but if he could really get them off the island, she'd prefer the kettle of his ship over the fire of the island. She took a breath. "What do you suggest?"

Florian arched an eyebrow. "Give them a show, Duqatun. You're good at that."

He tilted his hat, hopped up on a boulder, and bounded down the mountainside, pausing only once to check if the men were following. Chenzira strode to Aviama. "Give them a show. He's right, you're good at it. I'll leave Umed with you and the girls and take Manan and the brothers with me. Manan and Sai found a rendezvous point, so Sai can lead you there, and Manan will make sure the ship is positioned at that spot when night falls."

Aviama's stomach knotted. "You're not staying with me?"

Chenzira sighed, and his lips flattened. He cast a dark look down the mountain. "I'm not letting this guy out of my sight.

And we don't know our new additions well enough for me to leave them behind, either. Husani has the food, and he can stay with you. Bring him when you come. Or don't. But make sure to get the food."

He pulled her in, kissed her forehead, and wrapped his arms tight around her, the little girl squeezed in between them. "I'll find you. Don't do anything stupid while I'm gone, okay, Tally?"

Aviama hugged him back hard with her one free arm. "Stupid is my specialty."

"You really need to stop taking over my areas of expertise. It's annoying."

Aviama smiled. Chenzira pulled away and glanced down the mountain, where the red feather in Florian's hat bobbed farther and farther away. Chenzira tipped up her chin and kissed her soundly on the mouth. "I'll see you soon. Be safe."

"You too."

Chenzira called Osahar and Zahur and gestured for Manan to follow before running down the mountain after Florian. Manan glanced back at Aviama, and she nodded. He took off at a sprint, leaving Durga and Aviama behind and the little girl in Aviama's arms. The mountain precipice fell away to their right, and the sun sank into the horizon in ever-deepening hues of marigold, blood orange, and pomegranate.

A shout rose with a clatter from around the bend. They turned together toward the sound, and people spilled around either side of the rock formation before them. Bodies rushed toward them in a wave of white linen and sun-kissed skin, some old, some young, some well-muscled, others frail—and all of them screaming as one.

"Duqatun Elwehi!"

"Duqatun!"

A flutter in her chest seemed to whisper to the power in

her blood, sending a tingle up and down her arms. She could do this. She'd done it before. Florian was right—it was time to put on a show.

Aviama gave the little girl a kiss and shoved her into Durga's arms. Durga held the girl half-away from her body, eyes bulging as if a deadly feral creature had been dropped in her lap.

She gaped up at Aviama. "No."

Aviama leveled her with a look. "I need both hands free if I'm going to give them a show."

Umed and Teja sprinted toward them on the left, but the first of the crowd overtook them, swallowing them like a surging wave. On the right, Aviama caught a glimpse of Sai with her hand gripping Husani's tunic, but the next moment, Husani ducked and was gone, and Sai was alone.

And still the mob came.

Aviama threw up her hands in a tight bubble around herself, Durga, and the baby. Two young men faceplanted into the barrier and dropped to the ground, a woman hitting the invisible wall only an instant later. She ricocheted off the surface, stumbling back into the crowd.

The glint of steel flashed in the golden light of the sinking sun. Aviama dropped the barrier, enveloped the knife in a cushion of air, spun it round, and delivered the handle into the palm of her hand. She thrust it into the air.

"Silence!"

Teja ran forward, screaming the translation. "Alsamto!"

Another knife sailed through the air, this time at Teja. Aviama dropped it to the dust with a flick of her wrist, but a whistling wind and a *thud* sounded behind her as she moved toward their interpreter. She spun back to see a man lying on his back against a rock two paces away. Blood poured from a wound on his head. He did not move. Durga dropped her hand as Aviama turned.

No, no, no. Durga had used windcalling—the power the people only attributed to Aviama—and killed a man. One of their own.

Aviama whirled to take in the response of the people. Had they seen it? How long would it take them to—

By the time she registered the spear barreling toward her heart, it was too late.

But a handsbreadth from her breastbone, a glowing hand snatched the spear from its path. The body attached to the hand rolled through the momentum and popped up right beside her.

Husani. *Biscuits.* The kid's reflexes were lightning.

"La telmasi qayidu jeh shi fideyika!"

Teja stood, shaking like a leaf, between Husani and Aviama. She bit her lip. "He says, 'Do not touch the commander of the army of your redemption.'"

Aviama pursed her lips. People really needed to stop saying things without consulting her. "Okay, fine, I can work with that. But it's my turn. Translate what I say."

She hurled the knife into the midst of the people with a strength worthy of an assassin's pupil. The spin was beautiful. The blade cut through the air with the grace of an Iolani tail, the poetry of song.

It was a shame she had to ruin her best throw.

Aviama threw up her palm and caught the knife in a current of air just as a grizzled older man registered its tip flying a single meter from his jugular. The blade spun over backward and rocketed up over the crowd, tumbling end over end, until at last it stuck upright, blade downward, hovering over the heads of the waiting mob.

Aviama held her hand out, palm up, as she commanded

the wind to her bidding. She raised her voice, and Teja translated her common tongue to Keketi. "Don't you think if I wanted to escape, I would be gone already? Don't you think if I wanted to kill you, you would be dead already?"

"Sifal," someone cried. "Sifal!"

Aviama arched an eyebrow. She needed no translation for that word. "Was Raisa's magic sifal, or tabeun? Did she destroy magic because it was sifal, or because even the natural, even the tabeun, was abused? But when the four famed melders of The Crumbling infused their magic in artifacts, it was a failsafe, a means to escape tyranny should no other option remain."

Aviama danced the knife blade over their heads. "Tyranny has reached this island, has it not?"

An uneasy hush fell over the crowd as they strained to hear Teja's translation. They might not all agree on who she was or what should be done about her and her power, but they seemed to have this in common: they did not like the monarchy. And despite their slave trade—and if Florian was to be believed, their burning of traitors—they saw themselves as victims.

"Raisa died to protect the innocent, did she not?"

Murmurs wafted through the people. Expressions were mixed. Aviama cleared her throat and tried again.

"The oppression of the regime grows, but the power of Raisa is here! Would you destroy the commander before the army strikes? Any man who lays a hand on the commander loves the king! Any man who objects to the power of Raisa betrays Jazir!"

A wizened old man with long spindly limbs jabbed a knobbed finger at her chest, the deep wrinkles of his face pulling the corners of his frown into an impossibly deep displeasure. He spoke slow, deliberate words.

Teja's face paled three shades. "He says the altar is ready. You cannot be out of sight of the altar until the ceremony is complete."

Sai's mouth parted. "Ceremony for what?"

Bile flew up the back of her throat. Aviama didn't know, and she didn't intend to find out. But she did intend to *pretend* she knew, and to stall. She lifted her chin.

"I will not draw closer until I see the preparations are correct. Your altar needs more wood. I want every surrounding island to see the smoke."

Murmurs grew to rumbles, anger etched into the faces of some, fear painted on the blanched faces and whites of the eyes of others. Some shifted their weight, nodded, or glanced back down the mountain as if calculating how long it would take to bring more kindling from town.

"The first time you met Raisa, her power was limited. Now, it is not. What is wind? What is wind but that which touches all things?" She didn't know what it meant, but it sounded good. Hopefully. She kept going before she could talk herself out of her own nonsense. "All of us are connected by its force. It bears the power to destroy, or to save."

Aviama dropped the knife, and it plummeted toward the people. Shrieks went up and the mob scattered, but Aviama swept a gale through their midst, catching the blade in its path and weaving the wind among them so that each felt its power before she took hold of the blade again.

She tossed it to the ground. "My fight is not with you. And you shall be rewarded. Tonight, I will give you a show. For those who doubt. For those who question me. We will light the fire. We will dance before its flame. And you will see what the second Raisa is capable of."

And we will run like a rabbit from the den of the fox.

She left off that last bit. Better to leave some surprises for the show. But even as the crowd roared with approval, fists pounding the air, pearl-white teeth flashing smiles, she imagined those teeth sinking into her flesh. Chenzira was right—these were not her people. This was not her world.

If she didn't tread carefully, the fox could catch the rabbit and tear it to pieces.

There were many things Aviama did not know, but two certainties spun over and over in her mind:

Her show had better be good.

She had better be on time to meet Florian at the rendezvous point.

12

Roars went up from the crowd. A chill ran down Aviama's spine.

Excitement. Dark glares. Hope. Fear. All of it flickered across the faces of the people, sometimes one after the other on the same face.

Umed pressed back a few stragglers as they tried to edge closer to Aviama. Durga strode to Sai and dumped the baby into her arms. Durga turned to Aviama.

"We've got to get everybody back on the far side of the mountain, so our path out of here is clear."

Aviama nodded. "Teja, tell the people we will oversee the altar improvements from up there"— she gestured to the large domed formation above the plateau they'd set up in before— "but will not come down until it's ready."

Teja delivered the message, and Aviama gathered a great gust of wind around her. She ran to the rock and jumped. The power of the wind increased around her, lifting her higher and whipping her clothes and hair as Sai and Durga added their energy to the blast. Aviama alighted on the top of the domed formation, three meters over the heads of the islanders.

Umed, Husani, and Durga ushered the people around the sides of the formation and back to the slope of the mountain they'd been on before—the side facing the center of the island rather than the coast. Sai held the little girl, and once the people were gone, Aviama helped Sai up with another gust of wind added to Sai's own. The girl reached for Aviama, and she took her and held her close.

Aviama ran a hand over her face. "What kind of show can I put on? There's nothing here but dirt and rocks. I can't just do more shapes."

Sai stretched out her arms over her head and leaned this way and that, as if limbering up for what was to come. "You claimed to have more power than the first Raisa. Husani is a quakemaker. Durga and I are windcallers like you. Play with the fire when they light it and use all our powers together."

An unladylike groan came from behind them, and Aviama turned as Durga clambered up the rock. "Next time I get to be the duchess goddess person, floating everywhere, and you can do all the climbing. This is ridiculous."

Aviama rolled her eyes and held out a hand. She half expected Durga to smack her hand away, but the girl took her hand and pulled hard as she made her way up onto the dome with Aviama and Sai.

"Least you could do, really. Have you got the food yet? Never put on a show on an empty stomach, that's what I say. And since we'll be doing most of the work, I think it's only fair we get the biggest portions."

The food. Aviama's heart stopped. She glanced in both directions. Umed was on the plateau beneath them, with Teja. Where was Husani?

Had Husani been wearing a bag or satchel of any kind when she saw him with the mob? She couldn't remember. Had he stashed the food for himself? But then why come back at all once he had the gold bracelet from Chenzira?

Aviama spun.

Durga moaned. "You lost the food."

Sai shushed her. "He's here. It's here. Keep it down."

Aviama let out a breath. On the end of the dome, Husani kicked at a kid maybe two years younger than himself that was trailing him, and spidered his way up the cliff. Aviama arched her eyebrows. Not only did he have fast reflexes, but he was an excellent climber.

Husani rolled to the top of the dome and folded his legs in a crisscross sitting position, fist still fastened to the spear he'd snatched before it skewered Aviama through the chest. He popped the spear upright and leaned on it.

"Why did your boyfriend take Osahar and Zahur and not me?"

He sounded like a wounded puppy. Aviama pressed her lips in a flat line, willing herself not to smile. "He probably thought a few men should stay with us women."

Durga scoffed, and Aviama shot her a look. Let the kid feel good. Let him feel useful. Until he did something stupid, they were giving Husani a chance and bringing him along. Although, Durga was right—Chenzira never would have trusted the skinny newcomer kid with their safety. That's what Umed was for. And they'd yet to see how precise Husani could be with his tabeun ability.

Chenzira barely trusted Husani to get provisions, though to his credit, he'd come through. Aviama cleared her throat. "He also wanted to make sure we got the food. You have it, right?"

To Aviama's relief, Husani had a bag slung across his body. He twisted, opened the bag, and pulled out a wrapped pack. He pulled his shoulders back and lifted his chin. "Yes, but I'm in charge of it. You can have some, but we have to ration it."

Sai made eye contact with Aviama and widened her eyes for a split second. The meaning was clear. *Is this kid serious? Did he really just pretend he was in charge of something?*

Husani glanced at Sai, and Durga puffed her chest out and made a pretentious expression while his back was turned.

Aviama bit her lip. "Yes, thank you. We've eaten moldy bread for months. We won't eat it all, but if you don't give us each an equal portion"—here she shot a glare in Durga's direction—"I'll feed you to Durga."

Durga's scowl at the word *equal* brightened at the concept of permission to take Husani down a peg. Or three. She grinned.

Husani eyed her, adjusted the headscarf over his hair and tossed over his shoulder, then opened the pack. "I got us some salted meat. Let's start with that."

The teen passed out portions of the meat, and it was all Aviama could do to take bites rather than inhale the whole thing and choke to death. Her mouth watered at the sight of it, and the glorious smell made her head swim. Umed and Teja joined them a moment later, Teja taking a seat next to Sai, and Umed eating his portion from a standing position on the rock where he could see all the Keketi on the mountainside, and the altar as more kindling was added.

The next few minutes were spent planning the show and subsequent escape. Husani had an extra headscarf in his bag, which they cut into long strips and wrapped around Sai and Aviama's bare feet. Durga and Umed still had decent shoes, and Husani's were in good shape, but Sai and Aviama's had been stolen and destroyed on the voyage over in the cargo hold of *Raisa's Revenge*. Running down a rocky mountain would not go well in bare feet.

As for strategy, with the firebloods down the mountain with Chenzira and Florian, and no water source close enough to use, controlling any fire the people lit on the altar would be fruitless. At best, they could bat the flames around with wind and make it a little bigger and more dramatic, but the best options were to lean into the resources they had: wind, wind, and more wind. Oh, and whatever quakemaking abilities Husani had.

Husani insisted he had great control and the best quakemaking she'd ever seen, but his cocky demeanor did little to inspire confidence. Quakemaker abilities were dangerous, and with an entire mountain of rock, steep cliffs, and crags, he could intend to scare the people and end up sinking their legs into the mountain or killing them outright with a landslide.

Some of the people had gone into town for more wood, but some overprepared islanders had brought extra, so the stack of kindling on the altar was looking pretty intimidating as it was. Aviama's gut pinched. How long would it take a person to fry to death in a blaze of that size? She shuddered.

"Sai, are you *sure* you can find the rendezvous point in the dark?"

Durga tilted her head at Sai. Sai scowled.

"You've asked me twice. How much do you think my answer will have changed since then?"

"Well, if you can't, and we miss the boat, we're all as good as dead." Durga sniffed. "So you'll forgive me for making sure."

Teja cleared her throat and turned to Husani. "Do you have family here?"

The boy winced. "No one who would care if I was gone."

Teja offered a pained smile. "You know, once we do this,

there's no going back. Me, I haven't lived in Keket since I was a child, and the only other family I have left is in Radha. But you're different. You live here."

Husani stared at her for a long moment, eyes empty of mischief, glassy with numbness. He licked the salt off his fingers and dusted his hands on his trousers.

"It's not living."

Silence descended like rain, chilling the air and filling the space around them. Durga shifted her weight and dragged a finger through the dirt in swirling circles. Sai grimaced. The baby tugged on Aviama's hair.

Chattering voices drifted up to them from the crowd below, none distinct enough to pick out one over another. Lumber shifted and clattered to the rocks as some of the wood overflowed the altar. Someone swore, and three islanders yelled in the face of a fourth.

Umed cleared his throat. "The sun just set. We have maybe half an hour before nightfall. If we're lucky."

Aviama's stomach churned. "How long do you think it'll take us to make it down the mountain?"

Durga scrunched her nose. "Do I *look* like I hike mountains? Please."

Umed walked backward until he could hear the conversation, keeping an eye on the people. "Too long."

"When would we need to leave?"

"Maybe ten minutes ago."

Sai's jaw dropped. "But that's impossible. What kind of show can we put on without any time?"

"Florian only just left." Durga paused. "He can't possibly have meant at nightfall when he'd barely make it down there himself by then. Could he?"

Umed shrugged. "Either way, Commander, you need to start the show now, and it needs to be fast. End it with a strong finale. Cause enough of a ruckus that we can run and disappear into the night before they find us."

Aviama groaned. "No pressure."

"None at all."

Biscuits.

Aviama stood and passed the little girl to Sai. "Teja, you ready?"

Teja nodded.

"Good." At least one of them was.

Aviama nodded at the little band with her—Umed, the melderblood from Onkar's crew on the *Wraithweaver,* who'd learned basic thievery and pickpocketing alongside her in the kitchens. Sai, her maidservant from the House of the Blessing Sun, previous informant to Prince Shiva. Durga, her maidservant informant to Queen Satya, turned lackey to Shiva, turned ally of convenience on Keket. A freed slave woman without tabeun abilities, whose mother had been murdered just that morning. And Husani, the newcomer teen Keketi boy with an existence he would not classify as living.

Down on the mountainside, the squabble over the wood on the altar escalated, and one of the men punched another across the jaw. Others jumped in, and before Aviama could blink, a brawl had broken out. Durga had already killed a man today, with power ascribed to Duqatun Elwehi. How many more would die before nightfall? If anything went wrong ...

Umed crossed his arms. "We don't have time for the whole show, Commander. The sun is set. Darkness will fall. Skip to the end."

The end? Now? Aviama swallowed. Large-scale wind-calling spent her energy differently than small gusts or short, powerful blasts. She generally dismissed it and recovered when she had the time, but just how big of a show would she need to make the statement she intended for the Jazir islanders? How drained would she be for the flight down Mount Zobaat toward the rendezvous?

"Any day, Commander."

Right. Of course. Thanks, Umed. Aviama stepped forward until her toes brushed the edge of the rock. Her foot kicked a pebble, and it skittered off the formation, dropped to the edge of the plateau, and tumbled over the edge.

Inhale, exhale. Inhale ...

She spread her hands, palms up, and closed her eyes. *Focus.*

What a strange sight she must be to the several hundred people down below. A woman in a billowing white tunic and trousers, no shoes, and cloth wound around and around her bare feet. Golden hair spilled over her shoulders, her skin red from the start of a sunburn. She carried no weapons, only an odd yet beautiful battle horn fit for kings and royal halls, hung across her torso and resting snug against her hip.

But none of them saw her. The shouting grew louder, and the thud of bodies bashed this way and that reminded her of battles and narrow escapes. Sounds of combat were not foreign to her. She'd heard her brother train with the guards all through her childhood. She'd mostly been spared from seeing or hearing the few quick skirmishes by rebels around the castle over the years.

Until the assassin army descended on Shamaran Castle. Until Semra smuggled her out, and she learned what it meant to be on the run with a killer. A killer with a heart of gold. It sounded like a contradiction. Was it possible?

Those memories seemed so far away. Back when she was helpless, naïve, and afraid. When she cowered behind her brother's sword and her sister-in-law's dragon. But now that she had power, she also had blood-soaked hands.

Shiva's face flew to mind. His body tumbling over the rail

of the *Wraithweaver* into Iolani-infested waters. A death sentence.

Was she a killer with a heart of gold? Or was Chenzira right—that he'd seen something dark in her that day, the day she planned to murder Shiva before she lost her own life to whatever enemies would mow her down? Was the thrill of her power tabeun as well, or did a natural ability fill her with an unnatural drive to abuse that power—as so many others had done with sifal magic? Were tabeun and sifal magic sources really so different?

Her brow furrowed, and her eyes squeezed tighter shut, as if by mere willpower she could block out the emotions rolling through her. But she needed a storm. A *great* storm. She needed to command the attention of all, convince them of astonishing power, and escape in the blink of an eye.

When had her power been strongest, but at her Awakening? In the storm that killed the innocent servant boy? Was she willing to let her storm rage again with such peril?

Enzo's decapitated head stared up at her from the silver platter in her mind's eye. Bhumi's smiling face and bright optimism were replaced with the ghastly pallor of death. Bodies littered the sand and the docks in Radha. Swords glinted in the starlight of the slums of Rajaad, as the heavy boots of the royal guard swept through every alley to destroy melderblood scum. Laksh's corpse lay on the deck in a puddle of burning oil, under a sun he would never see again.

Her chest hitched. Wind swirled around her, and a rush filled her ears. Air whispered along her skin and whipped at her hair from all directions. A lump formed in her throat.

With it, a sneering accusation intruded into her thoughts like a slithering hiss. *You are no Duchess of the Air.*

Of course she wasn't. She wasn't a duchess of anything.

She had never claimed to be Duqatun Elwehi. Aviama was no goddess, nor did she want to be one. But the hiss continued.

Death, death, death.

Blood, blood.

Destruction.

What had been whole that she had not torn to splinters wherever she went? What lives had been lived that she had cut short? What buildings, what families, what peace had she not torn asunder?

Duchess of Death.

The lie of her identity burned in her throat like fire. The anguish of konnolan used to slaughter melders, a weapon she'd handed Shiva without a thought, ripped through her body like the crumbling of brittle bones underfoot. A sob caught in her chest, but even as a tear escaped down her cheek, the gale surrounding her whisked it from her face the moment it fled from her lashes.

Don't fight it. You know you need all the power of devastation. You know your undoing is the fuel you need. You remember the smithy? You remember the pure might of your Awakening. Lean into the pain. Do it again.

Aviama couldn't shake her head. She couldn't do anything but draw comfort from the rhythmic rush of the wind about her ears, the power of the force pressing in around her body. The strength of the storm mounted, and the ache in her chest came alive like a fuse lit in the center of a dam.

She reached one thumb over to touch the ring she'd spent so many hours leaning on for support. For that last connection to her murdered mother. For the solace of one single familiar thing rooting her to the ground.

It wasn't there.

Her mother was dead. Her father was dead. The cavern within herself yawned wide, her flimsy attempts to fill it decaying into dust. A colossal rush of air lifted her from her feet, fed by a bottomless pit of despair. The force of it chilled her to the bone, even as adrenaline flooded her blood with tingling anticipation.

Hello, darling.

And then the dam broke.

13

Aviama saw the flame ignite on the altar just before the storm burst. When her eyes opened, a whirlwind several stories tall held her in its midst a meter up from the rock. Sai and Durga stood behind her, their hands lifted in her direction, their silhouettes visible only through wisps of swirling wind as Aviama turned her head.

Down by the altar, a man placed his hand on the wood, and fire leaped from his touch. It was at this moment that Aviama released the chains of the whirlwind, reacting to the information of the fireblood at the altar as if in slow motion. Fire enveloped the dry kindling and went up in a whoosh, lighting up the dusk of the evening with dancing flame and a tower of smoke to challenge the revolving whirlwind as it shattered across the rock of Mount Zobaat.

Screams came in eerie spurts as the wind battered their sound in every direction, amplifying some and smothering others. Men, women, and children dove to the ground at the onslaught of the windstorm's gale cutting across the mount. Flaming logs tumbled from the altar like missiles pursuing bodies blown into the sharp rocks.

Out of the corner of her eye, she saw Umed fall. Fire exploded from three new positions in the crowd, and the mountain shook. To her right, rock shifted and split apart, breaking into boulders that rolled down into the islanders with all the ingredients for a blunt-force trauma death and corpses flattened to pancakes.

Aviama's feet hit the rock again, and the mountain bucked in a rolling wave. Two firebloods threw balls of fire into the blaze on the altar, doubling its size. Three men in long robes and gold hovered at the edge of a precipice to her left, gaping wide eyed at the scene. One ducked behind a boulder, scribbling notes in a leatherbound book.

They didn't look like citizens. They looked like government officials.

A dozen islanders rushed the firebloods, screams and shouts and blows filling the air. Winds blew from every direction, knocking Aviama sideways. The sky grew dark. Pleading eyes searched for Aviama up on the top of the mountain, screaming for Duqatun Elwehi.

Teja touched Aviama on the shoulder. Her hand was cold. "They're crying out for mercy. Some ask you to bless them with powers. Others call you traitor."

Time to go.

Durga caught her eye. "Blaze of glory?"

She nodded. "The biggest."

Aviama lifted her hands, Sai and Durga funneling their own wind into hers until it tripled in strength. She launched it into the burning pyre already towering over their heads. Its height leaped as their wind fed greedy fingers of flame that sucked up the air around it and licked at the sky. Heat radiated from the glow at an alarming rate, casting her skin in red-orange and surging up to the heavens. The ground beneath her feet shifted again. More screams.

Aviama retreated from the edge. Umed regained his feet, scooped up the little girl, and ripped his khopesh from its sheath. "To the boat. Now."

No need to ask her twice. Aviama ran to the edge and jumped. Sai grabbed Teja and followed, Durga joining them as the windcallers slowed their descent with an updraft of wind. Umed took a flying leap and a skid, his feet already rolling into a sprint by the time they touched the ground. Husani was close behind, and they were off like a shot down Mount Zobaat.

Aviama's feet slapped the rocky pass, grateful for the thick cloth strips wrapped around her soles and ankles. Dust kicked up behind her, but after the market that morning, her whole body ached. She had to move faster.

Shouts and screams trailed them as the strange band darted down the mountain: three women, a man built like a tree, a teen built like a twig, and a toddler.

A few persistent believers still called out for Duqatun Elwehi. Aviama hadn't a clue what else they were screaming, but she imagined it was colorful and rather less than respectful—and it was growing closer.

Aviama pushed off a rock as she rounded a bend and tripped her way down into the darkness. Sai was up front with Teja and Umed, leading the way to the rendezvous point, Husani close on their heels, Durga just behind Aviama. Durga shoved Aviama forward from behind.

"Don't look now, but they're chasing us."

"I know they're chasing us."

"With torches."

Great.

Ahead of her, Husani twisted around, glancing over their heads in the direction they'd come. "And melderbloods."

Aviama chanced a look back. It was a terrible decision.

Her heart stopped. A hundred people scurried down the mountainside. Torches lit the dark and spread out like vines in every direction. Fireballs hurled this way and that, cutting a blaze of light through the night before smashing into boulders and disintegrating in a cloud of sparks.

Biscuits.

Florian had said if they didn't come alone, he'd take his ship and go. Aviama had a feeling they wouldn't survive the night if they were left on Jazir.

A flash of light seared the air by Aviama's ear, shattering against a rock and showering her in embers. Durga threw up a barrier behind them.

"Go, go, go! They've found us!"

Aviama bit back a retort to Durga's remarkable deductive powers and launched forward with every last ounce of energy in her body. Her calves burned. Her heartbeat battered her ribcage. And still their pursuers gained. They weren't going to make it.

Much less alone.

Aviama seized Durga by the wrist as another fireball exploded against her air shield. "There, the drop-off—do you see it? We're taking it."

Durga's gaze darted in the direction of the drop-off as a fresh fireball lit the area for half a second. She snatched her arm back. "Are you insane?"

"Not half as insane as I'm going to need to be."

Durga swore. "You're going to get us killed."

"Would you rather I leave you here?"

Durga scowled. "I hate you."

"Thanks."

Aviama ducked under another ball of fire and threw up a barrier against another, stopping it a handsbreadth from Durga's face. Her eyes popped wide, and the next moment, darkness hid her expression again. Aviama had lost all sight of Husani, Sai, and Umed. But their location was already known, so she shouted above the din.

"Umed!"

The long scrape of a skid in gravel. "Commander?"

"Bear left. We're going over the cliff."

Aviama slammed into a body. Husani cursed and swatted at her arm as he stumbled down the slope, but it was too late for Aviama. Her feet tangled with his ankles, and she fell. Her heart flew to her throat. She threw her arms out sideways for anything to stop her descent, but all she found was Durga. They fell together, tumbling over and over as they slid down the slanted ground.

"Cliff left, affirmative." Umed.

Aviama's cheek slammed into something hard, and the heels of her hands grated against the coarse, rock-ribbed ground. Durga let out a grunt. Husani wriggled free from somewhere under her legs.

Up the slope, their pursuers had doubled. Wind whistled through the swirling slopes of the mountain's corners and crags. Fireballs burst no longer in every direction, but like arrows after a deer—a single identified target. Four hit the rock they'd been standing on a moment ago, before Aviama sent them sprawling.

Aviama wrenched herself upright and dusted her hands on her trousers.

"The ship does *not* leave without us on it. Do you understand me?"

A large, warm hand gripped her elbow. Umed's voice was low and firm at her ear. "The ship will not leave."

Aviama felt along his arm and broad shoulders in the dark. "Where's the baby?"

"Sai has her. Go."

Her arms ached. Her legs burned. Her pulse pounded. But she went.

It wasn't until they'd been running another several minutes that Aviama realized she'd lost all bearing on where they were.

"Where's the cli—"

Her foot swam into nothing, and she tipped forward. Umed's strong arm shoved her onward with a dragon's might, out over the yawning abyss, out from the safety of dry ground, over an onyx sea of rock and mist and air as cold as the grave.

Wind rushed in her ears as she fell, end over end, through a haze of sea spray. A light twinkled from somewhere in the bleak below, though from which direction she could not tell. Her mouth went dry. Goosebumps fled along her skin.

Falling bodies. Rocks. Foam. A child's terrified scream. Candlelight.

It all filtered into Aviama's consciousness like puzzle pieces without a home. Except one.

Rocks.

If she didn't slow them down, they were going to die. But where were they all? Had all five jumped? Were they close together? Were their skulls about to bash into one another?

A wall of inky black etched with jasmine-white lace rushed toward her. Time was up. She threw up a bubble of air around her, pressing it outward as far as she could before she hit the water.

Bump. Kshhhhh.

Now Aviama knew that the darkness of night she'd been in before was not in fact true blackness, for she descended at that moment into a tumult of deepest obsidian. On impact, the protective shield around her had hit something hard, harsher than water, and knocked her sideways. The bubble burst.

Frigid water smacked through her defenses and soaked

her to the bone as the last of her air escaped her lungs and flew to the surface. Cold whirled around her body like ice talons, sinking deeper and deeper toward her core. She threw her hands out to summon the air, but from which direction?

Aviama's lungs burned. She was going to sink. She was going to die. She was going to—

She froze. *Sink*. It went against every instinct. Her brain begged her not to do it. But she did. She went limp in the water, willing herself to imagine she floated in a tranquil sea rather than a watery tomb.

Slow and steady, she gave herself over to the whim of the water. Her body drifted this way and that, and just as the first desperate urge hit to pull water into her lungs, she began to sink. Down.

Which meant the other way was up.

Aviama thrust both hands upward and pulled with all her might. *Come to me*.

Blessed air surrounded her, and she gasped long drags into despairing lungs. Up she went, up, up, until she broke the surface. Several other dark forms dotted the water around her. Fire rained down on them from above, each blow accentuated by cheers and shouts from the top of the cliff.

And there, in the distance, was the silhouette of a small ship—pulling away into the night.

14

Aviama glanced up to the top of the cliff, only to be greeted by a ball of fire plunging straight down at her face. She ducked down into the water a split second before it hit and came up sputtering.

"Umed!"

"Commander?"

Relief washed over her. He was a few meters off, but close enough.

"The ship! Do you see it?"

"Yes, Commander."

"I don't have the strength to stop it with wind. Please tell me you're a crestbreaker."

It hadn't occurred to her until now that she'd never seen Umed use his abilities. He'd always been in the thick of things, and Onkar seemed to only have melders on his crew. Manan had said he thought Umed was a crestbreaker, but he could have been wrong.

"Yes."

Aviama struck the surface of the water in victory. "Everybody here?"

A child cried. Aviama's heart broke. The little girl had endured so much, all without a peep. Until she escaped a shower of fire when the person holding her jumped over a cliff into a freezing, pitch-black sea.

"I have the translator girl. She's not good."

Husani's voice. It dipped into a gargling sound on the word good. Water rippled. A splash followed, and on the next fireball, Aviama caught a glimpse of him—halfway under the water, struggling to keep Teja's limp frame above the water.

Aviama swam toward him, and in a moment, the group was together again. With Durga's help, Aviama enveloped them in a bubble of air, as Sai held the little girl, Husani held Teja, and Umed gathered the waters around them and propelled them toward the ship. Florian was going to get a piece of her mind when they got there.

Right after she collapsed on deck from exhaustion.

Water foamed at the boundaries of the bubble Aviama, Durga, and Sai held firm. Husani gripped Teja and stared down at the translucent floor of the air pocket slipping across the surface of the water as Umed called to the sea and pushed them along toward the ship. It wasn't far. Aviama could make out the shapes of men along the rails. One of them would be Chenzira, waiting to pull her up, furious at Florian for departing the island without her.

Behind them, the blaze of the altar fire lit the night from Mount Zobaat. The signal would be seen for miles in every direction. What would the rest of Keket make of it?

Torchlight still dotted the top of the cliff, but no one else had dared make the leap after them. The firebloods had given up, and Aviama hoped the Jazir were reasonable with them in the aftermath. If they believed Raisa had given them their powers, maybe they would change their minds about melderbloods.

Or maybe Aviama's escape stunt would break the facade of her ever having been Raisa to begin with.

The ship rose before them, and Umed slowed their approach. Men shouted from the main deck. Lanterns swayed this way and that as sailors scurried to throw ropes overboard to help them up out of the water. Umed's arms bulged with the exertion of commanding the sea for so long to bear such weight. Haggard breathing revealed the toll it had taken to bring them so far.

Aviama looked up at the ship looming over them. Her stomach dropped.

No black hat. No red feather.

And no Chenzira.

"Stop. Nobody get on the ship."

It was too late. Teja and Sai were already halfway up the ropes, the little girl still in Sai's arms. Husani scurried up next, and by Umed's dark eyes and sagging shoulders, he couldn't continue the way he had been on the water. He needed to rest. But if this wasn't Florian's ship, there would be no resting.

Aviama grabbed Durga by the elbow. "Something's wrong. This isn't our ship. Keep an eye out."

Durga shot a look up the side of the ship, and a shadow fell over her face. "Then why are we boarding it?"

Aviama gestured at the group already up the side. Teja's feet disappeared over the rail onto the deck. Durga groaned. Aviama's hand rested on the Iolani battle horn, and she hesitated. It was too conspicuous. She needed a way to hide it.

"Husani!" she hissed. His satchel might hide it. But he probably wouldn't give it up. "Husani!"

He glanced down at her but continued up the side without a word. Umed grabbed a rope.

Great.

Aviama snatched a rope, and she, Durga, and Umed made

the climb up to the railing of the vessel's main deck. The higher she went, the further her heart sank. Where was Florian? Where were Chenzira, Manan, and the twins? Whose ship was this?

Strong arms pulled her over the railing when she reached the top, and she shifted the horn from her hip to slightly behind her, keeping her back to the railing as she straightened. Orange lanternlight swayed toward them in the hand of a man dressed in a white schenti, thick belt, and brass guards on his calves and upper arms. A wide brass collar, half ornamental, half armor, lay across his upper chest, exposing the rest of his torso. His khopesh was sheathed, but as he lifted the lantern with one hand, the palm of the other went to the hilt of his weapon.

Durga let out a long breath. "I'm really getting sick of ships."

Aviama knew the feeling.

The guard scanned the group as they stood on the deck. Water *drip, drip, drippppped* down their clothes and hair onto the wooden planks, forming a puddle at their feet. The man spoke to them all in Keketi, and Sai and Aviama exchanged a glance. Whatever he said, it sounded important. The little girl reached for Aviama, and Aviama took her without a second thought. The girl hid her face against Aviama's shoulder. It wasn't until Aviama's arms wrapped around the small body and hugged her close that she thought about the horn at her back, or the gale she may need both hands free to call.

Three more guards in the same dress strode forward. Sailors looked up from their work to see what the newcomers were like. Aviama pursed her lips. *Drowned rats, that's what we're like.*

The man spoke again, and Teja's eyes widened. Husani

gaped. Teja spoke quickly, words spilling out in a flood. Aviama shifted her weight. Durga sucked her teeth.

How well did they know Teja? She was a slave who they'd set free. Not a melderblood. And she was Keketi. And her mother had just been killed. She might not be thinking straight. She didn't know who Aviama was, but she had plenty of valuable information to share. As did Husani. And without Chenzira, there wasn't a soul on board Aviama trusted who spoke the language.

The guard's eyes swept over Umed, Sai, Husani, Durga— and stopped on Aviama and the girl. He jerked his chin at her and said something else. Aviama dipped her head down. No need to show too much spirit. Not when she didn't know what they were saying.

Teja cleared her throat. "He wants to know who we are, and what the fire on Mount Zobaat is for. He wants to know why we came to their ship. I told him there was a scuffle of some kind this morning at the slave market, and the people are making an offering to Raisa."

Aviama looked at her and shrugged. "Well, that's what happened. Why doesn't he look satisfied?"

It wasn't a particularly detailed account of what happened, but it was the truth. If that really was what she'd said, she did a great job. Aviama glanced at the guard again and jumped to find him standing closer than he had been before, staring daggers straight into her soul.

"He, um, doesn't believe you are Keketi."

"So?"

The guard looked her up and down, from her pale skin to her light hair, strange foreign clothes, and strips of cloth wrapped around bare feet.

Teja winced. "I think he thinks you're a runaway slave. And the rest of us too. And he thinks we're lying to save our skin."

Aviama clenched her teeth. She needed to get some Keketi clothes and a head wrap. And then she needed to leave Keket. Fast.

Husani stepped forward and bowed his head. He spoke quickly, and the guard tore his gaze off Aviama and turned his scrutiny on the boy.

Teja interpreted in a soft voice. "He says he and I are traveling together. That I am his aunt, and his father is abusive. That you are slaves, a gift from his mother, and that his mother sent him away during the commotion in hopes his father wouldn't notice he was gone until morning. He says his mother will meet him on Anhiraf."

The guard tilted his head. He questioned Husani again, and Husani answered. Teja explained.

"He asks Husani if he thinks he can swim from here to Anhiraf. Husani says no, we had a small skiff, but it had a leak we were not aware of until we were far from shore. It sank, and we swam to the ship for help."

Aviama kept her expression neutral, playing with the ends of the little girl's hair. Husani's story was good. Aviama had tried to think of one, but her mind spun, and nothing believable came. It was much better coming from Husani, who was Keketi, dressed Keketi, spoke Keketi.

The guard still didn't look convinced.

Aviama glanced back at the mountain. The fire still raged, a beacon screaming high into the night to tell the whole world of what had happened there. Of the slave girl who had destroyed the market, broken a statue, and claimed to be Raisa reincarnated. How fast would word travel? How often did people go from Jazir to the other islands?

The three officials at the edge of the crowd filled her mind. They would make their report with haste. She'd be lucky if she had until morning before word reached the governor, and then the king.

Onyx waves lapped at the base of the ship, sprinkled in mottled moonlight that drifted down through patchy clouds. The last of the torchlight on the cliff wove its way back up the mountain toward the other side and the city beyond. To the left of the cliff, the sea stretched out to meet a hidden horizon under the stars.

And on it sat the shape of a small ship.

Aviama's pulse quickened. She whipped her head back to the guard. Had he seen her notice it? Did the others see it?

She caught Umed's eye. His head was always on a swivel, his gaze moving this way and that. Had he seen the second ship? But if he had, he made no indication of it.

"Chisisi's feathers, what a surprise."

A new figure emerged from the dark recesses of the ship, dressed not only in the white schenti Aviama had grown so accustomed to seeing on the island or even on the guard, but a gold gem-studded collar across his naked chest, a gold band around his forehead, and matching bands at his biceps and forearms. The belt he wore sparkled with gemstones set on a crimson background inlaid with gold. He ran a hand through his dark beard, and Aviama couldn't help feeling as though she'd been in this exact position before.

Examined by the guard, by Abasi, by Onkar, by Makuakan and Limakau, and the Radhan royal family before that. Why must she always stand somewhere, waiting for others to make determinations of her? Of what to make of her? What to do with her?

The way the man carried himself, chin high, chest out, a swagger to his step, Aviama didn't need to see the jewels to know he was a man of authority. The guard dipped his head and stood to one side, and the newcomer flashed a pearl-white smile at Aviama.

"Welcome. I hear you come with news of our island friends on Jazir."

His Keketi accent was noticeable, but his command of the common tongue was excellent. Aviama half-dropped into a perfect curtsy before thunking her foot down on the deck and transitioning into an awkward bow instead. She had to stop being the perfect princess. Diplomats and politicians knew protocol. Servants knew protocol. Did most people know it? Should she look like she knew it, or only look like she felt she should know it, but wasn't sure how to go about it?

The others fell into similar dips and bobs of respect. The man in gold turned his eyes on Husani, but he continued in the common tongue. "If they are your slaves, why is your aunt informing them of everything you say?"

Husani shifted his weight. "Perhaps I treat my slaves better than others on Jazir. They've been through a lot today. They deserve to know what's going on."

"They most certainly do. As do I." He cleared his throat and cracked his knuckles. "Let's start with something easy. What is that one's name?"

He pointed at Aviama. Her breath caught.

Husani's jaw went slack. "I don't know. We only got her today."

"And your aunt, did you only get her today too?"

Husani's eyes bulged. "Sir?"

"Never mind. Your story is yours, and you can keep it if you'd like." He smiled and spread his hands wide, gesturing across the sea in either direction. "I'll take you anywhere you want to go with no further questions, but I'm going to need some information in return. From each of you. I have reason to believe the chaos on Jazir is related to a rebellion. Part of my duty is to keep the peace. I'd love to hear each of your eyewitness reports. Individually."

A chill chased a bead of salt water down her spine. They hadn't prepped a story, and there was no way their accounts would match. Unless they told the truth. Which was not an option.

Aviama swayed side to side as if rocking the little girl, who had inexplicably dropped into the long, deep breathing pattern of sleep. At the edge of her sway, Aviama tossed a glance back toward the ship she'd seen earlier. It was closer, wasn't it?

This time, when she caught Umed's eye, he was looking directly at her, firm and steady, unflinching as iron, and she was certain he'd seen the ship. But when she turned back to the man in gold, her mouth went dry. He'd seen it too.

The man's smile widened, and he tented his fingers before him. "What a long ordeal you must all have been through. Soaked to the skin in the dark of night, with a small child to care for. Two relatives and their four slaves, escaping an evil abuse of power. That deserves all the help I can give. I'll let Tarik here gather the story from the Keketi, and since I speak the common tongue, I'll start with the slaves."

His gaze fell on Aviama. "Let's start with you."

15

Aviama hugged the little girl tight, afraid her trembling might show if she let go. She took a half-step back, and the Iolani horn bumped into the railing. The moment he saw it, any hope of selling the slave lie would be gone. At best, she'd be a thieving slave, and Teja and Husani's story would be ripped to shreds.

She licked her lips and nodded to the little girl. "She's asleep. I'd like to keep her here a few more minutes. She sleeps better when I stand and sway."

Aviama had heard a mom say something to that effect once at home. A servant who'd recently had a baby had come back to work with her little one strapped to her chest. She hoped it was true, and that she sounded convincing.

The half-naked man in gold collars and armbands shook his head. "Oh, I insist. No need to leave the child in the cold wind. Let's get you warmed up with some blankets, make you comfortable, and you can share your story while we're on our way to Anhiraf. And if you'd prefer to stand, by all means, you may do so."

Biscuits. They were going to be separated. Aviama couldn't let that happen. In fact, last time they were threatened with separation, she freed nearly a hundred slaves, burned down a town-square platform, and started a revolt. It hadn't even been twenty-four hours.

Yet if she called the shots now, she wouldn't be believable as a slave. And if they told their stories, they'd be exposed as liars. If they were separated, there was no guarantee they'd be allowed together again. And once they left the upper deck, if Chenzira was on the other ship, there would be no way for him to find them.

And no way off the ship to get to him.

Aviama resisted the urge to count the stupid things she had done since sunup. *He doesn't call me Tally for nothing.* Did it count as all happening in one day if daylight had already gone?

Her gut twisted. If she gave the word, the others would follow her command. All eyes were on her, both from her own little loyal band and the decorated official with his guards. Could she stall?

She dipped her head again. "Thank you, sir. May I ask who I am speaking with?"

"You may." His eyes glittered with mischief. "May I ask the same?"

Stalemate. *Biscuits.* She couldn't give a Keketi name. That had not gone well last time. A Curion name would probably work, except all the ones she knew were famous.

"Lesala."

Nobody would know that name. Nobody but Semra and Siler, who had helped the girl escape the dragonlord at the tender age of four, as they themselves made their way out of the assassin academy of Mount Hara. Nobody but Zephan, her brother the king, or the Rinabs, who had taken her in. How old would she be now? Eight? Nine?

It was strange to think of Semra finding Lesala in the mountain and running with her out onto the plateau. Lesala had been the push Semra needed. Couldn't the nameless little girl in Aviama's arms be her own catalyst? The linchpin in her mind, proving she must not go below deck?

The toddler was not going to be orphaned again. She was not going to be dumped into the hands of just anybody for whatever evil purposes they could contrive. Teja would not be abandoned. Husani wouldn't escape abuse at home, only to fall into the hands of a new tyrant. That's what had happened to Aviama—from the kettle to the fire, from Queen Satya's dark oversight to Shiva's snake-like arms. He'd been a python, and he'd nearly crushed her.

"Lesala ..." The man tilted his head. "What sort of origin would that be?"

Aviama set her jaw. "The sort that lands you on a slave ship, apparently. I didn't think slavers cared much where they got their merchandise."

Husani sucked in a breath, and the man's eyebrows soared.

As the shock wore off, the man laughed. "Nonsense! When I purchase a piece of furniture, its history is half the cost. Have you never haggled with a supplier for a lower price, only to be spun a tall tale of a fascinating but sordid history?"

"Would you like a tall tale? Or sordid history? If sordid history is what you seek, I imagine that the island of Jazir has it in spades without any need for falsehood."

She knew it was the wrong thing to say the moment the words left her lips. Sai stiffened, Teja faltered back a step, and all the blood drained from Husani's face.

How long had she lasted with the demure submissiveness before the facade fell away? Five minutes? Aviama bit back a groan and swallowed hard. She shifted the little girl onto one hip, supporting her with one arm and leaving the other mostly free. Behind her back, the toddler's foot nudged the battle horn.

The nameless man's smile tightened, and he stepped forward. "Do slaves talk this way where you come from?"

Aviama stepped back until she bumped up against the rail. "Where I come from, people are not sold like cattle."

The man ran a hand through his short, trimmed beard and gave her a long look up and down. "You are out of your depth here, I see. Let me tell you something about Keket. We don't take advice on how to run a kingdom from people who can't even manage to wear shoes."

She swallowed. "Thank you for the education."

Sai sidestepped next to her, her arm brushing Aviama's, and a whisper of wind left a trail of goosebumps up her arm and through her hair. *Shall we?*

"Oh, it's my honor. A slave of your caliber deserves more than kings, does she not? Whims obeyed, ideas accepted, knowledge given." He smiled. It looked like oil, and it turned the stomach sour. "Please, I can't let a young mother and a stolen child stand out in the cold. Stand or sit, but you will come with me below deck."

Aviama bristled. "I did not steal a child."

The official crossed his arms. "Neither are you her mother."

Her stomach dropped. He was toying with her. As long as the game was fun, he'd allow it to go on. The moment it wasn't, heads would roll.

"Why take such an interest in a slave?"

He grinned. "Maybe I'm in the market."

The man reached for her then, and Aviama blasted him backward with a gust of wind she hardly registered sending. Power rolled down her arm and shot through her fingertips like an arrow. The official was on his back before she could blink.

The closest guard whirled and struck with his spear. Umed crashed into him like a human boulder, knocking him off course and into a second guard. Sailors rushed forward, and Durga shot a wall of wind toward them, toppling two over the opposite railing. The next instant, Durga fell over the side of the ship into the black sea below, hit by some invisible force. The official's hand flew up into the air, and in an acrobatic move, he was on his feet again and barreling toward Aviama.

She threw a hand up and called the wind, but not before the official shoved her hand to one side and spun her around. The solid frame of a man's body pressed into her back, impeded only by the little girl's foot, the prongs of the Iolani horn, and Aviama's own elbow. One arm held behind her back and the other around the toddler, Aviama wrenched forward, but to no avail.

The man's grip tightened. Aviama slammed her head back into the man's skull as a gale from Sai swept them both sideways into the railing of the ship. His hold loosened, and he staggered back. Umed flipped a guard onto his back and tossed him to the deck with a reverberating thud. Aviama slipped her free hand tight around the little girl, stepped on the chest of Umed's latest victim, and launched up to kick off the rail and fall into the sea.

But just as she began to topple, a wall of frigid water smacked into her with the force of a giant club, sending her straight back to the ship deck. The girl in her arms let out a cry. Aviama rolled on impact and popped back up.

Three more guards rushed toward her. Sai sent one sprawling, but then a gust from a guard knocked her into

Husani. A tower of water rose up on one side of the ship, shutting them off from escape, with Durga on the other side.

Aviama tucked the girl into the crook of one arm and threw up a blast of air at an oncoming guard. The guard matched her blow, two gusts of air meeting in the middle, tension building at an ever-increasing pressure.

Her pulse pounded in her ears, muscles tense. Realization struck her in the face like a bucket of ice water. They were melders.

Husani threw a jab at the nearest sailor. A fireball pitched him overboard in reply, the flame extinguishing in the tower of water with a sizzle. Husani's body draped over the railing as he was whipped backward into the water and ricocheted off it like a ragdoll toward the ship again. Teja threw her hands up. Sai sidestepped next to Aviama as Umed ducked beneath a fireball aimed at his head.

Aviama tossed up a barrier around them in a sphere. "There's another ship. We need to get overboard."

Sai shook her head. "Windcalling isn't getting through the water."

Aviama flinched as blasts of air and fire hit the edges of the barrier. "Umed, we need a chink in this armor. Just for a moment."

His breath came ragged, and he winced as he moved his arm, but he nodded.

Four hits against the barrier, and the shield burst. The official lunged toward her. Sai blasted the fireblood backward as Umed surged toward the ocean barricade. A hand brushed Aviama's arm as she twisted after Umed and Sai. The wall of water split like a crack as Umed stood in the gap at the rail, redirecting water on either side of him. Over his shoulders, three meters high, the width of his torso, a blessed sliver of hope rent through the prison wall.

Umed yelled at Teja. Teja seized Husani and shoved him overboard, and the two fell together. The crack in the ocean wall shuddered, and the sliver narrowed. Umed's arms shook. Sai ran toward the opening, but hesitated.

Aviama's scream cut the air like a knife, the rasp of it burning the inside of her throat. "Go, go, go!"

Umed dropped to one knee. Sai launched herself forward, planting one foot on his knee, one on his shoulder, and she was gone. The opening wavered, and Umed let out a guttural cry as he fought to keep it open.

Two guards gathered their feet and surged toward him, curved blades extended. Aviama darted over injured men littering the deck and leaped for the gap. The first guard's blade sliced into Umed's arm. Fingers caught in Aviama's hair and closed into a fist. Her head snapped back.

The gap disappeared. The wall surged higher.

The child in her arms cried.

Aviama's heart burst. Heat flushed her face. Panic chilled her to the bone.

A thought tugged at the edges of her mind. She shouldn't. She couldn't.

The hand in her hair wrenched her backward, and the official's other hand pressed on the toddler's back, guiding the two of them away from the rail toward the center of the ship deck. At the touch of his hand on the little girl, fire and fury blazed from a molten volcano inside herself Aviama didn't know existed.

Oh, but she would.

Aviama's lip curled, muscles strained, and she whipped in close to the man. Her scalp burned with his iron grip in her hair, but she didn't care. Nose to nose, the cool of the moon mixing with the eerie flickering glow of lanternlight, Aviama pressed the palm of her hand up under the cool metal of the golden gem-studded collar over the man's chest.

She could feel his heart hammer against her hand. Every line of his muscled chest beat against her palm. But beyond it, sweet victory, was the man's breath.

A rolling heat roiled Aviama's belly, bile threatening her throat as her nails raked against his skin and called the wind out from his lungs.

His hold on her hair dropped away. The wall of water fell.

Aviama left him on the deck, ran for the railing, and leaped over the side.

16

Cold. Dark. Aviama yanked down a bubble of air from the surface and checked the baby in her arms. She was crying, startled, cold, and clutching at Aviama like a life raft. But as the bubble around them formed and began to move under the water, the girl stared open-mouthed at the starlight playing with the waves overhead. She reached a finger out to test the barrier, and the water vibrated like an ocean giggle at her touch.

Two more air bubbles appeared beside them, one containing Husani, Teja, and Sai, and the other Durga and Umed. A spear plunged through the water and burst Sai's protective shield around them as she struggled to maintain it. Neither Sai nor Durga had much experience using their wind-calling abilities for something like this. They'd been able to feel it out after the jump from the cliff, when Aviama formed it and they helped maintain it, but this was their first attempt at their own air pockets.

Umed held one arm close to his body and used the other to call the water around them. Aviama cradled the girl against her chest and held up her hand toward the shadow of the second ship, directing the bubble of air around her through the water. Silver flashed across their path, and Aviama's heart lurched to her throat as images of sword blades, spearheads, and shimmering siren tails cycled through her mind. But the little girl wrapped an arm around her neck and wiped the tears from her face with the other, pointing at a school of fish scattering before them.

Aviama's chest hitched. What would her mother have done?

She smoothed the girl's hair and leaned in close. "They're pretty, aren't they?"

The girl nodded. Aviama was startled to see her respond to the common tongue. She forgot the girl had come with her mother from Radha and may have learned the common tongue alongside Radhan in the area she lived. But if she understood the common tongue, why hadn't she said anything?

Still, that wasn't all bad. Aviama pressed her lips to the girl's soft cheek. "We're going to have to be quiet when we get to the ship, okay? We're going to a different ship. Hopefully, a better one, without mean people on it. I'll keep you safe."

The girl nodded and craned her neck around Aviama's shoulder to watch the last of the silver fish wriggle out of sight. The shadow of the belly of the ship grew larger, and Aviama slung the girl onto her back and positioned her arms around her shoulders. "I'm going to need my arms. Hold on tight."

Her arms and legs ached. By the time she broke the surface, she felt like she was treading water with limp noodles dragging through mud. The ship was smaller than any of the vessels she'd been on in the last six months, with two modest decks, a bowsprit extending out over the sea about the same length as the hull, and a single mast reaching up into the night.

Black sea lapped at the hull. Aviama glanced up at the railing as two ropes sailed through the air from above and slapped against the side of the ship. The silhouette of a feather bobbed from a hat as a man peered over the edge.

Aviama snatched the rope and looped her foot in it. Long pulls drew her upward as two other air pockets burst up to the surface and the others reached for the second line. A chill breeze wafted over her soaked skin. Goosebumps cropped up along her arms as every square inch of the light tunic clung, cold and clammy, to her body.

She couldn't pull herself up or help the men as they hauled her onto the vessel. Arms limp and muscles weak, it was a mercy she could even maintain a grip on the rope. All she knew was a pit in her stomach and a scorching need to see Chenzira's face.

Solid arms took hold of her at the rail and toted her over the side and onto the ship as she cradled the girl to her chest. Wood planks welcomed her weary feet, and someone threw a large blanket around her shoulders. Osahar and Zahur stood at the railing. The two of them must have been the ones to bring her up. They reached down the side again, and plopped Teja, Sai, Husani, and Durga on deck beside her a moment later, one after the other. Umed was last, and hauling his sturdy frame over the side involved a hefty number of grunts and groans, but they met with success in the end.

Florian tipped his hat. "Glad to have you aboard."

Aviama glanced across the deck. Where was he? Where was Manan? Had they made it on board?

The pit in her stomach grew. What had Florian done to them? What if—

Corded arms enveloped her, and Aviama whirled into the threat. But when two hands slipped around her face and neck and warm, familiar lips pressed to hers, the knots in her stomach exploded into butterflies, and she leaned into him. He smelled like freedom, and he tasted like home.

Aviama sagged into Chenzira's arms, and he tucked her under his chin as if hoarding a treasure he'd searched for far and wide. She let out a long sigh, and the pressures of the day caught up to her as his safety allowed her the space to breathe. She burrowed closer against his chest. "You scared me."

He shook his head against hers and ran a hand through her sopping wet hair. "Says the woman who made me watch her plunge off a cliff."

Zahur handed out thick blankets to the others, and Florian wiped stray sea spray from his dark jacket. He planted his feet a shoulder's width apart, crossed his arms, and arched an eyebrow.

"For the sake of realistic expectations, do you always do things the hard way? Because we were docked precisely where we said we would be, and instead of waltzing on over like a normal person, you opted to sprint down a mountain in a hailstorm of fireballs and jump off a cliff. And then board the wrong ship. I've not led a revolt before, but I imagine even rebel leaders can afford simplicity once in a while—like stepping onto a stationary ship instead of chasing after moving ones."

Durga shivered and tugged her blanket closer around her. "Moving ones that want to kill us, you mean."

Florian pursed his lips, drew out a handful of sugared ginger from a pocket, and popped a piece in his mouth. "It did appear that there was a scuffle. What happened exactly?"

"A royal envoy happened, that's what!" Husani tousled his wet hair with the dry blanket and frowned at his dripping wet satchel. "We almost got killed!"

Umed's gaze darted back out over the water at the enemy ship. "Set sail. They're not done with us yet."

Florian nodded at the helmsman, who was little more than a shadowy shape down the deck and waved off the concern. "You're safe with the queen."

Aviama's mouth went dry. She couldn't stomach the clutches of another pernicious queen. And after the snatches of information she'd gathered from Chenzira about the Keket royal family, she wasn't eager to meet them. "You sail for the queen?"

"Not *that* queen." He spread his arms wide, indicating the ship. "*Malika tul Barqa*—the *Lightning Queen*. You're standing on her."

Sai's brow furrowed. "Won't they chase us?"

"They're welcome to try." Florian grinned and patted the thick mast of the vessel. "They're no match for my baby. She outruns every seaworthy thing in Keket."

"Normal ships, maybe." Aviama swallowed, glancing around the group. "They're melders. All of them."

Chenzira's fingers turned to ice on her arms. When he pulled back to search her face, his eyes were piercing. "All of them?"

Sai nodded. "They had all different melder powers, too. Wind, fire, water—they've got everything."

Chenzira's lips flattened. "Maybe not everything."

Florian jerked his chin across the deck. "Let's get you out of sight. I'll get us past the envoy and get you all settled shortly."

Zahur strode past the rowboat tied to the center of the deck and pulled up a hatch. Chenzira took the little girl from Aviama's arms and carried her down to the deck below, leaving Aviama's arms free to work the ladder. Barrels were stacked on either side, with a spare cannon and two rows of bunks at the far end.

The others followed, and Chenzira led them to the bunks.

Aviama dried off the little girl as best she could and tucked her into a bed, piling an extra blanket on top of her. By the time Chenzira passed out water and Aviama turned around again, the little girl was asleep.

Durga scowled down at the filthy, ruined outfit she'd worn for weeks on end. "We need new clothes. Preferably dry ones."

Sai set her jaw. "Maybe we could escape the royal envoy first before we care what we look like."

Durga tugged at the Radhan dancer attire she wore and arched her eyebrows. "Does this look Keketi to you? Or does it stick out like a sore thumb? Look at Aviama. She's white enough to blind the birds, and she's in *trousers*. And a weird, fancy tunic."

Aviama froze. Her lips parted, and her eyes flew to Durga. Manan smacked Durga in the arm, and her hand flew to her mouth. She swallowed.

Teja's face drained of color. "Did you just say her name was Aviama?"

Chenzira passed a hand over his face and groaned.

Husani glanced around the room. "Who's Aviama?"

"Sands, I've got outstanding timing." Florian's boots hit the floor, and the hatch *thunked* shut after him, the wind from its closure wafting through the feather in his hat.

Umed and Manan rocketed to their feet from bunks opposite one another, crossing their arms between Florian and Aviama as the seaman swaggered down the deck toward them in the wavering lantern light. Chenzira shot Durga a withering glare, and her shoulders sagged.

Aviama crossed her ankles from her seated position on one of the bunks and glanced at the girl on the bunk behind her. "Stop stomping around like a bahataal. She's sleeping."

If she was going to have their plans upended, at least she could curb the yelling.

Husani leaned toward Teja. "Who's Aviama?"

"Don't you know?" Florian swept his hat from his head and sank into a dramatic bow. Aviama set her jaw. Florian straightened. "Aviama is a Jannemari name. But this is *the* Aviama—Her Royal Highness, Princess Aviama Shamaran of Jannemar, the kingdom to our southeast across the Aeian Sea. Home of the Origin Wellspring and the resting place of Aurin's Spear these past six hundred years, if the legends are to be believed."

Teja shook her head. "Can't be. I thought she was getting married to the Radhan prince."

"She's got bodyguards. Don't you see that's what these two are?" Florian gestured to Umed and Manan. "When they call her commander, she doesn't flinch. When I said she was the princess just now, she was annoyed, but not surprised. Everyone looks to her for what to do. Didn't you ask who she was before signing up to chase her around Keket?"

Husani's eyes bulged. Teja gasped. Aviama's stomach knotted.

"I'd wager she isn't here for whatever you think she's here for. And while you all look to her for the next steps ..." Florian paused and nodded at Chenzira. "The only person *she* looks to is *him*."

He pivoted on his heel toward Chenzira. "Which begs the question, who are *you*?"

Husani gaped at her. "Wait. Are you really the princess?"

Aviama twisted the skin on her finger where her mother's ring should have been and pursed her lips. "I'd really love it if everyone would stop calling me that."

The boy's eyes narrowed. "Because it isn't true, or because it is?"

"I knew it! I knew you were somebody special." Teja

leaned forward, eyes alight. "You're supposed to be in Radha. Where's your fiancé?"

Durga snorted, and Chenzira silenced her with a look. It would be hard for any of the three of them to forget Durga trying to force Chenzira into a compromising situation—and Chenzira slamming her into the barrels of the *Wraithweaver* cargo deck, Aviama's wind holding her there, his hands digging into the vulnerable skin of her throat. At that time, Durga had tried to blackmail Chenzira and failed, and ultimately gave up information about where the magna was stored. Now, she'd do well to keep what she knew to herself.

Chenzira cared less about civility than Aviama did. Durga knew it. She sobered.

Aviama shook her head. "I have no fiancé."

"That may be true, but you did. Radha can't be happy about that." Florian plopped himself on the edge of the nearest bunk and dropped his chin into his hand. He wiggled his eyebrows. "Do they know about your new suitor?"

Aviama and Chenzira exchanged a glance, but said nothing. Sai shifted in her seat.

Florian slapped his knee. "They do! How delicious." He wagged a finger at Manan, Umed, Sai, and Durga. "And these four all know about it."

Teja bit her lip. "So you're not going to free the slaves?"

Husani eyed her. "Are you here to lead a rebellion?"

Husani had come because he believed she would lead a revolution. Osahar and Zahur had joined for the same reason and had abandoned their jobs and risked their lives using melder powers on Jazir to follow her. Teja was there because she'd been kidnapped into the slave trade, her mother had been murdered, and she'd almost accidentally found herself entangled with three troublemaking melderblood windcaller women at the market.

What *were* they doing? What was the news from back home? Home, where Radha's army marched as they spoke. Perhaps war had already broken out. Had Radha captured the Horon Mines? Would they get enough wyronite to make sifal magic housing artifacts? When Shiva had said every Shamaran would burn, were the artifacts a prerequisite for that plan, or only icing on the cake? Had Murin gotten there in time to warn her brother, or had they been blindsided by the first attack?

Aviama's head throbbed. Her stomach dropped, and her mind spun. She twisted behind her to stare at the little girl, her damp matted hair splayed out on the pillow, sleeping soundly. Calm in the storm. Softness in an arena of blood. Innocence.

Innocence worth protecting.

But what was she supposed to do with an orphan toddler? Without a mother, without a home, without a family? What of those who had chosen to follow her? What obligations did she have to them?

She'd need a ship to get home, but what could she do on her own other than die next to her brother and sister-in-law? She wouldn't get there in time to stop an onslaught on the mines, not even if she left that same night. Zephan and Semra could take the dragon and fly away, but they never would. They'd never abandon Jannemar.

Just like Aviama could not abandon those who had fallen into her care. But finding out what to do with them didn't mean she took on the responsibility of overthrowing a government. She'd already disrupted a tense peace with Radha. How many more enemies could Jannemar survive?

Aviama shut her eyes tight and sucked in a deep breath. A lump lodged in her throat, and her eyes burned. If she'd only been more afraid of Queen Satya and scurried off home before handing over the secret of konnolan to Shiva. If she'd only escaped Radha before the army departed. If she'd only killed Shiva when she had the chance back in Radha, before he set out for Ghosts' Gorge.

No. She couldn't think like that. She'd killed him in the end, after all. Wasn't his life on her conscience enough? Did she dare add more red to her ledger? What would the officials from the mountainside tell the gold-gilded crestbreaker they'd met on the sea when he arrived to gather their report? She'd be hunted. Rebel or not, she'd disrupted the peace. Abasi was dead, Masud was dead, and at least one other man had died on Mount Zobaat at Durga's hand. All attributed to Aviama.

She would be marked as a criminal of the highest order. If they found out who she was, Keket would wage war on Jannemar. A war Jannemar could not afford.

Chenzira placed a warm hand on her shoulder and squeezed. "We've had a long night, and it isn't over. Let's take a break, get some sleep, and we will tell you all what you need to know before we dock."

Florian moaned. "Boringgg! Is no one else interested in the identity of the man she ditched the world's most powerful prince for?"

"We're paying you for safe passage. I'd recommend you focus on sailing. You could also make yourself useful and find a medical kit of some kind for Umed's shoulder."

Florian cast a sideways glance at Umed. "I do have a small medical supply."

Umed winced. "I'm fine."

Chenzira arched an eyebrow. "That is the kind of talk that a brave man says before an infection kills him, and he ceases to be of use to anyone. Take the medicine."

Umed's mouth twitched. "Medicine it is."

Chenzira gave a curt nod. "Manan, you're taking first

watch. The rest of you, get some rest. Durga, if you do anything stupid, I'll kill you myself."

Her eyes widened in challenge, but she tucked her feet underneath her on the bunk. She'd comply. For now.

Aviama leaned into Chenzira's arm. Nobody provided the kind of rock she relied on like him. If she'd listened to him from the start and hadn't flown off the handle and revealed melder powers—if she'd waited just a little longer for him to find her, or for her to find him—they wouldn't be in this mess. There would have been no scene. No escalation. No one would know anyone interesting had arrived in Keket.

But she could never have watched the little girl get sold and disappear forever into a life of bondage. She couldn't have ensured she would see Sai and Durga again. For better or for worse, for good or for evil, they had each served as her maidservants. Aviama had always been protective of her maidservants. Murin had become a close friend.

Sai had also become a friend. Even Durga had helpful moments when it served her. Besides, she'd been as good as dead in Radha. What choice had she had but to find someone powerful to protect her and keep her alive in a kingdom that destroyed melderbloods?

Florian skipped off for a medical kit, and the moment he was out of sight, Chenzira held his hand out to Aviama. She let him pull her to her feet and followed him back toward the ladder. As desperately as she needed sleep, they needed a plan more. And to be out from under prying eyes and ears.

Chenzira went up the ladder first, and as she moved to follow, Florian appeared out of the shadows and caught her by the elbow.

"They're nothing without you. Like it or not, you're the face of a rebellion. And to think—just this morning you were a slave. Amazing how quickly our fortunes can change."

Aviama's chest tightened, her heart racing like the pounding hooves of a stallion with a zegrath on its tail. Fatigue tugged at the edges of her consciousness, begging for reprieve. She lifted her chin. "What are you trying to say?"

"I'm saying you need to think for yourself." He cast a glance up toward Chenzira. "Do you know who he is? Who he *really* is? If you want to get home, I can help, but I can't do it with him around."

Aviama placed a firm hand on Florian's and plucked it from her elbow. "I'll keep that in mind."

She left him there in the dark and followed Chenzira up the ladder. But as she did, a chill ran down her spine, and a gnawing began to eat at her insides. Chenzira offered her a reassuring smile and took her hand.

His touch was cold.

17

Aviama's mind whirred in a tug-of-war between exhaustion and adrenaline as Chenzira led them to the rowboat lashed to the center of the deck and sank down on the floorboards, leaning back against the rowboat. Aviama sank down beside him and stared at the cannon in front of her, aiming at invisible enemies in the dark of the sea. Her gut pinched, and the gnawing sensation worsened.

Florian said he could get her to Jannemar. But did he want to separate her from Chenzira because he had reasonable suspicions about him, or because he saw Chenzira as a threat, a protector, that he needed out of the way before exploiting a young princess for his own ends? Chenzira had shown her no reason not to trust him. He hadn't told her what he'd run from in Keket, but he'd promised he *would*.

They hadn't had time, that was all. Keeping his identity secret was a safety measure for all of them, just as keeping her identity secret had been—a security Durga had just blown to bits. Which meant time was running out. If Keketi leadership clocked her as a rebel leader, they'd hunt her down. And she'd need a ship.

"We need information on Jannemar."

"We need a diversion."

They looked at each other. Both had spoken at once, and from the look on Chenzira's face, he hadn't expected her to say that. He frowned. She winced.

"We have people around us—Husani, the twins, Teja. We aren't doing what they want. They could turn on us at any moment. Durga's likely to sell us out to the highest bidder the minute she gets the chance. The more people who follow us, the worse off we are. Meanwhile, Jannemar is under attack, and if we're going to get killed here, we might as well go there."

Chenzira pursed his lips. "I can't leave without Rana."

"Your sister?"

He nodded. She sucked in a deep breath. Of course he couldn't leave her. Or, at least, not again—he'd left her once already. His forehead creased, and he stared down at his hands.

Aviama bit her lip. How much time would it take? How would they do it? Where was she?

"Okay. I said I would come with you to get her, and I will. Can we dismantle the slave trade while we're here?"

"Sure, right after we establish world peace. We'll be done by lunch."

Aviama rolled her eyes. The corner of his mouth twitched. But it wasn't funny.

She pinched her ring finger and swallowed. "You really aren't going to do anything?"

"I'm not sure what you expect me to be able to do. We don't have an army. Keket isn't just Jazir. As you found out this evening, there are quite a few melderbloods working for my family. This is no ragtag group of ruffians or disorganized criminals."

"If that's true, how are we going to get your sister? Do you know where she is?"

He hesitated. "Maybe."

"So let's just tell the crew the truth." Speaking the plan out loud soured her stomach. If Husani really did escape abuse, what was he supposed to do now? If the twins returned home now, would they be burned, or would there have been enough melderbloods on the island to change the culture?

Maybe melderbloods would start killing everyone without powers. The potential chaos was mind-boggling. Maybe they made peace. Maybe ...

She shook her head to clear it. They didn't have anything real to offer anyone following them. Nothing at all. And every fresh lie they told or encouraged would only add to a deeper betrayal on the back end.

"Once we land, we'll tell everybody we're sorry we disrupted your lives, but we wish you all well, and we have some business to attend to. We'll melt away into oblivion, the rebel leader they're chasing will disappear, we'll extract your sister, and snag a ship to Jannemar."

Chenzira ran a hand through his beard. "Umed and Manan won't leave us. And I wouldn't want them to stay in Keket."

Aviama shrugged. "Sai might not either. Anybody who wants to come would be welcome. I wouldn't feel right ditching them after all of this if they wanted to stay. But the more people we have with us, the harder we'll be to conceal. And what are the odds the newer ones will stick around after they find out everything we did was for show? Let them find a better life for themselves in Anhiraf or Siada or wherever the wind takes them."

"And the baby?"

"Okay, yes, well, there's that." Aviama bit her lip and grimaced. She glanced at Chenzira. It was a terrible idea. She was certain it would sound even dumber out loud. "I was thinking maybe she comes with us."

"I was afraid you were going to say that." He leaned his head back on the rowboat and closed his eyes. "My sister isn't lying on a barge, being fanned by servants all day. I imagine she'll be hard to find, and if anyone realizes where we're going and why, there's a pretty high chance we'll be chased or killed. How do you think that'll go with a toddler?"

"Probably not great." Aviama tried to imagine tossing air shields left and right with a baby on her back, or jumping through a window and fighting off a horde of Keketi melderblood soldiers with a toddler in tow. What if that innocent face, with her soft cheeks and large, searching eyes, were the next to appear in her rotating nightmares of the dead?

A lump lodged in her throat. Whatever might come, she couldn't abandon the girl. She would do what she must to protect her or die trying. And if she died trying, she wouldn't have to live with the guilt if she failed. Aviama blinked back tears and stared out at a sliver of onyx ocean she could see through the cannon gunport across from where they sat.

"I don't want to regret anything else, anything more than I already do. I never thought I'd be that person—someone with regrets. With blood on my hands. With a list of nightmares to revisit at night. I know Semra still has them, sometimes. Most of the time, she's fine, but every so often, her past catches up with her. Memories. I never thought that would be me. But while she went from dark to light, I feel like I'm moving from light to dark."

The sea lapped at the *Lightning Queen* as she cut her course through the water under a blanket of starlight. A soft splash signaled jumping fish somewhere along the surface, any sign of them obscured by the sides of the sloop hemming them in. The ache in her chest widened again, and she wondered if the emptiness would ever leave, or if it would one day expand so much that it enveloped her completely. Could sorrow eat at the emptiness, filling her with pain so that the oceans could not contain her tears? Or would the emptiness win, creating a cavern within herself until she was invisible beneath its yawning abyss?

"You miss him. Admit it."

He drilled her with an intense stare, a darkness in his eyes. She was startled at the look of him, as his biting tone brought her back to their conversation.

"Miss who?"

"Shiva."

"What?"

His jaw clenched, and he shifted toward her to look her full in the face. His voice softened, but he couldn't mask the bitterness seeping through. "You collapsed in my arms after he went overboard. You cried for him. A lot. You regret it. I know you hated him, but maybe another part of you didn't."

Aviama gaped at him. "You're kidding."

"I'm not."

Her chest tightened. Her face flushed hot. He'd lost his mind. Wind whispered across her fingers, winding its way around her hands and through her hair. A fire lit in the abyss of her soul, licking at the edges of her consciousness, hungry for the chance to burn.

"You think I miss him? That's why you think I was crying?"

Take it back. Tell me you didn't mean it. Tell me I'm not invisible. Tell me you understand.

Tell me I'm not alone.

He shrugged. "You blasted him over the railing, and something in you changed. And the minute we were through the Gorge, you wept and wept. I held you. I didn't say anything. You weren't in a talking mood. But what was I supposed to think?"

Idiot.

The fire in her chest exploded in a burst of rage. She swung at him then, and he caught her fist a hair from his own nose. The gathering wind in her palm escaped in every direction with a *whoosh* as her knuckles hit the meat of his hand.

He dropped her fist and tilted his head. "Would you like to try again?"

Aviama shot him a dark glare and bit back a retort. The blaze in her heart lived on, leaving an ashen land of loneliness in its wake. She was *not* like her sister. She was *not* like Durga, or Shiva, or anyone else who would have taken the bait and risen to the challenge he'd presented. They would have jumped on the chance to exert power, no matter the cost, no matter how much kindling they might dump on a pyre of animosity. Better to put out the flame inside herself and redirect to something productive.

"No. I didn't mean to hit you. I shouldn't hit people. Even stupid ones. And if I wanted to hurt you, I wouldn't use my fist."

She'd use the wind. She'd starve his lungs. She'd leave him on the deck, like she had the official in the other ship ...

So much for putting out the flame. Had the thought of hurting him genuinely just flickered across her mind? Aviama wavered as the blood drained from her face. She lurched to her feet and lunged for the railing. Air. More air. Sanity. She was going crazy.

He caught her elbow. "Look, maybe I misunderstood you. Don't run. Just tell me what it was about, then, if not that."

Tears burned her eyes as she spun on her heel, hair whipping him in the face as she whirled and came nose to nose with him under a shrouded moon. "Laksh's body was still on the deck! Bhumi was dead! Shiva's fleet of pawns was at the bottom of the sea! What was I supposed to feel?"

She flung her arms out sideways, chest heaving. "What emotions would have been permissible? Was I supposed to celebrate killing him? Was I supposed to be happy? Maybe some people don't have reactions to killing anymore, but I still took a life. My hands did that. Mine. And yeah, I was upset about that. I was upset about Enzo too. Seeing his head on a platter staring up at me. I was upset about Sai's bruises and Makana's enslavement. I was tired of carrying the weight of everyone's lives on my back and still losing as many as we lost. They're dead. They're not coming back. Like Sona and Liben. Like the melders at the dock in Radha. Like the little girl's real mother, who Abasi murdered on the ship. Like Teja's mother, who died this morning before we disembarked."

Aviama choked on a sob and swallowed hard. "Death is supposed to bother me. I'm scared that if I lose that, I'll change. That I won't mind it. I used to think it was never okay to kill. I don't agree with that anymore. And that scares me. If we have to kill sometimes, how long will it take for me to justify enjoying it? What if the power I have drives me mad? What if that's what happened six hundred years ago—people like me, normal people, woke up and realized a long-dormant evil awoke, not because they were worse people than anybody else, but just because they had the opportunity? What if good people aren't good at all, but are too weak to do any damage? What if power corrupts everything it touches? Who am I to think I can escape that? What if I *am* Shiva?"

She stared up at him, chest heaving, tears streaming down her face. Chenzira blinked back at her as if he'd been struck.

Nothing. No words. No comment. No denial that she could turn into the monster he hated so much.

Aviama turned away and covered her face with her hands. Her chest hitched, and she threw a hand out to the railing to steady herself against the lull of the rocking ship and the rolling wave of emotions threatening to drag her under.

Chenzira cleared his throat. "Oh."

She might have felt victorious over the bashfulness of his tone if she wasn't simultaneously furious that he had nothing further to say. He'd been knocked down a peg, sure. But where did that leave them? On opposite sides of a chasm, the weight of the world ripping a crack between them?

He shifted his weight. The movement grated on her. His silence grated on her. Everything he did bothered her—how he stood, the way he tugged his fingers through his beard, the roaring quiet he maintained. The gall of this man to think she'd been upset over losing an oppressor rather than losing her soul. She had no fondness for Shiva. She just didn't want to become him.

Aviama gritted her teeth and swatted a tear from her cheek.

Chenzira stepped closer, bumping the side of his arm into hers. "Hey. I'm sorry. I was wrong."

She took in a shaky, sniffling breath. "Yes. You were."

"I was."

He put his arm around her and kissed her on the forehead. Aviama leaned into his solid frame and let out a long sigh. Then a thought dropped into her mind. She tilted her face up toward his.

"Why are you still competing with a dead man?"

Chenzira startled, then looked down at her. He opened his mouth, then closed it. "I don't know."

Aviama pressed her lips together. "I think … I think what you said was about you. It wasn't about me."

He hesitated, then gave a slight nod. "Yes. But you trusting me is still something we need to talk about while we're in Keket. So we don't have another Jazir situation."

Aviama thought of what Florian had said. Did she know who Chenzira really was? She dismissed it but didn't share it with Chenzira either.

"Okay, sure, but if we don't have a chance to plan something together, you have to know I will do what I think I need to in the moment."

His mouth twisted into a lopsided smile. "I know." The smile faded. "Speaking of plans, I don't trust Florian with your identity. At all. He'll sell that information, and there are plenty of people who would pay a pretty penny for it. He'll describe the rest of us, too, and if he finds out where we're going or what we're doing, he could send soldiers straight to us. We need to blend in and disappear, to find some place to hide away while we get information about Rana."

Aviama nodded. It made sense. "How well do you know Anhiraf?"

"Pretty well. We'll need to move fast to get clothes for all of us that look Keketi so we can move around a bit easier. And we need a shawl or something to cover your hair." He tugged on a lock of her long golden waves.

"Reasonable. In the morning, I want to lead the meeting with everyone. And if we can keep Florian away during that time, all the better."

"Done." He lifted her hand and pressed his lips to her knuckles. "Let's get some sleep."

Sleep. On a bed. Not urine-soaked straw needles. She might faint at the thought.

"If you insist." She smiled, and his answering smile lit the night. The emptiness inside her fled as she basked in the warmth of that smile and those soft, cinnamon eyes. The look that said she was known, and loved, and cared about.

Florian be hanged. Nothing would separate her from that smile.

Chenzira led her back to the hatch, down the ladder, and they walked together down the cargo deck to the bunks. They might not have much of a plan, but they'd figure it out. Side by side.

Because Florian was wrong. Working with Chenzira didn't mean she wasn't thinking for herself. It meant for once in her life, someone saw her as more than a princess. She wasn't a helpless valuable to be stashed away in danger, and she wasn't a trinket to be bartered for larger political means.

For the first time, she was an equal partner in a worthy endeavor. Chenzira had deferred to *her* when the islanders thought she was Raisa. Just as he'd stepped back on the *Wraithweaver,* happy to let her lead and be called commander. In return, she'd leaned on his expertise and skill in the Gorge, and would do it again in Keket, on Chenzira's home turf.

If anything, it was Aviama who had not respected Chenzira's opinions enough, rather than Chenzira not respecting hers.

Yes, he wanted her to be safe. Yes, he wanted her to be reasonable. But didn't she want the same for him? Isn't that why they'd started tallying their dangerous tendencies to begin with?

Death-defying feats were their specialty. From the arena to the sea, from the sea to the islands, only one constant remained: Chenzira.

So she would sleep tonight, soaking up every minute of her long-awaited rest. And in the morning, come what may, they'd face it all as a team.

Aviama squeezed his hand in a silent goodnight, and they parted in silence, drifting off to different bunks. Chenzira took the one next to Umed, the two of them placing themselves between the ladder and the rest of the group. The twins, Husani, and Manan were next on the right, with Sai, Durga, Teja, and the little girl opposite them on the left.

Chenzira slipped under the blanket and disappeared. Aviama sank down on the edge of the little girl's bed, reaching out to sweep a rogue lock of hair from her face. The little one reached up in her sleep and clutched at her hand, snuggling it against her cheek. Aviama's heart pinched.

Slowly, she moved to tug her hand free, but the girl held it fast. Who was she to disrupt one of the little girl's few comforts? Aviama slipped into the bed beside her, tucking the blanket carefully around the small body, and laid her own head on the pillow beside her.

News of home. Rana's location. Escape from Keketi officials.

Uncomfortable confessions.

All problems for tomorrow.

Aviama took a long, deep breath and drifted off to sleep. She dreamed of freed slaves, living parents, and a full belly. She dreamed of a world where these were not luxuries, but common.

She dreamed that the darkness in her soul did not deepen, that her power was safe from corruption, and that allies were trustworthy.

And then she woke up.

18

"Pssst. Aviama. Psssssssssst."

Aviama cracked one eye open. The haze of early dawn sifted down through the hatch. Bodies lay sleeping on bunks. Durga flicked her in the forehead, and Aviama smacked her hand.

Durga grinned. "Awake?"

Aviama groaned. "No."

"Too bad. Because we're here. And something's wrong."

Both eyes flew open. Aviama sat up. The little girl still slept beside her. Husani, Teja, Sai, and Zahur breathed deep from their bunks.

"What is it?"

"His H—erm, Chen—well, your boyfriend jumped up like he found snakes in his bed and ran up the ladder. Osahar yelled at someone. I think Florian has a few other crewmen on board somewhere, because the only other person I've seen is the kid he's got, the boy from the mountain, but Zahur said the sloop needs at least a couple of people to man it. Anyway, there were some harsh words. And Chenzira hasn't come back down for an hour."

Aviama slipped out of bed and crept along the deck toward the ladder. She hadn't missed Durga's slip. She'd almost called Chenzira His Highness, and then nearly resorted to his name. What were they supposed to call him, if not by his name? It must have been weirder for Durga, a servant in a palace, who could have been flogged for addressing a royal or dignitary without proper respect.

She glanced back at the sleeping forms behind her and picked up the pace toward the hatch. "How long ago did the ship dock?"

"Maybe ten minutes."

Aviama's jaw dropped. "He's been gone over an hour, we've already docked, and you didn't think to wake me until now?"

Durga shrugged. "You're much easier to deal with when you're unconscious."

Aviama rolled her eyes. "Funny you should mention it. I feel the same way about you."

She crept closer to the ladder and climbed the first couple of rungs, leaving the hatch down and peering through it as best she could. Running footsteps thudded across the deck, and for a moment, Zahur's massive frame blotted out the dawn and cast the ladder in shadow. Words flew like knives, at least three voices, fast and all in Keketi.

Durga cleared her throat from below. "Well?"

Aviama winced. "I can't understand anything. They're angry, and they're in a hurry. That's all I got."

"Wow, you're a genius. I'm so glad I woke you up."

"You're so helpful. I'm so glad Onkar sold you to Abasi instead of letting you rot in the *Wraithweaver* brig."

Aviama grimaced. It sounded a lot harsher than she'd meant it. She glanced down at Durga. Durga snorted. "He didn't want to deal with me."

True. Durga had been nothing but trouble, and Onkar had

probably been eager to be rid of her for a few coins. Aviama squinted back up through the hatch. No good. She shoved it open and started to climb up.

Florian, Chenzira, and Zahur stood in a huddle near the mast, their gesturing hands nearly as loud as their voices had been a moment ago. Florian glanced up, and his expression turned to flint as his eyes fell on the princess. "Sands, are you trying to get us killed? Get below."

Aviama clenched her jaw. "Why? What's going on?"

She craned her neck around the mainsail to take in the view. The sloop was anchored just offshore in a small cove. Ruddy cliffs the color of desert sands rose up around them, hemming in the sloop and blocking out a view of the rest of the isle. Azure waters sparkled around them like crystal, bumping up against land to feed wide leafy palms and lush foliage cropping up unexpectedly here and there among softer slopes and clefts of the rock.

Not a soul in sight.

Aviama spread her hands. "Who's going to see me?"

Florian glared at her, his smooth exterior cracked for the first time. "Everyone. Literally everyone. You're a beacon from a hundred meters off."

Chenzira jerked his head in their direction, beckoning her closer. "You could get behind the sail, or head back down the ladder. The kid will be back any minute now with some clothes."

Florian scowled. "She sticks out like a camel in a fish tank."

Aviama skipped up behind the large sail and crossed her arms. "Rough night? Or are you always this pleasant in the morning?"

Florian ignored her and turned to Zahur. "We need to get the sail down."

Zahur squinted up at the sail and across the cove. "I thought we needed covered. To hide."

"We need to look like we don't need the coverage." Florian stuffed a hand in his pocket and produced a silver coin, tossing it in the air and catching it. "If the women stay below deck"—here he shot a look at Aviama, and beyond her to the hatch where Durga's head was poking out—"I can bring down something to eat, we can bring in the sail, and Amon can bring down the clothes when he gets back. The moment you all are dressed, I want you off my ship."

Aviama's eyes narrowed. "What were you arguing about?"

Chenzira ground his teeth. "We're not on Anhiraf."

Her gut wrenched. "What?"

"He brought us to Siada."

The main island. The island of the royal family. The island of Chenzira's parents and all major governing bodies. The military center. Florian had delivered the foreign princess rebel leader to the king's doorstep.

She shook her head. "But we said we needed to get to Anhiraf."

"Yes, and I said I'd only take you on board if you came alone." Florian rolled the coin in his fingers, tossing it up again and snatching it from the air. "But you did not come alone. You brought a horde of angry islanders and fireballs after you, not to mention I still came and saved you after you *fought* with a royal envoy. Like an idiot."

Aviama glanced at Chenzira. "I think I liked it better when he was pretending to be nice."

Chenzira's mouth twitched. "I don't. I like my cowards to show themselves early rather than late."

"I like to be alive. Free from prison, preferably." Florian crossed his arms. "I have a business to run, a new ship to acquire, and a crew to feed. I've got a schedule to keep and a reputation to maintain."

Aviama pursed her lips. "Then why did you offer to take us?"

"Are you kidding? If you're going to start a rebellion, do it here in Siada, in the thick of it. Leave Jazir alone. They're insane. If you could have gotten away without setting the whole place on fire, that would have been better. I do good business there. If they start hunting melderbloods, or melderbloods turn the place to ash, I'll never work there again."

Chenzira ran a hand through his beard. "What kind of work do you do, exactly?"

"The kind that doesn't need to draw a lot of heat. And you and your little band are basically a firebrand."

"Ohhh." Realization dawned. Aviama sucked in a breath. "The boy's a fireblood. If they hunt melderbloods, he won't stand a chance."

Florian nodded. "Jazir is out of the way and a great resupply and business opportunity for us. Keeps food on the table and is a necessary stop on our route. Now I'm not sure when or if I'll be able to go back there, even after getting you out."

"But maybe they'll realize that melders aren't bad, and it'll even out. The dust will settle." It might take a while, but it would. After the initial shock, they'd catch up with the rest of the world. Aviama tilted her head. "They couldn't live like that forever, in an old lie in a bubble all their own."

Florian's head snapped up. "Let me tell you something, Princess. Dust over here only settles in blood."

Aviama swallowed. She planted her hands on her hips, then folded her arms instead. "It doesn't matter. We told you Anhiraf. You should have taken us there."

"I did. But it's too close to Jazir, and word had already gotten out about you." Florian wagged a finger at her. "*You* are the talk of the town. The docks were full of people looking for you, even so late. I turned off and came here. Call it an executive decision."

Biscuits.

Zahur cleared his throat. "Boy is here. Not alone."

Florian swore and strode to the railing, calling out orders as he went. "Get her below. Now."

Chenzira put a hand on her back. "Come on. It'll only be for a few minutes. I won't let anything happen."

Aviama lifted her chin and looked him in the eyes. "Neither will I."

She liked to be cared for, and it felt good that he wanted to protect her, but just that moment, it felt a lot like she was being sequestered away. Getting stuffed in a room while excitement happened somewhere else had become her least favorite experience.

Chenzira sighed. "Get everybody something to eat and check on the girl. We'll probably have to get the anchor up and dock somewhere else. I'll be down as soon as I can."

Aviama peered around his shoulder. Florian's boy, Amon, sprinted around the bend with a bundle on his back that looked nearly as big as he was. Beyond him, several adults in traditional Keketi white came running.

Chenzira tapped her on the back, a gentle push toward the hatch. "If they see you, they'll know you're here. I'm a native. I don't stick out as much. That's all this is."

As much as she hated it, it did make sense.

"Fine. But if you don't come down soon, I'm coming up."

"Deal."

Aviama hurried across the deck and down the ladder, shooing at Durga to get out of the way. The hatch shut her into the cargo deck with a soft *thunk* as Aviama's feet hit the floor. Durga arched an eyebrow.

"I could have let you sleep, huh?"

"They don't want people to see me. They're running after Florian's kid. Also, we're on the wrong island."

"Fantastic. Are you sure you can trust your boyfriend?"

Aviama set her jaw. "I'm not sure I can trust *Florian.* But I trust Chenzira a thousand times more than I trust you, if that tells you anything."

"It doesn't. You don't trust me."

"I'd agree the bar is low."

Durga pursed her lips. "I'm just saying your choice in men hasn't been great so far."

Heat flew to Aviama's cheeks. "I could say the same about your choice in overlords. First the queen, then the prince you are misinformed enough to say that I *chose.*"

Durga held up a hand. "Fair enough."

"There's nothing fair about what happened to me. And while you're questioning my decision-making, consider that I could have killed you on the *Wraithweaver,* and I let you live."

The girl opened her mouth, then planted her hands on her hips. "I'm not sure that counts as a wise move."

Something about the blatant honesty struck her, and Aviama laughed. "Me neither."

For all Durga's many flaws, her frankness was oddly refreshing. There would be no brown nosing or coddling by Durga.

Sai and Husani were sitting up when Aviama and Durga reached the bunks again. Teja stretched and sat up, rubbing her eyes, and Husani hit Osahar with a spare pillow. Umed examined the belt and khopesh at his side. He tensed when he saw Aviama and kicked Manan's bed. Manan grunted from a precarious position on the edge of the bunk and fell onto the floor. The only person still left undisturbed was the little girl, her chest rising and falling peacefully with each deep breath.

Aviama cleared her throat as all eyes bored into her. She twisted the skin around one finger and grimaced. "We're on the wrong island."

Sai's brows soared. "Excuse me?"

"Florian anchored the sloop at Siada instead of Anhiraf. He sent Amon ashore for some supplies, and the kid is sprinting back now, bringing curious onlookers after him. They asked me to get out of sight so as not to draw more attention."

Umed frowned. "Why would anyone follow a random kid?"

Aviama shrugged. "That's a good question. I don't know."

Could Amon have contacted people on Siada somehow in the short time they'd had since anchoring? Did Florian want people in an uproar? Were they looking for Aviama or something else?

Manan winced as he jerked himself upright and gathered his feet. "What's our next play?"

Durga plopped on the edge of Osahar's bed. Osahar pulled back, and a shadow of a smile flicked across her face. She let out a dramatic sigh. "Hiding like moles while the kid of the man we don't trust brings us clothes."

Umed spun to Aviama. "Where is he?"

There was no questioning who he meant. Aviama gestured above deck. "Above with Zahur."

Umed cursed and broke into a jog across the deck toward the hatch. Aviama resisted the urge to follow. Aside from the clothes he wore, Umed looked like he could be Keketi. And if Chenzira was alone above deck with Florian and Zahur, nobody trustworthy was with him. He was alone. Aviama's stomach dropped.

Who had been on watch when the sloop docked? Anyone? Or had they all just fallen asleep and failed to wake the next watch?

Umed disappeared up the hatch, and Osahar and Husani exchanged a look before jumping up to follow him. Manan turned to her, silent but expectant. She jerked her head toward the stairs.

"Stand guard by the hatch. Listen and be ready. Nobody gets to us that you don't know."

He dipped his head and trotted over toward the ladder, grateful to have an assignment, if not a more active one. Manan adjusted his wrinkled tunic as he went and stood straight as an arrow on the opposite end of the ladder.

Thud.

Aviama jumped at the sound. Distant shouts carried toward them from the direction of the shore. Running feet pounded the planks above them, shaking dust down into the cargo deck from overhead. The little girl stirred and whimpered. Aviama reached for her and pulled her into her lap.

Teja sat next to Aviama and the girl, patted the girl on the arm and raised her gaze to Aviama. "They shout, 'Thief, thief.'"

Aviama groaned. "The kid. Florian sent him for supplies, and he stole them all."

"Spectacular." Durga shook her head. "It was getting boring around here. I almost got half a night's sleep."

Sai glared at her. "What? Nightmares of your betrayals keep you up at night?"

Durga sniffed. "No, reminding myself how smart I am lulls me to sleep like a baby. It's everyone else's stupidity that keeps me up at night."

Aviama held up a hand. "Shhh." She slid the little girl off her lap toward Teja and crept across to Husani's bunk. His headscarf was bunched up into a makeshift pillow at the end of his bed, the actual pillow tossed aside. Aviama snatched it up and laid it over her hair, arranging it to hide as much of her golden waves as possible.

When she turned, Teja, Sai, and Durga all stared at her in horror. Aviama glanced from one disgusted face to another.

"What? If we have to run out of here, I should cover my hair so I'm not so obvious when we leave, right? I'll give it back. I don't even want the head wrap. I don't think he'll mind."

"It's not that." Teja pursed her lips, and Sai's nose scrunched.

"You've never worn one of those before, have you?"

She shifted her weight. "I mean, a couple of times, but I didn't put it in. I've done my own hair before, though."

Durga snorted. "How noble. No, really. It's *noble.* Highbrow and fancy. You've done your own hair a few times, have you? Congratulations! How smart and talented you must be!"

Sai waved her off and summoned Aviama to come closer. "Please don't go out like that. It's embarrassing."

Aviama sank onto the bunk Sai indicated, and Sai got to work fixing the headwrap, arranging it with expert fingers. A moment later, it felt secure in her hair rather than falling out, and probably even looked good. Heat flushed her cheeks.

"Thanks. Sorry."

Sai smiled and patted her on the shoulder. "It's fine."

Durga rolled her eyes. "She means her expectations of you are low at this point."

Sai glared at her. "That's *not* what I meant."

The ship lurched, and the shouting outside ratcheted up— but this time, sound came from both directions. Manan ran two steps up the ladder when the hatch ripped open from above and Florian's voice floated down to them above the din.

"We could use some windcallers!"

Aviama directed Teja to stay with the girl and sprinted with Durga and Sai down the deck to the ladder. Durga beat her, but let Aviama scale the ladder first as Manan stayed behind to watch their progress up through the hatch.

Florian reached a hand down and pulled her up. Aviama shoved away from him and straightened her filthy trousers out of habit as if they were velvet skirts. "I thought you wanted me out of sight."

His eye caught the motion, but he said nothing, casting a quick glance over his shoulder instead. "Yes, but I like my ship more. She's one of my favorites."

Aviama frowned. "Why would you lose your ship?"

She craned her neck beyond him. Amon was at the helm, like a twig-sized captain in a grown-up's world. Chenzira and Zahur wrestled with a winch to bring up the anchor, muscles bulging as they strained to hurry their progress. Onshore, twenty or thirty people had gathered, shouting at them in Keketi. Cliff walls banked them in on every side, hiding the sloop away from the prying eyes of popular docks and fishing spots. But there, out toward the mouth of the cove, a larger vessel moved to cut off their escape—running up the Keketi colors and crest of the royal family.

19

Aviama whirled to Florian. "Why would they seize your ship? Why is the royal family looking for you?"

Florian ran his thumb and forefinger across the brim of his hat. "They don't approve of my adventurous business deals."

"You've got to be kidding me."

"Not in the slightest. And I'm afraid Amon has been recognized by some people we may have slighted before."

Durga gaped at him. "What does that mean?"

Aviama leveled her with a look. "He's a pirate."

"Privateer, thank you very much."

Aviama rolled her eyes. "Yes. The respectable kind who are wanted for crimes, chased for theft, and keep fast getaway ships ready at the drop of a hat."

"That's ridiculous. I would never drop my hat. Now, if you would be so kind, we need to turn this headwind into something more in our favor."

He gestured toward the bow as though he were ushering them into a banquet instead of asking them to expose their abilities to avoid his own arrest. If they hadn't been so keen on avoiding any governmental body, Aviama would have rather let Florian hang himself for his own crimes. As it was, after last night's shenanigans, she could only imagine consequences for capture would be worse for her than for the pirate.

Sai and Durga fell in behind her as she strode toward the mast. Her heart hammered in her chest. She stopped at the mast and lifted her hands. No need to go to the bow. No need to be so visible.

Osahar and Umed stationed themselves at the bow instead, as Chenzira and Zahur finished securing the anchor. Husani stood at the railing, taking it all in, eyes wide. Shouts continued from shore as the band of angry islanders vented their frustrations. Chenzira glanced up at the oncoming ship, scanned the cove, and locked eyes with Aviama.

He ran forward and touched her on the arm, leaning in to whisper in her ear. "Get us to the side of the cove, and we'll make our way off. I don't trust Florian, but we can't get caught by the royal envoy either."

Her gut twisted. "It'll make a scene. I'll have to show off our abilities."

"Better that than execution for leading a rebellion. It won't take them long to figure out who you are once they're upon us."

She glanced back out at the mouth of the cove. "Maybe I can get us past the ship."

"In a natural wind this strong going in the opposite direction? That ship is almost here. We can't let them see our faces. Even if we aren't caught, if they see our faces, we're in trouble."

Sai tapped her on the shoulder. "What should we do? We're running out of time."

Aviama glanced at Chenzira and back to Sai. "Push to the

edge of the cliff. On the other side from the shore. We'll need as much distance as we can get. Manan!"

Manan popped up through the hatch.

Aviama jerked her head toward Amon, who sat in a coil of rope, gnawing a piece of bread with the satchel over his shoulder. "Give him some food, but take the bag."

It felt wrong to take it from a kid. But then, everything he took was supposed to be for them anyway, wasn't it? Food and clothes? How he got it wasn't their concern. Was it? Maybe they could return it all someday.

She shook her head, but the guilt still plagued her as she lifted her hands and called to the wind. Manan rolled out onto the deck, and Chenzira ducked back and out of the way as the three windcallers took up their positions. Sai and Durga stood on either side of Aviama, and a rush of air whirled about them as the energy of the gale built stronger and stronger. Sai glanced at her, but Aviama gave a slight shake of her head to indicate not to release it to the sail. Not yet. The energy gathered easier on its own before fighting against obstacles.

Florian's hat lifted a hair off his head, and he smashed a hand down on top to halt its escape. "Any time now!"

Aviama lifted her hands higher, the surge of tabeun energy running along her skin like electricity on an eel. "You should never have brought us here. We should have been on Anhiraf."

Florian crouched by the mast, hand on his hat, under the might of the gathering gale. "You'd be stupid to go to Anhiraf. Word had already reached them, and there was no safe place to dock."

"It wasn't your call. You should have asked where else to go." Heat flooded her chest as the wind washed over her, swirling in powerful arcs around the three women. Aviama lifted her voice to shout above the din of the rushing air. "Siada is the last place we should be!"

Florian edged closer, eyeing the wind. "Which is why you *should* be here. Nobody would expect it. Besides, did you tell them where you were going? The royal envoy from last night?"

Aviama gritted her teeth. She wouldn't answer the last question. The one that would make her look stupid. Because Husani *had* said exactly where they were going. "Expected or not, I wouldn't call this a covert landing on Siada, would you?"

The ship crept across the mouth of the cove, now entirely blocking their exit. If they hoped to pass, they'd be clipping the side of the hull. Were there melders on that ship, too, as there were on the last ship of the royal guard? It looked to be the same type. What if they had five windcallers to their three? What if they had crestbreakers?

She looked across at the ship. Archers fell in line at the railing. They were out of time.

"Now!"

Aviama snapped her arms forward, angling them into the sails, Durga and Sai following suit. Florian toppled sideways on the deck as the wind whipped over his head, filled the sails, and tugged the sloop out and further away from shore. The royal envoy at the mouth of the cove angled toward them. Archers notched their arrows at the railing.

The *Lightning Queen* bore hard to the starboard side, tilting at a steep angle into the water. Ripples of ocean waves ran across the surface of the sea from the enemy ship, counter to the current. They had a crestbreaker.

Aviama's stomach twisted. She glanced at Umed. He saw it too. Umed lowered into an engagement stance, feet set wide apart in a half-crouch by the railing, keeping his center of gravity low and balance strong. His hands were moving, low and invisible to anyone outside the ship. Another ripple of water coursed out from the *Lightning Queen* to meet the one from the ship on the opposite end. The opposing currents mixed and spun together, creating a small whirlpool between the two vessels.

Her mouth went dry. Was anything more dangerous than melderbloods? Every attack, every violence, was escalated. But if tabeun power existed in the world and was used for evil, that reality demanded a counterbalance on the other side to oppose it. To keep it in check. To keep tyrants from rule.

Perhaps the four famous elemental melders had been right about The Crumbling all those years ago. About destroying magic. But if there was no way to destroy it again, there had to be a way to survive in a day and age when such power had awoken.

If the ship was using crestbreakers and archers, they weren't ready for a full-scale attack taking on melders. For whatever reason, they still hoped to be covert. That worked in their favor.

Unless it didn't. Unless they changed their mind. Did they have windcallers and chose not to use them? Or did they not have any? Were they only waiting for the right—

A gale knocked Aviama off her feet. She hit the deck, and the wind in her hands escaped in every direction. The wooden planks scuffed the palms of her hands as she shoved herself up. So much for the enemy not having melders. She squinted into the distance toward the other ship. Whoever they were, they were good. Precision this far away to send a wind that strong around Aviama, Sai, and Durga's currents into the sails and still hit Aviama hard enough to knock her down required substantial control.

Aviama threw up a barrier in a semi-circular shield around herself, Sai, and Durga as Sai and Durga continued funneling air into the sails. She gathered her feet and strained against the pressure testing her air shield. Someone was trying to break through it. And now they were down a windcaller working on the sails.

Manan joined Umed at the railing, the two crestbreakers working side by side. Aviama glanced at the expanse of water between them and the other ship. The whirlpool had doubled in size, and without the wind pushing as strong against the current, the *Lightning Queen* was starting to succumb to its pull.

Chenzira yelled at Husani, and he dropped below the railing just in time for an arrow to whistle past his ear. Chenzira ducked down, back against the side of the ship, hand on his khopesh. He called to Aviama. "We can't pass them. They're too close, and if they have crestbreakers, it's too dangerous. We have to disembark. Now."

Florian adjusted his hat, red feather bobbing in the rushing wind. He shook his head. "I'm not bringing my ship ashore. If we ride the edge of the whirlpool across, the girls can do wind stuff to push us up and out. We'll have the element of surprise. We can make it out."

Chenzira glared at him. "You just don't want to get caught."

The pirate ignored him, looking hard at Aviama. "Remember what I told you. What I can do for you."

There could be no questioning what his implication was. *I can get you home. Chenzira won't.* But Florian didn't know that. And Aviama didn't trust Florian.

Aviama winced as a punch of air slammed into her barrier. Harder than she expected. She repaired the weakness, where air had dissipated from its protective place at the strength of the blow.

Florian popped his head up over the railing to look at the ship's position, the whirlwind between them, and the archers on the side. He dropped back down and held up a hand.

"We're lighter and smaller and have better maneuverability than they do."

"Get us out of here, Tally. Close to the cliff."

Osahar and Zahur stood at the bow, weapons in hand. Amon, Florian's kid, sat rooted to his spot in the coil of rope, gaping at the scene before him. Aviama, Umed, and Manan were losing the crestbreaker battle, and there was no guarantee the three windcallers could save the *Lightning Queen* from the pull of the whirlpool before it spun off into the rocks on the far side and destroyed the hull. Especially if the windcaller on the opposite ship kept forcing them to split their attention between sails and shields.

So far, no fire. Zahur had one hand in a fist, and he looked like he was itching for excitement. For involvement. Anything but stand and do nothing. Aviama knew the feeling. And he wasn't the only one. Chenzira raked a hand through his beard and clenched his jaw. A muscle in his neck tensed.

Another gale punched at Aviama's barrier. Another. Even as energy rolled off her to fuel it, Aviama felt the drain as she pushed herself to keep Sai and Durga safe and protected.

"To the cliff!"

"No! To the sea!"

Aviama's blood boiled at Florian's commanding voice. She opened her mouth to retort, then shook her head. It wouldn't do any good. And Sai and Durga would still do what she asked, not what Florian said.

Durga lifted her chin. "If you want to be in the sea so bad, feel free to jump in."

The corner of Aviama's mouth twisted up. Florian kept one hand on his hat as the wind whistled around him and placed the other on the khopesh at his side. Durga rolled her eyes.

He couldn't possibly be that stupid.

The sloop rocked, and the wood creaked as the whirlpool

tugged them to port, and the wind in the sails pressed starboard. Wind whipped the taut sails, and Sai's shoulders began to sag.

Aviama sidestepped next to her. "Throw up a shield just between us and the archers. Let me take the sails."

A simpler, straight shield should be easier to maintain, and could take the windcaller on the other ship a few minutes to find. But they'd be vulnerable to attack from gales on the sides. She'd have to move fast.

Wind pooled in her palms as Sai nodded and refocused her attention to block the archers. Aviama joined Durga and was struck by the might of her windcalling. The Radhan girl might not yet have finesse, but she had power in spades.

Aviama stepped toward the bow, separating herself from Durga, making two separate targets for a single windcaller. "Umed. Manan. Stop adding energy to the whirlpool. Stabilize the ship and ride the edge."

Manan glanced at her, unsure. "They'll draw us closer to them."

Florian held the helm, eyeing them closely. Chenzira moved up beside him and nodded to Manan. "We'll redirect before we reach them."

Umed dipped his head. "They're right. We're only building it now. If we ride the edge, we can use our momentum and pull off to the side and out, and we'll be free."

Aviama glanced up. The other vessel maintained its position, floating just at the entrance to the cove, blocking escape. Slowly creeping up on them from the safety of quieter waters. The *Lightning Queen* was in an uproar, and the royal envoy only sat back and watched the show.

The sloop pulled in toward the whirlpool, leaning into the wind. Wooden planks creaked. Sea spray tossed, coating them with cool saltwater. Wind surged into the sails. They were picking up speed. Fast.

Florian strained at the helm, glancing down at the whirlpool and back up to the ship. "Slow us down. You're going to slingshot us straight into them."

Chenzira shook his head. "Hold."

Behind her, Sai let out a scream and slid down the deck. Aviama spun just in time to see an invisible force slam into Durga's chest and blast her backward. The tabeun wind abandoned the sails as Chenzira caught Sai around the waist and Aviama dove to catch Durga before she toppled overboard. The ship rocked sideways, tilting toward the funnel of water pulling down, down, into the bottom of the cove.

Florian ripped his hat off, threw it in a nearby barrel, and gripped the helm with all his might. "Exit the whirlpool!"

Chenzira set Sai on her feet. "Hold."

Aviama shifted her weight as she summoned the air around them with all the vehemence she could muster. The whirlpool yawned ever wider before them. He was waiting too long. But then, blessing of blessings, Chenzira gave the order.

"Now!"

The sloop cut out of the whirlpool, and Umed and Manan bent all their energy on a current to carry them to the cliff. But Florian was right. They were moving too fast. The sloop surged over rippling choppy water that cropped up out of nowhere as the whirlpool dissipated in their wake and they barreled toward a towering wall of rock.

A soft, muffled cry pierced the air.

Aviama froze. A chill ran down her spine. She looked at Chenzira. "The girl."

Chenzira's gaze swept the deck. He cursed. "Where?"

"Below, with Teja."

Chenzira glanced up at the cliff face rushing toward them,

back at Aviama, and dove across the deck for the hatch. Her heart stopped. If they ran into the rocks, and the hull broke apart, anyone below could be skewered by splintered wood and rock or trapped underwater.

A wave of water bashed against the sloop, rocking them sideways as they careened toward the rock face. Chenzira wrested the hatch open and disappeared. Aviama stumbled backward as the ship tilted under her feet.

Durga flung her arms around the mast, and the wind died down. "Can't you just crush their lungs from here?"

Aviama's back hit Zahur's knees as her rear hit the deck and she skidded backward. By the time she looked up, the sloop's prow grazed the rock. She threw her hands up as Zahur hauled her to her feet, sending a barrier of air to cushion the prow and slow their approach. But the ship was big, and her energy was dropping.

"No, I can't. They're too far for something so precise."

Durga flung a hand up toward the approaching cliff, and a blast of air shot from her palm. "Isn't it worth a try?"

Whoops and hollers came from the shore behind them as the prow scraped the cliff face, the front of the bowsprit snapping to splinters. Aviama grimaced as she worked to slow them, but they'd hit the side pretty hard. Had the hull been damaged?

"If you're so convinced it'll work, do it yourself!"

Durga scowled. She'd never had that kind of control. Aviama tossed a glance this way and that. Ahead, sheer cliff and more sheer cliff awaited them. Wind rushed by her ears as she called to the air and Umed and Manan coaxed the ocean to pull the ship off its course.

Further up and to the left, the royal guard ship edged closer on tranquil waters clear and crystal as smooth sea glass. The archers stayed their hands, but their arrows remained in place, their iron tips trained on the modest pirate sloop. Florian beckoned to Amon, and the boy ran to his side. Whoops and hollers rose from the shore far behind, their cries growing all the more distant as the wind and waves over-powered the sound.

Raised water ran along the surface between the two vessels, like the crest of ocean rolling off an eel coursing just beneath the face of the sea. Aviama turned to look, and the raised portion swirled this way and that, deliberate patterns swirling their way into seafoam. But as she kept her eye on the design, a chill ran down her spine.

They were letters. In her language.

RAISA.

20

T he guard ship wasn't here for Florian. It was here for her. But if that were true, how did they find her so fast?

"Aviama! A little help?"

Aviama snapped her attention back to Durga and the sloop and the cliff. *CRACKKKK.*

What was it? The hull? The figurehead? The mast? No, the mast was in place. And there were another two hundred meters before the cliff gave way to palm fronds and a sandy beach. Where the guard ship patiently waited to pick them up when the sloop broke apart.

A knot formed and doubled in her stomach in the space it took for her to take a breath. Stale air swept past an ever-expanding lump in her throat, threatening to strangle her. Her mouth went dry.

Florian was screaming from the helm, Amon attached to his side. "What are you doing? Get us off the cliff!"

Durga strained against the mast, hands up, as the ship grated against the cliff. "Aviama!"

Sai abandoned the air shield to help Durga cushion the

sloop from the rock. Manan and Umed doubled over the railing in their efforts to manipulate the surf. Husani, Zahur, and Osahar were red in the face, hands itching at their sides, helpless.

Where was Chenzira?

Aviama ran forward to stand beside Durga, looping an arm around the mast to steady herself as she thrust both palms toward the cliff. "Umed, Manan, keep us close. Just a little space between us and the wall. Target the enemy currents between us and the ship, not just the water right around us. There, we have it—steady as she goes!"

The hatch flew open with a bang. Chenzira emerged with the toddler on his back and Teja in tow, white as a sheet.

A low rumble shook the cliff.

Snap. Crunchhh.

The *Lightning Queen* jolted to a stop as large juts of rock shot out like cannons from the cliff face and embedded in her hull. Aviama's breath caught. She locked eyes with Chenzira. They had a quakemaker. And the closer the guard ship got, the more accurate their melders would be.

Water gushed into the hold below, and no shore was close enough to swim to. They were running out of time.

Chenzira glanced up at the guard ship. It had angled toward them during the sloop's collision with the cliff and now made a beeline right for them. He adjusted his grip on the girl, whose eyes were wide, skin flushed, skinny arms wrapped tight around Chenzira's neck. Aviama threw up an air shield between them and the oncoming ship, abandoning the sails as Chenzira lifted his voice to the little band on the dismantling ship.

"With me!"

In a flash, he broke into a sprint, the little girl's knees in the crooks of his elbows as she bounced on his back, his palms out toward the cliff. With a bound he leaped to the railing and launched toward the cliff out into nothing—nothing, until a slab of rock jerked outward just in time to meet his feet. Aviama ran after him, a blast of air knocking against her shield as she went. Slab after slab met their feet as Chenzira pulled out rough steps climbing higher and higher up the cliff.

Aviama's cloth-wrapped feet slapped the cool stone as she left the sloop behind. Fire exploded a handsbreadth from her nose as she ran, shattering into sparks against the rocks. Her breath caught, and she jerked backward away from the shower of embers, knocking her off balance.

Durga slammed into her back, and Aviama rocketed forward again like whiplash, both of them tilting precariously over the cliff. They each threw a hand out, cushioning their fall and blasting themselves upright with a gale of air before they could plummet to the broken ship and rocky surface below.

"Watch it! You almost took me out!"

Aviama ignored her, trying instead to focus on jumping for the next slab, but her pulse pounded in her ears. If she didn't get her head in the game, they might not make it off the cliff.

Kshhhhhh.

Another ball of fire shattered against the rock wall from somewhere behind them. Husani shrieked. Umed's booming voice called out from the rear.

"Commander! Cover us!"

Aviama threw up a barrier on their left between them and the ship. "Windcallers, air shields up! Do not return fire! Do not—"

But they already had. Zahur and Osahar shot flaming balls of fire down at the ship, eager to finally join in on the action. The archers released a volley of arrows and ducked below the railing of their vessel. Sai and Durga threw up shields of their own as the group ran, step after step, up the steep cliff.

Below, the enemy ship grew smaller and smaller. Above, the cliff was running out. Leafy green palm branches peered down at them from the top, wafting lazily in the morning breeze. Chenzira passed the girl to Teja, and Teja took her without a word and climbed the last two steps to the top. Their group dotted the cliff like mountain goats, leaping from place to place.

Chenzira's chest heaved, breathing hard, muscles flexed with the exertion of his work. He reached out and took her elbow. Fatigue tugged at her lead calves, her sagging shoulders. His eyes held the same weariness she felt, but still his gaze swiveled in all directions, first to her, and then to the group and the threats on the water below.

The ship had come upon the sloop, and men pooled by the edge of the ship as if preparing to disembark.

Aviama gripped his arm. "Don't let anyone follow."

"I won't."

Aviama turned and moved up and off the cliff, maintaining the air shield as best she could for the troop still climbing beneath her. Durga and Sai climbed up next, followed one by one by the rest, until only Chenzira remained. As she looked out at him, her heart stilled.

He stood against the light of the morning, sunlight edging his hair with gold. Sweat beaded his brow, and the muscles of his strong chest and arms tightened as his intense gaze fixated on something far below. In a flash, he clenched his fists, and the mountain shook.

The ground beneath her feet trembled as a great crumbling sound ripped up and over the crest of the cliff. Men screamed, and with a mighty crash, their cries were silenced.

Chenzira looked out over the crystal waters of his homeland. Palm fronds beckoned from above. A whisper of soft sea surf murmured against the rocks below. Aviama's heart utterly failed her as she drank in his powerful stance, the cut of his jawline, the strength of his body. Something about his ferocious protection, his commanding presence, in contrast to his deliberate softness with her, captivated her completely, body and soul. Her gaze traveled over his sun-kissed skin, glistening with sea spray and sweat. His lips parted as he turned, breathing hard. Solemn yet resolved.

No regret crossed the hardened expression on his face for the destruction he'd caused below. Chenzira turned on his heel, bounded up the final two steps to the top of the cliff, and strode toward the ragtag band staring at him open-mouthed. The people he'd just saved. Even Florian gaped at him.

He looked through them all—*through* them, as though not really seeing any of them—until his eyes rested on Aviama. Her stomach flopped, and a fluttering sort of warmth exploded in her belly, knocking the wind from her lungs. His gaze was impenetrable and piercing, like a spear through the heart. She felt almost as though every secret she'd ever known was laid bare before the eyes searching her soul, an inescapable pressing in on all sides.

He was beautiful.

She was vulnerable. Exposed.

She couldn't breathe.

Durga shifted her weight and coughed. "Welcome home."

Chenzira cut her a dark glare. "Lucky me."

The sun was rising ever higher in the sky, but as he spoke the words, a shadow seemed to fall on the quakemaker prince. The darkness of it sent goosebumps across Aviama's skin. Chenzira turned on his heel and set off at a brisk pace through the dust, green palm, and lush foliage.

What would Keket do to him? What had Keket already done to him?

And why had Chenzira left home in the first place?

Aviama swallowed hard, gathered the little girl into her arms from Teja, and strode after him. But as they left the royal guard ship behind and kept a pirate in their company, the shadow that had descended over Chenzira seemed to spread over her as well, like dark clouds ahead of a storm. Her mind spun with unanswered questions and images of bodies crushed between rocks and shattered ships. The faces of the dead cycled before her waking eyes, and she replayed the scene at the cove a hundred times over.

The guard ship from the cove had accomplished melders of every element. In Radha, she'd had the upper hand by being a melderblood at all, and with Darsh, she'd gained respect by her power and control. On Jazir, she'd been hailed as a goddess because of that power, and the illusion was fueled in part by her impulsive nature and in part with the help of other melders lending her their aid.

But the mysterious opponents that came against them in the cove were strong, coordinated, and capable melders in their own right. They knew who they were looking for, where Aviama would be, and they weren't afraid of her power. But Aviama's crew had already tipped their hand by showing which of their own company had what ability—and they still didn't know who was after them.

Her heart sank.

Welcome to Keket, indeed.

21

P alm trees and lush greenery waved at the group of newcomers as they passed. What, Aviama wondered, could spoil a day as beautiful as this one? Onkar had sold six of them from the *Wraithweaver* to Abasi on *Raisa's Revenge,* but now their numbers had doubled. Florian and Amon likely didn't count, but they were traveling with them for now, since Florian didn't want the royal guard to catch him, and his ship was lost. Reluctantly including them brought their number to thirteen.

Azure skies and bright sunshine warmed their faces from above as their feet kicked up dust at Chenzira's brisk pace. Husani had taken control of the food rations again and passed out small portions of bread and salted meat. Traveling with children made them both slower and more conspicuous than they already were. Manan had the bag of whatever Amon had stolen that morning, but no one mentioned it.

No one mentioned anything.

Aviama shifted the little girl's weight, stopped to move her to ride on her back, and finally gave up and put her down and let her walk, the little hand secure in Aviama's larger one.

Everyone's pace slowed, but Teja was breathing hard, and Aviama was certain she wasn't the only one grateful for the rest.

Florian took up the rear with Amon, but so did Umed—each wordlessly fighting each other to be in the back until at last they settled for walking side by side. Manan and Husani walked behind Chenzira, the women two by two in the middle, with the giant twins towering over them on either side. Durga edged closer to Zahur and smiled. He grinned. Osahar glared at him.

In the midst of it all, a tiny hand clutched hers. The little girl stumbled over a root, and Aviama pulled her up, instinctively catching her and setting her on her feet again. Large eyes looked up at her, and the grip on her fingers tightened. Something in her chest broke apart.

She sucked in a shuddering breath and let it out. The little girl saw her as trusted. Safe. But with the islanders chasing Florian as a thief, and the royal guard chasing Aviama as a rebel leader, was anyone safe if they were close to her?

Her throat squeezed shut, and her eyes pricked. This is why Aviama was always stuffed in a room somewhere during danger. She was the little girl. Throughout her childhood, throughout the battles over Shamaran Castle before The Return—her whole life, until recently—she'd been the helpless innocent thing everybody else had stowed someplace out of the way for safekeeping.

It made sense. If she trusted anyone enough to watch the little girl, she'd stow her there in an instant. But the few people Aviama trusted were either with her, and therefore too close to Aviama to be a safe place for the toddler, or too far across the sea to be of any use.

The trees dwindled as they made their way down the slope, until they turned onto a natural landing overlooking the harbor and the sea. Boats swarmed a bustling wharf—everything from modest fishermen's sailboats to sloops and ships. Many were flat across the top without railings, its occupants perching directly on top save a cabinlike structure on one end, and paddles lining the sides. Bright-red paint shone at them from the sides of a barge moving past with massive golden columns laid across it.

But nobody paid any attention to the barge. Not today.

Osahar whistled. "That's three times the normal number."

Chenzira peered over the ledge, scanned the scene below, and gestured to Manan. "Everybody get dressed. It's time to blend in."

Manan dug into the bag he'd snagged from Amon and passed out clothes. Osahar, Zahur, and Husani didn't need anything, but Teja's dress looked more Radhan than Keketi, and the ripped trousers and scorched tunic Aviama wore now were a far cry from expected female attire on Siada. Durga and Sai stood out nearly as much, and the men from the *Wraithweaver* weren't much better.

Aviama set the Iolani horn on the ground, tugged at the headwrap over her hair, and held up the wad of white gauzy cloth she'd been handed. "Please tell me there's more to this."

Durga snorted. "You don't want to reveal all your secrets?"

Sai smacked Durga in the arm and tossed Aviama a white sheath dress. "There is. This goes first. And also this." She passed Aviama a simple collar of colored clay designs.

Durga shrugged and tugged the sleeve of her tunic then and there to start undressing. With seven men standing right there. Aviama grimaced, gathered the horn and the clothing items in her arms, and marched several paces away. When she looked back, Chenzira had turned away, busying himself with another look down at the wharf. Zahur was staring at Durga, and Manan snapped his fingers in front of the man's face and shoved him toward Chenzira.

Sai and Teja hurried after Aviama, the little girl toddling along behind. Aviama had no interest in Osahar or Florian or any of them looking at her the way Zahur looked at Durga. Somewhere in the back of her mind, a needling thought prodded at her that she didn't particularly want Chenzira seeing Durga undressing either, but he'd turned his back. It was fine.

Her stomach twisted. She glanced back through the waving palm trees. Florian arched an eyebrow at her from down the slope. *Biscuits. Not far enough.* Aviama recoiled from his ostensive stare and stepped further away from the group with her armful of foreign items, beyond another cluster of trees.

Aviama changed out of her shirt and trousers and into the light sheath dress. The sleeveless dress hugged her body from shoulder to calf. She ran a hand down the smooth fabric. She was used to beautiful dresses of the highest quality, but though her gowns back home might have been fitted through the torso, they often flowed away from her body to the floor, or at least dropped from her waist to her toes in a river of velvet. Even the harem style pants Shiva had gotten for her on the *Wraithweaver* had been loose, as had been the trousers she'd just set aside in a neatly folded stash at the base of the cluster of palm trees she stood behind.

The clay collar with its colored accents lay cool against her chest and collarbone. A simple belt wrapped her waist and dropped down the center of her dress. The gauzy layer was next, a transparent swath of breezy cloth that draped her bare shoulders, left her elbows and forearms uncovered, and fell to her ankles.

Aviama replaced the Iolani horn across her torso and

straightened to survey her companions. Sai wore a similar outfit, but without the gauzy layer, and Teja was handing Aviama a pair of sandals. Aviama untied the cloth bound to the soles of her feet and ripped them off. They were a bit loose, but workable. The little girl smiled and reached for her. Aviama bent down and the girl poked at the painted colors of the collar.

Florian's voice cut through the trees. "We don't have all day. In case you've forgotten, we're being chased both by land and by sea."

Aviama cleared her throat and stood, taking the little girl's hand in hers. "Right. We're ready. Sorry."

She strode back through the palm trees, the breeze in her hair, followed by the scent of salt and sea and green things bursting with life. The toddler's hand squeezed hers, and she squeezed back. The soles of her shoes padded along the dirt and dust, and the closeness of the fabric to her body from shoulder to ankle made her squirm a little—but she also felt like a woman.

Her arms were bare, but she wore real shoes, and though she was certain she'd miss having pockets, part of her loved being in a dress again. Even if it felt a little bit scandalous.

She took the last steps past the trees obscuring her view from the rest of the company. All heads swiveled toward her as she approached.

Husani whistled. Umed socked him in the stomach. Florian arched an eyebrow, then jerked himself upright and composed himself.

A smile the size of the kingdom broke across Chenzira's face as his gaze swept over her.

"Sand and sea," he breathed.

Aviama's stomach flopped, and butterflies exploded in her chest with a side of whatever sort of warm, gooey dessert might fill the body with heat from head to toe. She'd nearly lost her own breath at the sight of him. He wore the traditional white schenti of his people, a decorative belt wrapping his waist and dropping down the middle, ending just above the knee. Not a stitch graced his upper half, exposed in all his defined-muscle, cut-chest glory. She shifted her weight and adjusted the decorative collar along her collarbone.

She should look away. She should probably look anywhere but at him. But the instant she did, she found herself drawn back to his face, his shoulders, his chest.

Chenzira drew himself up to his full height, took four long strides to meet her, and offered her his arm, as if they were headed into a ballroom rather than down a dusty mountain with a ragtag group of pirates and rebels.

She knew she was blushing. But she couldn't stop the heat in her cheeks any more than she could stop the beaming smile from creeping over her face at Chenzira's attention.

Manan coughed. "Where to, Commander?"

Aviama looked at Chenzira. "Where to?"

Chenzira stared down at her. "Aviama and I have an errand to run." He shook himself, reluctant to look at anyone else, and addressed the group. "We'll get off this rock and closer to town, and then split up until tonight. With the heat on Florian and the guard looking for Aviama, it's best not to have them both in one place. And speaking of distinctive people, maybe you should lose the hat."

Florian gasped. "I would *never* lose my hat."

Umed crossed his arms. "You're wearing a dark jacket, a black hat, and a red feather. You're worse than a blazing beacon in the middle of the night."

"As enjoyable as our little tryst has been, I am a busy man, and our business is done, so I'll be parting ways with you now. I know you'll miss me, but who else can keep the guard in as good a shape as I do?" He winked at Aviama. "Because they never catch me."

Durga groaned. Aviama pursed her lips but said nothing.

Florian offered her a dramatic bow, gestured to Amon, and adjusted his black hat. "Until we meet again, Your Royal Highness."

Her gut pinched at the use of her title, but his cavalier manner reminded her of Onkar, and she was almost sorry to see him go. Further evidence of her naivety, perhaps. Onkar was a cheat through and through, lining his pockets with gold before attending to the needs of anyone else—if indeed he knew how to care for others at all in the long run. His stupid note and stupid wooden carving left much to be desired as a parting gift when he sold her and her friends into slavery just outside Ghosts' Gorge.

One hand in the crook of Chenzira's arm, the other holding the little girl's hand, Aviama watched as Florian sauntered off in the direction they'd come, Amon skipping along by his side. Onkar was gone, and so now was Florian, whatever his real name may have been.

Maybe the pursuers would catch him after all, or at least see him, and he'd give them a good chase. Wear them out, draw them away. That would be helpful. But unless Chenzira had a lot more cash, it wasn't likely Florian was motivated by anything other than his own interests. Just like Onkar. Or, more accurately, Grigglor.

The little girl grinned up at Chenzira, and he stuck his tongue out at her. She laughed and hid her face against Aviama's leg, before emerging to examine the Iolani horn resting on Aviama's hip. In the space of a minute, Florian and Amon's absence brought their number from thirteen to eleven. But one of them was a child traveling the speed of a tortoise, and the size of the group was still far too noticeable.

As if reading her thoughts, Chenzira ducked behind Aviama and scooped up the girl, plopping her on his shoulders. She squealed and patted him on the head, and he winked at her. Aviama laughed. He was good with kids. She'd never seen that before. In that moment, he was light, carefree. Totally focused on the game.

Walking together, with the distraction of something innocent and beautiful in the midst of their hardships, was like roses growing among thorns. Threats were present, but velvet petals blossomed all the same. Sometimes, there was even time to stop and drink in their magical aroma.

He whirled halfway backward and forward again until the toddler rocked back and forth on his glistening bare shoulders. She giggled, seizing his hair in fistfuls to stay upright. The light in his eyes and the levity in his face were the sort that erased the wrinkles of age or the darkness of sorrow. Aviama leaned against his arm and sent a whisper of wind through his hair, just glad to be a part of it all.

A devilish grin fell across his features as he turned from the toddler to the woman beside him. The ground beneath her feet rolled, and Aviama yelped as she tripped her way over the moving land.

Chenzira caught her by the arm and tucked her hand firmly back into his elbow. "You're awfully clumsy today. Let me help."

Aviama's jaw dropped. "Rude!"

He shrugged. "It's not my fault you don't know how to walk."

"But it *is* your fault I tripped."

He pursed his lips, a twinkle in his eye. "All I saw was someone walking alone and then being saved by a handsome man."

"Is that what you saw?"

"Mhmm. Yep. And before you think about retaliation, you should remember I'm carrying a kid."

Ha! She arched an eyebrow. "Retaliation for what?"

"Oh, just whatever you're blaming me for. Needlessly, no doubt."

She started to yank her hand free, but he squeezed his arm tight against his body, trapping her to him. She froze. A shiver of fear pricked at the back of her mind.

Shiva had demanded she be near him. Shiva had required she show her affection. How many times had Aviama had her hand on his arm, only to be paraded about on his terms?

But Chenzira's arm loosened, and she kept her hand where it was. When she dared to glance at him, he was studying her. Cinnamon pools of tender watchfulness.

Aviama let out a breath. No, he wasn't Shiva. He was nothing like Shiva. He was teasing her and would let her go the moment he knew she was uncomfortable. She bit her lip and stared down at her toes.

Chenzira shifted beside her, and she chanced a look at his face as they walked. He glanced at her but said nothing. She dropped her gaze to her hand on his arm.

Aviama's knuckles were white against his bronze skin. A jolt of realization lurched her heart to her throat. She'd been clutching at him like a cornered cat, hackles raised, nails biting into whatever was in reach.

Biscuits.

Slowly, she released her grip. Blood flooded into her aching, tingling fingers. Aviama grimaced. She glanced over her shoulder. Directly behind them, Sai walked with Manan. Beyond them, Durga was trying to strike up conversation with Osahar, who wasn't having it. Zahur watched her progress, amused, while Teja and Husani took up the rear with Umed. None seemed to have seen Aviama's moment of panic, but any of them could have been playing it cool for her sake. Except maybe Durga, whom Aviama was certain would have snatched up any opportunity to poke at her.

Aviama cleared her throat and focused her gaze on the palms before them, the slope of the ground, and the glimpses of ocean on their left as they worked their way downward.

"Sorry."

He sidestepped into her, offering a gentle nudge with his arm. "If you think a scratch or two is going to scare me off, you don't know me very well."

She swallowed and dropped her voice as low as she could manage. "There are worse things about me that could scare you off."

"Like how terrifyingly bad you are at directions?"

"That's not funny."

"It's a little bit funny."

Aviama scowled. The air around them shifted, and she hated the tightness in her chest, the seriousness that fell over them. It was her fault. She'd stopped the fun they were having. Maybe that's who she was. The wet blanket that squashed happiness for people.

Chenzira hopped off a rock, bouncing the little girl on his shoulders, and reached up to hold the girl's ankle to keep her secure. He glanced behind them at the troop following their footsteps, and when he spoke again, she had to strain to hear him.

"It is true that I'd like you to stop trying to die, if that's what you're referring to. And that you need to figure out what that's about. But *you*—your character. Your love for people. Your dedication to the good things in this world, and how you fight for that hope you have—it's admirable."

Her stomach twisted. "Naïve, you mean."

He shook his head. "No. I mean admirable. Yes, you were

naïve when you first came to Radha. But I also think I'm too cynical sometimes. You've shown me that. Sometimes, the best solution is in the middle. Sometimes, hope exists. Sometimes, people can be redeemed."

"Maybe not. Shiva never redeemed himself."

"But you believe people *can* be redeemed."

"Maybe I was wrong."

Chenzira took a breath. "Aviama. You welcomed Durga along with us with open arms. You hold me back when I want to jump to the most severe punishment. You connected with Makana in a way no one else could. You could have been angry at the world and stayed in your room on the *Wraith-weaver,* but instead you created a network of people who love you and fight for you and follow you. And when you couldn't get me out of the dark, when I was in the brig, you sat with me in it."

Aviama eyed him, but he looked away. He ran a hand along his nose, as if he had an itch, and sniffed. The one eye she could see glistened. Chenzira cleared his throat.

"You keep me from the dark spiral. You anchor me to the sun."

Breath left her body at the emotion in his voice. This wasn't the butter-soft tenor of a well-rehearsed psychopath. The rough edge to his words sounded like shattered ceramic patched with gold, the kind that made a thing more beautiful for having once been broken.

But he was *her* anchor, not the other way around. She relied on him, perhaps more than she would have liked to admit. Could it be that he relied on her just as much? If he did, what would it do to him when she failed?

A fist-sized lump surged to her throat. Tears stung at her eyes; tears she batted back with a vengeance until they receded back into the abyss.

A muscle in Chenzira's neck bulged as he clenched his jaw. She felt the intensity of his gaze, like the searing sun on a tender burn. He sidestepped from her so that her hand fell away, and her heart ached at the rejection, until his large hand slipped around hers and his fingers intertwined with an urgency that said it might never let go.

"Maybe you've decided you don't deserve light. But you're made of it. You emanate light wherever you go. Maybe it's time you kept some for yourself."

22

Aviama had never heard words that made her heart race and slow down all at once. Chenzira's assessment of her situation was both remarkably accurate and painfully impossible. It complimented and destroyed her at the same time, because though, somehow, he believed she could choose to hold onto the light—a light she supposedly had—Aviama had no idea how to do that or if she really had any at all.

She'd had light once, sure. But it had dimmed almost four years ago now, when her windstorm killed the servant boy by the smithy. And in the months between when she met the soul-sucking Radhan prince and fed him to the Iolani, whatever light that remained had flickered and gone out.

Levity came now in spurts of vacation from reality rather than a settled thing she could trust to stay. Yet, with her hand in Chenzira's, and the little girl reaching down from his shoulders to tug at the scarf wound around her wavy blonde tresses, she thought maybe the two people beside her were the ones made of light.

Perhaps in Aviama's hands, light was a ray filtered through

a thick net of branches overhead, visible only in spots swiftly changing with the clouds, the wind, the rain. But Chenzira and the little girl were lanterns, lighting her way even when the sun sank into a melancholy horizon and the nights grew cold.

They walked in silence from then on, except for the little girl's occasional giggle when Chenzira poked her or bounced her on his shoulders. She'd said hardly anything the entire time Aviama had known her, though her age would suggest she should know more words. But though Aviama had only rarely heard her whimper or cry, she'd not heard her laugh at all until today. The sound was like rainbows on a prism, brighter and longer with every giggle, each just as mesmerizing as the last.

The cool of the morning gave way to a harsh and unforgiving sun, and Aviama found herself grateful to be in thinner layers than she was used to. As scandalous as it felt, it was practical, and by the time they reached the fringes of the palm-tree forest on the outskirts of the city, her new clothing was all but forgotten, except for the edges of her head wrap, which she arranged to cover the tops of her shoulders to keep them from being scorched by noon.

Chenzira split the group into two: Sai, Teja, the little girl, Umed, and Zahur in the first, and Manan, Durga, Osahar, and Husani in the second. They'd be less recognizable in smaller numbers, and Chenzira gave painstaking directions for each group to wind through the city to specific people that may or may not still be living in the specific places he outlined for them. Reluctantly, Aviama removed the Iolani horn at her hip and hid it in Manan's satchel, as Chenzira and Aviama were more likely to be recognized and stopped than the others and would be taking greater risks.

Durga hadn't liked the idea. "Shouldn't we be the ones taking on the risks if you're so recognizable?"

She wasn't the only one. Umed had called her "Commander," but shook his head with a pursed lip. "It isn't safe. It isn't smart."

"The risk is necessary," Chenzira had said. "I'm the only one who knows the person we are going to find."

"Then leave Aviama with us and take Umed," Sai had returned. "The baby likes her, and she'll be safer here with us if you're going someplace dangerous. If we lose you both, we'll be in trouble."

They'd both answered at once:

"I'm going."

"She's not leaving my sight."

Manan wanted to know what would happen if they didn't return. Husani asked how finding one person would bring them closer to overthrowing the monarchy. "No offense to present company, but is it a *real* commander? A retired general? Oh! A master melder?"

Chenzira hedged, promising only that the person they were going to find was a crucial first step to any dealings with the royal family, and that the person could provide the sort of inside information they would need. The nonanswer caused Husani to trade the spark in his eyes for a disappointed frown, and Durga went so far as to cross her arms and tap her foot.

Osahar and Zahur exchanged looks every few seconds throughout the exchange. And Chenzira's plan—or apparent lack thereof—wasn't the only issue to be had. No one was lost to the fact that Chenzira's groupings separated the twins. Durga had tried to push to be in Sai and Teja's group, but Chenzira had flat out refused, and Aviama backed him, not because she knew why he'd done it, but because she assumed he had a good reason, and all the heads in their little band had swiveled toward her for the final say.

Still, an hour later, they had all eaten a ration of the provisions from the satchel, Manan's group had headed for the more dangerous route closer to the wharf, and Umed's group had set out through the city, navigated by Zahur. Aviama had given the little girl a hug and a kiss, clutching her close and trying to remember the feel of the small arms hugging her back. Strange to think how little time had passed for Aviama to feel so attached, so obliged to return for her. Her stomach was in knots at leaving. The girl went willingly to Teja, but her large eyes followed Aviama every step until she'd been carried out of sight.

Did she understand the common tongue? Did she know that Aviama had promised to come back for her? Was it better if she did understand, or if she didn't?

What if—

Strong arms wrapped around her, crushing her against Chenzira's solid chest in a great bear hug. Aviama snaked her arms around him and held him tight, suddenly desperate for his closeness. The lump in her throat was back, and her heart had dropped like a stone.

He squeezed harder, and she squeezed back, holding on for dear life until the moments passed like rain and the tension of uncertainty and chaos melted away in a single exhaled breath they shared together. Her body relaxed into his like a sigh, and his arms dropped to her waist as his shoulders caved in around her.

But before she could ask him what it meant, if it were relief or sadness, his hand trailed up her spine to capture the nape of her neck. Aviama's breath caught, and when his knuckles brushed her chin and turned her face up to meet his gold-flecked cinnamon eyes, she forgot how to breathe entirely.

A soft gasp escaped her lips, but her arms pulled him tighter. She let her lips linger ajar, an open door, a ruby-red invitation, and tilted her head up further as her eyes searched his. The whisper of a wind bearing secrets and lullabies played in the palm fronds overhead as Chenzira pressed his mouth to hers.

Delicate as lace, sweet as honey, his kiss was like rubies falling on soft velvet. Aviama pressed into him. Her fingers wound up into his hair, tugging him lower as she reached up on her toes. An electric shiver took him over at her touch, and he pulled her in with new fervor, one arm winding low and tight around her hips, the other roving across her back, as if the heat of a thousand suns burned beneath.

She could see it now, as their lips moved in an intricate dance bursting with life and love, and colors not yet invented danced behind her eyelids; he was the anchor to her tossing ship, and she, the lighthouse to his dead of night. Aviama deepened the kiss, and Chenzira followed her lead with an ardor as though he'd saved it just for this moment.

A twig snapped. Aviama's racing heart faltered, and the two of them broke apart. Pirates, islanders, and royal guard all had their eyes peeled for the troublemaking Raisa impersonator. They'd pressed their luck too far. Someone had found them.

Aviama spun this way and that. Whoever they were, they were well hidden. She'd need a shield around—

Feathers fluttered overhead, and she flinched. Chenzira's hand jerked her closer at the sound, and she grinned. "Who's jumpy now?"

He pressed his mouth into a flat line to suppress a smile. "It could have been a lot worse than a bird." The mirth left his face, and he scanned the trees again. "We've got to go."

She nodded, still breathless from their kiss. He took her

hand and set a brisk pace along the tree line. When she stole a glance over at him, his chest rose and fell with the thunder of a rising storm—and when his gaze met hers, the gold flecks in his warm brown eyes were ablaze with the sparks of an unquenchable fire.

He forged ahead, tugging her along behind him, then turned to look at her again. "What?"

Aviama grinned. "You're breathing hard. Do you need to slow down? Maybe I can take your pulse?"

Mischief lit Chenzira's face. "I think you know it wasn't our pace that took my breath away."

Aviama skipped along beside him, swinging their hands between them, and flashed a smile. "It was me."

"Yes." He twisted her hand up to his mouth and pressed his lips to the back of her hand. "You're my favorite reason for my heart to race. But I think if we stopped now, I would just go on kissing you until the world ends. We would never save my sister, you would never get home, and we would almost certainly be found and arrested."

She scrunched her nose. "That does sound unfortunate."

"It does."

The cover of the palm trees waved goodbye, and Chenzira dropped her hand to place his hand at the small of her back instead as they left the greenery behind for the dusty streets of the seaside town. Aviama adjusted the wrap over her hair and tried to imagine she'd lived there all her life. She wouldn't gawk at the lithe bodies under thin white sheaths, or the bare bronze arms sporting bands of shining brass or gold. She'd walk with purpose, not pausing to take in the long-legged, short-haired cats that leaped from the tops of adobe buildings to play with children in the street. She'd be too busy with her own life to trouble about the man at the market stall handing strands of glittering jewels out toward her, or the woman who gave him a hearty and too-familiar shrug as she asked Chenzira if the lady might need a hair piece.

To Aviama's surprise, Chenzira paused at the woman's booth, dug out two coins from inside the waistband of his newly donned schenti, and snatched a black-haired wig from her long spindly fingers. The wig vendor flashed a smile at the coins, and when her gaze swept over Chenzira's splendid half-naked form, Aviama swore the woman stuck out her already-prominent chest and batted long lashes lined with heavy black kohl.

The vendor held up a thick beaten-brass armband with the frightening image of a half-crocodile, half-human creature depicted on it, dangling it from one finger.

"A prince of a man to care for his woman. Come now, that's all you'll get your lady? She looks like she could use a few luxuries." She leaned across the table, offering a good look at more than just the bauble. "And you look like you have some to spare."

Aviama blanched, and she imagined her skin lost any meager color it had ever possessed. Chenzira's lip flinched upward in an infinitesimal note of disgust before washing away into boredom. He ignored the vendor's offering, both of herself and of the brass, and reached instead for a golden cobra snaking around into two coils, tail draped downward, head raised, hood flared out from a diamond-shaped head.

"This one."

The woman's lips twisted into a smile. "You have excellent taste." Her glance flickered to Aviama, and the smile soured. She returned her focus to the glorious male specimen before her, drinking him in like water as if he were an exhibit and she the sole proprietor of the display.

Aviama coughed. Why was he entertaining her at all? Why

weren't they walking? Weren't they supposed to be avoiding attention, instead of drawing it the second they arrived?

Chenzira dug out several more thick, heavy coins and dropped them into the woman's waiting hand. The vendor passed the cobra to Chenzira, and he promptly turned his back on the woman and strode away, wrapping his arm around Aviama's hips. Aviama fought the urge to look back at the vendor. She was pretty sure she was getting a death glare, but she didn't care. Chenzira hadn't given two figs for the woman's forwardness.

Chenzira lingered by two more stalls on his way through the bazaar, purchasing a steaming skewer of lamb chunks for the two of them to share, and then crossing the aisle to wave a white shawl in her face. Aviama shook her head, but she couldn't help her smile.

Still—shouldn't they be going?

Aviama glanced behind them. The wig and jewelry vendor was out of sight, and the crowd started to thin as the first of the merchants packed up their wares for the morning. The sun beat down in scorching rays of fire, lighting the adobe houses and white schentis and dresses, tanning bare skin accustomed to the harshness, and promising to stifle anyone who remained on the streets in the roasting midday hours.

Chenzira appeared at her shoulder on her opposite side and brought her hand to his lips, intense dark eyes never leaving hers. A bead of sweat dripped down her spine, but it still couldn't chase away the involuntary shiver that took her over at his touch. She glanced sideways. Biscuits, there were people everywhere! What was he thinking?

Something cool and round slipped over her finger, and Aviama turned to find a lapis-lazuli ring staring up at her from the index finger of her right hand. Chenzira grinned, glanced over his shoulder, and steered her through the scattering marketplace as she blinked down at the accessory. The stone boasted deep, rich hues of royal blue kissed by midnight swirls and a wisp of storm-cloud gray set in simple silver.

Aviama glanced up at him. "Where did you get money for this?"

He shrugged. "I figured Florian owed us for dropping us off on the wrong island. Plus, he's a reaver, so it probably wasn't even his to begin with."

Aviama's brow furrowed. "Reaver?"

"Pirate."

"Oh."

Chenzira tossed another glance behind them, and this time Aviama followed his gaze. Two men armed with a khopesh, wearing armored calf and forearm guards and the wide distinctive collar of the royal guard, scanned the bazaar. Chenzira whipped back around, moving slowly, almost dawdling, at the last table before suddenly pulling off the main street into a narrow back alley and ducking between lines of clothing hung to dry.

Aviama dipped behind the cloth barrier. Her heart pounded the beat of an ancient drum, and she craned her neck around the cloth in spite of herself. "Did they see us?"

"They will if you keep peeking out. Stop that." Chenzira tugged her back behind the drying clothes and yanked a long frayed thread from the hem of a stranger's clean shirt. "Here. Braid your hair as tight as you can and tie it off. You should wear the wig on the way out. And give me the headscarf. We need to look different walking out than when we walked in."

She unwrapped her hair and got to work braiding as quickly and tightly as she could, while Chenzira lifted the headscarf over his own head and broad shoulders. He hovered protectively, blocking any view of her through the laundry with his own large frame, sandwiching her body between himself and the wall of the nearest building.

The first time she'd seen him shirtless was the moment they'd met—or not *met,* exactly, but when she saw him, and he saw her. He'd been devilishly handsome then, if not terrifying. The look of him had sent a jolt to her core then and had much the same effect on her now. Except now he wasn't an unknown danger.

Make no mistake, Chenzira was dangerous. She'd known it then, from the ice in his eyes to his bulging muscles. She'd known it when he slammed her up against the wall in the Radhan king's private study when her espionage had interfered with his. And she'd known it in the cages of the menagerie, when he'd told her a fight to the death between them would end in her body on the ground.

She hadn't even known he was melderblood back then. Having seen him in action now, Chenzira was ten times more deadly than she'd imagined. Aviama shuddered to think how many sailors he'd killed just that morning with whatever avalanche he'd sent down from the cliff on the pursuing guards. But the ice in his eyes melted when he looked at her, and the fight in his body was *for* her, not against her. When he said he would find her, she believed him. And when he claimed to defy death, she knew he would, because he had.

Chenzira's perfect bare skin glowed with the luster of unreached treasure as a sweat bead made its way slowly down his body. Maybe it was the heat of the day, or the spices of the vendors in the corner of the market, but he smelled of allure and entanglement and stolen kisses in dark galleon ships. He turned, and the warrior edge to him softened as he caught her staring.

Aviama sucked in a breath. Heat flooded her cheeks, but the smile he gave her was dazzling. He looked like the sort of dream she might stay asleep forever just for the chance of seeing again.

He tapped her fingers, and she jumped. She'd been fiddling with the end of her braid. How long ago had she finished it?

Chenzira leaned in close, and his breath tickled her ear. "I'd love to let you keep on looking, but we really do have to go."

Her lips parted at his forwardness, and she almost snapped back with a retort, but the denial died on her tongue. Aviama bit her lip, grimaced, and wrapped her braid into a tight bun at the nape of her neck. She pursed her lips. "Get me another string."

He pulled one free from the fraying shirt on the line, and she tied her hair in place, took the wig from his hands, and set the black wig over her golden waves.

"How do I look?"

Chenzira slipped the cobra armband up over her elbow to her upper arm, stepped back, and looked her up and down. A rogue expression flitted across his face. "You look like someone I'd love to have stare at me, if only so you're close enough that I can stare back."

Her stomach did a somersault. She knew they were being chased but couldn't resist pressing into the feeling. "You like it?"

He stepped closer, so abruptly close that she stepped backward into the wall. Chenzira planted one hand on the wall by her head, and she was pretty sure she stopped breathing. "I do."

She tilted her face up, but he jerked himself upright as if woken from a reverie and cleared his throat.

"I can't be seen kissing a girl with black hair. I'm partial to blondes lately, and I know one that gives nasty side-eyes to anyone who flirts with me. I can only imagine what she'd do if she saw me kissing you."

Aviama rolled her eyes, but she didn't miss his quick glance toward the market before he guided her through the laundry and down the side street in the opposite direction.

"The wig girl looked like she wanted you for breakfast."

"Yes, well, she also slipped the word *prince* into conversation, which I found substantially more concerning."

Biscuits. Aviama had barely noticed. And when she had, she'd dismissed the thought as paranoia.

She twisted the ring on her finger, almost surprised to find a real ring there waiting. He nodded at the stone.

"Do you like it?"

"It's unnecessary, but beautiful. I love it." And she did. Not only because of its mesmerizing colors and the blue that reminded her of her mother's sapphire, if only vaguely. But it had come from him. And the way he'd slid it onto her finger had made her feel like a child with a sweet and a woman in a ballroom all at the same time.

He worried his lip and dipped his head. "You'd tear your fingers up if you didn't have something on your hands. I know you miss it. Maybe one day, I'll get you a nicer one."

23

Tall buildings toward the center of town displayed paintings of battle victories and heroes fighting against ancient beasts. Beautiful people in white moved like stars under the sun, a strange contradiction as they went about in a bustle of errands run late, acquaintances to greet on the street, and children to usher in for unfinished chores. Aviama twisted the new ring on her finger, wondering what he meant by getting her a nicer one.

When was one day, exactly? Did he really plan to propose, or was he caught up in the moment? Or maybe he'd given her what he considered to be cheap market jewelry and felt bad about the quality, and he planned to upgrade her to something else without any other promises attached.

If he was worried she didn't like it, his concern was needless. She caught herself staring down at it every few seconds, turning it in the light, examining its swirling storm-gray and ebony-black ribbons against the rich royal blue. It felt good to wear something beautiful again. And to have something to turn on her finger.

They weaved through the city, left and right through alleys

and squares, passing kittens and children and bare-backed men steering ox carts of burdens. An hour passed before Aviama realized if anything happened to Chenzira, she'd be utterly hopeless at making her way back—or to whatever rendezvous point he'd explained to the others while her eyes glazed over at the litany of instructions her brain refused to turn into anything usable.

Chenzira stopped at the back door of a line of shops near the city center and rapped twice, twice again, and then once, in quick succession. The door jerked open so hard it reverberated in the hand of the old man who held it. Wizened, leathery skin stretched across a tiny face into a beaming smile so wide that his pure-white teeth overshadowed his enormous gray beard. The man glanced down the alley in both directions and ushered them inside.

Gold dripped from floor to ceiling along midnight backdrops almost completely obscured by trinkets and baubles. Rows of necklaces, bracelets, earrings, and headpieces made of gems and precious metals lined the shop. A long-nosed woman with sharp eyes sat on a stool near the door, reminding Aviama of a Keketi version of Durga, but if she noticed the shop's guests, she didn't show it.

The old man swung the door shut behind them and shooed them to a corner of the shop glittering with sashes, belts, collars, and armbands. He clapped Chenzira on the back, nearly rising on his toes to do so from his shrunken stature. Colorful tapestries lined the few bits of wall space not filled with wares and partitioned off a section in one corner. Chenzira smiled, leaned down to clasp the man by the arm, and leaned in close to whisper something in Keketi.

The shopkeeper eyed Aviama, then nodded and waved a head toward the corner. Aviama started to follow, but Chenzira put a hand on her arm. "He knows who I am and can't be seen talking with me. But he's also very selective with who he allows in his inner sanctum. I'll be right back."

Aviama's stomach knotted. What if guards came in while he was gone? What if the woman by the entrance noticed her, knew she wasn't Keketi, and passed the information on to the guards? How many foreigners came to Keket?

She swallowed and dipped her head, eyeing Chenzira and the older man as they disappeared into the sectioned off room. She then busied herself with a detailed study of random items on the wall. Anything for an excuse to keep her face turned away from the entrance.

Birds, bugs, moon, stars—if it creeped or flew or shone in Keket, it was emblazoned on some belt or ring or bracelet or other. The craftsmanship was exquisite: carved gemstones smooth as sea glass and purest gold to make the sun jealous. Intricate statues stood on the floor or hung from the ceiling. A jade eagle coursed overhead, chasing a school of carnelian fish suspended in the air above an ornamented weapons display. Gilded khopesh swords and ivory-handled knives flanked ruby-studded double axes. Between the figurines, the jewelry, and the armory, Aviama wasn't sure there was any object the shop did not customize, enhance, and bedazzle.

When Chenzira finally reemerged, the worry lines of his brow had deepened, and his mouth tugged down into a frown.

"Let's go. Our next stop isn't far from here."

Aviama followed him out the back door and down the alley again, and soon they were weaving once more through street after sunbeaten street.

Her stomach turned as she glanced up at his face. "What happened?"

"My sister recently tried to find our mother. She went to the midwife, who lives here on Siada. Bassel, the jeweler back there, has been a trustworthy informant for me for many years. But if Bassel knows she's back on Siada, he's not the only one."

"That's good news, though. We have a lead. We can find her."

He winced. "Our mother was always a weakness for my father. His marriage to Heba, the queen, has been up and down over the years, but ever since Rana left, it's only gotten stronger. And by left, I mean when my brother tried to kill her, and my father agreed to help me hide her."

Aviama worried her lip as they turned a corner and ducked under a line of laundry. Chenzira doubled his pace, and she hurried to catch up. "But she was safe, wasn't she? Just sequestered away, in hiding? Why would she come out?"

"Our mother died when Rana was a baby. I never met her. My brother, Sutekh, was born first, and Heba and my father were already married. My mother was always the scandal everyone worked hard to erase. But she had made him swear that he would raise us in the palace and give us all the benefits appropriate to children of the king, and he agreed. Heba resented him for it. Sutekh picked up on her sentiments and kept them, even when Heba softened."

Chenzira sucked in a long breath and took her hand as they walked. "Rana's always been obsessed with the idea that our mother was alive. That we had someone who loved us who might take us in if we ran away. She's a runner. That's what she does. But she just couldn't handle the fact that our mother really was dead, and wasn't coming back, and we were alone."

Aviama's chest wrenched. She had grieved two parents and would continue to grieve them until her dying days. Sometimes, she almost wished the memories wouldn't hit so hard, but the moment she thought it, she hated herself for the thought, because memories were all she had—and they deserved to be cherished. She couldn't imagine the hole without the memories to grasp on to.

She sent a whisper of wind against his cheek, flowing through his hair, and squeezed his hand. The ground beneath her feet trembled as he squeezed back. Warmth at their bond mixed with sorrow as her heart ached for him. But a needling thought would not leave her mind.

"If Rana has been in hiding all this time, why would she come out now?"

Chenzira wiped a bead of sweat from his brow, and she swore his bronze skin lightened a shade. "Rana must have been keeping tabs on the midwife too, just as I had been before I left Keket. But while I did it to make sure she was protected from my father and brother, and to keep alive some small illusion of connection I had with my mother, Rana did it in hopes that the midwife would one day make a move. That something that would change, and she would seek out our mother, and Rana could follow."

Aviama kept her left hand in his but reached across now to touch his arm with her right. "And?"

Chenzira swallowed hard as he stopped by the gate of a simple two-story adobe dwelling. "Yesterday, the midwife made a move."

A heavy iron lock hung from the gate. He swept his hand toward it. "Would you do the honors? Quickly, before we're seen."

Aviama stepped forward, summoned the wind, and sent intricate fingers of air through the inner workings of the lock until it released with a soft *click*. Chenzira opened the gate, held the door open for her, and closed it behind them the moment they were both inside.

About ten meters separated the front gate from the door to the house. A small garden grew on the left of the home, and a small wood-fired mud oven sat across from it. A wisp of smoke curled up from the oven. Someone was home.

Chenzira strode across the courtyard and through the front door, releasing her hand to open it. His hand went to the hilt of his khopesh as the door swung inward, and he stepped inside. Aviama followed. A large slab of stone connected to the wall on one side—about the height for sitting down on—and was set with ceramic vases. Two companion stools lined the wall to one side. A single pillar with red markings rose up through the center of the room, mirrored only by artist renderings along the border of the upper wall, by the ceiling, that were painted in the same faded crimson hue. Facing the room, one door led to one side of the house in the back right corner, and another to the opposite side in the back left corner.

Light footsteps padded in from the right side of the house, and a middle-aged woman appeared. Gentle wrinkles spread from the corners of eyes that had worn many smiles, the warm ocher of her eyes the softest Aviama had ever seen. Strong, calloused hands gripped a clay jar as the woman glided in like a great cat, lithe and almost totally silent. A quiet determination set the lines of her face—until she saw Chenzira and Aviama.

The woman froze, and the jar slipped from her fingers. Chenzira dove to catch it before it hit the ground, and Aviama threw out a cushion of wind that stopped the jar's descent midair and held it aloft for Chenzira.

"You're her." The woman gaped at Aviama as Chenzira straightened with the jar in his hands. She glanced at Chenzira. "You shouldn't be here."

"It's all right. We had to check on you—word on the street is you're moving, and if we know it, we aren't the only ones."

Chenzira shook the jar. The metal of coins clinked inside. "Your leaving is more than a rumor, I guess."

The woman snatched the jar back, glancing between Aviama and Chenzira. Her gaze landed on Chenzira, her fingers tapping against the side of the jar. "You shouldn't be here," she repeated. "Guards are looking for someone in the streets, and I'll bet the contents of this jar that the someone is *her*. Now that she's here, I've got to get out even faster."

She turned her back and padded back through the doorway into an adjoining room. Chenzira followed, and Aviama trailed him into a bedroom. A myriad of items, from clothes to lotions to papyrus, were laid out on a sleeping couch. A hair comb carved with painted white lilies sat next to a short, stout container of face powders decorated with carvings of delicate women in Keketi sheath dresses and deep-kohl eye paint. A bag yawned open next to the items on the sleeping couch, ready for packing.

"Nailah."

The midwife busied herself pouring coins from the jar into a smaller pouch, not bothering to look up as they entered the room behind her.

Chenzira put a hand on her shoulder. "I need to find Rana."

Nailah stilled. "Maybe she doesn't want to be found."

"I can't leave things the way they were left." Chenzira let out a breath. "She's always been a runner, but never from me. And trying to find Mother will not end well."

Nailah shifted her weight. Her gaze darted around the room, as though seeking escape. She picked up a stack of three folded clothing items and stuffed them into the bottom of her bag. The woman clenched her jaw, but her eyes misted at the word *mother*.

But something didn't feel right. Nailah's fingers shook, and she pressed her lips together, as if willing herself to hold in the confidence of a friend.

"Biscuits." Aviama's stomach turned to knots. "She's alive, isn't she?"

Chenzira screwed his face up in response. "That's ridiculous."

Nailah stuffed the powders into her bag, abandoning a larger bottle with a blue bird on it in favor of a small one with a caracal, its long ears up, its long teeth exposed in a smile. Next, she fastened a necklace over the one she already wore, but her hands trembled.

"That's why you're running. For her. For their mother. Something's happened. And when it did, Rana came to see you."

Nailah shook her head, but her shoulders sagged.

Chenzira glanced between them and turned to Nailah. "When did Rana come?"

The midwife swallowed hard and stared at the floor. "If I tell you, you'll go after her. But you've made an enemy of every kingdom strong enough to rely on. You're dangerous."

"Yes, I am dangerous. You forget yourself."

Aviama sucked in a breath and winced. She placed a firm hand on his arm. *No.* But the damage was done. Nailah's eyes flashed as she jerked her head up to look Chenzira in the face.

"You're the one who left. You're the one who cemented your brother's control over your father, over the crown. Weeds have choked out the power you used to hold, dearie. What? You thought in the four years you were absent that Sutekh would let the people mourn you as a martyr? You've got no ground to stand on." Nailah swept a hand in Aviama's direction. "You think your new girlfriend will help you? You think a few melder tricks and a rebellion will do anything but get her killed? She ruined Jannemar's tenuous peace with Radha, and you removed yourself from the running to impact Keket. You've abandoned your nation and thrown Keket into Radha's waiting arms. Mark my words, your presence here will only solidify a deadly and devastating alliance."

Aviama staggered back. For a commoner, Nailah was far too comfortable snapping back at her prince—even a disowned one. But what assaulted her mind the most was Nailah's summary. It was remarkably accurate.

Chenzira's eyes blazed. "You think I wanted to leave? You think I didn't run through a thousand alternatives first, before each one went up in smoke?"

Nailah clenched her jaw and stuffed another handful of items into her bag. "Making yourself a victim doesn't change what happened here at home. Tell yourself whatever you want. You did have other options."

Aviama cleared her throat. "How many people know who I am?"

"It doesn't take a genius, dearie. Not for anyone with contacts. Radha brought four girls, one from each bordering nation, to compete for the prince's hand, and they sent three home. The Jannemari princess stayed, and the wedding preparations began. An alliance with Jannemar would go with the union, but then Radha attacked Jannemar, and the prince set sail not south toward the war front, but west, and has not been seen or heard from since."

Nailah looked her up and down and pursed her lips. "Now you show up, fair-skinned, melderblood, and clueless. You don't speak Keketi. Your accent is Jannemari. You are stupid enough to try to destroy our markets. Yet while you're worrying about everybody else's kingdoms, your own falls."

"What have you heard about Jannemar?"

"Jannemar is small, broken, and out of resources. A horrible choice for a prince to ally himself with, particularly when they've got enemies as powerful as Radha." Nailah shot Chenzira a look, then softened. "Radha's made contact on your northeast side, and it doesn't look good. I'm sorry."

Aviama bit her lip. "The mines?"

Nailah nodded.

"Word travels fast, but not that fast." Chenzira plucked the comb with the lilies from the bed and twirled it between his fingers. "You still have contacts inside the palace."

"Yes, and the palace still has eyes on me. They always have, just as you used to, before you left. But when you left, so did Sutekh's motivation to stay away. I've been watched, followed, hounded. He's been looking for you. He thought you'd come here if you ever made it back to Keket. He was right."

"Which means he already knows I'm here."

"Yes, and it means my life is getting shorter by the minute. As I said, you shouldn't have come."

Chenzira stared down at the carved comb in his palm. "My mother always loved lilies. It's one of the few things I know about her."

Nailah shifted her feet. "Yes, well, that was hers. I'm sentimental." She closed Chenzira's hand over the comb. "Take it."

Chenzira caught her hand between his. "Is she alive?"

Nailah looked up at him and shook her head. "Rana has gone to the Khurafa Temple. If you go quickly, you may still catch her."

A muscle in Chenzira's neck twitched. But this was good, right? They knew where Rana was. Unless Nailah was lying. Which seemed entirely possible.

Aviama spun the lapis-lazuli ring on her finger. If Nailah was telling the truth about Jannemar, her home was under attack, and the Horon Mines had fallen. If the mines fell, Radha would seize the wyronite. How long would it take them to force melderbloods to make housing artifacts out of it, so that those without tabeun powers could access those abilities with forbidden sifal magic? Wyronite conducted magic better than any other substance discovered to date and lessened the negative effects of using housing artifacts. But magic had returned less than four years ago, and there were no conclusive findings on the long-term impact of using wyronite as a melderblood magic conductor.

Chenzira studied Nailah for a long time before he finally dipped his head. "I'm sorry we had to come by. I hope I see you again."

Nailah smiled, relief relaxing her shoulders. "I wish you well. Now go, before your sister slips away for good."

Chenzira took Aviama's hand and turned for the door. But as they went, Nailah's soft voice called after them once more.

"Be careful. Rana hasn't been the same since you left."

24

S weat dripped down the nape of Aviama's neck and made little rivers down her back, and her white sheath dress clung to her body as they approached the temple. It had taken only twenty minutes to reach it by foot and was impossible to miss. The structure stretched to the sky in a triangular-shaped top set over a cube base rimmed with columns all the way around. Steps rolled out from the columns like carpet.

Two identical huge statues guarded the front entrance at the top of the stairs, one on either side—a beast with the body of a great cat, the extended feathered wings of a mighty bird of prey, and the head of a woman. Each stood four meters high, the wingtip of one touching the wingtip of the other, creating a doorway six meters high beneath their wings. The statue sentries towered over Chenzira and Aviama as they moved up the steps.

Shadowy figures moved about between the columns. Gauzy golden veils and clinking jewels obscured the faces of the women, and the men wore hooded cloaks the color of clay and camel.

The hair at the base of her neck stood on end, and her scalp prickled all over despite the heat. Aviama's stomach knotted as she cast glances from one side of the temple entry to the other. Figures drifted to either side of the entryway as Aviama and Chenzira strode in. A smaller cube stood several meters in from the bordering columns, with rooms wrapping around its circumference. A spiral staircase moved up into the triangular top of the structure and down into its belly.

"What is this place? Are you safe here?"

"Khurafa Temple. My people worship many things, many creatures. The khurafa are a popular choice, the most famous of which is called Chisisi. Legends tell of her demanding, possessive nature, but those who come here claim her as their protector. Chisisi loves to play games, and her acolytes are no different." Chenzira drifted apart from her as they passed under the wings and into the shadows. He adjusted the head-scarf he had wrapped about his head and over his mouth and nose, concealing half his face. "No, we are not safe here. But it's a good choice for anyone who wants to hide."

Eyes followed their every movement. The silence was palpable as their sandaled feet slapped cool stone. Gone was the noise of the bazaar, or the soft city sounds of people talking and children playing through courtyards and open windows. A breeze wafted through the black hairs of Aviama's wig, wicking at the sweat on her brow and neck.

No one spoke. No one greeted them. But every shrouded eye saw, and every neck turned, if only slightly, before returning to whatever business their work at the temple required.

Did they know their missing prince had returned? How many of them were paid informants? Did Chenzira's family already know he was there, as Nailah had believed?

Two women exited one of the enclosed rooms, leaving the

door slightly ajar, and walked in lockstep rhythm around the corner and out of sight.

Aviama blinked. "You could walk by your sister a hundred times and never recognize her here."

"She won't be up here." Chenzira never broke stride as he crossed the open space and stepped onto the spiral staircase. He hesitated, glancing up first, and then down. Both options were endless stairs leading into darkness.

A muffled scream. Aviama froze.

Chenzira stiffened. "Did you hear that?"

She nodded. "It came from below."

Together they flew down the swirling steps, melting into the darkness until nothing but the chill of the stone wall and the echo of each other's footsteps guided their way. Her sandals slapping against the stone felt wrong in a place so silent. Chenzira was heavier, but somehow more solid and level than she, his steps sounding like a low *thud* rather than a raucous *thwap*.

He threw an arm out, and she ran into it, ricocheting off him and into the wall. Her shoulder burst with pain as it connected to the hard stone. The stairs branched off in two directions. They'd heard no more screams since entering the stairwell. No more sounds at all.

But now, a red-orange glow licked at the dark stone beneath them—and a crackle broke through the shackled quiet.

Chenzira's knuckles brushed her hip as he reached for the hilt of his khopesh. He was a powerful quakemaker, but using his powers here would only collapse the building on top of them and bury them alive. But wind could whistle through the smallest of spaces. Aviama lifted one hand, palm out, at the ready.

They descended slower this time, soft as a leopard's paws on the prowl. Aviama's heart hammered in her chest, thrumming the ancient tune of every creature who had looked into the face of death and expected to meet it again. The glow blazed brighter around the edges of a door at the base of the stairs. The crackle escalated to a muffled, snapping, sizzling sound. But no smoke came through the door.

Chenzira reached a hand toward the door handle, but if there were flames on the other side, it could burn his hand. Aviama summoned the wind and opened the door with whirling tendrils of air. The door swung open with an eerie, elongated *creeeeeeeaaaak.*

Aviama gasped. Stairs led down through the doorway into a reversed dais, a lowered section in the middle of the floor of the basement room. From their elevated position, Aviama could make out the design marked out in leaping, crackling fire on the floor below. The outline of a lily. And there, in the center of the fiery blossom, lay the charred body of a woman.

The moment Aviama stepped through the doorway, a wave of heat rolled out from the center of the room in a mighty blast that sent her reeling backward. Aviama threw up her hand in a wall of air, pushing back against the heat and flames. The stench of burnt flesh and hair mixed with the copper of blood and a wisp of something like incense.

Billowing black smoke rolled up and over them as if set free from an invisible dam. Aviama shielded herself and Chenzira with a bubble of clean air around them, but when she looked up, Chenzira was gone—forging through onyx smoke in a mad dash toward the center of the flames. Aviama leaped to her feet and threw the air forward, stretching her shield bit by bit, searching, searching ...

Where was Chenzira?

She stumbled down the steps toward the charred body on the ground, visible only in snatches as the rest of the black smoke barreled headlong over her. Aviama coughed against the smoke, but clean air was coming through the stairway in narrow whispers while the black airborne ash gushed out of the chamber, filling it almost completely.

Smoke and ash stung her eyes. Aviama blinked against the harshness of it. And then she saw him. Chenzira, leaping through the fire to the center of the lily.

If she didn't move quickly, he could be dead in minutes. Aviama flung up both hands and blasted him over the corpse and out of the way onto the steps on the far side. She sucked in a deep breath with the last of her clean air, leaped to the ground beside the body, formed another bubble around herself and the charred woman, and sent all the air out. She had to starve the fire.

The edges of the bubble compressed around her. Her arms shook. Her lungs burned. The flames rippled and wavered.

And then they extinguished.

Strength left her body, and Aviama collapsed on the stone next to the ash-covered body of the dead woman.

BURN. Ache. Pain.

Strong arms wrapped around her body and pulled her into a broad chest. Light danced behind her eyelids, flickering like the flames that had nearly taken their lives. The crackle of fire still taunted her from the distant corners of the room.

"Tally."

Aviama loved the sound of that voice. She loved its honeyed tones, and the intense care lining every syllable. Maybe if she kept her eyes closed, he would keep holding her and talking to her and calling her Tally, and she could drift off again to sleep.

"Tally!"

Less honey. More urgency. Her eyes fluttered open. Chenzira searched her face, and the worry lines of his brow softened.

"We've got to get out of here."

A deep hacking cough racked her shoulders and burned her lungs like fire, accentuating his point. Aviama winced and sat up. Smoke still curled around the top of the basement room. With a wave of her hand, she sent it shooting out through the doorway and up the stairs in the direction they'd come.

She reached out a hand to steady herself and snatched it back as her fingers brushed the flaky black ash coating the body beside them. The woman's face was burned beyond recognition, and her body and the stone beneath her were blackened—perhaps the work of an accelerant. In the middle of the victim's chest, a fiery red mark broke up the ashes along what used to be skin.

In the shape of a hand.

Aviama's jaw dropped. Her stomach churned, and bile shot up the back of her throat. "She—it's—"

No use was what it was, because another round of coughs overtook her. She doubled over. Aviama stared down at the body, unable to look at anything else as the image engraved itself in her tortured mind.

Another death. Another body. She couldn't decide if the woman burned to a crisp beyond recognition was a blessing or a curse, as the visage of the corpse cemented in her memories.

Chenzira placed a hand on her back, and she straightened. And looked straight into the eyes of a young woman standing in the doorway opposite the one they had come down.

She was a couple of years younger than Aviama, with gentle flowing waves of deepest brown hair. Red-wine lips parted slightly in surprise, set against a backdrop of rich, warm, perfect skin. Golden gauze wafted gently around her in the dress of the other temple women as the last of the smoke swirled up and out through the doorways.

Her gaze fell on Chenzira and Aviama and down to the blackened body on the floor. Her expression hardened to flint. In a flash, she hooked a jeweled veil back into place over her mouth and nose and disappeared up the stairwell.

"Rana!"

Chenzira's deep bellow rumbled through the chamber. Aviama forgot to breathe. That was Rana?

Chenzira took off into the stairwell, and Aviama followed close on his heels—only this stairwell didn't lead up more than a couple of steps before rolling out into a long, flat tunnel. Ahead, the outline of a woman sprinted into the dark.

"Stop her, Tally! Stop her!"

Aviama lifted a hand and sent a gale swirling after the escaping woman. The woman stumbled but did not fall. But the wind had been strong. How could she not fall?

She tried again, this time throwing up both hands and feeling her way—she was the wind, driving down the tunnel, running along the rough walls and dirt ceiling, hungry for something to catch up in its mighty current.

A grunt. A scream. A body hit the ground.

Aviama's throat constricted. Her heart dropped to her toes. No, no. It hadn't been that strong. It hadn't—

Chenzira was yelling.

"What did you do? What did you do?"

Aviama opened her mouth, but no sound came. No excuse. No explanation. She had none.

A moment later, they tripped over the body in the dark.

Chenzira scooped her up without a word, and on they ran toward whatever end the tunnel might have. Aviama sent out a river of wind to feel out the course of the passage, a hand on Chenzira's arm to guide him. If the movement of the wind around Chenzira and the woman in his arms was any indication, Rana was utterly limp. Lifeless.

It took all of five minutes at a full-tilt sprint to reach the end of the tunnel. A door spilled out into a dark, stone room lit by torches along the sides, carved all around with images of people doing anything and everything—farming, fishing, ruling, fighting. Families, warriors, battles, children. The room was narrow and contained two rows of benches and a small table adorned only with dried flowers and a single unlit candle.

Chenzira lowered Rana to the floor. Aviama knelt beside him, then sucked in a breath. "You're bleeding. She's bleeding. Oh—"

She stilled. A knife protruded from the young woman's neck. Blood soaked her neck, her gold gauze cape, her sheath dress, and ran down onto Chenzira's arms and chest.

Aviama swallowed. A lump lodged in her throat. But where had the knife come from? If she was stabbed, it wasn't Aviama that had killed her. Who else had been in the tunnel?

Chenzira reached down with trembling hands and removed the jeweled veil from her mouth and nose. He froze. Slowly, he turned to Aviama. "That's not her."

"But if that's not Rana ..."

Aviama couldn't bring herself to finish the question. Chenzira paled in the orange glow of the torches and stepped away from the body, shaking his head. "It's not—that doesn't—"

"The scream in the tunnel wasn't Rana." Aviama swallowed. "It was her."

Chenzira ran a hand through his beard, staring down at

the unknown woman's corpse. Suddenly, he snapped upright, as if shaken, and strode from the room like a rolling storm.

Aviama followed him, out of the room and up stone steps to a trapdoor that opened into another modestly sized rectangular room with a series of identical trapdoors along one side, and several more benches and tables on the other.

Chenzira walked as if in a daze, through the room, past its carvings, and out the door into the afternoon light. He stopped. "She's gone."

Aviama scanned her new surroundings. From the outside, the structure was adobe, and stood like a single flower in a field—one of several dozen identical structures laid out on a flat plain. Dust, rock, and adobe, next to more dust, rock, and adobe.

"What is this place?"

"*Mastaba asuhul*. The Plain of the Tombs."

A chill ran down her spine. "We're in a crypt?"

"Essentially. Each one of these are privately owned family tombs."

Aviama shivered. "What now?"

Chenzira shook his head. "It doesn't make sense. None of it makes sense. Rana would never—something is wrong."

That, they could agree on. Something was very, very wrong. They'd followed Nailah's directions and waltzed into a blazing murder scene. The work of a skilled fireblood, by the looks of things. Aviama still didn't understand how the smoke had remained in the chamber until they crossed some invisible barrier that set it all free. And how was it that Rana was the first person they saw walking into that space?

Why had Rana fled? Did she kill the temple girl in the tunnel?

If she had, maybe Rana wasn't who Chenzira thought she

was, sister or not. But one glance at Chenzira's face told Aviama now was not the time to voice those fears.

Aviama quickened her steps, taking two strides to match one of Chenzira's. His face set, and the steel in his eyes reminded her unnervingly of the look she'd just seen on Rana, in the basement of Khurafa Temple.

"We have to get to Nailah."

25

B y the time they got back to Nailah's, Aviama was panting from a full-tilt sprint as she tried to keep up with Chenzira. Twice they evaded guards roaming empty streets, but none saw them. Three streets over from the house, smoke twirling up into the sky indicated that perhaps Chenzira was right, and Nailah was still at home, cooking some last provisions for the road. But as soon as they turned the corner, Aviama's stomach dropped.

Black smoke curled out the windows of the center of the house, whisking away any hope they still had of finding the midwife. The lock on the gate was bashed in, and the gate hung askew on its hinge.

Chenzira skidded to a stop at the gate, staring at the house. "Adobe is fireproof."

Aviama glanced back toward the residence. Smoke still wisped up from the windows, though more like evidence of a snuffed-out campfire than the billowing top hat to a roaring flame. The house itself was not engulfed, and now that she considered it, Aviama couldn't think of much that could have been flammable inside the home, either.

A movement in her peripheral vision reminded her that soon locals would start to ease out of their houses again for the afternoon. Someone was watching them from the neighboring house. Did that same someone see them come to visit Nailah before the Khurafa Temple? How many eyes had tracked them on Siada without their knowledge? Had the jeweler in the bazaar really recognized Chenzira?

Aviama pushed the gate open. It gave way with a creak, and she hurried across the modest courtyard. Turning her back to the neighbor's window, Aviama reached for the door and sent an eddy of wind through the windows to blow it open from the inside. Maybe Chenzira was wrong, and something was burning inside.

But the door was tolerable to touch, though warm, as it bumped into her waiting hand. She shoved it open and slipped inside, holding it ajar behind her only for a moment as Chenzira crossed the courtyard and scooted into the house behind her.

The door swung shut. Aviama turned to face the room. And stared wide eyed into her second murder scene in the span of an hour.

A bed of kindling smoked from the stone slab against the wall, a few final, lazy embers still glowing deep in its recesses. On it, a woman lay dead. Nailah.

Burns covered her arms, legs, and clothing. Her face remained untouched, glassy eyes staring up at the ceiling. A knife plunged hilt deep into her chest, blood trailing down the stone slab and dripping slowly onto a growing crimson stain on the floor. Nailah's hands were folded neatly in front of her, oddly serene considering the chaos of the rest of the room—smoking kindling and broken crockery scattered across the small space.

Aviama glanced up at Chenzira. He stood ramrod straight,

stiff as a corpse, and rooted to the spot. Aviama's stomach turned over, but she swallowed her shock and stepped forward to get a closer look at the body.

The burns were irregular, some deeper than others, and in at least two places, Aviama could see the long, slender outline of fingers in the damaged skin or smoked linen of Nailah's dress. From the looks of things, she'd been tortured. Three of Nailah's fingers had been burned to ash, leaving nothing but a blackened nub where the rest of her digits should have been. And beneath those folded, mangled hands, Nailah's remaining fingers wrapped around a piece of parchment.

Aviama reached for the parchment. Suddenly, Chenzira was there, face set, his hand seizing hers. His iron grip crushed her hand with the weight of death and regret. She winced, and he released her—but not before gently guiding her two steps back from the body and snatching the parchment from Nailah's hands himself.

She clenched her jaw hard. Now was not the time to chastise him. But if he was worried about her being too fragile to see another corpse, he needn't be. At this point, she sometimes felt she had seen more dead people than living. If she counted her nightmares, it might almost be true.

Aviama cleared her throat. "You don't have to do this alone. I can handle it."

Chenzira's voice was gruff as he inspected the slip of paper, not bothering to look up. "You hate dead bodies."

"Yes, but I didn't know her. It's fine. Let me."

Chenzira opened the parchment and sniffed it.

Aviama folded her arms. "Congratulations. You've learned it smells like smoke. And ash. And maybe burnt flesh. Can I have it now?"

He shot her a dark look then, and she swore that glare could have curdled dairy.

"I'm checking for mujamada."

"Muja-what-a?"

"It's a poison some of my relatives have used. If inhaled, it paralyzes the victim, and the lungs freeze inside the body. Death comes by suffocation."

Aviama opened her mouth, then closed it. She swallowed. "And you just—you just thought you'd give it a big whiff, did you?"

He winked. "Worried about me?"

She slugged him in the arm. "Yes! You big fat idiot! We've seen two murders today, and you were all ready to be third on the list! I don't know if you know this, but as far as targeted killings go, two is my daily limit."

"You were looking pretty eager to get your hands on it yourself, Tally. I don't have a precise daily limit for murders I can stomach, but ever since I met you, I've developed a deep-seated fear I can't seem to shake. It's quite obnoxious. So, as discussed previously, I'd love it if you stopped doing things that might kill you."

"Says the guy who just sniffed poisoned paper."

Chenzira shrugged. "Not poisoned, as it turns out. And my tolerance for my own death is higher that my tolerance for yours."

She pursed her lips. "Doesn't that make you a hypocrite?"

"Some might say it makes me romantic."

"Should we do this in front of the dead body?"

He cocked his head. "Why? Do you think she's offended?"

Aviama blinked. Chenzira's mouth twisted as if unsure whether to laugh or to frown, and he coughed. "Sorry. There's only so many ways to survive horrible things. Weird comments come with the territory. I'm sure you'll be making them soon."

He waved the parchment in his hand to refocus her on the matter at hand, and she stepped into his side to read the note.

His Royal Highness, Prince Chenzira Bomani
Duke of Alrimal Wahab
Duke of Marfud
Earl of Tajama
Count of Khayin

together with

Her Royal Highness, Princess Aviama Shamaran
Duchess of Ramad
Countess of Alkharab

You are hereby cordially invited to a banquet held
in your honor
At sunset tonight
Special guest appearance: Kestrel
Don't be late.

Blood spatter soaked the edges of the parchment, which were already roasted brown and gently curled by a flame that had gotten too close. At its base, two wax seals overlapped—one in red wax, and one in gold.

The red seal depicted a tree with roots made of feathers and widespread acacia branches with leaves that formed the shape of a khopesh. A single drop of blood fell to the ground from the edge of its leafy blade. Inside the gold seal, an unblinking eye stared out at them from inside the borders of a diamond shape crowned with a royal diadem and flanked by a pair of outstretched wings.

Chenzira dusted the ash off the paper and handed it to Aviama as she re-read it a third time. "He knows we're here on Siada. He had people watching Nailah, waiting for us. He could have sent people to kill Rana and my mother and gotten more than he bargained for with my sister."

"You really think it was your mother that we found? That she's been alive all this time?"

He nodded, then swallowed. "I found a ring on her finger. It's a lily."

Aviama winced. "Lots of people like lilies. It might not have been her."

"It was her."

Based on nothing but intuition and an unrecognizable body burned to a crisp that he could compare with the zero memories he had of the woman. She scratched her head. "So you think the king sent guards to kill your mother and your sister, but only got your mother?"

He ran a hand through his beard. "Not my father. My brother, the crown prince. But yes. It would explain the dead girl in the tunnel. Maybe Rana acted in self-defense and was too scared to stick around."

Could be. But it could just as easily *not* be. Maybe Chenzira had created a narrative that felt better than a beloved sister turning into a monster after he abandoned her.

But what did Aviama really know of the girl, except that they'd come face to face when Rana walked into the temple basement to find them hovering over a dead body? What would she have thought was going on? Chenzira and Aviama were far more suspicious than Rana. No wonder the poor girl ran.

She probably believed her long-lost brother had murdered her mother.

Aviama squinted at the long, sweeping script on the parchment in her hand. "Does he really think we're stupid enough to show up at the palace like dinner on a silver platter?"

"He's claiming to have Rana. That's his bait. But we just saw her."

Aviama scanned the letter once again from the top. "Rana isn't mentioned."

Chenzira leaned over her shoulder and pointed at the line that read *special guest appearance.*

"She's the kestrel. Local birds of prey that pack a punch in a small frame. It's an old nickname."

"And—you're a duke? Twice? And an earl? *And* a count?"

Chenzira shrugged. "It's not so uncommon for royals. Aren't you duchess of anything?"

"Yes, but just one little area, and it doesn't mean much. I haven't actually managed it at all. And I'm definitely not duchess or countess of whatever this letter says I am." She waved the parchment in her hand.

"My list used to be longer. Looks like he's taken Muali. I knew he would. I'm surprised he hasn't taken Tajama. My father must have some sentiment left in him yet." Chenzira peered over her shoulder again and pointed to the last title under his own name. "This one, *khayin*, is the Keketi word for *traitor*. He's just being snarky at this point. 'Count of Treason.'"

Aviama arched an eyebrow. "And mine?"

"Don't worry, he didn't leave you out. He's named you Duchess of Ashes and Countess of Chaos." He grinned. "I know he's being nasty, but I kind of like the last one."

She pressed her lips together and glanced back up at Nailah's body. "We need to go."

Chenzira took the parchment, folded it tightly, and tucked it into the waistband of his schenti. "You're right. We've been here too long. They're probably watching the house to make sure their message was received."

"In the interest of full disclosure, if it looks like we're about to die, I will use whatever means necessary to get us out. Deal?"

His mouth twitched. "Deal. Stay close."

She swept her hand toward the door. "After you."

But he didn't go through the door. Instead, he walked through the doorway to the bedroom and slipped out the window to the back of the courtyard. Aviama followed, her feet hitting the dust of the little plot at the back of the house with a soft *pffft*. Chenzira bounded up two large ceramic jars and over the wall to the street on the other side. Aviama ran at the jars, planted one foot on the rim of the first, and leaped for the wall.

She fell short and swept a gale of wind to carry her over the edge so that she tumbled over to the far side, stopping herself with three long strides before landing in a heap in the dirt. Chenzira held out a hand, but she waved him off. "I'm fine."

Chenzira grinned. "Must be hard, being short and having little legs."

"I'm taller than most Keketi women!"

"Maybe. But you're a lot shorter than me."

Aviama rolled her eyes, but a smile threatened to break into her facade. Chenzira smiled openly, then tossed a glance at the streets around them. Four adults in traditional Keketi attire moseyed by on the far side of the street to their left, and three more paused to chat in the heat of the day on their right.

Chenzira stiffened, and Aviama followed his gaze to the rooftop of a building six houses down. Four male guards flanked the silhouette of a woman, arms bound, the naked blade of the first guard shimmering in the sun. Rana.

In a flash, Chenzira took off through the streets. Aviama's

stomach dropped. She sprinted after him, legs pumping as fast as they could go.

"Stop!"

Aviama reached for his arm, but her fingers only brushed his elbow and clutched at the empty air. "She's bait!"

But Chenzira didn't slow. If anything, he doubled his pace, flying ahead over rock and pebble and stone and dust, darting through streets and alleys he knew like the back of his hand. Aviama summoned a gust of wind at her back to quicken her pace, but her legs burned, and they were already making a scene as it was.

People poked their heads out of their houses, women stood on their stoops with brooms, children glanced up from their games. Their timing could not have been worse. Witnesses were everywhere—just as Chenzira's brother would have wanted if he planned to take Chenzira down for good.

Aviama chanced a look up at the rooftop. Rana was gone. The guards were gone. If Chenzira hadn't seen the same thing, she might have wondered if the stress of the day was getting to her, and it wasn't all a mirage.

She rounded the corner and skidded to a halt. Chenzira had vanished. Had he turned another corner? Gone up to a rooftop for a better vantage point? Had he even realized how far behind she had gotten?

Footsteps pounded the dirt behind her, and she spun. Three men in civilian clothing barreled toward her—the same three who had been down the street from their position as they left Nailah's. They carried no weapons, but the steel in their eyes said they didn't need any.

Aviama threw up both hands and sent a gale of wind spiraling down on them, only to have one of the three men throw up his own hands in defense. A shield of air formed a bubble around the three men, and her attack dissipated against its invisible surface. The second man threw a fireball at her head, and she dodged, but as she leaped sideways to escape the flames, the ground beneath her feet roiled and crumbled in on her.

Solid ground turned almost liquid, like a sand pit, opening wide to swallow her up. Aviama's heart lurched to her throat as she yanked one foot free, but the second was already caught as the ground solidified again around her ankle. Aviama's free foot landed hard, and the moment it contacted the ground, the dirt yawned open and captured it so that both feet were trapped above the ankle.

Aviama ducked out of the trajectory of the fireblood's second blow and formed a new attack. Vines of air spun behind the men. Long ghostly fingers wrapped themselves around their ankles and yanked them backward. All three hit the ground with a smack. Aviama sent a wall of wind into them, sending the men skittering backward like leaves in a fall breeze, clattering against the adobe side of the nearest house.

But her feet would not budge from their earthen prison.

Aviama yanked hard but was rewarded only with a searing pain that promised a sprained ankle if she didn't let go. She threw a slash of harsh funneled air down into the dirt. Soil rocketed in every direction, spraying her dress, her face, her legs, like a hundred stinging projectiles. One ankle wiggled a couple of centimeters. Victory!

But not nearly enough.

Just as one foot began to move, her adversaries recovered. A blast of wind knocked her backward as she worked, slamming into her chest like a sledgehammer. Aviama threw up a shield to protect herself, but the ground shifted again and swallowed her up to both knees the moment she straightened.

Aviama grimaced. The vines of air had worked—the men were surprised by any tactics requiring finesse and control, and more prepared for grand sweeping gestures of chaotic power. Still, three against one among melders of different types; she was at a disadvantage. She didn't want to use her last resort option. But if she didn't get free before—

Whack. Pain exploded at the back of her head. The world went dark, then light, and dark, in flashes as she fought to keep her eyes open. The ground beneath her feet loosened, and she scrambled away from the hole.

The outline of her favorite person smashed across her field of vision like a tornado, a fist connecting to a skull with a thundering crack. Whoever had hit her wouldn't be a problem anymore.

But then Chenzira fell, gasping for air. Aviama turned to the three men, her vision spotty as the pain of the blow still reverberated through her head. Ground swallowed two of the three as Chenzira returned the favor on her enemies, but the windcaller was crushing his windpipe. Aviama lifted both hands and ripped the air from their lungs.

The three men crumpled to the ground, and as the last of her strength fell away, the dark won.

Dark.

Her heavy lids lifted the blanket of blackness in a single flutter—just long enough to see Chenzira's form slumped over beside her. She couldn't tell if he was breathing, but his eyes were closed.

Cartwheels rumbled beneath them. Wood creaked. A donkey brayed.

She let her eyes flutter open once more. She lay on her back, staring up at the sky. Her hands were bound, not by rope, but by dirt and hardened clay molded around them up to the wrist. She called a whisper of wind, but nothing came.

Three men crouched around them in the cart. One of them hit the other on the arm.

"She's awake."

Wet cloth smothered her mouth and nose. Her scream stuck in her throat.

But she didn't have the energy to scream, anyway.

The world went black again.

Aviama came to herself like a foot dragged unwillingly from the muck of a mud-heavy swamp. *Don't move. Don't open your eyes. Breathe deep, like you're still asleep.*

She could feel her heart rate spike as whatever they'd drugged her with wore off and her brain reminded her body that she'd almost died—and might still, if she didn't watch out.

No sound of cartwheels. No natural breeze wafting in from open air and sky. Beneath her, the cool of silky cloth over a firm cushion replaced the rough wood of the donkey cart. Her skin felt smooth and clean, rather than the sticky sensation of grime and filth she'd grown accustomed to in the past months, but something cool and solid pressed down against her chest.

The room was silent, except for a light, rhythmic scratching. A moment later, a sheet of paper shifted on a hard surface, and she realized the scratching was a pen drawn across the page. But from the quiet scratch of the pen to the softness of the bed to the smoothness of her own clean skin along the cool silk, it was the aroma of the room that arrested her focus as she lay there in the mystery room, in the mystery building, behind the cage of her closed eyelids.

Deep, rich, and warm, the scent mixed sweet with spice in an elegant array of notes like transcendent five-part harmony. The lustrous aroma promised to transport her to a place of luxury, panache, and bad decisions; lovely, wild, and sparking her interest all at once.

Soft footfalls padded across the space, and a door opened and shut, leaving the room even quieter than before. Aviama took another deep breath in, hoping to identify the ingredients of the scent.

"Resin, myrrh, cassia, balanos oil—and a few extra treats thrown in just for you."

Aviama's eyes snapped open. Pure sky blue stared back at her across the ceiling, bordered by muted red-and-blue designs at the top of the wall, and large illustrations of the same colors splashed across the walls and around the sides of a stone bath filled to the brim, heated mist still rising from its surface. Vents at the top of the room allowed air flow, but more wall now sealed in the window casing on the far side where a view out of the room should have been.

"Sensual, isn't it?"

A young woman lounged on a sofa, long dark hair falling down her back. A thick gold band encircled her head, accented by a longer gem-studded piece extending down her forehead in the front. Gold dripped from her ears and draped from her neck in a metallic collar attached to her dress. The dress was white—fitting for anyone Keketi—with filmy, flowy strips dropping from the shoulder in the back. Blue gemstones interrupted the gilded collar at her chest, the bodice overlaid by gold in a design down the front that wrapped around her waist. Gold and blue decorated both wrists, and a gold armband graced one of the girl's slender upper arms. But where her bare feet kicked up on the sofa, two iron shackles captured her ankles, and the chain ran to a steel plate on the wall under the window that was no longer a window.

"Rana?"

"For as long as I can remember." She popped a grape into her mouth from the plate before her and scrutinized Aviama with an eye far too suspicious for a girl so young. Perhaps Aviama's sister-in-law, Semra, had been like this once—cynical, untrusting, distant. But Semra had been indoctrinated into an assassin program from the age of four, and Rana was a royal in a respected monarchy.

Aviama hesitated before she sat up, checking to make sure she was wearing clothes. Was the silky fabric on her skin a sheet or a dress? The answer, thankfully, was both—she did have clothes on, and there was a thin sheet over the top of that.

How long had it taken them to scrub the caked dirt, blood, and ash from her body? To wash from her hair the clinging stench of death and smoke from not one but two fiery murder scenes she'd visited that day?

She sat up and swung a leg over the side of the bed to examine her new attire. When she did, she exposed one leg almost entirely, thanks to a slit in her dress that ran halfway up her thigh. Upon further inspection, she found the opposite side held a symmetrical slit, the white cloth running up to a thick gold belt around her waist and draping down toward her toes in the front. White cloth crisscrossed in the front of the dress, fitted to her form. A gold collar lay cool against her skin from collarbone to breast, topping off the design.

But the shackles binding both her ankles were a less than luxurious change. Aviama's chain ran to the opposite wall, away from Rana's, meaning Aviama could probably reach the door but not beyond it, and Rana and Aviama were unlikely to be able to come into contact with one another. Looking up into the sharpness of Rana's knife-blade eyes, Aviama couldn't decide if that was a curse or a mercy.

"The slits were my idea." Rana sat up and leaned forward, taking in Aviama's reaction with a keen interest. "Beautiful, isn't it?"

Aviama swallowed. "Yes."

"I designed both dresses. They're mine." A devilish smile twisted Rana's lips upward as her gaze traveled over Aviama's body in her fashion creation. "I am sure my brother will approve."

"Which one?"

Rana shrugged. "Both. Who doesn't love a beautiful woman showing off long legs?"

Aviama's cheeks flushed hot. Okay, so Rana was nothing like Semra. But she *did* know a thing or two about design. Aviama had to admit, the dresses were stunning—even if she wasn't used to the style.

"You design too?"

"You design?"

Aviama squeezed her eyes shut and shook her head to clear it. This was all wrong. They shouldn't be sitting around in a lavish room eating grapes and discussing the latest fashion developments. They were shackled to the wall. She'd been abducted in the street. Chenzira ...

Her eyes flew open. "Where are we? Where's Chenzira? What happened?"

"We're home, dummy." Rana snatched another grape off the plate and threw herself back against the cushions of the sofa, as if all interest in Aviama died with mundane questions of survival. She waved a hand around. "My new room. Without a window, even though the courtyard down there made for a glorious view."

"Why did you leave?"

Rana shot her a dark look and popped her shackled ankle up on the arm of the couch, the slit in her own dress revealing most of her leg along with it. "Sand and sea, I don't know. I feel so welcome and free here. I clearly have such a loving, supportive family." She rolled her eyes. "They didn't even have the decency to gold-plait the chains. It throws off the *entire* outfit. *All* the metal I'm wearing is *gold*. It clashes."

Aviama pursed her lips. It was weird hearing the expression Chenzira so often used, but in Rana's snide tone. And as much as Aviama loved clothing and design, she was getting sick of the distractions. But if she didn't want Rana to shut down on her, maybe she had to play the game.

"You really think your brother will like this dress on me?"

"From the looks of things, I think he'd rather it be on the floor, but yes. I'm a mastermind." She tossed a lock of stray hair behind her shoulder. "You're welcome."

"It really is beautiful. Thank you for letting me wear it."

"Yes, well, your clothes were an insult to garments the world over. And they stank." She reached for one of two goblets set out by the platter of fruit, meat, and cheese.

Aviama's stomach rumbled. Rana lifted the other goblet in Aviama's direction. "You must be thirsty. Running around in the heat in the middle of the day, and all."

Aviama eyed the goblet. Her mouth watered, but she shook her head.

Rana rolled her eyes again and gulped down a swig from both goblets before lifting the second one back up toward Aviama. "Not poisoned. Satisfied?"

Aviama winced, but hopped off the bed and strode as far as her chain allowed. Both women reached toward each other against their restraints until their fingers just barely brushed, and Aviama had the goblet. "Thanks."

Now tell me where Chenzira is. And why we're here. And why you aren't freaking out.

Aviama cleared her throat. "Why do they want you? Why won't they let you leave?"

"I'm delightful company."

Aviama arched an eyebrow, and Rana laughed.

"It's okay, I wouldn't have believed me, either. I'm bait for you, obviously. Didn't you read the invitation? My brother wants a family reunion."

Everybody talked a lot about the crown prince. Why did they not mention the king?

"And your father?"

Rana scrunched up her nose. "The king focuses his time on what my brother wants him to focus his time on. Sutekh gets all the news first and gets first swing at all of it before filtering it and handing it off to the king."

"Sutekh makes all the real decisions." Almost like Queen Satya did in Radha, pulling strings behind the scenes with her web of spider spies. But in Sutekh's case, he already had ruling authority and would soon have all of it by rights—the moment his father passed it on to him or passed away.

Rana gave a nod. "He's smart. Sneaky. And ruthless. Bound to be wildly rich by the end of the year, especially after the king finalizes the alliance with Radha and Sutekh strikes a bargain of his own with their prince."

Aviama's lips parted, and for an instant, she forgot how to breathe. Nailah was right. Keket and Radha were joining forces.

"Considering you disappeared from Radha, and they attacked Jannemar, and you're in love with Chenzira, I assume the wedding is off." Rana snatched up a piece of meat and cheese between delicate fingers and took a bite. "Where is he, by the way? The Radhan prince."

Aviama took another sip from her goblet. Opulent, full-bodied red wine sweetened her mouth. She tossed it back and leveled Rana with what she hoped was a stare, both diplomatic and firm. "Where is Chenzira?"

She shrugged. "Maybe he left you."

"He would never do that."

Rana tilted her head back and, though she was sitting down at eye level with Aviama, still managed to look down her nose at her from beneath her impossibly long lashes. "I remember those days."

Aviama's heart wrenched in two, and her gut ached as if someone had slugged her in the stomach. Nailah had said Rana had changed when Chenzira left. How much had she changed? What had happened to her?

Aviama set her goblet down on the stand next to her bed and sank down on its edge. She folded her hands in front of her and leaned forward to search Rana's eyes. "He loves you. He regrets leaving you here. I don't know what happened when he left, but I know he wants to make it right, and he swore he'd come back for you."

A shadow flickered over the young woman's stunning features, soft and severe at once. For a moment, Aviama thought she caught a glisten in her eye, but the next moment it was gone. Rana waved her off and shifted in her seat, taking another bite of meat and cheese.

"He's doing a splendid job."

"Maybe he isn't done yet."

"Maybe I gave up waiting for him a long time ago and started to save myself."

"You're doing a splendid job."

The moment the words left her mouth, all breath left Aviama's body. It was the wrong thing to say. She needed an ally, and so far, it felt like she was dancing with an enemy combatant. No need to poke a chained zegrath.

But the next second, a surprised snort-laugh eased the tension in the room. "I guess I can't argue with you there."

Rana offered Aviama a plate and the platter of food, and after loading up on some of the items, the two of them ate in silence for several minutes. When she was finished, Aviama took a deep breath and tried again.

"You've clearly come into your own. You don't seem like you need or want saving—if anything, it's us who have needed the help since we got here. And if we hadn't come, perhaps Sutekh would have left you alone, and you wouldn't be here now. But maybe if we work together, we can get the three of us out."

"What did you have in mind?"

"That all depends. On what Sutekh wants, where Chenzira is, and what we walked into at the Khurafa Temple. We need to know the cards on the table, and I'll wager you know more than anybody else."

Aviama examined the shackle's lock around her ankle. It was smaller than the locks on the brig cell door, or on Nailah's gate, but she could probably get it open. Which means she could free them both. A valuable bargaining chip.

Rana cocked her head, following her gaze. "Windcalling can't break that chain."

"I don't need to break it."

The Keketi princess arched an eyebrow. "What would you do, then?"

Aviama grinned. "You first."

28

"You're wanted for anarchy and murder."

Aviama grimaced. It wasn't a great start, but it also wasn't entirely unpredictable. "Any chance explaining myself nicely will help?"

Rana snorted. "Fat chance. Especially since you're guilty."

Her jaw dropped. That she did not expect. "Nailah sent us to the Khurafa Temple to find you. When we got there, the room was already on fire. How do we know it wasn't you?"

"Because I've been searching all my life to find my mother. Why would I kill her?"

"Why would Chenzira kill her?"

Rana shrugged. "How should I know? I hardly know the man."

Aviama twisted the lapis-lazuli ring on her finger, grateful it was still there. "You ran from us."

The girl took a sip of wine. "People run from murderers. It's a thing."

"Says the woman who stabbed someone in the temple tunnels."

"Says the woman who just so happened to be on the scene

within minutes of two separate deaths and was seen at both covered in blood and soot, side by side with a fugitive."

Aviama sucked in a breath. Okay, so that didn't look good. She opened her mouth to speak, but Rana lifted a finger and cut her off.

"Oh, and she also started a rebellion on Jazir, stole and artificially freed a bunch of slaves, and pretended to be a goddess instead of a run-of-the-mill melderblood, managing to upend the entire island and disrupt peace and trade in the region."

Aviama threw her hands up. "You've got to be kidding me! Not you too."

"Much of our economy runs on the backs of slaves."

"Nobody should be a slave."

"I agree, but if I were to dismantle it, that's not how I would do it."

"How would you do it?"

She pursed her lips. "Doesn't matter. Anyway, Sutekh has some sort of offer for you. I'm not sure what it is, but he's very excited to meet you. So I assume we can expect that meeting any minute, since the servant left some time ago with the latest report and will be back shortly to check on your status."

"If I'm a murderer and an anarchist, why would he offer me anything?"

"People bound for death are more pliable."

The knots in Aviama's stomach grew. "More easily controlled, you mean."

"Obviously."

"That's what Shiva thought."

Rana hesitated, looking back up at Aviama with interest. A mischievous spark lit her eyes as she scooted to the edge of her seat, unable to conceal her eagerness. "And?"

Aviama couldn't help but feel a little proud, almost flattered by Rana's excitement. "He learned naïve princesses from Jannemar aren't as stupid as he thought."

The princess licked her lips and grinned. "Let's play a game. One answer for one answer. Chenzira is here, but Sutekh wants to keep you separate because your powers are too dangerous together."

Good. Finally, they were getting somewhere. "The queen carries a lot of pull in Radha."

Rana nodded. "We knew that. Next answer better be good. My turn—the air flow to this room can be filled with the same thing they knocked you out with, so if we cause trouble, they'll dump it down the vents and knock us out or kill us. It's called kululu, and we've developed an airborne version."

Aviama blinked. That was a good one, and she needed more answers on that level. Time to dig deeper. She needed to share something big, something juicy. But without all the details.

"Shiva wanted to prove himself. I rejected him, and he dragged us all to Ghosts' Gorge."

Rana's eyes bulged, and Aviama knew she'd hit the target like an arrow straight to the bullseye. "Ghosts' Gorge?"

Aviama nodded.

The young woman came alive, as if electric currents ran up and down her skin as she resettled on the edge of her seat. "How'd you get out? Where is Shiva now? Is he dead?"

Aviama held up a finger. "Nope. Your turn."

"Fine. All our guards are melderbloods, and Sutekh has built a specialized cage for each of the four types of melderbloods."

Interesting. She took another sip of the wine. "How do the guards keep melderblood prisoners in check when they're not in the cages?"

Rana shook her head. "Your turn."

Aviama shrugged. "I don't know if Shiva is alive or not."

Rana scowled. "Liar."

"Not a lie." And it wasn't. Not technically. She'd blasted him over the railing of the *Wraithweaver* into the hands of the Iolani, but she hadn't directly witnessed his demise.

Rana groaned and slouched back against the couch. "I'm bored with this game. Let's play dress up."

Panic welled up in Aviama's chest. She fought to keep her voice level and shook her head. "Pretty sure you already did that with me. And you haven't learned how I can get us both out of these chains."

"Pleaseeeee?" She pouted, and her shoulders sagged forward as if her greatest dreams had just been dashed to pieces. "Don't insult my creation. That dress deserves some accessories."

Aviama rolled her eyes. "If I do it, you owe me another answer. A good one. And I get to pick the question."

Rana perked up. "Fine. After that, get us out of the chains, and I'll answer one more question—anything you want to know."

"Anything?"

She dipped her head.

Aviama smiled. "Deal."

Rana rose from the couch, slipped on the sandals she'd left abandoned on the floor, and flew to a small vanity along the wall on the side of the room. Her chain allowed her to reach half the drawers, but not the other half. She rifled through several of them, dragging out gold bands, necklaces, and earrings before tossing her selections across the room to Aviama. Aviama caught about half of the items, and quickly gathered the rest of the fumbled jewelry up off the floor until she had everything: a pair of gold earrings, an elaborate upper armband, two ruby-studded wrist cuffs, and a matching gold

headpiece with a ruby centerpiece extending down the forehead in a similar style to Rana's.

Aviama put on the earrings, cuffs, and headpiece, but left
the upper armband in favor of the simple one Chenzira had
bought her in the bazaar.

Rana looked her over. "That armband looks like you were
born in a hole in the ground, but the rest looks absolutely
otherworldly, so I'll let you keep the ugly one. What's your
question?"

"What happened between you and Chenzira?"

Rana's expression soured, and for an instant, Aviama
feared she wouldn't answer. But then the words came—hard
as ice, acrid as a knife in the back. "He lied to me, abandoned
me, and gave up on Mom. He tried to hide me and failed.
Three months after he left, Nailah told me they'd found out
where I was staying. I got out, but they killed the family
anyway. I spent a year on a farm in the middle of nowhere,
and another year in a fishing village, waiting for him to come
for me. Then I decided to make my own way in the world. And
I've done it. And now he's back, and he's ruined everything."

A lump lodged in Aviama's throat. "Rana—"

"Don't worry about it. You asked, I answered. And now
you've joined him and made everything twice as bad. The
least you could do is take your turn and get us out of the
chains you put us in."

Aviama reeled backward. The poison in her tone and the
flash in her eyes sent a chill down her spine. Warning bells
rang in the back of her mind. Maybe she shouldn't release
Rana. Maybe whoever Rana had become was too shattered to
keep them both alive in an escape. But as soon as the thought
came to her, Aviama knew she had to let it go. She didn't trust
Rana, but Rana knew where Chenzira was being held, and
Aviama needed her if she wanted to save him.

Not to mention she needed the promised answer to one last question.

So Aviama gave Rana one long look, clenched her jaw, and turned her attention to the shackles around Rana's ankles. If the vents above them were being supervised, she'd need to be careful. Nothing too loud, and never drawing so much air through the vent at a time that anyone above would notice.

She lifted both hands, the thrill of a challenge, the tingle of power filling her body and soul. Softly, she crafted a narrow current of air and passed it between her palms, adding energy and strength to it with every pass. Then suddenly, with a flick of her wrists, Aviama sent the little channel of wind whistling into the lock of the shackle around the first of Rana's ankles. She could feel the mechanism turn until the latch released, and the lock opened with a *click*.

"Ow! You pinched me!"

Aviama glanced up at Rana's accusing glare. She'd just proved she could open delicate locks using tiny tendrils of precisely placed air currents. She had expected any number of reactions, but not this one.

"That's not possible."

The door to the room swung open, and as Aviama whirled toward it, something dark flew at her hands and latched on, securing them together before she could register what had happened. By the time she'd fully faced the door, a dozen guards swarmed into the room, and a mixture of what felt like soil coated her hands—surrounded by molded rock, perfectly fitted over her hands from fingertip to wrist as if cast from a mold.

Aviama whirled back to Rana, but her hands remained free. She rocked back on her heels and offered a small smile, rubbing the place where the shackle had been.

"Sorry. Question and answer time is over."

29

Aviama stumbled down the corridor, heart in her throat, pounding out the beat of a drum growing louder with every step. Her ankles still stung from the bite of the shackles the guards had removed. Rana and Aviama had both been dragged out of the room in different directions, landing her here—pulled down a long hall surrounded by half a dozen soldiers, hands trapped in an airtight chunk of stone.

She knew it was airtight, because she had been trying to call to the wind ever since she left the windowless room she'd been chained up in, and she hadn't been able to do it.

Three more halls and two sets of double doors later, and the guards led her into a large room with soaring ceilings accented by a long strip of glass overhead, pouring the fading light of evening into the space. Columns lined the long room, a room nearly as long as the throne room back home in Shamaran Castle. Each column depicted the carving of a warrior or king, towering twice as high as any of the mortals walking the Great Hall beneath them.

A circular fountain burbled in the center, its water glittering under the soft light streaming in from above. Two statues of the winged beasts with human heads, like those she'd seen at the Khurafa Temple, spewed water from their mouths in crisscrossing arcs in the fountain. Beyond the fountain, a small table, set for two, glistened with gold flatware and jeweled goblets, accompanied by twin empty chairs, as if a feast had been prepared to host a pair of ghosts.

Aviama's steps echoed along the tile floors, her light sandaled footfalls accompanied by the heavier thump of the guards' powerful strides moving forward in a perfectly synchronized rhythm. Her stomach churned, and she tried to reach for the ring on her hand, but her fingers were immovable in their bonds.

A flash of movement caught the corner of her eye, and she glanced sideways to see another half-dozen shirtless guards with collars, schentis, khopesh swords, and brass guards on their arms and calves leading another prisoner in their midst. Her lips were painted deep red, long golden locks spilling out in waves down her back beneath a jeweled headpiece adorning her brow. Rubies and gold sparkled from the Keketi collar hanging around her neck and the belt about her waist; her dress fitted to her body through her torso to her hips and dropped away to her ankles, the slits in her skirt exposing snatches of her legs as she walked.

She blinked. Head held high, shoulders back, no one looking on would have guessed at the tremble in her stomach or the wild beating of her heart.

Aviama glanced down the long room and saw a multitude of identical fountains emanating down either side, flanked by duplicate columns of duplicate carvings. Floor to ceiling mirrors ran just beyond the columns to her right and left down the full length of the hall. She stared at her reflection, taken aback by the sight of herself. She looked like a regal Keketi princess.

If only she could feel like one. All she wanted was to get Chenzira and get out. Back to Manan, Umed, Sai, Teja, and the baby. Biscuits, even back to Durga and the twins and Husani. What would they think when Aviama and Chenzira missed the rendezvous that evening? What would they do? How long would they last before the royal guards found them?

The guards escorted her to the fountain in the center of the room and abruptly split off in opposite directions, marching to either side of the room, posting themselves three and three next to the columns facing the fountain. Aviama turned around, but there was no one there. She stood alone, hands bound, in the visual crosshairs of the melderblood royal guard, as the fountain burbled softly beside her.

Aviama peered into the crystal-clear waters. The reflection of her face swam in a background of azure-blue sky, interrupted at the edges by the gentle rippling of the fountain where the streams from the statues' mouths poured back into the water. It occurred to her then that each of the two rooms she'd been permitted to see inside the palace so far—for clearly the palace is where she'd been taken—had contained water. The windowless room had held a large steaming bath, and the hall here had the fountain. The first had controlled air vents, and here her hands were bound.

Just a coincidence, or a strategic choice? How many of the guards were crestbreakers? What opportunity was there here for firebloods?

Aviama shot a look down the hall. Unlit torches hung from every column. *There it is.* Experienced firebloods should have no trouble creating and manipulating their own fire, but it was always easier to work with existing elements. Once the torches were lit, whether by a torch lighter or by tabeun power, they could be used to the melderblood's advantage.

Still, it was the water that featured most prominently. Windcallers could use wind from anywhere, and a powerful quakemaker could crumble the foundations of the expensive, luxurious palace, so wind, fire, and water would likely be in the highest demand in the service of the king. Or, in this case, perhaps in the service of the crown prince.

An out-of-pattern gurgle in the fountain brought Aviama's attention back to the water. A serpentine slither of water raised above its natural surface and circled in wide arcs and lines across its length, bumping up against the stone of its confinement. A shiver shot down her spine. She'd seen this before.

In the cove, from the deck of Florian's sloop. A masterful crestbreaker had drawn—

The hairs on the back of her neck stood on end as the same familiar letters took form across the waters of the fountain, as if embossed in tranquil tears. *RAISA.*

Aviama rocketed upright and stepped away from the fountain just as a shadowy figure materialized in the shade of one of the columns. With the mirrors on every side, how had she not seen him before?

Harsh green eyes stood out in stark contrast to his Keketi skin tone, piercing her through in startling contradiction with the confident swagger of his long, unhurried stride. A gold band wrapped around his brow, long dark hair falling past his shoulders and trimmed beard. A gem-studded gold collar served as the only adornment on his toned upper body, save for the armbands encircling his bulging biceps.

He swept his hand into a fist, and the letters in the fountain rose in a sweeping arc and dove into the water again, dissipating with a fluid grace as if they had never been disturbed at all. His eyes held her gaze as he came to a stop before her at the fountain. It was most certainly an intentional position, close enough to exaggerate his towering height over her small frame, forcing her to look up to meet his eye.

"If it isn't the barefoot slave girl." The man smiled in an effortless charm, a devious spark lighting his severe green eyes. "Lesala, was it?"

Aviama sucked in a breath. Biscuits, she'd met the man twice! But the first time had been dark, when they'd jumped off the cliff and found themselves interrogated on a royal envoy ship, his face lighted only by stars and the orange cast of the torches. And the second time could hardly be considered a meeting, since she'd never actually seen him in the cove. She'd only known a skilled crestbreaker was on the vessel, toying with her across the watery expanse.

She tilted her head. "And you are?"

His identity was obvious, but questioning it seemed like the most insolent option, and her diplomacy had apparently evaporated.

His smile widened. "Pleased to have caught the shiniest fish in the sea."

Ah, yes. Another exhibit for another menagerie. But she'd die before she went through that again, and she'd take as many with her as she could.

Aviama offered an answering smile. "If that is your opinion, I'm not sure you've seen much of the sea."

Sutekh arched an eyebrow. "I understand you've seen quite a bit of it. I'm looking forward to hearing more about that."

Aviama pursed her lips. How much did he know?

Sutekh swept his arm to the edge of the fountain, inviting her to sit. She didn't. He looked her up and down and ran a hand through his beard. Her stomach soured, and she fought the urge to shift uncomfortably under his penetrating scrutiny. He stepped closer.

"You look like you've stepped out of a dream."

"I think I've stepped into one. A nightmare, I assume."

"Maybe we can change that."

Aviama smiled sweetly. "I'm confident you can. Have your goons remove my shackles, let me go, and I'll be on my way."

Sutekh laughed. He waved a finger at her as though she were a naughty child. "You know, I would have preferred to hold this meeting without the shackles. Perhaps we still can. I do hope you will forgive me, but last time we stood this close to one another ... well, you took my breath away. And though I can honestly say you've done it again today"—here he swept his gaze over her again from head to toe—"I much prefer this means of stealing my breath away, as opposed to the trick you pulled last time."

She winced, but said nothing. He caught it and tilted his head.

"Did you not enjoy stealing the breath from my lungs and leaving me half-alive on the deck of my ship? Interesting."

"I don't enjoy hurting people. But I was confident your plans for me were unacceptable. I am just as confident of that now as I was then." Aviama lifted her bound hands, the rock around them heavy on her wrists. "Case in point."

"You haven't heard my plans yet."

"I'm pretty sure I don't need to hear them to know I won't like them."

"That's unfortunate." Sutekh clasped his hands behind his back and circled her slowly as she stood there by the fountain. "I think you enjoyed our banter, at the very least. You're sharp, which makes you interesting. A slave who was not a slave, with a stolen child who was not stolen, leading a group of miscreants off a cliff—well, it isn't something I see every day.

Watching you take that dive really did get my heart racing. Nothing like a near-death experience to wake up the body." He'd gone round behind her and stopped at her far shoulder, turning his head and leaning in to speak softly, close to her ear. She could hear the smile in his voice, even as she kept her eyes resolutely on one of the carved columns on the far side of the room.

"I think I've had my fill of those. No need to wake me up any further. I'm as awake as I can be, thanks."

Sutekh shrugged and completed the circle around her, crossing his arms in front of her and facing her once again. "I don't buy it. You're wanted for anarchy, two counts of murder, and association with a known fugitive. You blew up the fragile peace on Jazir and set yourself up as though you were a goddess. You destroyed the economy of an important trade-route stop and cost multiple lives while getting slaves and melderbloods under control on the island in the wake of your little show. Chaos follows you wherever you go."

She tried not to focus on his assertion that people had died getting the freed slaves and exposed melderbloods under control on Jazir. She lifted her chin.

"Countess of Chaos?"

The corner of his mouth twisted up. He spread his hands. "As you say."

Aviama glanced down the long hall. A door stood at the end. Not that it did her any good, with her hands in rock and unable to operate the handle. The set table opposite the fountain held two knives along with forks and spoons. But again, she had no hands or wind with which to snatch them off the table and drive the blade into Sutekh's blackened heart.

She cleared her throat. "Your sister said you had an offer for me. Would you like to lay it out, or would it be more expedient to reject it now?"

"I think I'd like to lay it out. Thanks for offering." He gestured again to the edge of the fountain. "But I do insist we sit. Perhaps later, we can free your hands and eat together like civilized people."

"I'll stand."

"I insist."

His eyes hardened as the levity in his demeanor cracked a bit. *There we are—the real you.* She'd played with snakes long enough, and maybe she was crazy, but she'd started to prefer the fangs to the game.

This was the man responsible for running Chenzira out of Keket. He wanted to kill Chenzira and Rana's mother and had pursued Rana. Had it been him who got to Chenzira's mother under the Khurafa Temple?

Aviama didn't bother with a smile. "I said I'll stand."

Sutekh clenched his jaw. "I think you forget whose palace you're in and who exactly holds all the cards here. When I say you sit, you sit."

He raised a hand, and a massive arm of water thrashed out from the fountain, wrapped around her torso, and yanked her down to the edge of the fountain.

With the shift in his expression and the force of the movement, the walls tilted around her. In the blink of an eye, she was back in Radha, in a dark circular room full of stars and a mirrored floor. Another man stood there, pretense melting off him in victory as he gained the information he needed to destroy her. She swung at him, and he held her fast.

Hot breath whispered *Lilac* in her ear as she struggled against arms too strong and threats too thick.

Convince me you love me, or I'll kill one of your servants. Convince me ...

Bhumi's decapitated head staring at nothing from the floor of the *Wraithweaver*. Shiva's mouth smashing into hers while her hands were chained, in the sight of all, baiting her to shove him away. The boom of the cannon. The weakness, the splitting pain of the konnolan.

Lips on hers, blackmail whispered like sweet nothings against the soft skin of her neck—every touch with the prince of coercion.

I don't hide my collections for special occasions. I wear them. And I will wear you on my arm.

Her pulse pounded in her temple. Heat descended on her chest like storm clouds.

Rough hands. Black eyes peering into her as though her soul would crumble into ash by hatred alone. It nearly had.

A roar split the air from her own throat, and she swung. But her hands weren't in shackles, and the wind ignored her cries. Stone sealed her hands together at the wrists. All the better for blunt-force trauma. She launched herself at the prince. She feinted high, and he dodged, but the rock around her hands was already plunging into his stomach.

He doubled over with a grunt, and she spun, bouncing on the balls of her feet. Guards converged from the sidelines. Shouts rang out around here.

Sweet, sweet music. No quakemaker would dare ruin the floor. No crestbreaker had any water but the fountain. It was deep enough to drown her in, but Sutekh still wanted to play. Fire she'd experienced before, and she'd just been doused with water. And windcallers would only add to the flame in her own soul.

A fireball whipped by her head. She ducked, the fire extinguishing in the fountain with a hiss. Aviama felt the wind change around her before the blast hit; she glanced up to identify the windcaller guard only an instant before he unleashed the gale. A third guard ran toward her.

Aviama took a flying leap off the side of the fountain and

wrapped her arms around the neck of the oncoming guard just as the windcaller's blow hit. A wall of wind knocked the two of them to the ground, but Aviama maintained her grip on the guard's neck. His hands flew to her arms around his throat, trying to loosen the seal on his windpipe.

Sutekh straightened his collar and held up a hand toward his guards. "Nobody touch her."

30

The guards shifted uncomfortably but held their positions in a semicircle on either side of Sutekh, facing her. Aviama still held the last guard's throat. He struggled, and she cinched his neck tight until he sagged. She brought him to the floor, arm still tight around his throat, but loose enough for him to breathe until he came to.

Sutekh cocked his head. "What a tortured soul you are. Does my brother know how tortured you are?"

She readjusted her grip on the guard's neck. "He knows a lot of it."

"But not everything."

Aviama hesitated. No, Chenzira didn't know everything. He knew of her nightmares. Back in Radha, before the arena, he'd overheard her screams for himself. But they'd mostly gone away since the *Wraithweaver.* He knew Shiva had forced her into situations she didn't want to be in. Just that morning, when Aviama flinched as he playfully grabbed her arm, he seemed to realize another layer of the impact Shiva had had on her mind.

He knew she hated being stuffed in a room away from

where the action was. He knew she hated killing people. He knew she'd gone unhinged when she blew Shiva's quarters to bits on the ship, dumped the konnolan overboard, and soared her way to the upper deck with murder on her mind. And he knew what she'd told him—that he was her anchor, her sense of steadfastness in a rolling sea.

But he didn't know the extent. He didn't know how often Shiva's iron grip bruised her mind still, even when his physical body was nowhere near. He didn't know how afraid she'd been in Shiva's clutches, how the hopelessness had started to taint her soul, how she wondered if she'd become him with enough time. How she had to remind herself who was safe, and who wasn't, when someone took her arm. How little it took to drag her back to that place of hopeless darkness in her mind.

Sutekh gave a solemn dip of his head. "I thought not."

Aviama tried not to grimace under the weight of the unconscious guard lying limp against her chest. She still couldn't call the wind and was woefully outmanned. Her attack was worthy of execution in any monarchy worth its salt, not to mention the crimes they claimed she'd committed. If she didn't find her way back into Sutekh's good graces soon, she'd be dead.

Sutekh motioned his guards to step back. They did. He stroked his beard.

"Rana was the same after she went through what she went through. Nightmares. Jitters. Jumpy. People who hadn't known her before might have thought she was clumsy or flighty. But she'd never been flighty before. The truth was, she'd been in danger so long, she didn't know friend from foe."

Growing up, Aviama had never been as steel-hearted as her brother or as confident as her sister. Whatever she felt, she'd felt with her whole heart and did little to hide it. People described her as a sweet, funny, innocent chatterbox.

Much had changed since those days. And the jumpiness had only come in the last five or so years—since the night the great black dragon smashed through her father's throne room. Witnessing the murders of both her parents hadn't helped, nor had being on the run with an assassin who slaughtered everyone in their path.

But when The Return happened, and she had her Awakening—when a windstorm killed a kind servant boy, and it was her own storm that did it—when she went to a foreign kingdom and was unraveled in every way, with death promised at every turn, spies in every corner—biscuits, none of it had exactly helped.

"You have a darkness in your soul. I can see it." He clasped his hands in front of him and knelt on the floor to look her in the eye. "You're a survivor. A fighter. I saw it when we first met, and I see it now. Fire."

Sutekh cocked his head. "But it doesn't come from light. It feeds on shadows."

Or the fear of shadows. She'd desperately tried to cling to the light. She'd seen how the dark could swallow a person whole, eviscerating the soul and leaving only a shell. Aviama couldn't afford to add another shell to her family tree.

"What say you put him down"—Sutekh nodded at the unconscious guard in her arms—"and we try this again. But I'm tired, so if you would indulge me, I'd prefer to sit."

A pit formed in her stomach. Sit on a fountain with the crown prince, or bleed out right here, right now, hands still enveloped by stone.

One gave her the chance to fight another day. To find Chenzira. To get back to the baby who still needed a name and someone to love her.

Aviama swallowed hard past the lump in her throat and eased her grip loose from the guard's throat. He slumped to the floor, and she slid out from under him and stood.

Sutekh seated himself on the edge of the fountain and angled toward her, ignoring the guards as they collected their friend. "You've been diplomatic a day too long in your life, haven't you?"

Aviama clenched her jaw, but she heard no sarcasm in his tone. She stepped to the fountain and sat, leaving a space between herself and the Keketi prince.

"I've done it for obligation. I've done it for family. I've done it with a knife to my throat. I'm good at it." Again, she tried to spin the ring on her finger, but her hands were as useless as those of statues. "I'm sick of it. All of it."

The prince nodded. "I know the feeling."

The guard stirred, and his companions helped him to his feet. Slowly, the six of them took up their positions again at the columns, while the two royals on the fountain's edge pretended nothing odd had happened.

Aviama pursed her lips. He was trying to find common ground, to get on her good side. If she humored him long enough, maybe he'd release her hands as he'd said he would, to eat together. And if he released her hands ...

"I think I'll hear out your offer now. I do hope you'll forgive my outburst."

Sutekh brightened. "Consider it forgotten! I understand better than my brother just what it means to leave a grudge behind."

Aviama doubted that, but ignored the dig. "You realize that whatever you're about to ask me, you're asking under duress."

He spread his hands. "You just attacked me and nearly killed my guard."

An impish quirk twitched at the corner of her mouth. "I thought you said it was forgotten."

Sutekh arched an eyebrow, a surprised grin stealing over his face. "So I did! All right, let's say the bonds are for my own protection, not because of anything that happened today—truly, you've been nothing but pleasant—but because of our last meeting, when you ripped the air out of my lungs and left me to die on my own ship."

She scrunched her nose. "That's not very diplomatic of you. Except for the lie, which was very diplomatic."

"Where did I lie, exactly?"

"I didn't leave you to die. I knew you would be perfectly fine. You're welcome."

He ran another hand through his beard. "And if given the chance again?"

Aviama shrugged. "You'll never know if you don't try."

"Why don't I lay out my offer first, and we'll see how things go?"

"Shall we shake on it?"

"I'm glad you're feeling more comfortable." Sutekh smiled. "Now, the offer. As you may already know, Radha has attacked Jannemar, taken the Horon Mines, and is sweeping down toward the capital as we speak. Keket expects a Radhan delegation any day, which is what my father is busy preparing for. Keket is on the brink of an alliance with Radha, which would be very bad news for Jannemar."

He took a breath. "I think you and I can save Jannemar, acquit you of your crimes in Keket, and put you in such a position that Radha wouldn't dream of coming after you. You'd be safe on every side, ready to put your nightmares behind you and have a life of your own."

Aviama dipped her head, steeling herself to present a neutral expression despite the goosebumps crawling down her arms. "How sacrificial of you. I accept your acquittal of any and all crimes, including those I did not commit."

Sutekh knew her pressure points, and to offer so much, he must want something big. Something unreasonable. If he tried to marry her, she'd strangle—

"Marry me, and all of those things happen at once."

Aviama moaned, a guttural, rumbling disdain from deep in her throat. As if she'd spilled boiling-hot tea, swept a plate off the counter in her effort to clean it, broke the cup, slipped on the mess, landed in the steaming spilled tea and shards of crockery—one last mishap she couldn't possibly be expected to put up with. If her hands hadn't been tied, she would have run them over her face. As it was, she wiped her brow with the back of her arm and let out a long breath, willing herself back into a pleasant discourse.

It had been a knee-jerk reaction, and the wrong one.

Sutekh stared at her, his expression so mixed with emotions she couldn't have plucked one out if she tried. He cleared his throat. "I admit, I mentally prepared for many reactions from you, but this was not one of them."

"Forgive me. May I be frank? Thank you, I think that's best." She surged onward before he had a chance to say no. "I've already been through this with Shiva, but I'm smarter now, and I've given a lot of thought to what I would do if I had the misfortune of being forced into matrimony again. If you blackmail me, I'll refuse. If you threaten to kill me, I'll do the job myself and save you the trouble. And if you believe we can learn to be a team, I'll tell you that you would not enjoy being married to me, and if you tied yourself to me for the rest of your life, I'd likely make it so miserable that you would want out. You're a prince, with power and authority and experience of killing people. Which lands us right back here, with me on death's door. Why go through all that trouble?"

Sutekh blinked. A moment later, the prince descended once more. He folded his arms, all poise and composure.

"You're that convinced you'd make a terrible bride?"

"No. I'm convinced I'd make *you* a terrible bride."

Sutekh pursed his lips. "Because I'm not my brother, and you've not yet discovered him for the liar he is."

Aviama's stomach twisted. She set her jaw. "Because relationships built on manipulation make people want to die. Been there, done that. Didn't like it."

"I wasn't making a declaration of love. I was offering a solution to a problem. It doesn't hurt that you're easy on the eyes, but marriages at our level are rarely for fun. Do you have a better solution? Without me, I'm afraid you're dead in the water. Pardon the expression."

Aviama opened her mouth, but no sound came. She didn't have anything valuable to offer. Alliance with Jannemar was less than desirable, considering Jannemar was broke and struggling in a new war, and Keket was in the process of securing an alliance with Jannemar's attacking enemy. Keket already had melderbloods—well trained ones, even—so training seemed an unlikely avenue, even if she was willing. Which she wasn't.

On her part, if she'd been in a position of power, she would have made many demands: free Chenzira, Aviama, and Rana; clear them of all accusations; put pressure on Radha to withdraw from Jannemar; end the slave trade. All of them were insane.

Sutekh sighed. "You understand I need something valuable from you. If you won't provide it, you'll be executed for your crimes."

She was the one who needed many things. Sutekh held all the cards—and the greatest one. Chenzira. He had no reason to give her anything she asked for.

Her mouth went dry. "I haven't committed any crimes."

"Are you still claiming the rebellion on Jazir wasn't you? Because we both know it was, and I was the one who plucked you out of the water off its coast. Or are you referring to the murders? You were spotted fleeing the scene of an arson with a dead woman inside, and a temple girl was found stabbed to death in a mastaba. You were next seen leaving the house of another burn victim, with blood all over you." Sutekh shook his head and tsked at her, as if she were a child who'd stolen from the cookie jar. "Not a good look."

Aviama twisted her lips. "You're proud of yourself, aren't you?"

He grinned. "Maybe a little."

Why didn't he end it? Why didn't he kill her and Chenzira and be done with it? Why the theatrics, the effort of—

She stopped. Aviama knew all the demands she would make if she were in power. But what was Sutekh after? Beneath the bravado, the marriage proposal?

"What are we really doing here? Are you proposing to punish Chenzira? You imagine I'll say yes to save my own skin, and trap myself to you, and you'll trot him out and gloat before you chop off his head?"

"That's not an entirely unappealing idea." He angled his body further toward her, green eyes boring into hers with lightning intensity. "Keket may be smaller in land mass. We may be an island nation. But we are mighty. The water has been our home since before Radha or Jannemar existed. Keket was once the most powerful empire this side of the Great Sea. I want the respect that is our due."

"You want the sea." And an empire. Free roam on the Aeian Sea. Valor. Victory.

Sutekh lifted his hand, and a tower of water rose from the fountain and formed into the shape of a palace, with city upon city of tall pillars and regal statues stretching across the full surface of the water. "Keket will return to her former glory. And anyone who stands in the way makes themselves our enemy."

The watery cities burst in explosive pops, one after the other, until each one plopped back into the burbling fountain.

He pictures himself as a conqueror. What about the king? What about—

Aviama tilted her head. "I don't understand. I can't possibly be threatening to you. I'm from Jannemar, a nation under attack, with few resources."

Sutekh snorted. "Jannemar, the birthplace of magic, has few resources? The Origin Wellspring is there. One of the original four housing artifacts is there, if not more. The last keeper is there. Radha sees Jannemar for its full potential. They were right to attack it."

Aviama drew back. Sutekh wanted housing artifacts, objects infused with the tabeun power of melderbloods to offer magic to those without it or to greatly increase the strength of the natural powers within a melder. Jannemar had wyronite, the best conductor of magic with the least amount of negative side effects from its use. And, hiding in its forests around Ellix, at the base of the Origin Wellspring, was Frigibar—Aviama's mentor and trainer, "keeper of magic, scholar of ancient melders, and the most knowledgeable person alive" if he did say so himself, regarding the formation of the world and the magic within it.

An alliance with Radha would get Keket access to Jannemar's wyronite, only they wouldn't have to pay for the bulk of the war effort or get their own hands dirty. They'd also link themselves to the world's strongest navy. Sutekh was in it for the long game. He'd find a weakness in Radha and exploit it until the oceans were his.

Aviama clenched her jaw. "Radha wants to kill melderbloods."

Sutekh smiled. "You're still here, aren't you?"

"No thanks to Shiva."

"What did happen to him, by the way?"

Aviama lifted her stone-captured hands. "Maybe if you release me, I'll be in a more talkative mood."

He eyed her, a spark of interest coming alive in his gaze. She could feel the air in the room changing, like the fresh scent of a rainstorm before the first droplet fell. A thrill ran through her, and she held her expression firm, but patient. Like a bird on a branch, as likely to sit for an hour and enjoy the breeze as it was to swoop down and snatch its prey from the air.

Sutekh shook his head. "You won't tell me."

Aviama lifted her chin and smiled sweetly. "You've built your entire defense system around melders, and you're vulnerable. Radha can incapacitate all your best fighters. You haven't killed me, because you need me. You need information that I have. I've been on the inside of both Jannemar and Radha. I know more than I should about both. And as much as you think you need me, I'm certain what I know is worth double what you expect."

"You've grown awfully cocky since attacking my guard."

Aviama let her smile drop and looked him up and down, as though he were the prey, not her, and he was hardly a morsel worth the effort. "I'm surprised you thought I'd be interested in marrying a second fiddle."

Fire blazed in his eyes. He lurched to his feet, water from the fountain towering over her unbidden, matching the emotion of its master. Sutekh's hands balled into fists. The shadow of the wave, frozen in place, fell over Aviama's form as she sat at the edge of the fountain. A single drop of water fell from the wave suspended above her head, dripping on her forehead and running down her face.

Her heart pounded to the steady drum of a funeral procession. Victory mingled with terror at the impact her words had caused. But oh, she'd gotten to the heart of the matter.

Sutekh caught himself, realizing his mistake too late. His face changed to mask the rage roiling beneath, but his cheeks were still flushed, and his bare chest heaved with heavy breathing. Sutekh left the wave hovering over her, as if he'd created it intentionally—drip, drip, drippping on her forehead one droplet at a time as she looked up at him.

She steeled herself not to move, not to flinch.

He stepped forward and brushed away a rivulet of fountain water from her cheek with his thumb. "I'm not second fiddle to any man. I'm the whole orchestra. You will play my tune, or you'll be released from service to this world."

Aviama leaned away from his touch and stood to meet him until they were almost nose to nose as he peered down at her. She searched his eyes. "Was Chenzira first fiddle? Did your father like him best? Is that why you chased him away?"

Sutekh studied her for a long moment. "You don't know?"

"Don't know what?"

The pit she'd been fighting in her gut all day doubled, the ache spreading through her belly and constricting around her heart.

The edges of his mouth twisted into a smirk. "Sands. He hasn't told you." Sutekh raised his voice and turned to the mirror. "Why haven't you told her?"

31

T he reflection of the hall with its columns, the fountain, and the Keket prince and Jannemar princess shimmered and shook. It took Aviama a moment to realize what was causing the movement. Two of the guards had taken hold of a section of the mirror and were sliding it across the floor as though it were set on unseen wheels. The section of mirror tucked neatly into a hidden space beyond the columns, exposing a view of—

Breath left her body.

Chenzira hung over a vat of a dark and bubbling liquid, strapped to a board tilted forward over the vat so that he was positioned almost, but not quite, upright. Bands of leather secured him to the board—Sutekh wasn't stupid enough to restrain a quakemaker with stone—and his hands and forearms were encased in a hardened silvery substance up to the elbow.

Sutekh glided across the tiled floor as if he were an entertainer, the entire room his stage, and the time had finally come for his great finale. His eyes glittered with cruel mischief as he breathed in deeply through his nose, as if soaking up the addictive, seductive scent of victory. The prince swept a hand toward his half-brother hanging over the vat.

"May I introduce you, Your Highness, to the man who was a criminal long before you met him? Tell me, were you an anarchist before, or did he taint you over time?"

Aviama stared at Chenzira, mouth agape. Agony rippled through her body with the paralysis of hopeless pain—the sort that one can do nothing about and may well have been one's own fault. She imagined the sensation in her chest was akin to if someone had ripped her chest open, wrenched her heart in two, littered the pieces amid her remaining organs, and haphazardly sewn her back up with a needle the size of her arm.

"Oh, look at her," Sutekh crowed. "She looks stunning in Keketi, doesn't she, Chen? Rana really knows how to dress a woman. It's good to see something lovely before death. Something to distract from the coming pain. If only she'd shut her mouth occasionally."

Aviama glanced sideways on either side. The six guards stood motionless. The door at the end of the room to her right, on the far side of the little table set for two, was unguarded. But there was no hope of her living to make it there, and she wasn't willing to try without Chenzira by her side, anyway. She looked up at Chenzira and found his gold-flecked cinnamon eyes boring into her soul.

They were made of deep beauty, the kind that is only developed through the refining furnace of escaping death with scars. As if he'd been wounded, again and again, but patched up with gilded steel stronger than what had been there before—until his brother recreated the scene of the crime in his mind, ripping open age-old ills.

She'd expected to see the fire of the fight in those eyes, but instead she found sorrow and softness, as though he silently begged to pull her in for a tender kiss goodbye. As though he had already given up.

As though she already believed the words coming out of Sutekh's lying mouth.

"Justice has never been Chen's strong suit," the crown prince was saying. He clasped his hands behind his back and paced, as though giving a grand presentation before a host of generals. "Not when he himself is so often on the wrong end of it. No, he'd rather triple his kill count to escape a gracious sentence than stand up like a man and accept his conviction."

Aviama shook her head. "Whatever happened, I'm sure four years of exile are enough. Particularly if you layer in the torture you have him in now. Let him down."

Chenzira winced. Sutekh grinned so widely she thought his face might split in half.

She wasn't that lucky.

"What, this comfortable place in the gallery where he can watch the show? *This*? Torture? Please, don't be ridiculous." Sutekh flicked his wrist, and the bubbling liquid in the vat splashed up against Chenzira's exposed torso.

A guttural howl of pain escaped his throat through clenched teeth. His body trembled against the leather restraints biting into his skin. Aviama rushed forward, as if there were anything she could do against such reckless sadism. But the liquid returned to its vat, the only evidence of its escapade in the blistering red trail leading up Chenzira's stomach. A sizzling wisp of smoke wafted from a section of the leather strap around Chenzira's torso, where whatever substance was in the vat had eaten it away like rats on rags.

Sutekh caught her around the waist and dragged her back. She swung her bound hands, but he trapped both her arms with one of his and gestured at the damaged leather. "If you really want me to let him down, I can arrange for that. But I'm not sure the result would be particularly pleasant, except that the screams would be drowned out. He'd be dead in seconds."

No trace of fear crossed Chenzira's face. Only pain and sadness. Regret, maybe, though for what, she couldn't tell.

Aviama's chest heaved with the exertion of panic and spent muscles and sagged against Sutekh. He brushed his lips against her neck. A sliver of ice shot down her spine, dragging with them a torrential flood of swirling thoughts.

Freeze. Freeze. Don't move, and he won't kill you. Freeze. Freeze ...

Kill. Kill, and no one will touch you again. Kill, even if they kill you ...

Scream. Scream, and maybe someone will help you. Scream, even if they slash through your throat ...

But she'd sworn never to freeze again, as she had with Shiva. And if Aviama was dead, Sutekh would have no reason to keep Chenzira alive to toy with. And the baby with Sai would remain nameless and abandoned. And the last Shamaran would indeed burn, which would make Shiva grin from the grave.

And there was no one who might hear her scream who would come to her aid. It would only give Sutekh the satisfaction of seeing her broken heart and a crushed spirit on display.

Aviama choked on the terror of losing Chenzira. She was losing herself too. She could feel it. His eyes were sad, but steady—always steady, her anchor in a raging sea. For her part, she guessed her own eyes were frenzied, like a flailing, flapping bird fowl next to a bucket of the heads of its companions. All negotiation, all strategic tactics, all gimmicks fled her brain. She was dangerously close to falling to her knees to beg the royal pig for Chenzira's life.

And from the sly grin on Sutekh's face, he knew it.

He released her, and she staggered sideways. Sutekh rubbed his hands together. "Now. My dear brother was about to tell us all how he got kicked out of Keket. Please, do tell."

Chenzira opened his mouth as if to speak, but before he could get the words out, Sutekh leaned over to hiss in Aviama's ear. "He murdered someone."

Aviama jerked away from Sutekh's closeness, her stomach twisting at his nonsensical words. Sutekh clapped his hands. "Oh, isn't it delicious! A young woman who keeps the secrets of her tortured soul away from her love—but tells me, whom she claims to hate. And a killer who betrays his woman just as easily as he betrayed his country."

She clenched her jaw but couldn't help glancing Chenzira's way. "It's not like that. He doesn't enjoy hearing about Shiva. I didn't want to add fuel to the fire."

A storm cloud seemed to pass over his face, interrupting the sorrow he wore. But where there was a storm, there was lightning, and she was glad to see he had some sparks left.

"No, I can't imagine he would." Sutekh tented his fingers and paced one direction, then the other. "You aren't going to ask me who he killed?"

She shrugged. "Seems like a waste of time. I wouldn't believe you, anyway."

The door on the far side of the room swung shut, and Rana swept in like a swan spitting fire from its mouth. "You should. He's the only one telling the truth these days."

Aviama sucked in a breath, and Chenzira's head snapped to the side to take in the sight of his sister in all her regal glory —and wrists unfettered by any restraint.

"Rana!"

It was the first time Chenzira had spoken, and it stung a little that he'd said something to Rana and not to her. Had she insulted him by telling Sutekh about her so-called tortured soul?

But showing her hurt would only give Sutekh more ammunition. Better to be united, for the few opportunities of it they had left. Aviama ignored Rana and turned to Sutekh.

"What do you have on Rana?"

Aviama was no idiot. Rana had yelled to let everyone into their room earlier, when Aviama unlocked her ankle shackles. The girl was in on it. But was she coerced, or acting of her own free will? The lack of restraints didn't bode well for the answer to that question, but she couldn't know for sure.

Sutekh shrugged. "You noticed how easily you told me your troubles. Rana has found me to be fair and comforting, now that she's given me a chance. And oh, she did have grievances to share! It's a shame my half-brother kept us divided for so long."

Aviama rolled her eyes, but Rana crossed the distance in effortless glory and held up a hand. "It's true. Chen had me so afraid of Su, but it was Chenzira I should have feared. It's easy for naïve little girls to be confused about traitorous men."

Here Rana shot a knowing look toward Aviama, somehow looking down her nose, even though the younger princess was shorter than the older.

Biscuits, if this was an act, Rana was the best actress Aviama had ever seen. Derision rolled off her in waves, as though she'd fed on nothing but bitterness over the last four years and now, at last, released it—in a volley of poisoned arrows.

Chenzira shook his head. "He's lying. You saw all the guards trying to capture us when I got you out. Six guards, dead. Sutekh's page, dead. The falconer, dead. All for failing the man who pretended to be the king."

Chenzira's lip curled, and his chin jutted toward Sutekh on

the word *king.* But Rana was shaking her head before he'd even finished speaking.

"You killed them, Chen. I saw you kill four of the guards; we were together for that. The other two would have been easy enough to take care of and plant when you slipped away from me, leading me past their bodies to convince me of Sutekh's intentions. The guards were there to keep me safe, not to kill me. To keep me safe from *you.* And the page was only a boy."

Sutekh winced as she spoke, brow furrowed in what he probably hoped looked like grief and pain. Aviama glanced between them, from one to the other. She didn't know the story at all, much less the true version from the false ones.

Chenzira groaned. "A boy who knew too much! Rana, listen to yourself! You're smarter than this. You're only alive now because he needs you for something. What does he need you for, Rana?"

Rana looked at Sutekh and sighed. Sutekh wrapped an arm around her shoulders and pulled her in for a hug. "I'm sorry, Rana. I told you he'd never confess. He doesn't deserve your sympathy. Didn't I tell you? Didn't I tell you he'd play this game?"

"What game?"

The question had spilled from Aviama's lips before she could think about it. Standing quietly by the sidelines had not been her forte as of late, but even less when the man she loved was strung up over a death vat beside her.

Sutekh pursed his lips. "We knew Chenzira would try to rip us apart. To convince Rana he was acting in her best interests, that he hadn't murdered so many in cold blood. That taking Rana away wasn't vengeance. The king had offered him a third of the kingdom and a host of slaves to cultivate it. Chenzira spat in his face. He wanted more. *More* than a *third* of the kingdom, as the illegitimate son of a peasant!"

The crown prince flicked his wrist again, and Chenzira cried out as the bubbling mass beneath him shot up in a spurt against his ribs. Aviama flinched and bit down so hard on her tongue she feared she'd bite it clean off.

The same leather strap around Chenzira's torso took another hit, and from the looks of it, the last fibers couldn't take much more before they snapped. How much more of Sutekh's random retribution before Chenzira fell from the board to his death?

The position of the board also meant that even if Aviama could figure out a way to release Chenzira, he'd only fall into the vat. She glanced up at the board. It was secured to a heavy wooden stand behind the vat, the board branching off to extend over the boiling liquid. She couldn't see its base. Maybe it had wheels, and she could push him away from it. Or maybe, if she got her hands free, she could blast him backward away from it.

Sutekh wasn't done. He wheeled on his heel, eyes ablaze, and glared at Chenzira. "He threatened to crumble my father's kingdom. My inheritance. He demanded more power, and when he was denied it, he slaughtered half a dozen guards, poisoned Rana against the rest of the family, and ran off—with something important."

Chenzira clenched his jaw and shot his half-brother a withering glare. "As much as you may hate it, he's my father too. Where did you hide him, so you could do this to me under his nose?"

"You're changing the subject."

"From what? Your invented myths?"

Sutekh spat, spittle hitting Chenzira on the cheek. He turned his head but couldn't move to wipe it off.

Chenzira ignored him, turning to Aviama and Rana instead. "The king had doubts about Sutekh being handed the entirety of the kingdom after him. Sutekh has always been hot-headed and proud and way too eager to go overboard on everything—"

Sutekh's face flushed red. "That's enough!"

But Chenzira didn't slow. "He once lost three duchies to a gambling debt. So Father wanted a workaround to give me more control in the kingdom and save some of it from Sutekh."

Sutekh balled his hands into fists. "Lies! He knows I'm the only true successor! He wouldn't dare!"

"Maybe not anymore." Chenzira's eyes flashed. "Not after you tried to off him twice already. Has he been more docile for you since I've been away?"

Sutekh's fists squeezed tighter, and the vein in his neck bulged just before he made his move. Aviama's stomach dropped. She lunged, and her stone-encased hands made contact with his temple just as the boiling substance burst up in another splash toward Chenzira.

Chenzira cried out in pain as the liquid hit his abdomen. Sutekh doubled over as the rock smashed into the side of his head. And a wall of wind knocked Aviama sideways.

She careened into the side of the vat, the force of the gale sending her half over the side, so that her arms and nose hung parallel to its bubbling surface. Sweat broke out on her brow as steam from the boiling mystery substance hit her in the face. A putrid smell assaulted Aviama's nose. Her head swam.

Another blast of hard air hit her back, and she crashed again into the side of the vat. This time, her wrists swung down, grazing the surface of the dark liquid. A shrill shriek screamed from her throat as fire like a thousand needles sliced through her skin. Angry red welts rippled along the smooth skin of her wrists as she jerked herself away from the vat and summoned a deluge of air.

Someone was screaming her name.

It didn't matter.

The boiling vat had cut through the stone around her wrists like butter. Stone exploded from her palms in shrapnel, flying in every direction.

The wind had answered.

32

A viama's ribs smarted, but the pain was nothing compared to the power flooding her palms. The guards were nearly upon her, but with a twirl of her fingers, she pulled the air from their lungs. They collapsed, unconscious—for now. She hadn't killed them. Not yet.

Her chest burned. Her skin tingled with magic. Her breath came fast. This was it. She'd destroyed all chance of peace, while they were too far inside the palace to have a strong escape route. Surrounded by specialist melderblood guards and enemy royals.

Don't think. Act.

Aviama threw a gale at the structure Chenzira was bound to. She needed to get him away from the vat before Sutekh recovered.

Sutekh can't recover. Steal his breath. All of it ...

But if Rana really had defected to Sutekh's side, killing him would also kill any chance of reconciliation Chenzira had left.

The wind smacked into Chenzira, and he grunted against its strength as the wall of air plastered him back against the board, but the structure did not move. Whatever fixed the thing to the floor was immovable.

Air crashed into Aviama like a tidal wave. She stumbled back against the side of the vat, but the burst dissipated as she looked up—straight into Rana's eyes. Rana's hand dropped, and she faltered back a step.

Biscuits. She was the windcaller. Aviama lifted both hands, letting the strength of the wind build in her palms as a shadow flickered over Rana's blazing eyes.

"Get out of here, Tally!"

Chenzira's call came too late. She hoped he'd know she wouldn't have listened, anyway. Wind ripped from her lungs in a harsh whoosh, coarse against her throat, until there was nothing but nothing.

Burning. Burning. Burning.

Excruciating pain tore her apart, from her throat down her windpipe to her starving lungs. Twice, her vision went dark. The world spun. Sutekh was trying to stand, steadying himself on the side of the vat, one hand against his temple. Blood ran down the side of his face.

The wind began to flee from her palms. If she was going to use it, it had to be now.

Chenzira was still tilted over the vat of a mystery, boiling, poisonous death. And Aviama was about to die in front of him, before Sutekh executed him and rid himself of his problems once and for all.

She could use her last blast of air to kill Rana, but Sutekh would only kill her the next moment, and the melderblood guards would come to soon enough. Could Chenzira handle Aviama murdering his sister?

In the heat of battle, indecision would kill faster than any blade. Her vision dimmed, and a tug on the bottom of Aviama's dry-heaving, hacking, empty lungs told her Rana was one hand-twitch away from ending it all.

Aviama swung both her hands in a wide arc and launched herself sideways. Rana screamed. The vat toppled with a crash. Aviama's shoulder slammed into the tile floor, and she gasped for breath in a heap as pain ricocheted through her body.

Bubbling, boiling slaughter sloshed across the smooth polish of the Great Hall. Sutekh shrieked the otherworldly, blood-curdling screech of a ghoul stretched between the world of the living and the realm of the dead as the poison he'd prepared for Chenzira swallowed his foot.

Scorching fire leaped from Rana's hands, a barrier ridge of flame leaping to her defense and cauterizing Sutekh's ankle in a swooping semicircle. Chenzira was shouting. Rana was screaming. Sutekh's shriek still echoed in Aviama's ringing ears. The blaze licked at the tile floor and sent the poison evaporating up in clouds of dark fumes.

The heat of the fire warmed Aviama's skin on one side, an odd contradiction to the cool of the tile underneath her. She rolled to one side, blinking at the destruction before her. The tile floor was rough and uneven where the vat had spilled, riddled with holes and lumps like moth-eaten cloth tossed over a pile of rocks. The air was calm around them, undisturbed by warring windcallers, though fire still burned in patches, feasting on little remaining puddles of liquid on the floor.

Rana huddled over Sutekh. One of his feet was missing, a blackened stub now replacing the place where his ankle should have been.

Aviama's pulse pounded in her ears as she shoved up off the floor, threw up an air shield, and raced to Chenzira's side.

Fingers trembling, she undid the leather buckles holding

him to the board. He was talking, but she only cared enough to note he was alive.

"Get through the door, down the hall, and out to the first courtyard to the right. A friend got word out about our situation, and they're supposed to be trying to set up an escape for us there by the wall."

Aviama blinked. "You had time to contact friends?"

He nodded as he half-fell off the board into her waiting arms. She crumbled under his weight, then pulled at his arms to draw one over her shoulders. They were still secured to his sides with whatever silvery substance had held them fast before.

"First, kill the guards and throw up a shield. I saw one move."

Aviama glanced toward the fallen guards, and Rana struggling under Sutekh's weight just as Aviama struggled under Chenzira's. Rana glanced up with massacre in her eyes, and Aviama bolstered the air shield around them just before a ball of fire flew at their heads. It exploded against the barrier with a shower of sparks.

Chenzira grimaced. "Apparently, she's a fireblood."

Aviama pursed her lips. "And a windcaller. She must have a housing artifact."

No time to kill the guards. She'd have to disable her shield to reach them, and there was no chance of her doing that with Rana in the room. But between Rana and Sutekh, they had three of the four elements covered even without the help of the melderblood guards. And considering the ruckus they'd just made, more would be arriving any second.

"Hold still." Aviama kept half the shield up toward Rana, and with her other hand, sliced up as precisely as she could. A sliver of wind blade raked across the silver substance sealing Chenzira's right hand to his thigh.

He winced, and a trickle of blood ran down his forearm—but he was free. His brows rose. "Wow."

Another shower of sparks cascaded against the barrier. Aviama refocused her energy on the shield, completely encircling the two of them. Chenzira reached his free hand to the floor. The tile shook, then cracked in two, and a shard of sharp rock flew to his hand. He slashed his other hand free and turned to his brother and sister.

Sutekh raised his hand. Rana lifted both of hers. The floor beneath their feet shuddered, and Aviama stumbled. A ripple ran across the floor, cracking tiles like dry twigs in a zigzag line from Aviama and Chenzira toward Sutekh, Rana, and the guards who were picking themselves up off the floor.

Tile and rock splintered apart and swallowed the six guards in one devastating fell swoop. The cries of the men cut off as they were buried in rubble. A vine of water wrapped around Aviama's ankle and yanked her off balance. Chenzira grabbed her elbow as she fell. She glanced down. Water had snaked from the fountain through the cracks under their feet, allowing Sutekh to attack from below.

But the moment Chenzira caught her, he fell next. Chenzira threw out a palm toward his brother, and the floor engulfed Sutekh and Rana together up to the waist. Aviama clawed her way back up over the shambled floor and wrapped an arm around Chenzira again. The blistering wounds along his torso weren't bleeding, but considering what the liquid substance had done to the floor, Aviama was afraid to ask what effects it might be having on his body internally.

He held onto her but didn't turn toward the door.

"Come with us, Rana." Chenzira's voice cracked on her name. "He's a liar. I only wanted to keep you safe. I'm sorry i'm late. I wanted to come sooner. But I did come back for you."

Rana's lip curled to a snarl as she swept a hand around the destruction of the room. "This is the real you, isn't it?"

"I don't know. Is this the real you?" Chenzira gestured at her, the last of her fire dancing in the space between them. "When I left, The Return hadn't happened yet. Melderbloods didn't exist. But Sutekh has always been a python. He knows what to say, how to draw you in, until it's too late. Tell me it isn't too late, Kes."

A storm rolled in across her features like clouds barely holding in the rain. Sutekh glanced at her face, then reached for the fountain.

"She's not your Kestrel anymore. She's come back home, and your sweet words will only kill you faster. You know Father will side with me after this. On everything. I've only got one more gift to give him—and I'll give you front-row seats."

Chenzira's dark eyes narrowed. "You'll have to catch us first."

A chill ran down her spine at the ice in his words, and Aviama barely had time to stabilize herself before the tile she and Chenzira shared shot across the floor toward the door, leaving Sutekh and Rana behind.

Fire and wind assaulted the barrier, and Aviama bent every last shred of focus on holding it steady. Chenzira reached for the handle, but it shriveled into knotted brass and dropped from the door like crumpled paper.

He swore and ripped the door from its place with a mighty wrench of its metal hinges. Aviama gaped at him. Only that morning, Chenzira had collapsed half a cliff onto his brother's men in the cove. But seeing him in action, the precision and power he wielded as a master quakemaker, took her breath away.

Until she saw through the open doorway.

Two dozen guards waited in the corridor, and over half of

them held up their palms rather than their weapons. Melderbloods. The tile Aviama and Chenzira still stood on broke apart. Chenzira wrapped his arm around her hips, and together they jumped through the open doorway. Aviama blasted several of them backward before re-forming the air shield on the other side of the door jamb, but not before a wall of fire leaped up along the floor. Chenzira split the floor left and right, the flaming rubble scrunched to either side as he swept the two of them along.

Aviama held up both hands against the pressure of wind and fire beating down on her air barrier. Chenzira zigzagged them through the mass of guards, knocking three down and blasting past the rest on a fresh chunk of tile, one arm still holding Aviama close against his body as they flew down the hall. But Chenzira wasn't the only quakemaker.

They slid through the double doors at the end of the hall, leaped off the tile, and took off running into a wide-open courtyard. Aviama's heart pounded in frenzied rhythm as her aching legs carried her through carved columns and mosaic renderings of ancient battles, over a flowerbed of red-and-blue blossoms, and out onto masterful stonework spilling down three steps and flowing around a large rectangular pool. The gentle breeze of chill night air wafted against her bare arms as they fled by moonlight, its illumination doubled by a perfect reflection in the serene, still waters beneath it.

A single door faced them on the far end of the courtyard, set in an arched alcove flanked by four pillars. The end of a rope whipped over the top of it, over the wall, as Aviama's rich borrowed sandals slapped the stone. Someone was waiting for them.

Fire roared in from either side just as they neared the edge of the water, three meters high, cutting them off from the stone pathways. Chenzira stopped short, the angry reds and oranges of the flame's light flickering across his skin. Aviama skidded to a halt beside him.

Heavy footsteps pounded closer and closer behind them as the guards navigated the ruins of the corridor and gave chase out to the courtyard. Aviama glanced at the pool.

"The water. I'll make a bubble for us and roll across."

Chenzira winced. "I'd rather take the fire."

If Sutekh made it out to the courtyard, his precision as a crestbreaker could be lethal if he caught them on the water. How good were the other melderbloods? The Return wasn't that long ago. Few had the chance to train as well as Aviama, though Keket had done remarkably well in this regard. Or was it only Sutekh and Rana who had done so well?

Aviama knew better than anyone how devastatingly dangerous an untrained melder could be. There was no good option.

She pooled the wind between her hands and shoved it into the heart of the blaze. Sweat broke out on every square inch of her skin. The blisters on Chenzira's torso took on a new color, pure crimson with lilac splinters spreading out from the wound. No, not lilac. Violet. Orchid. Mauve.

Anything but lilac.

"Behind us! Shield!"

Aviama pressed into the fire, but the flames were thicker than any she'd seen before. Keeping a thick enough wall of air between them and the flames had already set a tremble in her bones. She'd rarely felt such strain when using her powers in the open air, but she could feel the wind pulled in different directions, fickle in its choice, slow in its answer.

Windcallers had entered the courtyard. Many of them. Firebloods, too, must be working together, to hold such fierce, unyielding flames so thick for so long.

Aviama couldn't manage adding a shield. Beside her,

Chenzira held up both hands. Slim, smooth-cut slates of rock flew to his palms and melded together as one, wrapping his forearm like a perfectly fit shield, complete with arm straps. He leaned his shoulder into the stone and hoisted it at their backs. Showers of sparks exploded against it. Fire pressed in around it, and the stone of the shield moved almost like liquid to fend off attacks.

They were not yet even halfway past the pool of the courtyard, and already the shouts of the guards proved all of them had caught up and would be upon them—except for their own fire, keeping them at bay as it surrounded their quarry. The guards had the luxury of time and endurance and numbers. They could wait while Chenzira and Aviama exhausted themselves in the fight.

A blast of air smacked into the center of the shield with the strength of at least three windcallers, and the two of them fell headlong into the flames. Flames licked at her skin. Blackened stone pavement waited beneath as her body fell. Chenzira's full weight and the added stone shield tumbled over her from above.

Biscuits. I'm about to be a sandwich.

Aviama dropped the barrier completely and threw the last of her gathered wind at their plummeting bodies, just enough to plunge them headlong into the pool.

33

C old water smacked into her. The stark contrast from the scalding inferno to the chill water took her breath away. She tumbled down, down—until she no longer knew which way was down, or whether she spun in any particular direction at all but floated in a sea of oblivion.

Something seized her by the waist and pulled her sideways. Or was it up? She didn't know. She didn't care.

When she broke the surface, everything hit her at once. Aviama sucked in a deep breath. Water sloshed around her. Chenzira struggled to keep them both at the surface, lugging her dead weight. Fire still blazed on both sides of the pool. The rope still hung over the top of the building on the opposite side of the courtyard.

Aviama glanced behind them. Two dozen melderbloods lined the edge of the pool, momentarily distracted by two new figures approaching. The orange of the flames caught every piece of gold on the royal sibling pair as Sutekh and Rana moved into the courtyard, one of Sutekh's arms around Rana's shoulders. He used her like a crutch, swinging one foot to walk, and using her weight for the next stride, where his second foot should have touched the ground.

Except he had no second foot.

Chenzira swore. "Wake up, Tally. We're in the water. Get us that bubble and let's go."

Life rippled through her chest, the kind that blazed brightest right before being snuffed out. Currents of air whisked over her head toward the windcallers at the edge of the pool. Aviama treaded water with two legs and one hand, summoning the wind low across the surface of the water with the other. No use fighting for air against so many. A small bubble formed beneath their feet against the water, lifting them from the belly of the pool until she had both hands free again.

Fire shot across the expanse, and Aviama jerked them sideways out of its path. Chenzira lifted one hand toward the edge of the pool, rocking the footing underneath the opposition, but the Keketi quakemakers only bore down on the stonework until it was firm and immovable again.

"They've blocked me out. I've got nothing." Chenzira called for more slate, and a smaller shield flew to his arm as he fended off fireballs. "Get us out of the water, or we'll never make it."

Aviama spun the air around them and rolled the bubble across the surface of the water, picking up speed as they went. Chenzira pulled shards of slate from the stonework around the pool and shot sliver after sliver like volleys of arrows into the guards. Four fell before any of them realized what had happened. Until—

Bump. Kshhhh. A wall of water rose up, crashing against Aviama's barrier. Aviama and Chenzira fell back as they hit the edges of the bubble. Rivulets of raised water weaved around them like dozens of eels, taunting them. Aviama dragged more air into the bubble, forced it forward with greater strength, but it was like breathing through a thin reed. Rana and the other windcallers were doing their best work. There was little free wind to be had.

The water eels climbed the invisible edges of the sphere around them, choking their lifeline until Aviama and Chenzira were entirely shut off from the open air. Water surged over and around them. The light of the flames and dancing starlight fell dim against the inky dark of the pool. Up, up, they rose, as Sutekh and his crestbreaker minions lifted them high in a tower of water.

For an impossible moment, they hung in midair, except in water, until a sudden plunging motion sent Aviama's stomach toward her throat and the two of them hurtling downward into the depths. How deep was this pool, anyway?

Terror gripped her by the gullet. Her ears filled with the rushing of the water pressing in on every side. The boundaries of the bubble around them shuddered as her focus broke. Half of their precious air supply fled as she and Chenzira toppled head over heels, twice, three times, a collision of arms and legs and solid bodies that was sure to leave some bruises.

Chenzira was shouting, but Aviama heard nothing over the din of the water and the thundering crash of her own pulse striking a doomsday drum in her ears.

Focus or die. Focus or die.

Aviama latched onto the thought. Chenzira caught her as they fell, finally pulling her body against his, wrapping one strong arm around her hips, his chest firm against her back, his other arm tight around her midsection. Fear of crashing into each other removed, she concentrated all her sapping energy into the boundaries of the air around them.

Stay with me.

She couldn't tell if she spoke to Chenzira, or the wind, but both answered with mercy, hovering all around her like a cocoon.

Arena, brig, or depths of the sea, let me never be parted from you again.

The thought surprised her, in the midst of the chaos. But wasn't chaos kind of their thing? Why else did he call her Tally, if it wasn't for the two of them taking turns making rash, reckless decisions in the service of keeping each other alive?

Aviama's arms ached, her head throbbing with the strain of withstanding the pressure of the water threatening their air supply. Their one salvation from the water that would hand them over entirely to Sutekh. Aviama winced.

"I can't do this much longer."

Chenzira adjusted his grip around her, his voice rough against her ear. "When he's done toying with us, he's going to drag us backward and dump us at his feet."

"Maybe he'll toss is into the air again. If he does—"

But they were already moving. Sideways this way, sideways that way, in a wild, disorienting zigzag, and finally up, up, back to the surface.

Yes. A thrill ran down her spine. This was it. Her one chance. Now or never.

She took a deep breath and turned her head so Chenzira would hear her.

"Catch."

The bubble of air around them convulsed as energy ran through it, trapped yet whipped into a frenzy. With a snap of both wrists, Aviama shattered the bubble outward, disrupting the cohesion of the water around them. They broke free, the force of the blast casting the water in every direction.

"Sands."

If his mouth weren't right by her ear, the *whoosh* of the

wind and water would have swallowed Chenzira's muttering. Aviama smiled. He could do it. She knew he could.

And then he did. A sheet of thin stone slipped under their feet and skidded them across the water, expanding into stairs as they moved. Together, they ran up the steps as a fresh wall of water erupted up from the pool to meet their feet.

Their sandals hit the stonework on the far side of the pool, and the sheet of stone fixed itself upright in place behind them. The crash of the water clapped against the rock, but Chenzira and Aviama were already gone. And the rope dangled down before them.

Ten paces. Eight paces. Five.

Shouts. Screams. Pounding feet. Whooshing air. Blasts of fire. None of it mattered. Because Chenzira's hand had already sealed around the edge of the rope. He gave it a sharp tug, and Aviama leaped to meet him as the rope began to move, hauled up and over the wall of the courtyard by whoever awaited them on the far side.

Chenzira caught her in the crook of his arm, and she wrapped an arm around his neck and planted a kiss on his cheek. He grinned, and the light in his eyes could have lit her life for the rest of her days.

Her feet found the ledge of the wall, and new energy swirled around her like dawn breaking across a horizon long steeped in moonless onyx. Aviama threw up an air shield behind her as shards of rock, blasts of fire, and gales of wind assaulted them. Chenzira caught the shards and sent them spinning back on the Keketi guards.

The wall of fire on either side of the courtyard pool was gone, and the two dozen guards rushed toward them en masse. Sutekh and Rana stepped onto the water side by side, and Sutekh directed it to carry them across as ghosts might drift through a cemetery of their own making. Onward they came, Rana's free hand glowing with the power of fire, her hair streaming out behind her with the prowess of a skilled windcaller.

Aviama's older sister had experience with housing artifacts. Her stomach pinched as she regarded Rana for a moment. Using stored tabeun power bound in an artifact wasn't natural. It was sifal. Wrong. Dark. As a conduit of power, wyronite enhanced power running through it from a natural source. But using housing artifacts made of other materials came with side effects. And Keket had no natural wyronite resources.

Despite the dangers, the four melders of The Crumbling had still created housing artifacts. Aurin, Garjan, Dru, and Raisa. Semra, Aviama's sister-in-law, had Aurin's Spear. Or at least, she did when Aviama left Jannemar. But where were the other artifacts? Did Radha have one? Had more been found than those of the four final elemental melders?

"Aviama, now!"

Aviama ripped her gaze from Rana's scalding scowl and followed Chenzira four long strides across the wall and out over the ledge to freedom below.

Only, she didn't fall. She hung in the air, like a puppet on a string, yanked this way and that at another's will.

She reached for the wind, but it was not her wind that held her there. Aviama strained against it, but as she turned sideways, she caught sight of Rana holding one palm up toward her, and a line of windcallers adding power to the call of the Keketi royal.

On the other side of the wall, Durga, Umed, Osahar, and Husani stood with four horses. Osahar, Umed, and Husani pulled the rope that hauled Chenzira over the edge. One final gate stood open beyond them, waiting only for two more riders.

Durga blasted against the air surrounding Aviama, and Aviama reached out to touch it. The air around her split, and she half-fell before the windcallers behind her wrapped their air currents around her upper arms. Her damp skirts whipped against her legs in the wind, her hair billowing this way and that. But her hands were free.

Chenzira hit the ground on the far side of the wall and rolled to his feet. When he spun back toward her, his face drained of color. In a flash, fury replaced the fear in his eyes.

Melder guards poured out the double doors beneath Aviama. Chenzira yelled at Husani, and the two of them brought the structure crashing down. Half a dozen got out before the wall collapsed with a reverberating clamor of cracking pillar and stone that shook the ground.

Fire flew from Osahar's fingertips, meeting a stream of flame from over the wall. Aviama, with Durga's added power, wrenched herself free of the enemy's wind power, and dropped to the ground with a groan.

Everywhere she looked, fire and wind exchanged blows. Missiles of every color exploded in shattering rock, gales of wind, crackling earth, and spurts of water spiking up through the fissures from underground. Aviama launched herself onto the nearest horse, Chenzira climbing up after. She wheeled the animal round, but its hooves sank into broken soil like quicksand.

The horse whinnied and bucked, but the poor thing was stuck fast. Chenzira freed its hooves, but a fireball hit him square in the chest and he fell sideways off the horse. Aviama threw up a shield in the direction of the fireball, but a vine of water reached up from the ground and wrapped itself around her ankle, dragging her off the back of the horse from the far side.

Melder guards threw themselves over the wall, and in the

next instant, a dozen Keketi royal guards surrounded the six of them in the outer ward between the courtyard and the exterior wall of the palace grounds. Aviama slammed into the ground with only time to summon the slightest air cushion to break her fall.

Across the outer ward, the gate closed, sealing off their escape route. Archers popped up on the outer wall, three dozen at least, and launched volley after volley of arrows down on the intruders. Durga threw up an air shield, but with so many windcallers pulling at the air around them, her shield couldn't cover all the angles of the archers. Husani shot up clumps of earth to stop the progress of any arrows that survived her, Osahar aiding as he incinerated them with fire.

But that left only Umed, Aviama, and Chenzira to fend off the coming wave. Aviama ripped the air from the lungs of four windcallers. They dropped dead on the spot. A twinge of guilt settled into the back of her mind, but she couldn't afford to waste time on it now.

A ring of fire surged into being around the six prey. Osahar turned his palms toward it, but a chunk of rock flew into the back of his head, and he dropped like a sack of potatoes. Husani made a choking sound and fell sideways, unconscious. Umed still had a hold on a stream of water, hijacking it from the control of the palace crestbreakers, and three foes fell to his skill.

Chenzira, Aviama, Durga, and Umed formed a tight circle inside the ring of flame, backs to one another, facing outward, but the arrows were still coming. The ground was still shaking. The wind still whistled over and through the blaze, feeding the inferno and forcing Aviama to fend off the mightiest of its blows as Durga held up the shield against the arrows.

The ground split open between them, rocketing Aviama

and Durga to one side, and Chenzira and Umed to the other. Husani's body toppled into a deep fissure and was lost to the abyss. A scream tore through Aviama's hoarse throat, and she threw a gale straight at Sutekh. He wavered, and she ripped the air from his lungs.

She would leave nothing left. She would take it all. She wanted to see him crumble until all that remained was—

Pshhhhhhhhht.

Whistling air brought the same damp whiff of chemicals that she'd smelled in the streets, when a cloth had smothered her face. But this time, the windcallers sealed it in around them, smothering the area in a soft cloud of the stuff, until the taste of it was all her senses could handle.

Black spots interrupted her vision. Chenzira rocked on his heels. Umed threw a hand outward as he hit his knees. Durga had disappeared from Aviama's side.

And then Aviama sank to her knees, staring bleakly into the yawning fissure that had taken Husani. She lifted a hand to the wind, but as she did, she couldn't quite remember what she had been doing with her hand in the air in the first place.

Water crept up through the soil and wrapped itself around her ankles. A crackling fire warmed her even as the chill of water worked its way up through the dirt with an earthy smell clinging to the tangy bite of the chemical scent, sending her head spinning.

Aviama pitched sideways, and her body melted into the ground so that only her neck and head remained above it.

"Sands and sea." A man decked in gold and rich clothing sucked his teeth and gave a condescending shake of his head. "You don't know how to play dirty, do you? You only know how to bluff."

Aviama fought to keep her eyes open. It was important,

wasn't it, to keep her eyes open? Why was this man looking at her with such disdain? And why did he only have one leg?

The gold-collared man shrugged, as if disappointed in someone. "The guards from the hall inside are alive. You didn't even kill me when you could have. When you should have. Stupid."

He gestured to four corpses lying on the ground a stone's throw away. Aviama could hardly make them out in the dark from her position on the ground, and through the arms and legs of fallen friends around her. At least, she had a feeling they might be friends. Were they?

"This is a mild casualty report, at best."

Again, the man with the gold collar sucked his teeth. His arm was wrapped around the shoulders of a stunning young woman who looked like she'd eaten nothing but shards of glass for breakfast and feasted on fury for lunch. The important man glanced up at an assortment of people behind him and snapped his fingers.

"Summon the reaver. We set sail tonight." He drilled Aviama with a dark snarl. "It's high time we escort the princess home."

34

W ooden boards creaked. Muffled footsteps moved to and fro above her. The air tasted of salt.

Aviama groaned. Must she dream of *Raisa's Revenge*, after being trapped on it for so long, and escaping it only recently? She reached up to rub her eyes free of the remnants of sleep, but her hands stopped halfway to her face. A chain clinked.

Her dreams didn't usually include chains. They usually focused on all the dead she'd lost. If this were a dream, Husani should be making his debut appearance. Her stomach dropped.

And then she was fully awake.

Everyone stupid enough to have followed her from Jazir sat slumped against the hull of a ship, chained at the wrist, hands bound in an airtight quakemaker's contraption of thin stone so their hands looked like a roughhewn sculpture of hands slightly larger than their own. It was a more finessed version of what she'd been trapped in before, in the palace in Keket, and perhaps what they would have attempted then if they'd had more time—or if the quakemaker had had more skill.

The familiar rocking motion made her stomach churn, though less from seasickness as from the misfortune of returning to sea after escaping it so extremely briefly. The women lined one side of the gun deck at the far end of a ship, with Durga furthest into the most claustrophobic of the options, as the hull tapered near the storage room at the end. Teja sat beside her, shackled at the wrist but hands unfettered, with Sai positioned next, and Aviama at the end of the line of women and closest to the rows of sailor bunks.

Across from them on the opposite wall, Osahar's massive frame left his feet impeding on Durga's cramped space, with his brother Zahur beside him across from Teja, Manan across from Sai, Umed across from Aviama, and Chenzira at a diagonal to her at the end of the line of men. The little girl slept soundly, her feet tucked under Sai's legs, her head resting in Aviama's lap.

Aviama swallowed hard against the lump forming in her throat. Tears brimmed along her lashes. She blinked them back hard, staring up at the ceiling to keep them from falling. When had Sutekh found the others? How had Sutekh found the others?

Tears abated, she glanced down at the little girl's curly hair and soft cheek. Part of her was glad the little girl was with her again—she'd know Aviama hadn't abandoned her. But wouldn't it be better to be abandoned than to be used as a blackmail chip of coercion, witness to more death and destruction, and made to live in the squalid conditions of yet another abductor's ship?

The lump size doubled in her throat. She leaned her head back against the wooden boards at her back and shut her eyes.

How could it be that she'd traveled so far, learned so

much, and faced so many dangers, only to be returned home just in time to watch it burn? It felt like Aviama had left Jannemar a lifetime ago, and yesterday, all at once. She'd left home as a young naïve princess to compete for the hand of the Radhan prince and gain some inside information.

She'd won the competition but lost herself. And when she found herself again, it was through miscreant criminals who smuggled her in and out of the palace, and bathhouse magic lessons at night, and cooking lessons that were really pick-pocket and sleight-of-hand classes in disguise. But most of all, it was in Chenzira, and Sai, and Bhumi. And maybe even Durga.

The strange people she'd met along the way who she would never have had the pleasure or the misfortune to meet otherwise. A deep pang hit her heart as she thought of Laksh singing and Bhumi clapping as Onkar spun Aviama around in a dance across the kitchen floor on the *Wraithweaver*.

Chenzira had been the first one to frighten her in Radha. Now it was losing him that scared her the most. The mischief in his eyes, his unending quips, the way he pushed her buttons and pulled her in and made her want to settle in against his chest and kiss him until the sun went down. He made her ache and hope and yearn and love in deep ways she'd never experienced before.

He drove her mad, and held her close, until floating pieces of stolen dinner in the air across a dark brig became her favorite time of day on a long voyage. Even when they couldn't be together, it was the little things that kept them connected—the little things that stirred her heart and exploded her stomach with tingling warmth that filled her head to toe. Like the way she sent him a breeze the day they'd landed on Jazir, and the way he'd moved the sand at her feet.

The way she called him crazy, and the way he called her Tally.

The little girl was Aviama, but younger: an orphan, thrown into a ragtag group of people and dragged across the sea. Aviama had watched a knife blade bury itself into her mother's chest, and the little girl had watched Abasi's goons drag her mother away for execution. Aviama hoped the little one hadn't heard her mother's screams. Perhaps she had, and that's why she'd been so quiet. Perhaps those screams haunted her day and night, even at her young age.

She still needed a name.

Everybody deserved a name. Should it be Radhan, like her mother? Or Jannemari, like Aviama? Or Keketi, like the place where they'd met?

Yes, the little girl was a younger version of Aviama, in some sense.

But Chenzira? Chenzira was home.

The word was warm and soft like honey on fresh-baked bread, but the aftertaste was sickening and sour as old milk. Her physical home was under siege, and the Horon Mines had already fallen to Radha. Zephan and Semra would be on the front lines with Zezura, Semra's dragon. Who would be watching Shamaran Castle? Was whatever horrid vessel they were on now bound for the thick of the battle to offer aid to Radha and secure their alliance, or to strike the castle at the heart of the kingdom while it was most vulnerable?

And her other home, her heart home, was chained to a ship. Out of reach. Tortured, scarred, and hurting. Being sent away from his birthplace for the second time in four years.

She opened her eyes. Aviama hadn't noticed before, but it was light out. Rays of sun worked its way down through the hatch halfway down the deck, and the cracks between the boards over their heads spilled bright light. Gunports offered even more light, the first cannon positioned well out of reach, and the rest set at perfect intervals down the length of the vessel. Most of the bunks were empty, save a few sleeping souls draped here and there down the deck.

How long had they been unconscious? When had Sutekh caught the rest of her companions? How long ago had they set sail? How far from Siada had they gone?

Her gaze drifted back to Chenzira. His feet stretched out in front of him, his white schenti marred by scorch marks. The arms of the women were bound in front of them, but the arms of the men were bound behind them, just as Abasi had done with his slaves. Two golden upper armbands graced his well-defined biceps, but the collar so familiar to Keketi men had been stripped from him back at the palace. He'd escaped the palace with something else instead—the red blisters trailing along his stomach.

Escaped wasn't exactly the right word. They'd almost escaped, but in the end, they'd leaped from the pot to the fire. Although the pot had had a surprising amount of fire. Some of it from Rana, no less.

Aviama shifted her weight under the little girl's sleeping form and squinted across the small space for a better look at his torso. Well, not his torso specifically. Though she couldn't complain about the view. Corded arms, broad shoulders, muscled lines everywhere along his sun-kissed body ...

She squeezed her eyes shut and tried again. The welts. The blisters. Yes, there we go. They were angry red, but more than that, they were raised and splintered outward like violet spider silk.

The rest of him looked okay. More than okay, in her estimation, other than a few bruises. His beard was starting to get scruffier again, with less of the diligent upkeep he was used to, and his eyes—

He was staring right at her.

Aviama sucked in an involuntary gasp. Her stomach flip-flopped, and she swallowed.

"How are you feeling?"

"You'll have to be more specific. Do you mean how am I feeling about losing to my brother, or how am I feeling about being chained up without powers on a ship?" The corner of his mouth twitched. "Or do you mean how am I feeling about laying my eyes on a stunningly gorgeous woman in the royal dress of my homeland, slits in her dress revealing perfect legs, only to discover her deep green eyes looking me up and down first?"

Her lips parted. How could he do that? How could he turn her inside out with a word and a look, when they were chained out of reach on the precipice of death yet again? It wasn't fair. She cleared her throat.

"Um, all of those, I guess."

He let out a long breath, his eyes never leaving hers. "I feel pretty spectacular about the last one. It's the thing keeping me going despite the other ones. Good for the ego. Thank you."

Aviama pursed her lips, but she couldn't quite keep the smile off her face. She rolled her eyes to cover it up. By the twinkle in Chenzira's gaze, she'd failed entirely. Aviama cocked her head. "I'm all for helping out when I can. And how are you feeling otherwise?"

He started to shrug, then winced. "Less spectacular."

"It looks like whatever was in the vat caused a problem."

Chenzira glanced down at his torso. "It does look a bit worse than my other injuries."

"What do we know so far?"

"We're back on *Raisa's Revenge*."

Aviama snorted. "Yeah, the similarity hasn't escaped me.

Figures, right? Have you been awake long enough to notice anything about the crew, how many, or where we are?"

"No, I mean, we're literally back on *Raisa's Revenge*. It's the same ship. We're on the gun deck of a four-deck vessel, and the hatch you're sitting on was my ceiling for months and months. That gouge there in the floor was courtesy of Umed, when one of the sailors thought he was too spirited and needed to be humbled."

Aviama's jaw dropped. She glanced down the length of the ship. Stairs at the far end could be the same leading down to the trapdoor above the pit she'd been kept in for the months-long voyage from Ghosts' Gorge to Jazir, but it could be a lot of things.

Her gaze drifted down to the hatch beneath her legs, and wooden floorboards running toward it from the main belly of the ship. A half-inch deep gouge marked the floor two paces from the edge of the hatch, decorated by several scorch marks on either side. The inside of the gouge had rough edges, as though long splintered bits of wood had been hewn or twisted off.

"What happened when the sailor engaged?"

Chenzira grinned. "He was humbled."

Aviama bit her lip to keep from smiling. It didn't seem right to smile. They were in the pit of horrendousness. The slave ship of disgust. The ... why couldn't she think straight?

"I did kill someone the night before I left home."

His voice was solemn, and when she lifted her eyes to his, he stared down at the planks between them.

"I tried to protect someone. I didn't mean to kill him. At least, I don't think I did." He swallowed. "My father did offer me a third of the kingdom and a slew of slaves. That much is true. But I didn't want more land or more power. I told Father I would accept only on the condition that I could rule it without slaves and prove I could find a way to thrive economically without them, as a precursor to doing away with the slavery system entirely. I'd grown close with several of the slaves in our household, and they'd come to trust me enough to share their stories. I didn't want to be part of a system that would do to others what my father had done to them."

Aviama leaned forward over the little girl's slumbering form, intent on hearing every word Chenzira spoke. His voice was soft, and she needed every ounce of concentration to catch what he said.

"Sutekh said I threatened to crumble the kingdom, and I suppose in a sense I did—to put to death the only way of life all our region of the world has known for thousands of years. Nearly every kingdom of every color and creed has enslaved one another. Perhaps, once upon a time, kings thought themselves merciful to enslave rather than to kill those who were defeated in war. Perhaps my father thought the same, that the free labor boosting Keket's economy was a legacy of mercy, and that their work was owed in exchange for his continued kindness. But the stories the slaves assigned to me told me were not stories of kindness, and many generations had passed since any wars with their nations."

She hadn't thought much about it, but it was true. In her history lessons, all the ancient peoples had slaughtered each other for land and resources, and the victors often took the losers as slaves. Jannemar, too, had engaged in such practices at one time, but slavery had been banned many years ago now. Aviama hadn't ever considered how anyone could justify such a practice, however wrong that justification might be. She only knew it was wrong, and that anyone who thought otherwise was wrong too.

Chenzira continued. "Before I left, I purchased the freedom of my childhood servant-slave, Ozan. I'd tried to do so before, but had never been successful until I pushed for laws regarding the treatment of slaves as a small stepping stone toward their freedom. It took years. At last, there was an avenue to legitimately free a slave rather than simply transfer ownership, which had been the only option before. A slave could be given papers by his or her owner, sealed by the family's official seal, and could seek a life, even within Keket, as a free person. They could technically even own property, though none had ever been given the opportunity.

"When I gave Ozan his papers, Sutekh saw it as the beginning of the end. Of anarchy. Of his own slaves and the slaves in his provinces rising up and demanding their own freedom; of riots, of losing control, of having to allot a great portion of his budget toward employing slaves that had worked for free before. Many of his projects would have to be put on hold, perhaps indefinitely, if such a financial shift came about. And he wasn't the only one who reacted poorly.

"The guards and much of the nobility reacted with hostility to the idea, but I had gained enough pull with a percentage of the nobles that I knew Ozan's freedom could not be stopped legally. And once he was free, I had plans for the rest. It would just take time."

Aviama's chest tightened. She thought of her reaction to slavery when they'd landed in Jazir, and Chenzira's insistence that she couldn't rip down the system in a day. That attempting to do so would not only fail, but have disastrous consequences. She'd thought he didn't care enough to end slavery. In reality, he'd worked for years to overturn the system from the inside, and he was right—when she had tried to free the slaves on Jazir, Sutekh had only gone behind her and had many of them rounded up and killed. She had failed.

When Chenzira looked back up at her, his face was drawn, his eyes soft. "My father saw it as a rebellion, as rejection both of him and his offer of an inheritance of my own. He'd hoped I would carry on his legacy more reliably than Sutekh, and to preserve the kingdom from his arrogance, gambling, and extremist tendencies. But then Ozan presented his papers to the keeper of the house, and a guard attacked him.

"I heard the scuffle and ran toward the sound. Ozan was on the ground, bruised and beaten. His head was bleeding. I jumped into the fight and struck the guard in the temple with the butt of my sword. He swung for me, and I sliced him through the middle. I did not hesitate. My battle training kicked in, and when I saw a vulnerability, I took it."

He winced. "There were witnesses. Sutekh had me charged with murder, and it wasn't unfounded. The charge put my father in an awkward position—to carry out justice and thereby strengthen Sutekh's power, with me out of the way—or to go against the law, showing favoritism to his illegitimate son, and losing favor with half the nobles. Nobles whose support he needed."

Aviama chewed her lip. "So he chose Sutekh and the nobles."

Chenzira shook his head. "I didn't give him the chance to choose. I left that night. But Sutekh had attempted to kill my father once already, and I'd heard rumblings of attempts against myself and Rana. She wasn't safe there. So the only way I could get out of Keket with a clear conscience was if I got Rana out of the palace."

Except he hadn't left with a clear conscience. His guilt over abandoning Rana had eaten him alive since the day he departed.

"Why didn't you just take her with you?"

Chenzira sighed. "Her heart has always been in Keket. She wasn't ready to leave, and there was no legitimate accusation against her. I thought she could stay in our homeland, and maybe in time, the danger would pass." Chenzira laid his head back against the hull and closed his eyes. "I was wrong."

Aviama swallowed. What was she supposed to say? What would make it better? Had anything made it better for her when she handed over the konnolan solution to Shiva? When she'd hurt and betrayed everyone she loved, accidental as it may have been?

Better to keep her mouth shut. Maybe the right words would come later. She went in a different direction instead.

"And Ozan? What happened to him?"

"Sutekh destroyed his papers and re-enslaved him, assigning him to himself out of spite. It was Ozan who came to me when I awoke in the palace, strapped to the board in the Hall of Mirrors."

Aviama glanced around them. Nothing would have told her this ship was any different from a thousand others, but she was no sea captain. Both had cannons. Both had a crew of three hundred or so—the *Revenge* was larger than the *Wraith-weaver* had been, not only in length and width but by an entire deck. It was probably slower too.

"Why would Sutekh be on *Raisa's Revenge* instead of one of the royal envoy ships? A slave ship rather than an official Keketi vessel?"

Chenzira shrugged. "That's a good question."

Silence stretched between them. Heavy boots wore down the planks over their heads, crossing back and forth in long, purposeful strides. A scraping motion indicated a box or barrel being slid across the deck, accompanied by a few manly grunts. Several prisoners over from Aviama, Durga shifted and lolled her head to one side, with her ear closer to their conversation. Aviama wondered how long she'd been awake and pretending to sleep, to listen in on their conversation. Still, there was something Aviama needed to say to Chenzira.

"I don't see you any differently now that you've told me," she said. "Thank you. Thank you for telling me your story. Thank you for trusting me with it. And I'm sorry I didn't understand before, in Jazir. When I was angry with you. When I thought you didn't care. I was wrong."

She grimaced at herself for her own stupidity and for how gross the words sounded as they came out of her mouth. How could she have thought he didn't care?

Chenzira pressed his lips together, glanced up at her, then glanced away. "I'm sorry I didn't understand you before, about Shiva. I should have known my reactions would keep you from being able to tell me more about it. You're right, I wouldn't have taken it well. It's not like I'd taken it well so far, accusing you of missing him when you were mourning so many dead."

He looked up then, eyes glistening, a piercing intensity in his expression as though he didn't just see her, but saw deep inside, reaching beyond the veneer of the princess to the little orphan girl who wept for every new death she hadn't had the chance to grieve. "I was an idiot. I'm sorry."

Tears stung her eyes in a sudden wave of emotion she hadn't seen coming. Her stomach knotted and triple knotted, a lump bobbing to her throat. She swallowed. It hurt.

It had been a knife to the heart when he'd thought she was sad after the Gorge because some part of her loved and missed Shiva, rather than because her entire world had been split apart yet again, and more of her friends were dead, and she'd borne the weight of the world on her shoulders, trapped in a siren prison in the morning and handing a man over to his death by evening.

The betrayal from him, especially him, who was supposed to understand her best but instead got it so incredibly wrong, had hurt more than she'd expected. But hearing him now, she almost didn't regret sharing with Sutekh about her tortured soul, as he'd called it. Because Sutekh was despicable. But he'd been right about her. And Chenzira had gotten it wrong, blinded by his own jealousy. It had kept them apart.

Now, the only thing keeping them apart were the chains on the ship. And somehow, the marriage of tenderness and intensity in Chenzira's expression brought a healing salve to wounds she'd long fought to push out of her mind. Hearing how he knew her now, saw her, brought more closeness than his embrace after the Gorge ever could have.

Aviama's chest hitched in a half-sob she didn't quite let free, and she choked out a laugh. "You were an idiot."

He grinned. "I was."

She grinned stupidly back at him, maneuvering her bound hands to wipe a renegade tear from her face with the crook of her elbow. "It's okay. Me too. But thank you for saying it."

Manan's head slid along the hull as if searching for a better position, then stilled. Zahur sniffed. Chenzira cleared his throat and lifted his voice a little.

"We know you're all awake. You can cut the theatrics."

Everyone but Osahar came alive, opening their eyes, arching their backs, stretching their legs, and letting out grunts and sighs. Aviama's jaw dropped. She snapped it shut the next moment, hoping it covered her cluelessness. She'd thought maybe Durga was awake, but she hadn't realized all of them had come to during their discussion. All of them except for Osahar, anyway, who still breathed deep down on the end across from Durga.

Umed let out a grunt as he shifted his weight, repositioning with his arms still bound behind him. "What's our move?"

Chenzira glanced around the gun deck and sighed. "Not sure we have much of one yet. If we really are headed to

Jannemar, we have to wonder why Sutekh hasn't killed us yet —or at least hasn't killed the rest of you."

Aviama pulled back and arched her eyebrows. That seemed a little harsh.

He caught her reaction and lifted one shoulder, then let it drop. "I just mean that I'd expect him to want to torture me—killing me would mean having nowhere to funnel all his vengeful energy, and I'm not sure he's ready for that yet. Not to mention he can torture me to extort you"— he nodded at Aviama—"which kills two birds with one stone. So to speak. Keeping you alive also makes sense if he hopes to extract information about the layout of Castle Shamaran, or the structure of the army, or the habits of the king and queen. If they live up to their reputation, they'll no doubt be leading the charge themselves on the front lines, and any insider intel on weaknesses or patterns could prove invaluable."

"She's a softie. Doesn't like to kill people." Durga pressed her lips into a thin, flat line as she regarded Aviama. But her expression was matter of fact, rather than abrasive. "That makes her easier to manipulate. At least, that's what Sutekh will think. If direct torture doesn't work, he can kill us off one by one until she gives him what he wants. We're leverage."

Aviama didn't miss the "she." Durga still didn't know what to call Aviama. She'd stopped calling her "Royal Highness" the instant she was out of her servant role in the House of the Blessing Sun back in Radha. While Manan used "Commander" with ease, Durga would probably rather die than use that title. And yet, after months of avoiding the use of her name altogether, the only time Durga tried calling Aviama by her name, she'd exposed Aviama's identity to Florian.

Sai leaned into Aviama, arm to arm, in silent support. "It wouldn't be the first time we've all been used as leverage.

That's what Shiva did, and it's why Bhumi is dead. But we can't let that tactic work."

Durga shot her a glare. "You'd rather just give up now and die?"

Sai rolled her eyes. "No. But just as Sutekh may keep us alive long enough to use us for blackmail, if that's our only purpose, he'll just as soon kill us all when he gets what he wants. So if Aviama doesn't talk, we die slowly. If she does talk, we die all at once. I'm not sure that's preferrable."

Sai used Aviama's name naturally, with the warmth of a friend. And that's what she'd become. Aviama thought of how they had held each other, both of them lost to tears, when Sai learned Shiva had killed her parents. She knew about Shiva's blackmail in a more personal way than the others did. And she'd been closer to Bhumi than Durga had been.

Manan glanced from Sai to Durga, and back to Aviama and Chenzira. "Isn't this all a bit premature? We don't even know for sure that's what he's planning."

"No, but it's a good guess." Zahur's words were short, in the common tongue more foreign to him, but his tone was grave. He looked over to get his brother's take, but Osahar was still asleep. Zahur slung himself sideways and rammed his head into Osahar's with a crack. Osahar roared up from his sleeping slouch and whirled to face his imagined adversary, only to stop short at the end of his chains and take stock of his situation. He swore.

"Shhh!" Teja hushed. "Someone's coming."

Aviama turned to look down the gun deck, past the rows of bunks and barrels, to see three figures striding toward them. Two wore the regal attire of Keketi royalty, Sutekh's arm around Rana's shoulder as he practiced walking with a shiny new silver peg attached to the end of his mangled ankle. The third moved with the grace of a cat, his jacket black as night, a red feather bobbing from his hat.

35

A viama's mouth went dry. Florian.

He'd never exactly been an ally. She'd never trusted him. But somehow the sting of betrayal still soured her stomach. Had he taken them to Siada as a favor to Sutekh? Was the ambush in the cove pre-planned? Was he even a pirate?

Sutekh's new appendage clunked its way down the deck, adding a melancholy weight to the approaching footsteps. His face was set like chiseled stone, sculpted into an aristocratic scowl. Rana moved with a fluid grace, dark eyes fixed on Aviama, one hand around her half-brother and one resting lightly on a stunning conch shell studded with rubies and pearls nested against her hip.

The Iolani battle horn.

Aviama sucked in a breath, and the corner of Rana's mouth tipped up. She'd been waiting for her to notice. A burning set in her heart, but she'd already given Rana more satisfaction than she would have liked. Aviama turned her attention to Florian instead, his long, lithe movements putting Rana to shame.

But as he tipped his hat to her, the burning in her chest only swelled to a fever pitch. The little girl in her lap shifted in her sleep, grabbing Aviama's skirts in a fist and adjusting her cheek on Aviama's knee. Aviama rested her forearms over the girl's small body and glanced at Chenzira. The tension rolling off him eased as he relaxed, with effort, and leaned his head back against the hull as though the visitors bored him.

He played it well, but Aviama couldn't quite bring herself to do the same. She dropped her shoulders and straightened from her position on the floor, but a sliver of confidence was all she could manage. From the victory on the trio's faces, there was no fooling their captors.

Sutekh spread his hands, one arm still around Rana's shoulders. "Welcome to *Raisa's Revenge*." He smiled and nodded at Florian. "I understand you've already met my reaver."

Florian fell into a dramatic bow and winked at her. "*Pirate*, for my less sophisticated friends."

Aviama set her jaw. "The word is too good for you."

He shrugged, then reached into his pocket, pulled out a piece of candied ginger, and popped it into his mouth. The scent made her mouth water. How long had it been since they'd eaten? Florian licked his fingers.

"I'll also accept the word *captain*. Gotta get food on the table somehow! You weren't so opposed to stealing when my boy got you food and clothing. A time for everything, hmm?"

At this point, Aviama wasn't so sure Amon was even Florian's kid.

Sutekh cleared his throat. "I understand you know him as Florian, so we'll continue using that name. Now onto more pressing matters. I assume you've gathered that we are on our way to Jannemar. What you probably have not been able to gather is that we travel with a fleet of other ships and are already a day into our journey. It will take us some weeks to arrive, so settle in. If you get tired of your necks, do feel free to make a complaint, and we will make sure you have no more worries. As an added bonus, the more of you who cause problems, the less cramped it will be for you down here."

Chenzira tilted his head against the side of the ship and squinted up at his brother. "Can we skip the death threats and get to the part where you tell us why you're keeping us alive?"

Sutekh smiled, the thin kind of smile that didn't reach his eyes. "Maybe I'm doing it for fun."

He turned to Aviama. "Rana says you're an artist. You're a designer. You can probably draw. Draw me schematics of Shamaran Castle, of the Horon Mines, and of the layout of Ellix since The Return. And I've been to Shamaran Castle before, so I'll know if you fake it."

Aviama pursed her lips. "You've never been to Shamaran Castle. And I've never been to the mines."

Sutekh's lips parted, then flattened. "I *have* been to the castle."

"You haven't. I recognize most of the snooty people that visit. Usually, my father treats them well and then warns me about them, and I make a mental note. You would definitely be categorized in the warning category."

"Is this the same father who exploded? I heard his body shattered like glass. Did he forget to heed his own warnings?"

Sai stifled a gasp beside her, and Aviama's stomach knotted. *He didn't explode.* Other people did. Aviama remembered all too vividly the body parts flung through the smoke as she tore out the doors of the Great Hall and into the thick of the billowing gray. It smelled of ash, coppery blood, and burnt flesh. And her father's face, when she'd made it to his side ...

She swallowed and resisted the urge to lift her chin. Better to play it off as neutral as possible.

"That's not what happened. But I can understand why you'd think so. Truth has never been a high priority resource for you."

Florian laughed. "I told you she was fun."

"I've experienced her pleasantries before, thank you." Sutekh unwrapped his arm from around Rana and put a heavy hand on Florian's closest shoulder instead. "Speak out of turn again, Captain, and all you'll be captain of is the rowboat in the middle of the Aeian Sea."

Chenzira arched an eyebrow. "Don't get too upset, dear brother. Wouldn't want you to fall. You're looking a bit unstable these days."

Sutekh adjusted his standing position with a wince and glowered at Chenzira. Aviama wondered what magic he'd used to get his ankle stub ready for the fancy metal peg substitute foot. Even if there had been some miraculous healing, surely the pain was excruciating.

"Enough."

The bite in Rana's voice startled all of them. Even Sutekh nearly staggered at the suddenness of it. Rana stepped toward Aviama, crouched in front of her, and dropped her gaze over the girl.

Aviama's breathing quickened. The little one still slept, peaceful in Aviama's lap, oblivious to the crowd of killers assembled around her. What would Aviama do to protect her? What wouldn't she do?

But how could she protect the girl without giving Sutekh and Rana what they wanted? Were they cruel enough to threaten the baby too?

Sutekh locked eyes with Aviama. "Look at that. Fake mother and daughter reunited at last." His lips twisted into an eerie smile. "For however short a time."

Bile flew to her throat, and she froze. Yes, he was that cruel.

What Aviama couldn't quite decide was if Rana shared his ruthlessness. And if she did, did hers have limits?

Rana reached out, slowly, and brushed a soft curl out of the girl's face.

Aviama's heart stopped. Pain radiated from the lump in her throat. The hairs on the back of her neck stood on end. She could almost feel the others holding their breath as they watched the two princesses: one pristine in her long dress, gold belt, and gilded collar; the other with a nearly identical dress, belt, and collar, but stained with ash, soot, and blood spatter.

Aviama's gaze traveled beyond Rana's undecipherable expression and up to the blue gemstone against her forehead, set in her gold headpiece.

"My mother always loved blue," she heard herself whisper.

Rana's eyes flicked to Aviama's. The air around them tingled with energy, as though the fire in the young woman's soul flooded through her veins, oozed out of her body, and swirled between them, directionless in a disquiet sea. An unsettled feeling moved in Aviama's midsection, burning with a demand to be known.

And then she saw the ring. It was gold, like all Rana's jewelry, but the stones of the lily's petals sparkled dazzling white. The unsettledness in her core was shaken at the sight of it, tail-spinning into an uneasy imbalance, as though precarious scales expected at any moment to be knocked askew. The restlessness inside demanded a label, a name, a home, but Aviama stuffed it down. Whatever the sensation was, she didn't need it now.

"It's a beautiful ring. Your mother loved lilies, didn't she?"

Rana drew her hand back. Her voice was thick as her whispering reply barely escaped her teeth. "You know where I got this."

Aviama would have known it anywhere. It was the ring Chenzira had taken from the charred remains of their mother. Rana must have gotten it from Sutekh when they captured him and took anything he had on him.

"I do."

Any minute now, the stupefied reverie that had taken over Sutekh and Florian would erupt, and the tense moment holding Rana captive to Aviama's words would evaporate like mist. She had one chance to say something meaningful. To say the *right* thing. To start a doubt, without the others understanding. To connect without directly threatening. To question, not where she was *expected* to question, but to bring to the surface what Rana was too smart not to wonder about on her own.

Aviama leaned in, nearly nose to nose with the Keketi woman, searching her deep brown eyes, her words soft as a dying man's last breath. "The question is, why was she there to begin with? And if we didn't do it, who did?"

Sutekh popped Rana in the rear with his peg leg as she crouched on the floor next to Aviama. "Get up."

Rana hardly noticed, and Aviama didn't dare break her gaze. Had Rana killed her mother? She was a fireblood, after all, and her mother had clearly been murdered by one. Maybe it had been an accident, like the uncontrollable awakenings melderbloods sometimes had when they came into their powers.

But if she *had* killed her mother, Aviama's question wouldn't bewitch her so. Would it?

Rana had not blinked, had not breathed, since Aviama last spoke. Her eyes were deep pools of unsearchable secrets, her emotions cloaked by layers of something with the power to block out the world—a power desperate to remain in place, even as the world pressed in more and more, the weight of it expanding, its promised suffering lurking around every corner in the labyrinth of the human soul.

"Rana. Don't embarrass me. Get up."

Rana straightened, dusting the dirt from her skirts as if shaking off the last shreds of any emotion threatening her relationship with Sutekh. She couldn't afford to see him differently. Not now. But her fingers glowed a faint sunset orange as she smoothed her skirts again, hiding the insides of her palms.

Florian cast a furtive glance across the royals and gave a stiff bow. "I believe I'm needed elsewhere. We'll send some food soon, and someone to feed it to you. It's not a job I envy, and it won't be me. Your Highness?"

Sutekh waved him off. "Run away, Florian. We're just behind you."

Florian hesitated, but left. Chenzira eyed her and gave her a small nod. But was he nodding because he was thinking what she was thinking, or because he *thought* he was thinking what she was thinking, and wasn't? Aviama turned to Sutekh.

"I'll do what you ask. But not with you. With Rana. Also, the little girl stays with me always, and I spend my evenings here, for proof of life among us all."

Sutekh snorted. "You think I'll let you be alone with my sister?"

"You said yourself I had a tortured soul. Does it surprise you that I would refuse to relive those experiences?"

"You're not in a position to bargain."

Aviama shook her head. "I'm not bargaining. That's the point. I'm agreeing to what you've asked me to do, but telling you under which circumstances I will perform the required tasks."

Rana's eyes turned to slits, and Sutekh sucked his teeth, considering.

"Deal."

Sutekh glared at his sister, for it had been Rana who answered. Aviama blinked.

Rana waved him off. "Please. It'll be fun. You know she won't be able to touch me. And I want to hear stories about the Iolani." Her fingers drummed against the smooth shell at her hip.

Sutekh smiled, wrapping an arm around her shoulders once again. She swayed under his weight and repositioned her feet. He gave a short nod. "Very well. We'll send for you when we're ready."

36

S utekh and Rana must not have been ready for a long time, because no one came. Not the first day. Not the second day. Not the first week. Not the second week.

Three times a day, someone brought food for them, and at intervals, on a schedule, they were moved one at a time with their hands still bound and permitted to use a chamber pot. Whatever unlucky sailor was assigned to feed them, fed them all by hand. Sometimes the bread smelled like sweat. Sometimes there was dirt in it. Always, Aviama felt disgusted eating like a pet rat out of the hand of one of Florian's disgruntled ruffians.

The toddler remained unbound, which was a single small mercy—except for the couple of times she wandered off down the deck and no one could follow. Once she came back with a sleeping sailor's brandy flask, which gratefully she couldn't open. Another time, she came back with a roll of bread. She flitted between her fellow prisoners, poking at Chenzira's bruises, tugging on Umed's long beard, or giving Teja kisses on the cheek, but when evening came and it was time to sleep, she curled herself up in Aviama's lap or wrapped her arms around Aviama's neck and tucked her tender face against her chest.

The girl woke screaming, or frozen in terror but clammy to the touch, at least a couple of nights a week. Aviama half-wished she knew what nightmares haunted her, and half-knew she could hardly bear it if she did. Still, it was better for an adult to hear it and bear it than a child so small. But though she was old enough to be talking, she had hardly uttered a word. The dreams remained a mystery—a secret horror for her tiny body to carry alone. Aviama could only keep her close and comfort her as best she could between her own nightmares.

Aviama lost track of the number of escape attempt ideas that rolled through the group. Ultimately, none of them could figure out how to free their hands, and with not only their wrists restrained, but their fingers immobilized, there was little any of them could do. If they did get free, their reward would likely be a host of melderblood guards or sailors and a vast ocean. Not to mention Sutekh and Rana. There was no place better for a powerful crestbreaker than the sea, and Rana's combined wind and fire powers were formidable.

So they waited.

And waited.

Until a one-eyed sailor with a scar running from his temple and across his missing eye to his nose trudged his way down the gun deck one morning. He touched the chain where it attached to the side of the ship, and the chain dropped away as if it were butter sliced through with a knife.

He jerked his chin at the little girl. "Let's go. Her too."

Aviama staggered to her feet, then stumbled, her shoulder driving straight into the wooden planks of the hull. Chenzira lurched forward as if to catch her, but with his hands behind him, there was little he could do. The little girl clutched at her skirts and patted her leg, looking up at her with large brown eyes.

The sailor swung the ends of her chain absentmindedly, picking his teeth with what looked like a thin splinter of wood before stashing it between his teeth and out of his mouth. "Any day now, missy."

Sai edged toward Aviama, looking her over protectively. Satisfied her princess wasn't hurt, she turned her attention to the sailor. "Give her a break. She hasn't stood up in weeks."

He lolled the splinter to the other side of his mouth, regarding Sai with little interest. "Not my problem."

Aviama offered a halfhearted smile she hoped was reassuring and shoved off from the side of the ship. "It's okay, Sai. I'll be back."

Sai pursed her lips but settled back into her place on the floor.

Aviama could almost feel the eyes of her eight companions on her back as she moved down the deck. She instructed the toddler to place a hand on Aviama's leg, just to keep her close, and the girl did so without hesitation. The toddler didn't speak, but she listened carefully at least two times out of three.

Half-asleep sailors looked up lazily from their bunks as they passed. A group of men playing cards laughed as they huddled around a barrel on the end. Their friend scowled and threw down his cards, scattering them to the floor.

As they approached the stairs, Aviama saw the hatch leading down to the straw-lined pit she'd lived in for the months spent traveling from Ghosts' Gorge to Keket. Was she walking over the same planks the little girl's mother had walked when they dragged her from the pit and executed her for having powers?

But they didn't go down to the pit. Instead, they went up

the stairs, across the deck again, and One-Eye Toothpick Man rapped on a door on the end.

The door swung open, and Rana appeared. The princess was no worse for the wear of a long journey at sea. The woman looked elegant, fresh, and relaxed as the cool of a garden kissed by morning dew. The scent of bold, provocative spices wafted out of the room beyond, just enough to be inviting yet not overpowering.

Rana looked her over, pausing on the child, then glanced back up to Aviama. "Aren't you looking primitive this morning."

"Thank you."

"Well, don't just stand there. Get in and get washed up before your grime rubs off on me."

She jerked her chin inside the room, and Aviama and the little girl stepped inside spacious quarters with an easel, charcoal and pencils, and a bed dressed in onyx silks with gold thread designs. Furniture, too, was gilded midnight and accented by cobalt pillows. In the corner, a blue-and-gold screen partially obscured a bath with blue lotus flowers floating lazily in the perfumed water.

Rana lifted a goblet off a black wood-carved serving table, poured a vial of something into the dark liquid, and swirled it together with a golden spoon. She held it up toward Aviama. "Drink up."

Aviama stared at the dark drink, its contents still coiling inside the rim of the goblet. How many times had she been offered something she must eat or drink? Shiva had done it with magna. The queen had threatened poison. Neither experience made the beverage with its mystery substance overly appealing. But then, she'd waited to add the vial until Aviama arrived on purpose.

"It's magna." Rana watched the recognition light Aviama's

eyes. "You're aware of it, then. Yes, I thought you would be. Our growing alliance with Radha has come with quite a stack of benefits."

Biscuits, I'll bet it has. But how much did they know? And what updates had come from the House of the Blessing Sun, exactly? What other unsavory benefits had Radha shared?

Rana lifted the goblet to Aviama's lips, and Aviama drank, hands still encased in hard stone. A trickle of wine escaped her mouth and ran down her neck as Rana tipped the goblet too fast. Satisfied with the empty cup, Rana set the goblet down and turned to One-Eye Toothpick Man, still standing just outside the door.

"Effects are instantaneous, yes?"

"Yes, Your Highness."

Rana nodded and gestured to Aviama. The man touched the stone around her wrists, and they clattered to the floor. Her prisoner unfettered, Rana swung the door shut in One-Eye's face and turned toward Aviama, rubbing her hands together.

"Welcome. You're entirely too disgusting for this room, so I've arranged to get you cleaned up before we get down to business. Wash up, and then start drawing."

Aviama led the little girl behind the screen and helped her wash as well. A clean dress, from the looks of it also from Rana's wardrobe, was draped over a chair next to a towel for Aviama, so that by the time she bathed and dressed again in her lapis-lazuli ring, armband from Chenzira, and accessories from the palace that Rana had given her, she looked almost exactly as she had in the palace before all the violence. A shirt had been fashioned into a makeshift dress for the little girl, with cloth to crisscross across the torso and belt closer to her body so that it didn't gap so much. The little girl grinned up at Aviama in their freshly washed states, pointing at the similar clothes they wore.

Yes, baby. You and I are the same.

Orphan. Daughter. Prisoner.

But with someone who cared enough to protect them fiercely. For Aviama, that was Chenzira and the others. Manan, Sai, Umed. The little girl had fallen squarely under the protection of all of them, as though their fates were bound together by iron—or something stronger.

"Did the kid have breakfast?"

Aviama glanced up to find Rana rocking awkwardly on her heels, watching the tender display between Aviama on her knees and the little girl examining Aviama's jeweled collar and placing a hand on it and on her own, a simple gold collar she had found with her new clothes. Rana didn't strike Aviama as a kid person, but Sutekh would not have made these arrangements.

"Same as always. Roll of bread."

Rana pursed her lips, then gestured at a platter set out before a sofa and two chairs. "Help yourself."

Aviama tried to move slowly, but the sight of the meat, cheese, and fruit on the platter brought an irresistible urge, like a lush, impossibly soft blanket daring passersby not to reach out and feel it as they went along. She couldn't keep her eyes off it. Aviama ushered the little girl over to it, and she swept a handful of meat straight into her palm and shoved it straight in her mouth.

Rana perched on the edge of a chair and lolled her goblet between delicate fingers. "You need to draw. Sutekh will be here soon, and this page better be done by then."

Aviama swallowed a bite of cheese and popped two grapes in her mouth at once, barely swallowing before she answered. "What am I drawing?"

"Weren't you listening? The mines, the castle. You haven't had anything to do but think of our conversation those weeks ago. I'm surprised you've already forgotten."

Was that the reason for the wait? To let her ponder their last conversation? To increase intimidation and pressure? Aviama furrowed her brow and spun the ring on her finger, just once.

"And yet in all that reflection time, I didn't suddenly remember I had been to the mines when I hadn't."

Rana waved her off. "The castle, then. Just draw."

Aviama tossed another chunk of meat and cheese in her mouth and moved to the stool set before the easel. She tested out the pencils and the charcoals and ultimately went with the charcoal's soft strokes. The pencil may have been more precise for engineering-style drawings, but Aviama hadn't been able to be creative like this in months. She would play with light, with bold lines contrasted with soft shadows and a light source dimmed by evening and sorrow.

She took a deep breath and closed her eyes, reveling in the air flowing freely around her stiff hands and fingers. Aviama set down the charcoal, massaged her hands, and let her mind wander over sea and sand and green riverbanks, past the fishermen to the north, the farmland with its goat herds in the northeast, and the horse pastures outside of Haizlin. Down, down the Shalladin River until the sheer cliff came into view, the sparkling white stone of Shamaran Castle crowning the bluff, the underground Dezapi River pouring out into a waterfall just below it.

Aviama's eyes snapped open, and she sketched out the bones of the image—the line of the cliff at the top, with its tufts of grass all across, and falling vines on one side; the Dezapi breaking up coarse stone with a waterfall more wild and powerful, and yet more soothing, than any burbling foun-

tain she'd encountered; the spray of the water, the impressive
rise of the Great Hall from this side, and the towers on either
end; the balconies of the conservatory graced with velvet
flowers.

Out of the corner of her eye, the little girl climbed up on
the couch and started poking at Rana's jewelry. Rana drew
back awkwardly, then crossed the room to retrieve a small box,
and set it before the girl without saying a word. Aviama filled
in the columns along the Great Hall, pretending not to see the
Keketi princess's furtive glances checking on her progress and
the jewelry box she'd gotten out for the girl.

The little girl clapped and squealed, giving away Rana's
secret kindness as she drew out a bracelet with a handful of
baubles. Aviama suppressed a smile as she drew her mother's
favorite plants through the windows of the conservatory, and
the turrets gleaming in the light of the sinking sun. At the top,
she couldn't help adding a flag flying high in the breeze, with
its spear leading up to the nezil myansara flower, as though its
stem were made of steel and set on a backdrop of a dragon's
wings.

Jannemar had weathered many a storm before this one,
and always her colors still stood proud. If she never saw it
again, she would treasure the memory, recreating it here for
solace of her soul. But how many tragedies could one heart
hold? How many war-torn eras could a nation endure before
the kingdom itself was torn apart?

Aviama worked hour by hour, until lunch came and went,
until at last she sat back on the stool, examining her work.
Semra had become their myansara flower—the kind that
thrived in adversity, sprouting against all odds in rocky terrain,
beautiful and steadfast when all else crumbled around her.
Aviama couldn't hold a candle to Semra in physical combat,
and she still loved her dresses, but Aviama had stood her own

unusual tests and come out the other side. She'd lost count of the number of times she thought she might be about to die. Perhaps this time, too, a remarkable new solution would present itself.

She leaned forward and sketched one last piece of the puzzle of home: a great dragon flying overhead. If she'd had colors, she would have shaded her blazing blue with rose-gold accents and flame streaming from her mouth. Maybe one day, if she survived all this, she would draw the scene from above, now that she'd been on the dragon's back and seen Shamaran Castle from an angle only a handful ever had before.

The door swung open with a bang. Aviama startled, and the little girl jumped too. All three of them turned to see Sutekh sweeping into the room. The girl fled from the couch and contented herself among Aviama's skirts instead, twice as heavy as she'd been that morning after donning a dozen bracelets, necklaces, and other trinkets of every color of the rainbow.

Aviama set the charcoal down on the lip of the easel and dusted the residue from her fingers. She'd lost track of time completely, and she could have added more detailed shading and other specifics, but all the basics were there. The boring stuff Sutekh probably wanted. None of it would be overly helpful, considering it was only a slightly better view than they'd get from the river if they got that far, and it showed no interior layouts. Once she got to laying out the interiors, if Sutekh really hadn't been inside, she could swap out a few crucial bits in the drawings and no one would be the wiser.

She smiled at the dragon. *She's waiting for you, Sutekh. And I've seen what she does to enemies. Have you?*

Of course, that was assuming Zezura was at the castle. Which she wouldn't be, if Semra rode her into Radha's forces at the front lines near Horon. Aviama grimaced and turned her attention back to the crown prince.

Sutekh scanned his sister on the sofa, with an open jewelry box tossed into the sort of disarray one might expect if a burglar had ripped open its drawers in the dead of night. His gaze shifted from the evidence to the culprit, who promptly buried her face further into Aviama's skirts, and up to meet Aviama's eyes.

"You've only done one drawing?"

"Did you want *good* ones?"

"I want practical ones. I'm not hanging it on my wall."

"I didn't realize time was of the essence. You haven't seemed in a hurry so far. I'll double my production." Aviama cleared her throat and turned back to the parchment, drawing a quick diagram in the corner—a horizontal line with the cliff's drop-off, a rectangle at the top to signify the castle, and a semicircle boat with a triangular sail on a squiggle at the base of the cliff. "Now I've drawn two."

"I told you this was a mistake."

Aviama turned, but Sutekh's glare wasn't trained on her. It bored into his half-sister instead. Rana placed an earring back in a drawer and slid it shut, taking her time before tilting her face up at him.

"She's a skilled artist, just like I said. She knows the castle, just as *you* said. And you gave practically no instructions."

Sutekh eyed the easel, then Aviama. "Draw it again. Draw the interiors. Draw the layout. Where the gates are. Where the guards are posted. You do know where the guards are posted, don't you?"

Aviama chanced a glance toward Rana, her expression one of inconvenienced solidarity. "Does he expect you to be this stupid too, or is it just me?"

Sutekh's jaw clenched, but Rana rewarded her with a

twitch at the corner of her lips as she suppressed a smile. A net win, in Aviama's opinion. If she were going to get anywhere, it would be with Rana, not Sutekh.

Aviama cleared her throat and returned her attention to Sutekh. She could only push him too far before he did something crazy. "No problem. I'll do interiors next. How long do we have?"

"Not long enough. You may not have powers, but you seem too comfortable outside your shackles. Less ... motivated." Sutekh strode forward, ripped off the corner of the parchment where her snarky child's diagram was, and crumpled it in his hand. "Name a prisoner. Whom shall I decapitate first?"

The wind left her lungs. It was Shiva all over again. *Convince me that you are in love with me, or I'll kill one of your women. Cooperate, or a detached head will appear at your door.*

She had sworn never again. She lifted her chin to look Sutekh in the eyes.

"Aviama Shamaran."

37

S utekh smiled, the thin kind that Aviama imagined snakes wore. Serpents only looked like they were smiling when their mouths were open to eat fresh prey. Two long, uneven strides with his new peg leg, and he stood before her. In a lightning move, his hand shot out and gripped the girl's upper arm.

Aviama launched herself at him, and his balance was not yet so adept on his new foot to hold them both up; they fell back against the chair, the three of them knocking it over and tumbling to the wooden plank floor. Sutekh threw Aviama off him. The little girl screamed and scratched at him as his rough grip dug into her tender skin. Embers scorched his shirt.

The little girl's hand glowed.

Aviama blinked. Yes, it had definitely glowed. It wasn't glowing now. But she hadn't dreamed it. And from the expression on Rana's face, she wasn't the only one who had seen it.

Sutekh brushed the embers off his scorched shirt and spun toward Rana, who threw up a hand in his direction in the nick of time, the faint light of a soft flame barely contained in her bright palm. Rana shook her head.

"Not her."

"You're soft. She was dead before she got here. She was on a slave ship, and *this* one isn't her mother." Sutekh jerked a finger in Aviama's direction, his lip curled in disgust.

Rana let the glow in her palm burn brighter as she stared down her brother. "Even so."

Sutekh straightened, set the girl on her feet, and gave her a hearty shove back into Aviama's arms. "Fine. For now. I'll just pick another one. But I won't be responsible for what those little eyes see, if she lives long enough to watch her fake mother defy me again."

Aviama clutched at the little girl's small body, capturing her hands in Aviama's larger ones, drawing her into her lap, and wrapping around her in a protective hug. The girl's hands were warm.

Sutekh straightened his jeweled collar and leaned a hand heavy on the sofa where Rana reclined. She was pretending not to be bothered by what had just happened, but her chest heaved with rapid breaths. Rana snatched a grape off the tray and examined her nails, the way Aviama's older sister would have done when wanting to appear particularly pretentious.

But in the wake of his lost foot, her brother was less into appearances. He took a deep breath and crouched down low in front of Aviama and the girl until his nose was only a handsbreadth from hers. "Give me interiors," he hissed. "Good ones. Useful ones. And if you don't have one by the time I come back with a new specimen for slaughter ..." He licked his lips. "Believe me, yours will be the *last* head on the chopping block."

Sutekh stood, with effort, and thumped his way out of the

room. The door swung shut with a soft click, but Aviama still flinched.

And then it was silent.

Silent except for the jingling of jewelry as the little girl *thunked* her head back against Aviama's chest and twisted to look up at her. Big brown eyes innocent as doves peered into hers, round and young and somehow both full and empty at once. *Did I do something wrong?*

Aviama pulled her into a tight hug. "Keep the fire inside you," she whispered against the girl's ear. "Until it's safe."

The girl responded by patting Aviama on the cheek and slipping her arms around Aviama's neck.

Aviama's mind spun. The girl was a fireblood. With powers awakened already, at such a young age. Little was known about the development of powers, but Aviama's mentor, Frigibar, had implied that children with tabeun abilities grew into them rather than being able to have them from birth. Is that how her mother had been discovered? Had the little girl used fire and attracted the notice of Abasi's men? Had her mother pretended the child's flame was her own, and been killed for it, instead of for using her own powers to warm all the prisoners at night?

Rana jerked her chin in the girl's direction.

"Who is she?"

Aviama shrugged. "I don't know."

Rana arched an eyebrow. "I'd be an idiot to believe you. So why do I feel like I should believe you?"

"She's not mine. Not really. But she's more mine than anyone else's." Aviama rested her chin on the girl's head, the girl's small body tucked against her larger one. She had to be *someone's,* didn't she? Aviama was an orphan, but she still had her brother. Her sister-in-law. Chenzira. Sai. She had people.

Everyone needed someone.

Rana shut the jewelry box. "How long has she been calling fire?"

"I didn't know she could." Aviama swallowed, and a new thought stopped her cold. "The market. There was a fire on the platform, right after she was sold. Her real mother was already dead. The slaver killed melderbloods in his shipments, and her mother was a melderblood. A teenager took care of her for the rest of the voyage, and they were sold as a pair at the market."

The girl's arms squeezed tighter around Aviama's neck. Aviama hugged her back, hard.

"There was a fire, but none of us started it. She went under the platform, and the teen went after her. The platform started to collapse. The teen didn't make it. I got her out. She's been kidnapped, kept in a pit on this very ship, twice orphaned, and captured again. Fifty women were kept in there, with a hatch and stairs down to soiled straw like what you'd give a goat. You can go look at the pit. There's a hatch at the opposite end of the same deck from where you have your brother chained."

She couldn't help but remind Rana that Chenzira was her brother. The one who had taken care of her all her life. The one who looked out for her when Sutekh was threatened by her power. The one they tried to silence when she sought her mother.

And what had happened to her mother, exactly?

Rana stared at Aviama, the corners of her mouth turning down into a scowl before her gaze drifted to the circular windows in the side of the room, her eyeline boring a hole in the sea. The little girl scooted off Aviama's lap and tugged at the edge of Aviama's paper. Aviama lifted the large sheet, passed an extra sheet to the girl to put on the floor, and handed her a piece of charcoal. She picked it up and marked the paper, then grinned at her accomplishment and looked back at Aviama. *Did you see? Did you see what I did? My gray stick drew stuff, just like yours!*

Aviama smiled at her. She hoped the girl believed her smile, and not the goosebumps still running up and down Aviama's arms. She picked up another piece of charcoal and turned toward the fresh parchment. If interiors were what Sutekh wanted, interiors were what Sutekh would get. She'd give him more than he bargained for. More than he asked for. But oh, how accurate it would be. Even if it tore her heart out, she would draw the Great Hall precisely as she remembered it.

The Keketi princess reclined on the sofa with her goblet of wine, early in the morning though it was. Aviama could feel her gaze hot on her back, could see her outline in her peripheral vision as Aviama angled herself to see both the little girl on the floor and Rana's position in relation to her, while she drew out her next sketch.

"How'd you get captured in the first place? We heard you accepted an invitation to compete for Prince Shiva's hand in Radha, and then that you had won it and wedding preparations were underway. Next, the army heads out for Jannemar, the navy departs in several installments, and both you and Prince Shiva are missing. Imagine our surprise when you turn up barefoot to be sold as a slave on our most primitive trade island."

Biscuits, what a summary.

"That doesn't sound particularly normal, does it?"

The whole thing was ridiculous. The fact that any of it had happened at all was insane. Aviama caught herself wondering if Murin had made it home to Jannemar, ahead of the army, in time to tell Zephan and Semra what was really happening. Although, the last Murin knew, Aviama was still stuck in Radha. Everything was outdated. Aviama's lips twitched.

"Shiva wanted control of the Aeian Sea. Would Keket like

that? The island nation, known for their fishing industry and knowledge of the water, reduced to little more than a servant, a pawn in the hands of Radha—the power-hungry kingdom with the largest navy in the world, seeking control of the Iolani, to secure control of the ocean both from above and from below?"

"Radha wants a partnership. They have a strong naval force, but no one knows the water like we do."

"The Iolani would beg to differ. And what if Shiva gained control of the Gorge?"

Rana's goblet dropped to the end table with a reverberating *clink*. "He wouldn't. No one can."

"He tried."

Careful, Aviama. Running your mouth too much is exactly what got you into this position. You handed over the knowledge of konnolan to Shiva because you trusted him. Better to assume a snake and find a dove than to assume a dove and find a snake.

And Rana was no dove, no matter what pressures or confused delusions the young royal may be under. Aviama pursed her lips, considering her next words.

"Some creatures are attracted to bright colors. Bees, for example. Birds, who puff out vibrant feather chests to attract mates. But poisonous frogs come in the brightest reds and blues and yellows. Sometimes, we are attracted to things that are not good for us." Aviama paused. "That is what happened to me. And though I had been warned about him, I trusted him more than I should have. It is the deepest regret of my life. Many people have died, and will continue to die, because of my mistake. There's nothing I can do to make up for that.

"I watched my sister lose herself to a controlling mentor who told her what she wanted to hear at the beginning, just enough so that she would be eating from the palm of his hand and dependent on him by the time he told her to do things beyond her moral compass. By then, she'd allowed him to reshape her so that she didn't see wrong as wrong anymore. She saw pinpricks of light, and reason, and thought that was enough. It wasn't enough. She almost died, and she did not escape the consequences, just as I live with my consequences every day. Nightmares of the dead remind me every night of the gravity of my failures. People who cared for me were beheaded, their decapitated heads served to me on platters. Shiva will turn on you. Anyone who cares more for their power than for goodness will turn on you the moment you no longer serve their purposes."

Just like Sutekh. She let the silence linger, the implication to settle in Rana's mind without speaking the words aloud. Aviama drew another bold stroke of the Great Hall and turned to look Rana in the eye.

"But it's not too late for you to avoid the same mistake."

Rana held her gaze, and Aviama allowed the moment to stretch three beats after her stomach dropped to her toes before returning to her work. She might not be able to tell what Rana was thinking, but she had the rare opportunity to plant seeds in Rana while they were alone. Seeds of truth. Of hope. Of a different future than the one Aviama was already living.

Aviama was neither a bully nor a victim. She needn't rock the boat by being overly aggressive, nor tip the delicate scales out of her favor by proving a hapless pawn. Respect was a dangerous necessity. Demanding it without earning it resulted in revolution or violence. Not having it resulted in subterfuge, manipulation, and becoming an easy target to more powerful entities.

She had to earn Rana's respect without demanding it, *and* without being a doormat. But if she pushed too hard, too fast, it would translate as disrespect in the other direction, and Rana could lash out to reestablish control and dominance.

Aviama shut her eyes and blocked out the world. From the pot to the fire, from the chains of *Raisa's Revenge* to the Great Hall at her childhood home, the center of Jannemari government, the twinkling hall of parties and balls and galas. The place for jugglers' colorful balls tossed in arcs over trays of decadent hors d'oeuvres; live music, jesters, and dancing; diplomatic deals made with handshakes, drinks, and plastered smiles, while armed guards watched every calculated move; the place she'd learned to dance, and curtsied and nodded to high-profile guest after guest after guest.

The place where her mother had last smiled at her, with the beaming smile that reached her eyes and touched Aviama in the deep, warm place in her soul that felt more like home than any stone hall, tiled floor, rolling green hill, or twinkling starlit river ever could. The murder scene where the home in her heart had been strangled. Where her mother had collapsed in a pool of her own blood. Where dark had swept into Aviama's life while insolent golden sunlight still streamed in through tall windows.

"You still haven't told me how you ended up here."

Aviama opened her eyes and swallowed hard against a lump in her throat. The ache in her chest was back, and the swallow burned like salt on an open wound. She drew the charcoal across the page. "Shiva sailed for Ghosts' Gorge with a segment of his navy. All but one of his ships were lost to the sea. Shiva never left the Gorge."

Weight slammed into her chest as though a zegrath had sat on it, its spines spearing her through the heart. It was all technically true, but the specifics were probably better left unsaid. Maybe she shouldn't have said Shiva was gone. Maybe that would tip things too much. Rock the boat. Change the political landscape. But weren't the politics between Keket and Radha already headed for disaster? Maybe the high stakes, the rash power grab, and dire consequences of Shiva's ultimate failure would speak to Rana and help her rethink the similar path she herself was on.

Unless it didn't.

"And the slave ship?"

"The one surviving vessel escaped the Gorge and met *Raisa's Revenge* on the other side. The captain of the *Wraithweaver* was dead, and the man who took over sold my companions and I to Abasi."

Rana plucked the goblet back up off the end table and swirled the wine in her glass. "If that's true, he's an idiot. Selling a princess for a pittance and letting that horn you had out of his sight was the most moronic thing he could have done."

Yes, and where is that horn, exactly? Probably somewhere in Rana's room, unless Sutekh took it.

Aviama pressed her lips into a flat line and took a deep, measured breath. "I don't know why he did it, but the man is far from stupid."

Onkar, you swindling scoundrel. Why *had* he done what he did? She'd probably never know, but the mystery would haunt her. Still, his betrayal had no bearing on her current situation. He was probably off making deeper and better connections with his own loyal band of melderblood pickpockets, making a killing off thieving, black-market sales, and secrets.

Behind the first few parchments, a stack of thin semitransparent sheets peeked out behind the edges of the first stack. Aviama took one out and set it over her first sheet, intermittently drawing on the first layer, and then perfecting the second, shifting back and forth as she worked. It was a better, less inflammatory solution than the one she'd planned before.

It was a little less likely to end with one of her friends being murdered in front of her—as long as Rana kept what she saw to herself. It was a big gamble, but gambles were all Aviama had left. Shots in the dark were better than being swallowed by it completely.

Rana watched her work, and still Sutekh did not come. An afternoon snack was delivered, along with a fresh dose of magna for Aviama, which she drank without complaint. Aviama had three sheets she worked on now, moving from one to another and then back again. It was better to have two mostly done when Sutekh returned, but for Rana's sake, she wanted progress on the third.

The Great Hall done, Aviama leaned back. The base layer showed the interior as if in a painting from the perspective of a guest, with its walkway across the top leading from the guest rooms on the next floor up, over the gleaming floors of the hall with its high vaulted ceilings, and across to the door to the conservatory. A guard stood outside the tower door, and two more by the double doors of the main entrance to the hall; another set of double doors led out to the courtyard, and still another set to the right, on the opposite end of the long room.

But when she laid the semi-transparent sheet on top, the room exploded from its paper cage and came to life—or, perhaps, to death. Because there on the floor was her mother, Queen Sharsi Shamaran, with her favorite sapphire rings on white fingers, her kind eyes turned to glass, and an assassin's throwing knife protruding from her chest.

Rana lurched to her feet and toward the drawing. "Why did you do this? What is this?"

"This is the Great Hall, as I remember it. Just as I promised."

The girl stared at the drawing, chest heaving, sharp eyes glaring, palms glowing red hot. Aviama leaned away from her.

She'd expected anger, but this was more. Rana lifted a shaking finger and touched it to the page. Her lip trembled, and then her jaw clenched as if what was once tender had turned to stone all at once.

"What. Is. This." The princess said it definitively, as if it were a statement rather than a question, emphasizing each word.

Aviama didn't stop the tears misting her eyes, but took another slow, deep, deliberate breath in to steady herself before looking a wild Rana in the face and responding with quiet sincerity.

"This is my mother. She was killed by an assassin in the Great Hall, and ever since, I cannot see anything there but her. The person responsible for the hit contaminated my sister's mind. They destroyed my family. A small price to pay when it's other people's lives you're taking in exchange for stealing a throne and dominating others. To wrap oneself in pleasures and manufactured reverence through terror, to kill oneself just as much as killing others. I wonder what the person was like before everything. Before the dragon. Before the influence. If they had lovable qualities that they abandoned in the service of this goal. If succeeding would have made them happy. Do you think power provides happiness? Do you think if we were to get everything we wanted, that we would like it?"

Aviama couldn't decipher Rana's expression, but there was a crazed look in her eye. Her heart still beat hard and fast enough that Aviama imagined she could almost hear it. She could see the gem-studded collar move with every desperate breath the woman took in.

Was it wise to let her stew in such heightened emotion? Would it marinate into something productive, or would she reject the feeling so vehemently that she destroyed everything in her vicinity? Should she interrupt the moment, or let it lie?

Aviama didn't know, but she decided to say something anyway.

"I don't know the answer. But I know I will never walk through this hall the same again."

Flame leaped to Rana's palms. She ripped the top page from the easel, balled it up, and incinerated it in the span of a single breath. Sparks, ash, and a single wisp of dark smoke spiraled lazily up toward the ceiling.

Bang.

Aviama, Rana, and the toddler whirled as one to gape at the open door. Sutekh stood in the doorway, holding Teja by the nape of her neck.

38

All five people in the room stared at one another, frozen. A wisp of smoke still trailed lazily upward from Rana's palm. The little girl had her fist around a piece of charcoal. Aviama's charcoal still rested between her fingers, the stool scooted back as she had moved away from the flame. Sutekh's gaze moved over the women.

He threw Teja down, the only one of their company shackled without hands encased in stone. The only one without melderblood abilities. She caught herself on the corner of the sofa to keep from smashing her head into it and spun away from the prince's rage.

Sutekh *thunked* his way into the room, glaring daggers at Rana. "I let you monitor the prisoner for a single day and twice you lose control. What's wrong with you?"

"I didn't lose control. I stopped you from murdering a child, which would have been against our agreement, and I motivated said prisoner. But if you put me down in front of them again, you may see what loss of control looks like."

Rana's sharp eyes cut into Sutekh with unblinking intensity, but Sutekh only waved her off. "You're slipping."

Aviama cleared her throat and gestured toward the parchment. "Interior of the Great Hall is here, and a layout of the keep on this parchment here, but I wasn't sure about the dimensions. And there are several rooms in the servants' quarters that I don't really go into and can't remember how they're connected. Rana thought I was being untruthful because I washed out a line that I had put in the wrong place."

Rana's gaze flicked to Aviama but returned to Sutekh before he noticed. Sutekh wrapped his fist around the handle of the khopesh at his side, and the ship pitched sideways. Aviama lunged to catch the little girl as she began to slip, and Rana grabbed the easel. The ship settled again, and Aviama praised the girl's drawing efforts before refocusing her on her paper and righting the toppled stool.

Sutekh examined the layout, which was mostly accurate, save a few minor tweaks, and demanded more before declaring they were going to reach the border of Jannemar within a week. He sat in to watch her draw several more layouts, including the underground space the waterfall exited from beneath the castle. Few people knew of the expansive underground network of servants' quarters and small shops underneath Shamaran Castle. But the Dezapi River clearly exited from somewhere, and if she withheld other information, it might be just enough of a sacrifice to let Sutekh believe she'd earned her keep. Aviama drew a sketch of the underground layout, making the servant quarters only a quarter of the size, hugging the river itself, and leaving off the catacombs on the level below that led out to a narrow landing behind the cascading falls. The landing had become a permanent guard post ever since Semra became queen. No need to share that.

Teja crawled over to the girl and made quiet observations about her drawings while Rana and Sutekh scrutinized Aviama's diagrams. Sutekh was skeptical, but he was also excited.

His words came faster, and his eyes grew brighter, as pieces of a plan seemed to fall into place in his mind.

By the time they were finished, Sutekh was calmly cutting into the supper that had been brought and chasing down chunks of beef with fine wine, Rana was laughing on the sofa, and Teja still had a head attached to her shoulders. The one-eyed sailor returned with another man to retrieve Aviama, Teja, and the little girl and return them to the chains at the end of the ship below deck, where Chenzira and the others were being kept. When the prisoners were alone again, Durga couldn't help herself but to finally say, "Well?"

Aviama shrugged. "Nobody's dead yet. Rana might be softening. And the little girl is a fireblood."

Sleep did not come easily that night, and when it did, she dreamed of Rana—strung up upside-down with glassy eyes and smoking fingers, blood dripping from her neck into a tin bucket with a high, metallic sound to every drop.

Plink. Plink. Plink.

Sutekh strolled into the dark room, poured the blood from the tin into a wine goblet, and raised it toward Aviama with a smile. "A toast. To the woman who ferreted out my enemies. Who showed me who to trust." He turned to Rana's corpse, rotating slowly in the clutches of a chill breeze. "And to the weapon that brought me here. My fire brand, for however short a time. Cheers."

No!

Aviama had been too friendly. Rana had seemed too accommodating. Sutekh had turned the tables, using not only Teja and the other prisoners, but Rana herself, as his black-mail piece. He would know she wanted to save Rana. That Chenzira still loved her, and Aviama couldn't harm her. But had he lost faith in Rana? Had he ever had it to begin with?

Did rulers like Sutekh ever really have faith in people? Or

did they stack the odds in their favor, use them 'til they bled dry, and have an exit strategy to off anyone who tipped the scales in unfavorable directions?

Had Aviama tipped the scales out of Rana's favor? Perhaps it wasn't the prisoners down here that she needed to worry about most, but the woman above her who believed she was free. Who believed she'd found the truth.

When Rana told Sutekh not to put her down, why was the problem only that he put her down *in front* of Aviama and Teja? What did his put-downs look like in private?

How had Sutekh killed Rana's mother? He had motive; he had means. Did he get Rana to do it? Lie to her somehow about their mother, turn her against the woman? Perhaps she, too, was an assassin, though with less finesse than Semra's exceptional training. Perhaps the fire in her blood turned hearts to ash, and the target was dead before Rana realized who it was.

Sutekh smiled at her again in her dream, offering the goblet to her lips. Aviama tried to pull away, but chains wrapped around her whole body. The wind had abandoned her. She was alone.

"Her blood is yours. You earned it. Drink."

Aviama shook her head. Sutekh seized her by the hair, ripped her head back, and dragged the mouth of the goblet across her exposed throat. His lips drew close to her ear, and he spat out three words in a snarl.

"You did this."

Aviama awoke in a cold sweat.

39

Three days later, Aviama and the girl were summoned again, but Rana was not there. Sutekh and One-Eye supervised her progress on more sketches before sending her back to her chains in the cramped space at the end of the ship. She never saw the upper deck, and the other prisoners never left their positions except for their scheduled trips to the chamber pot.

After three more days, shouts interrupted their nightly routine of trying and failing to sleep. Running feet. Cannon fire. Swords rang out, but more than steel, it was the elements that clashed. The wind raged, and the ocean tossed the ship this way and that. Zahur hit his head hard enough to knock him out, as their bound bodies soared up off the ship with the momentum of a wave and slammed down against the hull again. Bodies fell to the sea, shadows passing by the gunport windows down the deck from the prisoners, followed by a tremendous splash.

For hours, the battle wore on, but then a blaze of light lit up the night, and the *whoosh* of a mighty windstorm ripped through the deck. The ship creaked. The ocean steadied beneath *Raisa's Revenge*, even as Aviama heard it batter an opposing ship. The crackle of fire and blood-curdling screams came to them through the night until at last all was quiet.

It was Teja that broke the silence. "What just happened?"

Aviama leaned her head back against the hull, eyes shut, as if pretending to sleep would keep the tears from streaming down her face. Chenzira's leg stretched out to reach hers, the largest gesture of being with her that he could offer.

"We have crossed into Jannemar." It was Umed's voice, solemn and soft. "Sutekh has overpowered Jannemar's border forces."

"Whichever ones were left," Osahar added. "They've bent all the military might they can manage to defend against Radha. Jannemar had no reason to suspect an attack from Keket."

"I'm sorry, Commander."

Manan. Sweet, kind, loyal Manan. The gentleness in his voice broke her. More of her people had died, and she hadn't even had the decency to die with them. She couldn't go down with the ship if she was on the winning vessel. Nothing was right. And Rana had helped. The wind and the flame were too great, too precise. Sutekh still had her in hand.

Alive, because she was useful. How long would Rana be useful? How long would Aviama be useful, or the others with her?

You'll be the last to die.

Why had Rana lost it when she saw Aviama's rendering of a murdered mother on the floor of the Great Hall? Had she been reminded of her own mother, scorched to ash on the floor of the Khurafa Temple? Did she realize that the corpse there really had been her mother? Had Rana carried out the hit? Did she want to?

Want to or not, Rana was now responsible for more families losing loved ones. Just like Aviama, but without the remorse. How many more?

Every Shamaran will burn.

Aviama may have destroyed Shiva, but it was Shiva who would have the last laugh.

And all she could do was sit. And watch. And wait.

viama didn't know how many days passed until the day the fire started. Whatever fleet accompanied Sutekh's flagship on the *Revenge* was formidable enough that the battles never slowed them for long, and the scant Jannemari forces left in the north fell to the fleet moving down south along the Shalladin River. Always, at the last, when the wind and waves had battered the smaller defending vessels within an inch of their lives, a blaze of flame would leap up and finish them off.

Jannemar had melderblood warriors, but not to the caliber or ruthlessness of Keket. Aviama couldn't help but wonder if Frigibar had been wrong about being the last keeper of tabeun secrets. Perhaps Keket had one too. But it was a passing thought, drowned out by the sheer numbers of Keketi melderbloods overpowering the dregs of Jannemar's minimal defenses as they turned their attention to Radha's attack on Horon to the northeast.

The armies would never make it back to the capital now if they tried. Even the dragon would be slow in coming from such a distance, now that Sutekh had snuck downriver and left no survivors from any ship along the route. And who would tell them there was a need?

The dark of night surrounded them, the prisoners at last falling into fitful sleep. The little girl had curled into Aviama's lap, but in her slumber half-fell off Aviama's legs, draping onto the wooden planks of the deck.

It was the twitching that woke Aviama from the dead of sleep. Jerking body movements flinched this way and that over her legs. She squeezed her eyes shut tighter, running her stone-covered hands up and down the girl's back as softly as she could.

Shhhh. Back to sleep. It's okay to be scared ... but you're safe.

Well, she wasn't, but what else was she supposed to think? She wasn't saying it out loud, so it probably didn't matter, but thinking about how they were all on the brink of death was not exactly productive, so she should probably—

Crackle. Pop.

"Ouch!"

Aviama's eyes flew open as something hot embedded in the skin of her forearm. Flames crackled along the wood of the deck, spanning across the entire width of the deck only a meter from where Aviama sat slumped against the hull of the ship. The very *wooden* ship. Her first instinct was to shout for help, but what would happen if they discovered she was a melderblood? What if they thought one of them had circumvented the stone shackles somehow, and Sutekh decided to kill them all for good measure?

The flames spilled from the young girl's limp, outstretched hand and out toward the rest of the gun deck—but stopped short of their maker and did not come nearer to the prisoners than the girl's palms. Both of her hands glowed red hot, almost white in the center. Her breath came long and steady in the rhythm of deepest repose.

Aviama kicked at Chenzira. "*Pssst*. Chenzira! Wake up!"

He grunted, shifted in his sleep, and his head lolled over into Umed's shoulder. Umed sniffed in his sleep, worming into a different position under the unexpected weight of Chenzira's thick head, and went still again. Aviama's mouth went dry. How long did they have until a blazing fire at night would be noticed? Already, the haze of morning light through the cannon ports warned that sleeping sailors would soon wake. But it was still dark enough to garner attention from soldiers and sailors on duty, if it grew loud or large enough to be seen through the hatch on the deck above.

She kicked him again, hard. "*Wake. Up!*"

Chenzira snapped upward, his head hitting Umed's on his way to straightening. His brow furrowed as he squinted at Umed, as if wondering how they had ended up in such a position, and then slowly turned to take in the scene around him.

"Sands!" Chenzira recoiled from the blaze.

"Are you always this jumpy?"

His jaw dropped as he gaped at her, then back to the fire, and back to her again. "Did you just say a ridiculous thing in the middle of us almost dying?"

"Maybe. Did I do a good job?"

"Yes." His mouth quirked into a half smile, then he checked on the fire again and froze. "But more importantly, whatever they put on my hands is wet."

"Why is that important?"

"Because. It's *melting*."

Aviama's lips parted. They'd never get a chance like this again. If they even had a chance now.

Chenzira twisted his body to hold his hands, still bound behind him in the silvery substance, to the fire. The metallic color glistened with a liquid-like sheen, and droplets began to seep off Chenzira's hands and onto the ship deck. Aviama spun to Sai and rammed her shoulder into her friend. Sai stirred, and down the line it went, until the group of hostages sat breathlessly watching the little girl still fast asleep, no longer twitching, draped across Aviama's lap as the flames licked along the floorboards—crawling toward the center of the ship.

Durga leaned forward. "I know we're all very excited that we will either be burned alive or be murdered very soon, but shouldn't we wake up the kid and make her stop?"

Aviama shook her head. "We need to wake her up slowly. If she scares, she could make it worse. She's so young. She probably doesn't have much control. And if she stops *all* of it, they'll kill her or all of us before Chenzira gets the chance to break free."

Umed jerked his chin down the deck. "Someone's coming."

With a collective cry, the ship awoke. Sailors yelled at each other from the other side of the flames. Any minute now, fire-bloods would be upon them to calm the blaze.

Aviama rested her stone-encased hands on the girl, glancing up at the shadows rushing to and fro beyond the line of dancing fire eating at the wood. Maybe she did need to wake up the girl. Maybe it was time to go. But what if she panicked? What if she ran off and Aviama couldn't stop her? What if she hurt someone by accident, half-asleep but with firebrands for hands?

She swallowed. "Chenzira?"

"Almost there."

Wind coursed through the gun deck, powerful as a river rushing unrestrained down a channel when its dam had just burst. Fire flooded their closed-in corner of the ship as the gale blew back the flame onto the nine remaining prisoners. Heat stung her eyes, embers raining down on her hair. Sweat broke out across her skin like steam from a boiling pot, her hands the only part of her protected from the fury of the fire.

"Auuuughh!"

"Get her up!"

"She's not a soldier!"

"But she's not *dead*, and she has powers!"

Aviama hardly heard her companions' urging as she tucked the girl's body between her legs and torso and brought her knees up, twisting her body away from the fire with the child folded securely into her lap. They couldn't wait any more. If Chenzira wasn't free, no one else could break free either. And if they were going to keep from burning alive, the only fireblood they had would have to do her best.

"Wake up! Wake up, baby! Come on!"

Biscuits. The kid really needed a name. She shifted in her sleep, her head burrowing against Aviama's torso, and a leg fell out of Aviama's lap to the other side. Aviama half lifted her up with her bound hands. Manan thrashed out with a leg and kicked the girl's foot, hard.

Her smooth little brow furrowed, and then her eyes popped open wide. She cast about, squinting in the light of the fire, until her gaze landed on Aviama.

"Amma?"

Aviama's heart stopped. She'd spoken. It was the sweetest sound Aviama had ever heard. And her first word in months was Aviama's name.

"I'm here, baby." Something in her chest constricted and broke, and she choked on the lump at the back of her throat. "We've got to get you up. Can you focus on the fire? Can you get it away from our friends?"

She clapped and pointed at the orange glow catching fire on Manan's trouser. "Fafa!"

Manan let out a yowl of pain. Zahur kicked at his leg, as if to beat out the flame, but all it did was add insult to injury.

"Yes, fire." Aviama nodded toward Manan. "Can you start there? Hold up your hand. No, not to me, over that way. There you go. Tell the fire, bad fire! Go away from my friends!"

"Fafa!"

A blast of wind knocked them all into the hull and to the edge of their restraints. Aviama's forehead bashed into Sai's bony shoulder and ricocheted into the side of the ship. Fire leaped up between the two sides of prisoners, separating the men from the women, and closing them off from the rest of the ship. Silhouettes of running figures with their hands out toward the captives laughed at Aviama through the wavering haze of flame.

Raisa's Revenge was awake and ready to defend herself.

"Now!" Durga screamed. "Stop the fire *now*!"

"No! Good job, little one, keep it going!"

Aviama whirled to Chenzira, who had spoken last, and squinted through the rising smoke and flame to get a better look at him. Her eyes burned. Her skin felt stretched, as though her hide had been cut from her body, beaten flat, and hung to dry in the blistering heat until it shriveled into old leather.

"Have you lost your mind?" Sai screamed.

"No want die, crazy man," Zahur added in his stilted common tongue.

"We won't last a second as soon as they get their wits about them enough to stop the fire and burn us to crisps directly. They've got windcallers and firebloods down here already, and that's plenty to kill us with."

Chenzira was still twisted on the floor, hands to the fire, when his mouth opened wide, and a guttural roar of agony ripped from his throat. A wooden plank beneath Aviama creaked, accompanied by an exaggerated *pop* from the crackling fire.

"Fafa! No, fafa!"

The girl threw both hands over her head, palms splayed out the way small children sometimes did when they tossed their hands up. The fire shuddered. Another gale swept through, and Aviama threw her hands up to block its path to the girl, but the wind knocked her over, and both fell into Sai together, landing in a tangled heap of limbs and chains.

The ship pitched sideways, and Aviama's body slung outwards toward the men, sandaled feet dangling into the fire. Fresh screams filled the air. And then her stone shackles broke apart.

In a flash, Chenzira was there, bare-chested and broad and glistening with sweat in the sheen of orange flame. Hands freed, Aviama threw up an air shield and dragged the girl behind it. And then there they were, seven adult melderbloods joined by a non-melderblood woman and a catastrophically powerful toddler, assembled behind an air shield, flanked by fire. Around them, the ship threatened to break apart, and before them, two dozen of Sutekh's finest trained melderbloods pressed in with their palms up to fight.

Osahar rubbed his knuckles and swore. "My hands hurt like—"

Chenzira cut him off. "We're going out the gunport. Manan and Umed, you're responsible for getting us up on the upper deck."

"Yes, Your Highness."

"None of that."

"Yes, sir."

"That'll do."

Durga cleared her throat. "We won't fit out the—"

Chenzira swirled his hands in circular motions, palms

facing each other, and the stone shrapnel of their shackles flew to his aid. Bits of chain still attached, he whipped the fragments into the melderblood opposition. Rough rock grew spikes at his command as it cut through the air, burying into the enemy like flails.

Sai and Durga threw up air shields of their own, and Aviama sent tendrils of wind to wrap around the ankles of the sailors and yank them down.

Crash. Crash.

One after another, they fell before the onslaught. Keketi firebloods worked to put out the flame, rather than feed it, leaving only a few to aid the windcallers in their attack on the escaped prisoners. But as the group stepped out of the charred remains of their imprisonment, the Keketi sailors regrouped to form a formidable wall of wind, fireballs flying over the top of it like cannon balls.

Chenzira leaned in toward Aviama, yelling into her ear over the din of the fire and the screaming wind. "I need the cannon!"

Aviama tested the Keketi windcallers' barrier. The cannon was beyond it, but if she could distract them ...

Osahar and Zahur lobbed fireballs over the air shield and to the left side, while Sai held their own barrier steady. Aviama sidestepped into Durga. "Airway to the cannon. On my count. One, two—I said on my count!"

Durga threw a torrent of wind through toward the cannon, and Aviama thrust both hands in the same direction, doubling her efforts. The enemy barrier wavered only briefly, but it was enough. Chenzira latched onto the metal in the cannon and ripped his hands toward the gunport on the other side of the ship. Aviama followed his lead with a blast of air, propelling it forward even further. The hull of the ship splintered outward as the cannon barreled through it and toppled over the side into the river, leaving a gaping hole in its wake.

"Now!" someone yelled.

Aviama lunged for the opening and whirled back just as Durga dove out the side of the ship. "Teja, the girl!"

Teja scooped up the toddler and jumped as a mass of flame burst from the little girl's hands and buried itself in a windcaller's chest across the charred aisle. The windcaller screamed, glowing embers marking a perfect spherical shape where the flame sank into his skin. Aviama's jaw dropped. She'd never seen a fireball sink into someone's body like that. The closest she'd seen was Chenzira and Rana's mother, where a fireblood had placed their hand directly on someone's chest.

Aviama felt the rush of energy gathering in the air before the blow hit her. She summoned a blast of her own and launched it at the line of melderblood fighters just before she dove through the opening in the ship and plummeted to the frothing water below.

41

Cold water surged over Aviama's head, washing her free of the sweltering inferno and sending chills down her spine as the river chased away the beads of sweat that had smothered her a moment before. But the moment she hit the river, the water was moving, tumbling, rolling, and taking Aviama along with it. Her skin relished the cool of the water as her lungs burned instead.

A mighty swell picked her up in its grip and rocketed skyward. Water exploded into morning light, and the escaped prisoners with it. Umed and Manan had done their work, and the element of surprise was still on their side.

Sutekh truly had brought a fleet of his own to Jannemar. Ship after ship crammed into the Shalladin River, restricted only by their size and the width and depth of the river to accommodate them all. *Raisa's Revenge* led the charge as the flagship, driving against the current to the soaring cliff, Shamaran Castle twinkling at the top.

Her childhood home, filled with laughter and love and security, under its second large-scale attack in five years. Semra had told her that, from above, the color of the newly repaired roof of the grand throne room had yet to fade to quite match the older stone around it. What other repairs would her home need by the time the sun set? Would she last long enough to see its ruins?

The wave of water carried them up and over the railing of *Raisa's Revenge,* just below a half-set of stairs leading up to Prince Sutekh and his royal sister standing side by side at the prow. They spun to the prisoners.

Aviama's breath caught. The Iolani horn slung about Rana's torso. Rana followed her gaze, and her hand went to the horn.

But no, it wasn't time for that. Not yet.

Chenzira flicked his wrists, and all the cannons on the main deck rearranged themselves from their gunports to aim directly at Sutekh. But Sutekh wasn't her primary objective. Manan, Zahur, and Sai followed Chenzira, Sai throwing up an air shield, and Zahur throwing fire to meet the stream of flame Rana unleashed down on them. Manan raised waves of his own to battle Sutekh's rising water on either side of them, as Aviama turned on her heel and swept toward the aft of the ship with the rest of their company.

Aviama threw a hand out to either side, and men fell to the ship plank floor as she moved. She didn't have time for gentility. Not today. Not at the threshold of her own home.

Sailors ran up the stairs from the gun deck, but together Aviama and Durga sent snakes of wind around their legs and waists and yanked them backward down the stairs and into each other. Umed summoned the river, and it washed half of Sutekh's men from the aft of the ship, knocking them sideways in the shock of his sudden blow. Aviama strode to the stairs—the stairs she'd been marched down when she was stuffed with fifty slave women in a filthy straw pit, a pit of death and disease and remorseless destruction of the human spirit, the stairs that sailors dared even now to march up to remove her humanity once again.

She threw her head back, arms spread wide, and called— no, commanded—a ferocious windstorm of ire and wrath. *Let* Raisa's Revenge *be mine. The wisdom they refused. The light they tried to snuff out.*

An electric tingling ran up and down her arms, across her chest, and from palm to palm. Durga staggered back, but Aviama leaned in as the heat in her soul lifted her to new heights. Her feet left the floor, and then she gave the order. Wind hurled down on the stairs. Blood spattered the wall where sailors careened into wood posts. One of the boards of the stairs impaled the one-eyed quakemaker as he sprinted for splintering steps. He dropped.

A sickening snapping sound rippled through the air, but to Aviama, it rang of freedom. She nodded at Osahar. "Light it up."

Osahar lifted a hand, and fire engulfed the mass of kindling that had once served as stairs from the upper deck down to the main.

Aviama jerked her chin at Florian, gaping at them from the wheel several paces off. "Durga, Umed, Osahar—take the helm."

Florian lifted his hands, brows raised as he eyed her, palms up in surrender. He stepped back from the helm with a half-bow. "No need to get handsy. I'm here for a commission, is all. Commission did not require I offer up life and limb on the paperwork."

"Yet you betrayed us without a second thought." Aviama strolled forward, Durga lifting a long finger toward his chest. Florian clutched at his throat, his breath halted mid-inhale. Aviama shook her head sadly. "If you have a next time, I recommend thinking a little longer."

Florian held up a finger, then pointed at his throat as his face drained of color. Aviama gave Durga a nod, and she released her hold on his lungs as Umed gave him a hard shove and took the wheel. Florian sucked in long drags of air, interrupted by hacking coughs. He held up a finger again.

"I know something you don't know. I can help you."

Aviama arched an eyebrow. "I sincerely doubt it." She didn't really want to kill him, but where could she stash the weasel that he wouldn't snivel his way out the moment he regained full consciousness?

Florian hesitated, glanced down the ship toward Sutekh, and licked his lips. "Why aren't you worried about your fiancé?"

Aviama's patience flattened to nothing the moment the word left his mouth. She raised a hand, but he shook his head vehemently.

"No, no, not fiancé. The Radhan prince. Why aren't you worried about him?"

"Because he's dead."

"How do you know?"

"I killed him myself."

Florian's lips twisted into a half smile that could have curdled dairy. "Boringgggg," he sang, wagging a finger at her. "If he were dead, then how did his new friend, the prince of Keket, receive direct word from him just before we set out from Siada?"

The excess energy of Aviama's windstorm streamed out from her in a *whoosh*, knocking Florian's black hat to the deck, red feather and all. It was a lie, of course. The odds were against them, outnumbered as they were with so many trained melderbloods on board. The obstacle Aviama had left on the stairs wouldn't hold the sailors down forever, and Chenzira wouldn't be able to fend off both Sutekh and Rana with her double powers once the other ships of the fleet got involved.

But still, a part of her shriveled like a grape instantly dried into a raisin at the notion of Shiva being in communication with Sutekh. Could it be that he had escaped Makuakan? Aviama had assumed King Dahnuk, Shiva's father, had been the one to tell Sutekh about the magna that dampened melderblood abilities. But what if it was Shiva?

Umed turned from the helm and delivered an old-fashioned slug to the gut that sent the reaver staggering backward. "Don't waste your time on him, Commander. I'll dispatch him for you."

Aviama drilled Florian with an icy glare. "If you're going to spout nonsense, you should at least be smarter about it. We're the only ones here. Radha attacked to the northeast, in Horon, and Shiva wasn't with them."

Florian wrapped an arm around his aching middle, nursing the memory of the broad-shouldered Umed's giant fist, and shot her a look. "You weren't at all surprised by just *how* alone we are here? How few skirmishes we encountered on the way in? How your brother's ships are all gone, and we've yet to meet even a single archer's arrow from the guard posts? Look for yourself. No one lines the walls. No one stands in the towers. Even stretched thin, no self-respecting governance would leave their kingdom's main castle completely unattended."

Breath left her body. He was right, and from the look on his face, he knew it. Aviama glanced across the river, up the cliff, to the castle at the top. She scanned all the usual guard posts. Nothing. If Radha's army was northeast, and no one else had attacked until Sutekh came through on *Raisa's Revenge*, why was Shamaran Castle so poorly defended? Not even poorly defended, but from the looks of things, vacant.

Was Jannemar's military so sparse after the war with Belvidore that they could not manage to leave even the appearance of reasonable forces behind? The Jannemari flag still flew, but the longer she looked upon the place she knew best in all the world, the flag looked more like a dare than an invitation.

And then she saw it—lilac vine, spilling over the balcony to the Great Hall.

Saeb, the housekeeper, may have been pleased to arrange petals tastefully here and there, or string up flowers for special occasions, but never would she sling a single mass of blooms over the side like that. After today, Aviama would see to it that not a single lilac petal was seen in Shamaran Castle again. But today was not over. And only one person could have left lilac for her.

Was she never to have a moment's peace? Was she only ever to gain enough hope for the future, so that she'd descend into madness when the past crawled up through the abyss to choke her out from behind? When all the hope would be ripped away? Were the past months of her life not payment enough for her evils? For her mistakes? For her failures?

Aviama moved as if in a daze, turning from the helm and leaving Florian staring up at the cliff behind her. Shadows of men rained down on her in the periphery, but as she walked to the beat of the drum within her own ribcage, hands outstretched at her sides, her adversaries melted away. A gale here, a body dropped there—none of it mattered as long as the lilac draped over the balcony.

As long as death beckoned like poisoned poetry.

Shouts followed her progress back toward the prow. Umed stayed at the helm, and Aviama was vaguely aware of Durga and Osahar following her. Teja and the baby had found some hole or other to hide in for the time being. That was for the best. Because where Aviama was about to go was no place for children.

Up ahead, Chenzira, Zahur, Sai, and Manan exchanged blows with Sutekh, Rana, and three other melderblood sailors on deck. Aviama stepped over three fallen corpses as she made her way toward them. There were two things she must do before she went up to rip the lilac off the balcony and pay whatever blood debt was required to unburden herself from her past failures.

She glanced out at the Shalladin River rushing by them. Images of its peaceful sparkling waters filled her mind— laughing with her sister Avaya, or splashing her brother Zephan as children on its banks upriver. Her mother, catching her up in her arms and spinning her in a circle, spraying their father with an arc of cold water until they all collapsed in giggles. Only this time, every memory turned the river to blood. Each iteration of the mirage turned darker and darker, until the figures within them slowly faded from view to the realm of the dead.

Every last Shamaran will burn.

"Stop! You don't have to do this!"

Somewhere in her brain, Aviama registered surprise that it was Durga's voice cutting through the noise. But didn't she understand? She, of all people? Who had been under the thumb of Shiva's mother first, and then Shiva himself, and knew the intricacies of the royal spiders under their command?

Aviama had thought she'd killed a spider. If Florian was telling the truth, that spider had had one last silk strand. And he'd used it, somehow. Slippery as an eel, cunning as a snake, spinning his webs until something big enough got caught up in it. Something juicy enough to save him.

What had he caught this time, to save him from the Iolani?

Aviama shook her head. It didn't matter. If she went up there, and he was there, only one of them would make it out alive.

Sutekh whirled his hands over his head and sent a crashing wave down on Chenzira and Manan. Sai threw up an air shield, but the wave was too strong. Her shield broke apart, and Chenzira and Manan fell to the ground. Chenzira released two of the cannons as he dropped to the deck.

Boom.

Booooom.

Sutekh swore and ducked, but the cannonball followed him—only narrowly missing his head and embedding in the forecastle instead as Chenzira hit the deck below and disrupted his focus. Rana raised her hand, and fire rained down on Zahur and Sai. Sai rolled free from the torrent and knocked her off balance, but only for a moment.

The thick of the battle raged, and still Aviama seemed to feel their eyes shift from each other to her as she moved with the steady onward motion of a dark cloud. What could redirect a cloud? What weapon could dispel it rather than move through it? And still it came, slow and sure as the moon, rising to preside over the time of the end of every day.

Was this the time of the end?

Would Chenzira come if she asked him? Would Durga? Would all of them?

Perhaps. But if they came, Sutekh would only come after them. He would regroup, and his men would make a cleaner assault. They'd breach the underground tunnels. They'd storm the castle, strengthening the enemy already taking up residence there. They'd chase her and anyone with her until no one was left.

Aviama gathered the wind and blasted at Rana. Rana skidded backward into the forecastle railing, but held steady, bringing a gale of her own to bear on Aviama. But Aviama wasn't trying to defeat her. Just occupy her.

Aviama sidestepped toward Chenzira as he gathered his feet. "Don't hate me."

He wrenched his hands apart, and chunks of cannon scraped free, flying at Sutekh like exploding shrapnel. "What's wrong? Something's wrong."

Sutekh shot another wave down on them, and Manan defended, but Rana swept his feet out from under him as he did, and Manan crashed to the ground. Sutekh's wave sent Sai, Manan, and Chenzira sliding down the deck as the ship tossed in troubled waters.

Aviama seized him by the wrist as he went by, hauling him up toward her with the help of a swirl of wind. "You don't think the current situation is wrong enough?"

He slipped one arm around her waist and shook his head. "We've done death-defying feats before. It's kind of our thing. You've got a look in your eye that I don't like."

Aviama shoved both hands at Rana, distracted by her victory over Manan, and the Keketi princess half-toppled over the railing before she caught herself. "Didn't you say something about me starting to sound ridiculous in the middle of death-defying feats?"

"Yes, but this doesn't feel like that."

Chenzira spun her like in a waltz on the floor, shooting a hundred sharp cannon chunks at Sutekh between them before pulling her to him again. Aviama threw up a spherical shield in a bubble around them, as if to stop the world for one last time.

"I'm about to go overboard in every possible way."

Chenzira pulled her into him and kissed her soundly on the lips. "Rattle some bones, my love. I'll keep them busy. What did you have in mind?"

Aviama smiled, as big as she could manage, and pulled him in to kiss him once more. "I need the horn first. But someone's inside the castle, so I'm going to start there."

Teja sprinted toward them with the girl on her back. With a slashing motion of both hands, Sai dropped Teja's two pursuers to the ground. Aviama stepped toward Teja, pushing the boundaries of the bubble to envelop the woman and the girl. She pointed at the cliff where the Dezapi spilled out beneath the castle and cascaded down the rest of the cliff face to the Shalladin below.

"Get Teja and the baby behind the waterfall. There, on the other side. There's a hidden cleft back there and a door to the catacombs."

Teja groaned, panting and out of breath. "Did it have to be catacombs?"

"Take it or leave it. It's your best shot." Aviama gave Chenzira a pointed look. "Don't let her leave it. Taking it is her only option."

Teja's face went white. Chenzira smiled. "You got it."

Fire blazed from Rana's palms. Aviama threw up a shield with one hand and snaked a vine of air around Rana's ankle with the other. Chenzira glanced toward her as she barreled after his sister, though from concern over her worrisome state or for his sister, she didn't know.

Either way, she didn't have time to debate the matter with him. And with the severe lack of quakemakers on either side, and Keket outnumbering them on a staggering scale, having Chenzira on the river fighting Sutekh was their best shot at surviving the morning.

Sutekh threw a wave at Manan, who rose in a tidal wave of his own, bearing him up above the deck. Behind them, toward the helm, victorious shouts from the rubble of the stairs suggested the sailors may have nearly conquered their latest obstacle.

Time was up. Aviama launched up the forecastle at Rana, ripping the air from her lungs before she hit the deck. Rana opened her mouth as if to gasp, eyes wide, clutching at her chest. Aviama gave a sharp tug—just enough. No more. Her eyes were half-closed, lashes fluttering, wind gushing from her hands in faltering, chaotic gusts.

Aviama slipped the horn tether over Rana's head and slung it across her own torso. "Sorry, friend. I wish I could have been gentler about it."

Strategists from then on could likely have debated the intelligence of leaving Rana alive. But she'd once left Durga alive on a deck just like this one, and Durga had become— well, not a friend, exactly, but friendly. Strange as it may seem, Aviama relied on Durga's relentless, no-nonsense approach and even her goading provocation to pull her out of wherever her brain had taken her, give her a good shake, and set her on her way again.

Maybe if they all survived, Rana and Aviama could be friends. But if not, and someone had to kill Chenzira's sister, Aviama desperately hoped that someone would not be her.

Sutekh spun toward her. Aviama lifted the horn to her lips. If they were outnumbered, perhaps all they needed was a little reinforcement. She wasn't sure how far a distance the Iolani horn worked in, or what sort of magic might be imbued in it, but she did know that Makana had told her help would come if she sounded the horn.

Sutekh's jaw went slack. The wave he raised from the river behind him doubled in size, frothing in angry, white-capped towers as his gaze fixed on Aviama.

No shield this time. Nothing could keep the sound from

carrying to Ali'i Makuakan and her siren friend Makana.
Aviama blew the horn.

42

Nothing happened. No sound. No shock wave of mysterious power. Nothing.

Nothing but Sutekh's torrential wave. The force of the blow smacked into her body like a hurricane plucking debris. Aviama's feet swept off the ship deck and over her head before she had the chance to breathe, a rag doll soaring through the air on the wings of a ravenous river seeking someone to devour.

Cannons fired. Flames showered the ship in a swirl of embers. Upside-down people fought one another, fireballs and blasts of wind, tumults of river and metal, dancing almost in slow motion as she tumbled through air and water. She managed only a whisper of wind cushion as she hit the Shalladin with enough force to snap necks. If the angle had been just a hair off …

Someone's dismembered arm plunged into the water beside her. As absurd as the thought was, she hoped it wasn't someone she knew. The last time someone's limb had flown by her, it had been in a cloud of smoke, and the victim had already been dead. If she were to lose an appendage, being dead was a foolproof way not to be bothered by the loss.

Aviama pulled a bubble of air down toward her—or sideways, or from whatever direction the surface was. She felt for the energy of the wind making its way to her and followed it to find which way was up.

Why hadn't the horn worked? Horns were tricky, but she knew she had the technique. Aviama had learned on her fair share of them since she was a girl, amusing herself with little hobbies of art and music and whatever was around, including the herald's horns and the military's bugles.

Biscuits, Aviama, what a dolt you are. It was designed for sirens. Why would a marine species design a horn to work on land rather than in the sea? Besides, sound traveled better in water.

An air pocket reached her, just small enough to take a breath. Aviama sucked in a lungful of blessed air and blew one more blast into the horn. This time the river around her shuddered, rolling away from her like an unfurled carpet flowing down a long marble staircase. A thrill ran through her bones, stunted only by the fact that it was utterly silent.

Either the horn was broken, or it was very different from any horn or bugle she had tried before. And if the latter, it probably wouldn't even matter. They were leagues away from Ghosts' Gorge. It was too far. The useless, last-ditch effort of a losing side.

You're not dead yet.

Aviama flung her hands in front of her, and a ball of air twice her height hurled its way down through the murky depths. She'd never attempted to fly as high as she'd need to if she wanted to hit the balcony. The entirety of the cliff loomed between her and the sandstone of Shamaran Castle.

Every last Shamaran will burn.

Flashes of blood in the river assaulted her mind again. Bodies washed up on the bank, flies swarming familiar faces. Teja. Durga. Sai. Chenzira. The baby.

A scalding blaze lit the blood in her veins. Her muscles grew taut as she tensed, closing her eyes to bend all her focus on the air beyond the surface of the river.

Come to me.

Wind wrapped around her like a garment. Down, down she went, to the bottom of the river. The air about her begged for release as the pressure of the river bore down on it. It begged to fly. It begged to launch out of the deepest despair of the cold, dank dark. But still Aviama held it firm. An element held in the palm of her hand.

She held it there, down, down further still, until her back rested on a bed of rocks at the bottom. The air twisted and twirled about her body, tugging upward in unspoken request, its energy rushing about her ears. Rivulets of wind spun downward like a whirlpool, gathering speed and strength, until at last Aviama sealed it off completely from escape. The full weight of the river played with the mass of atmosphere she'd drawn in around herself.

Visions of plastic smiles and bauble-studded canopies on the backs of Radhan beasts of burden found her there at the base of the Shalladin. Forced kisses, harsh hands seizing her wrists, feeling for her hips. Crooked smirks breathing threats in her ear like sweet nothings. Long silk gowns. Romantic gestures laced with coercion. The insufferable stench of lilac.

Konnolan, filling the air with bittersweet betrayal and helplessness.

No one knew. No one understood who Shiva really was. Not like she did. How could they?

Aviama wasn't new to mind games. Sutekh knew she was a tortured soul, and that her innocence had been crumpled by the Radhan prince. Florian had known of him as well. Was it beyond reason to think someone put the lilac there for no reason other than to draw her away from Sutekh and Rana and the river, and bait her into the Great Hall?

The thought came a nanosecond too late. A surge of adrenaline spiked the tense, charged air around her and lit the fuse on a world-class trebuchet of her own making—only the wind served as the mechanism, the river as the tension, and she was the missile.

Like an arrow from the string, the compressed air exploded up and out from the rock bottom of the river. Wind whistled past Aviama's face and through her hair. Her slitted skirts billowed about her legs, the Iolani horn hung by her hip, her palms directing the force of the air lifting her up, up, up. She'd been afraid of the height of the dragon when Semra took her on Zezura's back, but somehow this, with her friend the wind surrounding her and buffeting her upward at her command, sent a thrill down her spine.

Flame and towering water threatened the ships down below, but her concern was ahead instead. Her concern *must* be ahead, if there was any hope of those below her securing victory and keeping it. If Shiva was here, he'd have konnolan. And if he had konnolan, he could turn on Sutekh, and they were all as good as dead.

But he couldn't be here. Because while they might be as good as dead, Shiva was actually dead. Wasn't he?

You didn't see him die.

A swarm of sirens had attacked as he hit the water, when she blasted him off the *Wraithweaver* and into the sea in the belly of Ghosts' Gorge. Makuakan wouldn't be merciful to the man who kept his daughter captive for years and threatened his people and his children. But maybe Shiva had only been as good as dead, even then. Maybe he had tipped the scales in his favor. But what could have shifted those sands?

Vines bursting with lilac blossoms swayed in the might of her wind, showering her with purple petals as she flew up, up, past the waterfall, past the cliff, light as a feather, straight as a pelican's dive. A second burst of air boosted her up over the bastion to the balcony outside the Great Hall, carrying a whisper of Durga's voice sent along with the wind:

"I hope you know what you're doing."

Aviama's mouth went dry. *Me too.* But as her wet sandals hit the familiar tiles of home, she was not at all sure she knew what she was doing. *You should have told Chenzira what you were doing. You should have brought Sai, or even Durga. You should've—*

A shadow passed across the windows into the hall.

Every last Shamaran will burn.

Unless a Shamaran lived to rule in Jannemar, the kingdom would fall into ruin. Death and destruction on a scale like none she'd ever seen would sweep over the land. No one in Jannemar knew the gravity of the situation. To her right, where guards were always stationed, no one stood; to her left, nothing greeted her but vacant air and the desolate rustle of fallen leaves that had drifted over the wall from the northeast side.

Shamaran Castle sat empty, its defenders focused on Horon. Eerily empty. As if someone else had come in and cleaned house before she arrived.

Aviama sidestepped out of view of the Great Hall and tested the double doors at the enclave to her right. It was unlocked. Softly, softly, she turned the handle, and it swung toward her without complaint. Straight ahead, the hall would lead her past the anteroom and guard tower to the library, and down toward the receiving room and throne room. To her left, the double doors to the Great Hall loomed.

Somewhere out of her subconscious, a voice whispered: *Be surprising.*

She turned and strode into the stone staircase and up the guard tower. Her steps echoed in the narrow space, announcing her presence loud enough that she questioned the wisdom of entering a claustrophobic, closed-in place with no visibility out either end.

She reached the top of the stair and dipped into the guard room. Hooks for weapons, shields, and armor lined the walls. Three mugs served as the only decoration in the room—two on the table, and one knocked to the floor several paces away. A new gouge sliced into the corner of the tabletop, and five or six of the metal hooks from the walls lay misshapen and scattered across the floor near the door.

All the weapons were gone. All the armor. Nothing remained, save a scrap of parchment stuck under the base of one of the mugs. Her heart battered the insides of her chest as she stepped forward to read the ink scrawl across the paper.

Dearest Lilac,
I've missed you. Meet me in your family's lovely ballroom.
Let's have a party.

It was in his handwriting.

Aviama stumbled backward out of the guard room and down to the conservatory. She crept into the corner room of the conservatory, half-expecting an army to descend out of thin air to apprehend her. But this was a place of ghosts of memories, of altercations long past, the evidence left just for her. Spilled soil and plants littered the room, adding a dash of earth tones to the crimson of dried blood crusted on the low, round table and the long dragging marks on the floor. Shards of a broken ceramic pot shone up at her in white and blue designs, the insides of the pot still twinkling bright white behind splotches of caked dirt.

She crossed the room and tested the shards. Three of them came to a sharp point along the break. Aviama stashed two in her belt, clutched the third in her hand, and unlatched the door leading to a walkway over the Great Hall.

The design of the castle keep wrapped around like an armchair, the Great Hall serving as the middle, flush with the natural cliff, and the two halls extending on either side of it at an angle so that they were not quite parallel with each other. The courtyard where her father had been hit lay nestled in the center of the keep, touching all three sides. From the floor of the Great Hall, the ceilings soared high overhead from the sparkling floor, with a third-floor walkway elevated above the festivities of the hall to connect the conservatory, the king and queen's rooms, and the throne room on one side, to the guest hall on the opposite side of the keep.

If she was going to meet Shiva—or whoever was posing as Shiva—she wasn't going to go through the double doors to the main level.

A new thought dropped into her mind. What if it was Satya? If Shiva's mother had somehow heard what had happened to her son, she would stop at nothing to pack up her murderous hyena and destroy everything connected to Aviama—castle, family, kingdom, and all.

She'd prefer the outwardly sickening queen over her duplicitous, sneering son.

Aviama's sandals left light, damp footprints behind her from the conservatory, her dress still wet but wicked enough by the wind on her ascent that it was no longer dripping. The lever door handle was unlatched, and she slipped out the door to the walkway over the Great Hall. Chandeliers twinkled in cascading sunbeams pouring in through tall windows facing the cliff. Tile gleamed from the floors, with none of the foreboding evidence lurking in the guard room.

Wind whispered to her palms as she gathered energy around herself, soft and gentle as a morning dove, but consistent as a building wave. Cautious steps carried her out over the walkway, further from the conservatory doors, gilded molding along the wall to her right, and columns lining the dance floor to her left. Perfectly positioned tables sat under draped cloth along the wall, leaving the rest of the room open. The doors to the courtyard were ajar, and a cool breeze wafted in from outdoors.

The sharp edge of the ceramic shard bit into her palm as she clutched her hand around it. A rushing filled her ears, and it took her three beats of her pounding heart to realize it was her own blood and adrenaline filling her head over the silence of the phantom space. Aviama's sandals tapped lightly along the walkway. Whoever was here was toying with her.

Aviama called to the wind around her and let it carry her over the slender rail and down two stories to the ballroom below. She landed on her feet in the center of the room, shard still gripped in her hand.

"I missed you."

Her hands clenched, and her teeth set on edge at the sound of his voice. *Not possible.* It wasn't, was it?

But it was. Tone smooth as oil, lies slippery as an eel. It was him. A trickle of blood ran down her palm to the pristine floors from where the ceramic cut into her skin. She turned to face the arbiter of her nightmares: Prince Shiva.

43

I ce rippled through Aviama's veins. "Wish I could say the same, but then we'd both be lying."

Heavy double doors at the far end of the hall shut behind Shiva with a resonating thud as he strolled into the room. His face was drawn, features still chiseled as if from marble, the cut of his chest visible beneath a thin tunic of the Jannemari style, tucked neatly into pressed trousers and a regal navy jacket with gold embroidery.

Aviama steeled herself to keep from stumbling backward. She wasn't in Radha. She hadn't taken magna. There were no cannons in sight.

But if she had the upper hand, why did she feel like a mouse in a cat's game?

She jerked her chin at the jacket draping his shoulders. "You've been raiding my brother's closet."

Shiva flashed a devastating grin. "Oh, this? I thought it suited me. What do you think?"

"I think it would make more sense to dress a pig in pearls than to put you in royal finery."

"Ridiculous. My own wardrobe is made up entirely of royal

finery." Shiva plucked at the edges of his sleeves, the gesture uncomfortably reminding Aviama of her brother's mannerisms.

Aviama shrugged. "It makes no more sense there than it does here. You are not a king. You're a stuffed peacock parading around with other people's authority. And if one day you steal a crown, even then you will be not a king, but a tyrant."

"I'm glad to see murder on your conscience hasn't changed your fiery spirit."

"*Attempted* murder, and thank you. Were the Iolani more hospitable than I anticipated?"

Wind whisked about her hands, spiraling up and down her arms, wafting the hair about her shoulders in restless request. Why did she wait? Why not end him now? Snap his neck? What would conversation gain?

But an invisible force seemed to trap her hands in place and root her feet to the floor. What had happened when she stepped out of line before? But hadn't she defied him too many times now to care? How many times had she tried to kill the man? Twice, at least, now—even if the first attempt, on the *Wraithweaver* when she blew up the captain's quarters, had made Chenzira sincerely question her sanity.

A legitimate concern, if she was being honest.

Shiva clasped his hands in front of him and strolled toward her at a leisurely pace. Not so relaxed as to keep his hands behind him, but measured and slow. "They went for torture first. But Limakau wanted to make a name for himself, and he had enough backing to break me out."

"You can't expect me to believe that. Makuakan had firm control of the Gorge when we left."

The Iolani chieftain would have made quick work of the rebellion leader, whose alliance Shiva had courted while he and Aviama had been held in the underwater prison there. Makuakan's reinforcements had arrived just in time during the battle at Ghosts' Gorge, but they'd won the fight—and Makuakan was not known for his mercy. Had the war not ended?

Shiva smiled, his gaze sweeping over her like a man at an auction inspecting a horse. The fitted top of her dress clung to her curves, her slitted skirt falling from the belt around her waist to just short of the floor. Rana's jeweled collar and head-piece still graced her chest and brow, her upper arm and finger decorated by Chenzira's gift of the armband and lapis-lazuli ring. Golden hair flowed over her shoulders, the color deepened by her skirmish with the river water.

"I'm partial to Radhan fashion, but I have to say, there's something to be said for Keketi skirts." Shiva brought his eyes back to hers, taking his time as his gaze traveled back up to her face. "You don't have to believe it, dearest. Stroll out to the balcony with me and see for yourself. He and his sirens came with me to Jannemar. Their orders were to stay out of sight until you arrived for our rendezvous, and then to tear apart anyone and any ship not acting according to plan."

Aviama flicked her wrist, and with a blast of air behind it, sent the ceramic shard coursing toward Shiva's jugular. An answering fire blazed across the space into the ceramic shard, knocking it off its path to skitter harmlessly to the floor. Her stomach dropped to her toes. Had he just—

Shiva waved his hand in a flourish before him, flames dancing between his fingertips. "I see why you were so reticent to give up your power. It's intoxicating, isn't it?"

Her gaze followed the orange light of the fire bouncing off a jeweled cuff she'd never seen before wrapping tight around his wrist. She shook her head. "Sifal. Sifal magic. It will kill you."

"Yes, but even your sister-in-law uses the spear, doesn't she? Because it's made of wyronite and conducts magic without the side effects. I'll have the power transferred to wyronite soon. Were you worried about me?"

The topic was getting her nowhere. The revelation that Shiva was not only alive but had fireblood powers was enough to make her head spin. And if he had fireblood powers here in the castle and sirens in the water below, she'd need to create some other opportunity. If she could keep him talking long enough ...

She took a step back and cleared her throat. "Where is my sister?"

Shiva countered with two steps forward. "The dungeon, obviously. She was displeased with her circumstances. Told me the least I could do was light a candle to mask the smell. The dungeon is actually quite full; you should consider expanding it."

Aviama sidestepped out of his trajectory. "I'll make a note."

Power whispered to her every fiber. Was she the kind of person who killed people? Even if they were dangerous? She *had* been, and it had given her heaps of nightmares. But it had also provided peace. Maybe not peace of mind, for her, but physical safety to others. And yet many of them had been soldiers, doing only what they'd been told.

Chenzira had done it without a second thought. He'd done it in Radha. He'd done it in Siada with his brother's men.

But Aviama was not Chenzira.

Shiva smiled. "Trying to decide if you can kill me?"

Aviama called to the wind in silent request. *Stay with me. Until the right moment.* Rivulets of air currents ran along her skin in answer, sending goosebumps rippling up and down her arms. She tilted her head. "If I was, would you have any recommendations?"

Games. Games and more games. *Biscuits.* She was sick of them. She scanned the room. The marble floors and stone columns were to her advantage—they wouldn't catch fire. But the tables and cloths would, and fireballs could still shatter windows and burn her to a crisp. The image of Rana's mother, charred beyond recognition, reduced to ash and embers, surged unbidden from her memory.

Could she rip the air from his lungs without him intercepting with a burst of fire to interrupt her currents?

"You could try stealing my breath. I wouldn't fight it. Most people do, as a knee-jerk reaction, but I've spent my time training to meet you again, and I won't waste my energy or my power that way. I'll boil your blood instead."

Aviama blinked. "Can you do that?"

She regretted it the second the sneering smile crept across his despicable face. "Oh, I can. Like I said, I've been practicing. It's quite satisfying."

"How many?"

The words were out before she could stop them. It didn't matter. It *shouldn't* matter. What would it change about her interaction with him *now*, if he'd murdered five or three hundred since last they spoke? What purpose would it serve but to intimidate her and throw off her focus?

Shiva shot flames in a spiraling arc from one hand, over his head, and across the fingers of his opposite hand, like a juggler twirling colorful balls at a party.

"Limakau fears sifal as much as you do. He has plenty of his own power, and no motivation to risk it by playing with unnatural magic. But he doesn't mind me risking my own life, so once he smuggled me the artifact and we set a plan in motion, I started with the guard sirens." His lips twitched, eyes glittering. "I'm more thorough than you are. I made sure to kill Makana before I left. I didn't leave her corpse until it disintegrated into the sea, surrounded by ash flakes of skin and scales."

Makana. The siren Radha had captured and thrown in a glorified fishtank in a menagerie to show off to prestigious visitors. The Iolani chieftain's daughter, a warrior in her own right, who had seen through Shiva from the start. The one who nearly killed Aviama just by association with Shiva, but who ultimately risked her own life to save Aviama and Chenzira together in the arena.

Tabeun sister. The first time Makana had held up her palm to Aviama's and spoken those words, Aviama hadn't known what to say. But the two of them had become bonded in that moment. From the instant they sang together, a duet of legendary proportions, an offer of friendship between humans and sirens, they'd shared a remarkable understanding.

Both victims of Radha's brutality and greedy domination. Both held hostage far from home. Aviama had wanted nothing more than to free Makana, and she'd done it. Or had she? Had she, if she'd returned home just in time to save Aviama and her companions, only for Aviama to be sold into slavery and shipped off to Keket? Only for Aviama to pass off the perpetrator of her nightmares to Makana, where Shiva had boiled her blood and destroyed the hope of the Iolani and any chance at a genuine friendship between the peoples of the land and the peoples of the sea?

Power blasted outward from her in every direction, catching Shiva's body up off the tile floor. End over end, he spun up toward the ceiling. A deep ache awoke and beset her chest and throat, an everlasting companion brought back to the surface again. Makana's gift lifted off her hip, tugging at its tether in the wind, as if called home to a watery grave beyond the land of the living.

She'd hardly noticed when her hand had stretched

outward toward her most soul-crushing foe. She ripped her hand into her chest again, cutting off the wind and sending Shiva's body plunging back down to unforgiving marble floors. Shiva threw out both hands, and a gush of flame caught him and cushioned his fall. With a slashing motion, he extinguished the flames from the singed edges of her brother's coat —the coat of her most beloved family, one of the last of her Shamaran family, slung about the shoulders of her most hated enemy.

Shiva's expression hardened from graphite to impenetrable diamond, a catastrophic transition from gloomy and foreboding to impenetrable and deadly. The cut of his cheekbones stood out more exaggerated than she remembered, perhaps owed to the sifal magic he'd experimented with, giving his stunning visage a hollower look, haunted by shadows, as though vibrant life had cut a deal with death.

Little by little, centimeter by centimeter, he drew his head up and pulled his shoulders back, until his blazing eyes left the raging flames still burning in the palms of his hands to bore scalding detestation into the deepest abyss of her soul.

"Dearest lilac." He licked his lips, shades of carmine red, ravaging rust, and conniving fox playing in the lights of his eyes through the waltz of flames dancing between them. "That was foolish."

Blinding light bowled into her faster than she could blink. Searing pain exploded in her side. Flying. Backward.

If you hit the columns at this speed, you'll die.

Aviama snapped herself sideways with a wrench of billowing wind. Her hands hit the floor over her head, and she let the momentum of her body carry her into a cartwheel until her feet found their footing. She straightened, eyes latching onto her prey across the room.

"You said I was tainted. You called me a witch. You said

you would not stop until the last Shamaran burns." Aviama spread her hands. "Here I am, you dung-caked swine. Set the fire."

Shiva's stupid face split into a wide, leering smile. "You suffer from delusions of intelligence. It never ceases to amaze me. You think you can cow me with a few pitiful words?"

"I don't really care."

Aviama threw her hands out in front of her, and Shiva swung his own palms up to counter. Streams of air and fire shot out and met in a shower of roaring wind and flying sparks. A stray spark hit a tablecloth beyond the first row of columns, eating up the linen and rising to a fire in its own right. Shiva stepped, and Aviama stepped with him.

Muscles strained and taut, power emanating like a never-ending fountain of death, the prince of Radha and the princess of Jannemar drove into a dance all their own—a masquerade ball of precise footwork, approach and retreat, wind and flame. They swept across the ballroom of her childhood, a thousand invitations and a thousand bows and curtsies cycling through her memory. But there was another dance that pushed its way to the forefront, not at home but across the sea to a foreign place of fear and wonder and intoxicating mysteries.

He'd danced with the other three women already, the other contenders to be his intended. But when he'd extended his arm, and she'd slipped into his hold, he'd been perfect. Bewitching. Complimentary. A practiced man in footwork and flattery.

When the prince of that first dance had dropped his arm to press into her lower back, she'd been awkward, and he'd been lovely. She'd fumbled through apologies for knocking him over like a hurricane in a pristine afternoon tea when she'd first arrived in the House of the Blessing Sun; he'd only laughed and smiled and given her a spin and an intoxicating glance that had left her breathless. But even then, he'd had the keen observation of the eagle—and the penetrating gaze of a man experienced in more than women and waltz.

Shiva had led their movements then, guiding her this way and that, twirling her once, twice, rotating her into a graceful dip and back to himself in graceful, expert arcs. But a lifetime had come and gone since then. He wouldn't lead today.

Aviama shot a vine of air around his ankle. He blocked with a blast of fire, and she used the distraction to close the distance between them and angle for his chest. Could he feel the tug on his lungs?

His body shuddered, and he faltered. Shiva lashed out with a torrent of flame that sent her skidding backward along the slick floor.

Something in her chest felt wrong. Hot. Too hot. Spots dotted her vision, and her head swam. Aviama threw out a hand to stabilize herself against a column at the edge of the dance floor, but her hand missed the stone, and she toppled forward.

Sweat broke out on her brow. Pain screamed through her from the inside out, as if someone had snatched a butcher's knife from a furnace and begun to flay her alive. Aviama crumbled to the floor.

Don't clutch at your chest. Don't focus on yourself. That's what he said you'd want to do. That's how you die.

Aviama funneled every last shred of energy to cut through the wall of flame and assail her enemy's lungs. She tugged. Hard. The heat in her body shot up. And then went cold.

44

Cool marble caressed her cheek as she lay on the floor of the ballroom. Droplets of crimson decorated the polished marble. Where was she bleeding from?

It didn't matter. She couldn't move.

Out of her tilted vision from her position on her side in a heap on the floor, light still poured in from the tall windows on the northern side. Somewhere over there, beyond the balcony, beyond the bastion, and down the cliff, Chenzira, Durga, Sai, and the others would be fighting for their lives—seven melderbloods against Sutekh, Rana, and his Keketi fleet. If Shiva was telling the truth, Limakau and his traitor Iolani faction followers would be there as well, destroying anyone who dared to threaten Radhan interests.

And there, not but five paces from her, Shiva lay on his back, staring up at the soaring ceiling. His lips were parted, and his throat made a choking sound as if paralyzed.

Aviama rolled to her elbows with a moan as her body temperature began to settle from Shiva's blood scorching. If he'd continued another few seconds, she'd be dead. But the same was true for her, starving his lungs.

Shiva lolled his head to one side, umber eyes latching onto hers. His voice was raspy as he scratched out his next words. "You were always too weak to finish the job. That's why you blasted me over the railing of the *Wraithweaver* instead of doing what needed to be done. You're a coward."

She *was* a coward. She'd spent too long being afraid. She'd also been soft, perhaps both to her credit and to her detriment. Mercy kept her human. Mercy reminded her that humans cannot escape their humanity, no matter how hard they try, and carry within them powerful potential in every conceivable direction—the capacity for good and the capacity for evil. Her experience with hatred had taught her how close anyone was to falling into darkness.

Aviama had tasted the dark. It had scared Chenzira to see it and had almost enveloped her completely. But while she was in it, the dark had a numbing effect, so that she cared less and less about anything but the consuming object of her focus.

If she carried out justice, would mercy cry out to her forever? If she offered mercy, would withheld justice torture her and everyone she loved by visiting a restless evil upon them all until death carried them away?

Aviama shoved herself up into a half-sitting position and fixed her gaze on Shiva through wisps of messy golden hair obscuring her face. "I am not afraid to die. I'm afraid to live knowing I could have stopped you and didn't."

Shiva coughed out a dry laugh. "You lost. This is the way of the world. Whether today or some other day, when I die, another will take my place. Jannemar is a dead kingdom, and you will pass away with it, just as kingdom upon kingdom have faded before you. The best we can hope for is to gain what we can when we can and die with honor when the time comes."

Flame flew across the space between them, and Aviama threw up an air shield. Embers exploded against the barrier a handsbreadth from her face. She shot a blast at Shiva, and he slid along the floor before gathering his feet.

Slowly, they rose to face off once more. No, there had to be more to life than men rising and falling to take and to die, to give and to collapse. To win and lose 'til the sun set on one's final day.

She'd come to know a love worth living and dying for. Family, and friends who had become family. A little orphan girl who needed a mother. Her heart wrenched as she thought of the word Onkar's crew had used to describe a sameness of soul. *Heartmeet.* Jignesh had used it first, echoed by Umed and Manan. Makana had mirrored the sentiment in the way of her people when she offered a revolutionary friendship, palm to palm, as her tabeun sister.

As often in her life as Aviama had been seen as the naïve little girl to be protected from harsh happenings in the world, it now fell to her to protect *them* from experiencing the dangers she'd faced.

Who knew the Radhan prince's reprehensible nature like Aviama? Who understood his venom better than she?

Aviama dropped the shield and threw the ceramic shards still tucked in her belt, throwing a deluge of twisting air behind them as they sailed for Shiva's throat. Shiva threw himself into a roll and popped up again behind a burst of fire. The flames eating at the tables of the courtyard side of the room doubled in size as Aviama ducked and a fireball blasted into them.

Whistling wind raged to a roar. Aviama strode for the furnace of tabletop kindling and sent a mighty gale through the blaze, dashing the tables to pieces against the columns. To think she'd once been insane enough to allow the man's lips to touch hers. Her lip curled in disgust as she sent the wind to gather the flaming debris and hurl it at her adversary.

Shiva's expression contorted as he bent all his strength and will to the missiles headed toward him. One after another, he stretched his sifal power to explode piece after piece of flying lumber. One after another, Aviama bashed the tables to bits and launched them at Shiva.

The prince threw up a blast of fire a second too late, and a slab of tabletop slammed into him. He crashed through one of the windows, glass shattering with a cascading *kshhhhhh* as shards fell on marble floors, the stone of the balcony just above the bastion over the cliff, and other bits of glass. Aviama sprinted over flaming splintered wood and took a flying leap through the broken window and over the sharp smashed glass on the balcony beyond. She stretched out her hand to Shiva's chest as his back rammed into the balusters of the railing and ricocheted off it to the floor.

His eyes went wide as she came to stand over him. She could feel the air in his lungs, rasping in and out as she allowed just enough to keep him alive, cinching off the rest to keep him too weak to fight.

No man was any more than a sack of bones wrapped in a carcass, imbued with personality and soul and desires and experiences. The strongest of kings could die by eating the wrong plant, and the weakest of commoners could stand up against tyranny and change the course of history. She'd wished, perhaps, even back on the *Wraithweaver*, that Shiva might come to his senses before the end. Anything to stop her from having to kill.

"I wish I didn't have to do this." She shook her head. "I wish I could justify the time it would take to explain it to you. I wish all that was required was taking the time to walk you through it—through the joys of life, the things worth dying for, the things worth living for, and how the dying is a moment, but the living goes on and on. How death cements us as we are, but living molds and moves us. That nothing worth living for is big enough to deserve our devotion if we will not also die to protect it. That the living, and living *well,* is just as important a calling as the dying."

It was a waste of breath. A waste of time. But as she said the words, they breathed strength into her bones, and boldness to her blood. Truth she needed to speak to herself. Permission to do what she couldn't have done before.

Anger gave way to a sorrow she would have despised herself for having mere minutes prior. Wind gathered about her to carry her wherever she wanted to go, to do whatever she asked it to do. And she loved the wind in a new way—not for its exhilarating power or the thrill of its rushing, but for its ability to protect that which was worth living and dying for.

It was too late to protect her own mother, and too late to save her father. Her bodyguard, Enzo, had already passed into death, and Bhumi, Laksh, and Husani had joined him. No amount of begging would bring Makana back to sing again. Sona, the sailor on the *Wraithweaver,* could not be returned to his wife and children.

But there were others. Young, impressionable, powerful Rana was a motherless girl with too much grief and abandonment to hold in her body alone. If no one guided her in what to do with it, where else could it go, but to cause the world she touched to crumble as it had crumbled her? Durga had lived under Shiva's thumb and the domineering rule of his mother, Queen Satya. But freed from Radha, freed from their oppression, she'd come into herself. Sai would never be safe as long as Shiva was alive, and neither would anyone he touched or ruled or spoke to.

It was too late for many. For *too* many. But it was not too late for all.

Aviama clenched her fist, and Shiva's throat seized, dry-hacking and gagging at her command of his air supply.

"I do genuinely wish you could be redeemed. Because it isn't that people can't change. It's just that you have chosen not to be one of them. And if I were to try, you would only kill me and everyone after me once I was out of the way."

A door clicked shut from the guard tower behind her, off to one side. Light padding feet ran forward, velvet soft and fast. "Amma?"

Aviama whirled. The little girl hesitated two steps onto the balcony from the tower, her hair and dress still dripping wet from the waterfall they'd passed through to get to the catacombs.

Chenzira must have gotten Teja and the girl to the cleft, and they'd navigated the catacombs and stairs to the main level faster than Aviama would have expected. Why hadn't they stayed there until the fight was over? Why had they come—

A figure came into view then, sprinting through the Great Hall after the little girl. Teja, breathless, hair mussed in every direction, full tilt after the toddler. Teja disappeared into the guard tower and skidded to a halt in the doorway out to the balcony as she took in the scene of Aviama standing over Shiva's half-dead body, hand extended over his chest.

ow much death should little eyes see? And if they must be exposed to violence, should they be forced to see it doled out by those they love and trust? To see the hands of those who'd held her together rip apart another human being? Aviama froze, her hand still stretched out over Shiva's chest, the air in his lungs like clay in her hands.

But if she killed him now, would Aviama's face appear in the toddler's nightmares—not as her savior, but as the perpetrator? If she didn't kill him, what else could she do with him that would keep the girl alive long enough to dream at all?

Sharp blades sever in seconds. Arrows fly in the blink of an eye. And when an enemy is at the end of his rope, hesitation is death.

Aviama had hesitated.

The snake beneath her hand spewed fire like venom. A blazing stream flew past her toward the little girl. The orphan girl whose parents were dead. Whose mother had died for the crime of being melderblood.

Small, smooth hands cupping her cheek. Kisses good

night. Tiny fingers reaching out to grasp hers. Who'd been taken in Radha, when their prince had done nothing but add fuel to the furnace on the feverish greed for slave labor.

This prince. The one who had smiled at her, questioned her, kissed her, gotten answers from her, and made her feel as if she'd rather be dead than alive.

Aviama launched herself into the path of Shiva's fury, fiery deluge filling the entirety of her awareness. Flames engulfed her. Agony screamed through every fiber of her flesh as she leaped toward Shiva.

The shadow of a man rose from the stone floor of the balcony and lifted his palm toward her as her body rocketed toward him. Red hot agony exploded into searing, excruciating torture from the deepest parts of her, as if her blood might boil over out of every orifice and spatter across the cursed lilac draping the balcony.

"Amma!"

The toddler threw up both hands, releasing her own torrent of fire toward Shiva. Aviama slammed into Shiva at the exact moment the little girl's blow blasted into him, tripling the impact. The hold on her blood vanished, and the heat enveloping her body lessened, replaced by a glacial wind licking at the flames and the plummeting sensation of leaving her stomach somewhere high above her as she and Shiva blasted over the balcony and out over the bastion.

Strong arms wrapped around her like iron chains, flames still dancing on the hem of her dress and catching on the edges of her brother's jacket. Iron fingers dug into her ribs and the curve of her hip as Shiva crushed her against himself and the two of them tumbled headlong over the edge of the cliff.

Aviama fought to free a hand. She wormed one hand up to his chest and latched onto the air in Shiva's lungs. With a tug on his air supply, the fire all around her snuffed out into smoke. Her blood burned as he retaliated with fire at her core; her head swam, and her vision blotted.

Still, they fell. But Shiva needed her to cushion their fall, just as she had needed him to eliminate the flames. And now that the flames were gone, she had no need for him.

Just as he would have no need for her the instant they hit the Shalladin River.

Above, Shamaran Castle disappeared into a haze of morning light; beside them, cold spray from the Dezapi Falls sent a jolt of wakefulness through her, as if to remind her there was more work to be done before succumbing to the burning of her body. She had lost all feeling from one arm the moment she thrust it into Shiva's flame as it was on its way to incinerate the little girl. But she could still move it, and with a test she found that though the wind was erratic in responding to that arm, it responded nonetheless.

It would be enough. It would have to be.

Below, Sutekh's fleet had turned on *Raisa's Revenge.* Sutekh stood at the prow of a nearby vessel, Chenzira and the others fighting wind, water, and fire from the deck of the *Revenge* as sirens surrounded the ships and dragged sailor after sailor into the water. Rana was positioned not on the forecastle but on the figurehead of *Raisa's Revenge,* wind on either side protecting her balance as she sent a stream of fire and a blast of air toward Umed.

Cannons fired on the *Revenge* from the new flagship where Sutekh had set up his latest assault. The victim ship pitched sideways, and Rana lost her balance on the narrow figurehead.

Shiva's iron fingers gripped her like talons, scrabbling for purchase on his one lifeline as the two of them plummeted down the cliff, down past the Dezapi Falls, toward the rushing Shalladin River. Aviama's core burned as Shiva threatened her blood, ticking it up a notch—enough to warn, but not enough to incapacitate.

Save me. Save us, Lilac. And if you don't, I'll kill you before the river or sirens or rocks ever could.

That's when Aviama saw it—purple lilac petals drifting down from above them, floating demurely from the place where they'd been ripped from their blossoms hanging over the balcony. A drop of blood spoiled the pure amethyst of one of the deeper-hued petals.

Fury lit Aviama with another kind of fire. Lilacs should be left free to grow and bloom, not ripped from the bush, used until their inevitable demise, and tainted by the violence of others. The lilac bush could do even less than Aviama had believed she could do when she first landed in Radha.

But Aviama was no lilac.

The wind wrapped around Shiva and Aviama in a swirling mass from head to foot. Aviama's left hand slung around Shiva's waist, and her right slithered up over his chest. His umber eyes bored into her, the large oval stones of his bracelet digging into her back. *The artifact.*

She couldn't reach it. And he'd never stop.

A blaze exploded from his body as terror took him over and he lost control of the unnatural magic flowing through the object around his wrist. Any second they would hit the surface of the water, and he would kill her. The heat in her blood already intensified. Her vision swam, and she fought to keep her eyes open.

With a mighty yank, Aviama seized the air from his lungs like a fishhook snatching a fish from the depths. Shiva's eyes widened, mouth open as his air supply escaped him down to the last iota.

His eyes glassed over a fraction of a second before the two of them plunged into the river. Wheeling threads of air currents softened their impact, but the hit still knocked the breath from Aviama's body. Aviama sucked in a breath that accused her all the way into her lungs.

Thief. You stole his air. This breath was his.

But it wasn't, and she knew it. The moment Shiva laid the lilac over the balcony and left the note for her in the guard room, and lured her into the Great Hall, he had decided that one of the two of them would die today. He had made the unfortunate choice to attack both her and the little girl under her protection.

And there were no rules governing what one could and could not do in defense of one's own life. Her life was valuable. The toddler's life was valuable. And she would never again let him kill her, body or soul.

A strange numbness set in over her as she shrugged out of Shiva's frozen limbs and set him adrift in the river. His body sank slowly, his fingertips brushing hers as she pushed him away. A flicker of metallic silver and gold caught her eye, and Aviama glanced up through the thin buffer of air around her.

Sirens.

Shiva had been telling the truth. And if he was telling the truth, these sirens were loyal to Limakau—and Aviama was as good as dead in the water.

Three of them surged toward her, two silver, one gold, eyes glinting in the light filtering down from the surface. Aviama's stomach lurched to her throat as adrenaline coursed through her again, waking her from a blanket of numbness that covered her like a black cloud. In a last-ditch effort, Aviama rotated in the water and plunged down after Shiva's descending corpse.

His hand was cold, and the weight of his body pulled her down along with him. *Biscuits, he brings me down even after he's dead.* Aviama ripped the bracelet off his wrist and slipped it onto her own.

A wave of prickling fire rolled through her body, then localized in a burning pain around her wrist. The stones of the bracelet clung to her skin as if melded into it, and her palms tingled with beckoning power.

But she was underwater. What would flames do for her down here?

The sirens cut through the water like a spear, swift and strong. Aviama lifted both palms and summoned the wind. Sparks flew along her fingers in the air buffer around her, her tabeun magic mingling with the sifal of the fireblood housing artifact.

A stream of lightning-hot air blasted through the water. The blow hit the first siren square in the chest. The creature recoiled with a shriek, and Aviama sent two more after the remaining two sirens. One dodged, and the other fell back. The one that escaped spun in the water and came at her again from below, launching a spear from her palm and extending webbed claws toward her prey.

But strong as the Iolani were, and as long as they could hold their breath as a marine species, they still needed air. Which meant they had a weakness to exploit. Aviama caught the spear in one hand and flung her palm out with the other, pulling at the air in the siren's lungs.

The pull felt different somehow—more resistance, and a barrier as if there were a limitless reserve preventing her from stealing all the siren's air. Aviama had never noticed gills, and had seen Makana breathe air, but perhaps the Iolani had another or more robust means of breath.

Even so, the target siren writhed under Aviama's hand. Aviama summoned the wind, and it flew down from the surface to answer her call. The gale shot through the river to surround the siren with wind, immobilizing her in the water. Aviama's lip curled, and her fingers clenched as she hurled the ball of air, along with its screeching inhabitant, toward the rocks of the cliff at her back.

How many of these sirens had known Makana? Had forsaken her? How many of them remembered Aviama and Shiva coming to the Gorge, and knew that Aviama had claimed victory over Shiva then, and that Makana and the rightful chieftain, Ali'i Makuakan, had gifted her the horn now hanging at her waist? How many of them had expected Aviama to be dead and their new ally, Prince Shiva, to dispose of *her* body over the balcony?

But he hadn't killed her. Aviama had won. And she'd make sure every siren in hearing distance knew it.

A pang struck her heart at the thought of Makana. Makana, the chieftain's daughter. Makana, Aviama's friend and fellow captive from Radha, who had offered friendship to humans for the first time in centuries when she called Aviama *tabeun sister.*

What was it she'd said that day in the menagerie all those months ago, when Makana had sung and then ordered Aviama to do the same.

"When I sing, I learn. When you sing, I learn. You and I. One heart."

Something about the mysterious Iolani power allowed them not only to use their voices for the death lullaby that baited sailor after sailor to a watery demise, but also taught them something about the heart of a singer. It was not until after Aviama had sung for Makana that she'd cemented their friendship.

"Tabeun sister. You are true."

The siren princess had only concluded that Aviama was safe and meant her no harm *after* Aviama had sung.

But Aviama was not safe. Not to Shiva. Not to Sutekh. And not to these rebel Iolani, Limakau's scoundrel traitors.

The toddler remained with Teja up on the castle grounds of Aviama's childhood home. And Aviama intended to make the castle safe again or die trying. Her brother the king was risking his life with his dragonlord wife on the front lines near Horon, and Shiva had cleared out the castle in Qalea with such confidence in his sifal powers that he hadn't even cared to post guards nearby. Or perhaps he had none, being brought there by Limakau, and had swept into Shamaran Castle all on his own, his housing artifact and practical skill as a swordsman bringing him all the success he needed to empty the castle keep and Great Hall.

Sutekh and Limakau both remained threats to her home, her people—to innocents under her protection. And she would do anything necessary to end that threat.

Shadows moved across the deep of the river, glinting in copper, silver, and gold scales the closer they got to the surface. As long as they believed some allies remained on the surface, they would not use the death lullaby. Shiva would have expected Sutekh to be a friend, even if Shiva planned to turn on him in the end. That bought Aviama time.

Sirens flocked toward the dark hulls of Sutekh's ships. Aviama lifted the Iolani horn to her lips and let water surround her to carry the sound of it to ears more sensitive to hers—a herald of triumph, a dare to come against the daughter of King Turian Shamaran. The princess who refused to die.

Countess of Chaos.

I'm still here, guppies.

Aviama released the horn and adjusted her grip on the spear she'd taken from one of the attacking sirens. Between the dark shadows of *Raisa's Revenge* and the nearest Keket warship, a human female form struggled in the water between two sirens. Fire blasted from the woman at one of the sirens, but the water around it swallowed most of its heat, and the sirens held on.

It was time to demand the attention of the sirens and draw heat off Chenzira and the others. If Shiva had only needed a moment's hesitation from Aviama to turn the tables, maybe Chenzira could do the same if only he had a big enough distraction.

Could all sirens see into the intention and soul of a person through song? If Makana was moved to ally with Aviama all those months ago when she sang from heartbreak, and their emotions and purposes aligned, what would arrest the attention of traitor sirens more than music laden with threat?

Tortured soul? I'll show you what a tortured soul can do.

The thing about nightmares visiting each unconscious moment, the corpses of loved ones staring up from one's memory whenever stillness reigned for too long, was that terror and wrath lived only a hair beneath the surface at any moment. Aviama summoned the wind, breathed in deep, and leaned into both with every fiber of her being.

Burning fire flayed along her skin but did not harm her. Wind whipped around her like a cyclone. Rage shattered the cage of her mind, the limits of her power, like never before. Protective fury roiled in her chest like a mother zegrath whose pups had been stolen under her nose. Might, justice, and skill rolled into a venomous cocktail of deadly precision, pooling at her palms in a shower of embers.

Aviama Shamaran shot forward in the chill waters. It was time for a spectacle. It was time to demonstrate to any who dared come up against her exactly how the last Shamaran would burn.

It was time to ignite.

46

M elody hit her like the swell of a drum beating out the seconds before execution. Aviama let out the first notes, low and brooding, and cut off the sound. Again, she built on the song, so deep it was more of a rumble, and again she cut it off—cold and harsh as a freshly sharpened blade.

Mounting momentum funneled her forward as she crafted a wordless anthem made of fire and wind, tears and revenge. *I am Aviama Shamaran.* Minor notes blended with a colossal intensity that brought out a depth of emotion she rarely dared to face, the tenor and strength of it a quality she had never before taken into her hand and used to fuel the devastation of her power.

This is my home. You will suffer me. And at my hand you will fall.

The spear in her hand was light yet strong, cutting through the water with the grace of an eel. The wind at her back, the flame at her fingertips, drew every eye in the waters below toward a majestic warrior of a woman in the ripped, singed attire of Keket royalty. Aviama lifted her voice, and the river itself seemed to halt. She lifted one hand toward the sirens on either side of Rana. One tore away from her the instant Aviama locked eyes with her; the other raised a defiant hand, and Aviama commanded the fire to the siren's blood to boil her alive.

Arm outstretched, Aviama called to the wind, and the wind answered, sweeping a current down around Rana and carrying her to Aviama's waiting hand. Still, she sang. Still, her melody struck terror and warning, the herald of death, the promise of life extinguished and carnage ended.

Shall I burn, traitors? Would you like to see me burn?

Aviama shot out of the water, the remnants of an unfinished song hanging in unresolved tension at the surface of the river. She threw Rana to the deck next to Chenzira with an explosion of air around her that only barely slowed the woman's crash onto the floorboards of the deck. But Aviama soared to the rigging, lifting her spear for all to see.

Golden tresses flew out behind her, damp from the river, billowing back from the gilded Keketi collar that graced her neck and upper chest. Exquisite white linen crisscrossed her chest, torn, charred, and marked with blood. The garnet stone bracelet she'd taken from Shiva burned against her wrist, the sparks from her fingers bouncing red-orange light off the armband at her upper arm, the collar at her neck, the tone of her skin.

Angry red scar tissue ran up one arm from fingertip to elbow where she'd thrust her arm into Shiva's flames to protect the girl. But as she saw it in daylight for the first time, as jarring as the sight of it was, it didn't hurt. Now that she thought about it, she'd had feeling back for most of the time in the water. After she'd added the fireblood artifact to her wrist.

Perhaps the power that had inflicted the pain also lessened its effect, now that it had bonded to her instead.

The Iolani horn rested against her hip, her scorched skirts flowing about her legs from the slits on her thighs. Aviama lifted the spear in the air, then angled it at Sutekh as he gaped at her from the prow of the nearest ship.

"I am Aviama Shamaran. Shall the last Shamaran burn? Shall I burn?"

Aviama extended her hands out wide and fell from the rigging. Flames engulfed her. But this time, the blaze was hers. The fire was a friend. Air caught her a handsbreadth from the upper deck. The gust she'd commanded swept her upright and set her on her feet. She strode forward with the prowess of a ciraba, the force of a hurricane, the authority of a queen.

"Watch. Me. Burn."

Blaze shot out from her body in a flash of blinding light. Aviama reached out with her hands for the air in the lungs of the enemy. Half a dozen fell. Ten. Twelve.

Florian gawked at her from under the forecastle stairs. Rana picked herself up from the deck, brushed herself off, and stared at her in wonder. Sai's eyebrows soared.

Durga grinned. "Yessssss!"

Sutekh screamed something unintelligible from the opposite vessel. Cannons fired. Arrows flew. Wind and fire blasted from every direction around them. But this time, Aviama didn't fight the momentum of the blows. She absorbed the energy and spat it back out in the direction from which it had come. Wind and fire alike responded to her command now. Only water could threaten her, with too few skilled quakemakers to vie for victory. And Manan and Umed were already raising waves of their own to fight Sutekh's desperate walls of water.

Chenzira appeared at her side as the others fell in around

them. Sai, Umed, Manan, Osahar, Zahur, Durga—all six were alive and well, though Zahur had his arm in a haphazard sling. Umed had enough blood on him that it was unclear how much was his, or where his injuries might originate.

Chenzira stepped forward like a legionnaire straight out of an ancient legend. His bare chest rippled with taut, glistening muscles interrupted only by the gold on his upper arm and the schenti about his waist. From one hand, he swung the lone blade of a battle-ax. From the periphery, an unfortunate assailant had the gall to launch an arrow at the couple, and the blade flew from Chenzira's hands with a practiced elegance.

The weapon cut straight through the arrow and clean through the archer's neck before spinning round and returning to Chenzira's waiting hand. The man was magnificent. Stunning and imposing, gorgeous on a level that shook her to the core—but his dark eyes were set on her alone.

He reached out a hand, searching her face. Was he thinking of the last time she'd flown onto the deck of a ship? The time when she'd expected to die—almost *hoped* to die— and borne destruction aloft as her singular purpose? The time she'd scared him to the bone and nearly lost herself completely ...

She could see it in his eyes. Awe mingled with concern in the knit of his brow, the scrutiny of his gaze.

"Are you with me?"

Aviama returned his gaze with a steadiness and surety that had eluded her before. She had always denounced sifal magic and used it now only out of necessity. Only temporarily, to keep its power out of the wrong hands. She hadn't been turned. He had to know that.

She might be twice as dangerous, but she was also wiser. Smarter. Older, somehow, than mere months prior. Together, they would fight to the end, not only facing, but creating the ever-shifting sands of their story.

"I'm with you."

Aviama slipped her hand around Chenzira's neck and pressed her lips to his. A thrill ran down her spine as he twined an arm around the small of her back and pulled her close. A dazzle of sparks shrouded the two of them as they stood together on the deck of *Raisa's Revenge*. Wind spun about them, deflecting an arrow that broke through just before Sai's wind shield went up.

The deck of the ship shuddered, its metal nails frenzied, as if all the world begged for one moment more before the two of them parted. Aviama's gold collar fluttered as if it were a gauzy curtain caught in a breeze, rolling almost liquid as Chenzira deepened the kiss. He froze, and as he pulled away, he looked deep into her eyes for a moment before his gaze drifted down, over her lips, down her neck, to the Keketi collar draping her neck and chest.

The piece was solid again. Chenzira moved his hand from her back to her neck, trailing the metal with a finger. The gold rippled under his fingertip. He smiled and kissed her once more.

"Let's end this."

Aviama nodded, and together they turned toward Sutekh and his fleet—Chenzira with a battle-ax blade in one hand, and Aviama with her Iolani spear. A wall of water rose up before them, between the *Revenge* and the opposite vessel. Umed and Manan bent their focus on the water, and Aviama raised a hand toward the rebel wave.

She rotated her wrist in a tight spinning motion, and a funnel of air punched through the wave, assisted by Sai and Durga adding strength to the channel. Aviama nodded to

Chenzira, and he nodded back. The channel was for him, not for her.

Chenzira took a flying leap off the end of the prow and figurehead and across to the opposite ship just as Aviama swept a gale behind her up and over the towering wave. Chenzira landed in front of Sutekh, and with a mighty swing of his arm, the metal necklace collars the Keketi men wore grew razor-sharp edges and sliced clean through their necks. Heads bobbled to the deck of the ship, rolling with the tilt of the ship as Sutekh's wave crumbled.

The few sailors left on the ship, those either ruffian enough or poor enough to not wear even a basic traditional collar, belonged to Aviama. Her sandaled feet hit the railing, and she ripped the wind from their lungs. Bodies fell.

A celestial song rose above the din from the northeast end of the river from whence they'd come; Aviama glanced up to see a mass of serpentine creatures flooding the entire width of the river, bearing sirens on their backs. And there at the forefront rode Ali'i Makuakan and Aviama's tabeun sister, in the flesh, alive and well—spears outstretched, mouths open in a glorious battle song that stood her hair on end but begged for more all at once.

Shrieks filled the air as Limakau's sirens fled in a flurry of motion. They'd encountered Aviama's boiling fire and lung-starving wind and were only too glad to abandon her ship. But now they found themselves faced by the rightful Iolani chieftain and his daughter, come for revenge on a faction of sirens that could never hope for mercy. Whatever grace they'd received or wrath they'd escaped in the Gorge bore down on them with an irrevocable, constant pressing in like that of the rising sun—every moment bringing them closer to their fate.

Sailors across the remaining ships scattered. Some jumped overboard and were greeted by unfriendly sirens dragging them down to the bottom of the river; others saw the demise of their companions and opted instead for some dark corner of the hull of their ships. The furthest ships slowly turned about and angled to escape the river of death before the fury of the Jannemari princess and the forgotten Keketi prince caught up with them.

Fireballs exploded from Osahar and Zahur's hands, chasing down anyone insane enough to continue the fight. Sai threw up an air shield against a final volley of arrows and a few lasting melderbloods who had not worn traditional collars. Durga swept their legs out from under them, and Osahar finished them off.

Aviama ordered them into two groups: Umed, Durga, and Osahar; and Zahur, Manan, and Sai; each with a windcaller, fireblood, and crestbreaker, and directed them to sweep the remaining ships for survivors. If they chose the brig, very good. But if they fought back, they would be dealt with swiftly and severely.

As the teams moved on, one below deck and one to the next ship over, Aviama stepped to Chenzira's side. She glanced down at Sutekh's body. He'd been a visionary, in his own way, but without any moral code robust enough to keep him from an ends-justify-the-means approach to whatever goals he set before himself.

Aviama was grateful not to have to look over her shoulder for Sutekh or for Shiva. But with the relief came a sadness at evil so deeply entrenched in the heart that it became unstoppable. Nothing would have turned Shiva away from his aims. No one could have convinced him that what he was doing was not right, or could not have been just as right as the desire of any other leader.

Inevitably, someone would take their place. Shiva's father was not known for his kindness, and his mother Queen Satya was at least as bad as Shiva, if not worse. But perhaps, with the time to build up a decent force and a strategy, Aviama could aid in keeping such monsters at bay so that their power was stunted, stagnated, and stripped before they destroyed entire populations and kingdoms of innocent people. Perhaps she could help those with strong potential to grow in their leadership capabilities, able to stand up against evil with boldness and brawn, without sacrificing the softer things which the brawn was meant to defend.

She chewed her lip. Sutekh's body lay at their feet, severed at the neck. The jewel-studded metal collar that had been clasped around his neck slid over the end of his neck where his head should have been, and a blood trail led to his decapitated head, which had rolled a meter away and stared up at a blue sky he would never again see.

Aviama leaned into Chenzira. "Didn't you want a final word with him?"

Chenzira shrugged and wrapped an arm around her shoulders, resting his chin on her head. "There was nothing left to say. A drawn-out speech would only give him an opportunity to kill more of us. And I can't afford to lose you."

She smiled. Warmth filled her, but she still gave him a playful shove. "I can take care of myself."

"You're magnificent." He drew back to look at her, then pulled her in and planted a kiss on her forehead. "And I thank you for the opportunity to care for you, even when you don't need it."

Chenzira stared down at his half-brother's remains, and the corners of his mouth dropped into a solemn frown. "It needed to happen."

Aviama swallowed and looked away, out into the river —*her* river—filled with loyal Iolani chasing down the last of Limakau's rebels. "I wish it didn't have to happen this way."

Chenzira pulled her in tight as he turned away from Sutekh and looked out over the Shalladin. "Me too."

A tower of water bubbled up from the river, and there within it floated Makana. Spear in hand, white hair flowing, a bleeding scar across her cheek, Makana was every bit as fierce and formidable as Aviama remembered. She was also alive, her lavender eyes intense and unnervingly beautiful as ever.

"Tabeun sister!" Makana's solemn face broke into a wide smile and thrust her spear in the air in victory. "We hunt Limakau, but lose him. Horn help us find." Makana gestured at the Iolani horn at Aviama's hip. "We hear this. Keep it. Connect us always."

The siren lifted her palm up to Aviama, but instead of returning the gesture, Aviama ran forward to the edge of the ship and threw her arms around her mermaid friend.

"He said you were dead. He said you were dead ..."

Aviama fought the lump in her throat, the ache in her chest as the sorrow of the day mixed with the reassurance of her strange friend's survival and presence.

Makana hesitated, balancing in the water with a back-and-forth swishing motion of her long, muscular tail. At last, she hugged Aviama back, sending fresh rivulets of cool river water down Aviama's arms as they made contact.

The siren pulled away, an awkward half smile twisting at the corners of her mouth. "Tabeun sister?"

Makana lifted her palm again, and Aviama snort laughed in response as she lifted her own palm to touch Makana's, completing the gesture.

"Always. Tabeun sister."

"I speak with Father. We take care of own house, sink Radha ships in your country, then want meet with you. One month. Use horn."

Aviama dipped her head and wiped an escaped tear from her eye. "Thank you. I will."

Makana offered a nod, turned to go, then spun back toward Chenzira. Her gaze drifted from Aviama to Chenzira and back. "Spear man, why does tabeun sister have spear? You no have spear. In one month, you get new name. I will think of one."

Chenzira glanced at the Iolani spear still in Aviama's hand, and the battle-axe blade in his own. He laughed. "An excellent point. My name is Chenzira. You could try that one?"

Makana pursed her lips and shook her head. "I don't like. I will think of one."

With that, the siren flicked her silver tail and melted into the Shalladin River, calling her Iolani brothers and sisters to her, a pod of flashing scales of every color filling the water with radiant light as they moved as one under the ships and out toward the sea.

Chenzira took her hand, and together they turned back toward *Raisa's Revenge,* only to find Rana standing several paces off, staring at them.

"Was that what I thought it was?"

"Makana, warrior daughter to the Iolani chieftain? First siren friendship to humans in hundreds of years?" Chenzira nodded. "Yes."

Rana blinked, then turned to Aviama and gestured at the bracelet on her arm. "You got a housing artifact. Is that from Prince Shiva?"

"In a manner of speaking."

"Because he's dead, and you took it off him."

"Yes." Aviama stared down at it and paused. "But now that I think of it, I probably shouldn't keep it on. I know I'm not using the sifal magic anymore, and only used it for an hour or so, so I shouldn't have negative effects from it. But I don't really need it."

She reached for the bracelet and began to pull it off her wrist. Rana ran forward.

"No, don't—"

Aviama cried out, the burned skin of her hand and forearm lit with blazing agony, as if she'd just stepped into Shiva's flames.

Rana shook her head. "You can't take it off. It melds to you, somehow. I don't think it did before, but if natural melderblood powers mingle with the unnatural, and they're used together ... something about that causes an issue. That's how it's been with mine." She gestured to the stone in her headpiece dangling down her forehead.

Chenzira examined the bracelet and the burns along Aviama's skin. "We'll figure it out."

"Frigibar will know what to do. Maybe we can visit him soon. He was my trainer, my mentor—the last of Jannemar's keepers of knowledge of magic."

Rana opened her mouth to speak, then closed it again. She winced, then cleared her throat. "There are two in Keket. I can introduce you."

Aviama's jaw dropped. "Two?"

But it wasn't the number that surprised her as much as the fact that Rana had just shared a wildly high-value piece of information of her own free will. To Aviama and Chenzira, no less, whom she'd been willing to assist in capturing and watched her brother torture not long ago.

Rana nodded at the scar tissue along Chenzira's torso. "I know an antidote that can clear that up too. I smuggled some on board the *Revenge* before we left."

Chenzira's eyes misted. He blinked hard and swallowed. "Thanks, Kestrel."

Rana cleared her throat twice before giving a stiff nod. She looked away, then gazed up at the shimmering Shamaran Castle at the top of the cliff. "It's beautiful."

Aviama followed her gaze. "I've always thought so."

"Will you stay here now that everything is over?"

Aviama looked back at Chenzira's sister. "Is it over? I mean, you're not fighting us now. But I've been wrong before."

Rana nodded. "I was wrong. What you said about Shiva—the bright, poisonous colors—and listening to you while you drew on the easel. The drawing of your mother. The way you saved the kid. Sutekh never would have done that, and the more I saw how little he cared even about the baby, the more I knew he never cared about me either. Not really." She turned to Chenzira. "I'm still not sure what all happened when you left. But ... I think I'd like to talk about it."

Chenzira sucked in a breath and let it out in one long, rolling sigh that felt like life and breath and growing green things. "I'd like that. A lot."

Aviama could hardly believe it was over. Rana and Chenzira were going to get the chance to smooth things over and work toward answering questions on both sides. Shiva had told the truth about Limakau's sirens, but lied about killing Makana, and now neither Shiva nor his minions remained a threat. The remnants of Sutekh's sailors and soldiers were being sorted out, and after that, Aviama and Chenzira would have to figure out what adventure awaited them next. She had an idea what it might be, if Chenzira was willing. But whatever the future held, she knew it was a future with Chenzira by her side. And that was a future she could dream and live and love for all her days.

But something else needed to happen first. She turned the lapis-lazuli ring on her finger and looked up at the sibling pair.

"While we wait for you two to share stories, Teja and the baby are waiting for us in the Great Hall. And I need to free my sister and most of the castle staff from the dungeons. Want to come?"

Chenzira and Rana exchanged a look, and both turned toward her with glittering eyes filled with the warmth of home and reforged bonds.

"Always."

"Yes."

47

Aviama and Chenzira stood side by side on deck *Storm of the Seas,* the fastest ship among Sutekh's fleet that had still been seaworthy after the events of the Shalladin River battle over a month ago. After Aviama and the others had freed Aviama's older sister, Avaya, and the survivors from among the castle staff, they had waited for Semra and Zephan to return from the front lines where the Iolani had arrived to help finish off the Radhan navy. With dragonlord Queen Semra in the air, Makuakan and Makana in the sea, and King Zephan leading the remaining Jannemari forces on land, Radha's onslaught was crippled.

Jannemar's numbers had suffered greatly, and it would take a long time to rebuild the military to its former glory. But Radha had taken a massive hit, both underestimating the dragon and not expecting the Iolani. Jannemar would be safe to rebuild as Radha licked her wounds, less confident in the seas than they had been before Makuakan made a historic alliance with Zephan.

Aviama had reunited with her family, and her loyal servant Murin, and helped resettle everyone at home and swap stories. Chenzira fell into the family dynamic so comfortably that Aviama almost forgot he hadn't always been there, and by the time the two of them set out again from Jannemar, they left with a litany of promises to return, and a laundry list of unfinished game competitions that would require endless revisiting. The little girl, too, had made friends with all the servants' children, who had begged to have her back to play sometime soon.

The channel out to the sea opened up, and *Storm of the Seas* cruised gently out into the open ocean, a light breeze promising untold adventure. The toddler had begun talking more and more, and Aviama smiled at her as she tugged at the coil of rope Umed was teaching her to fold into various types of knots.

Flying fish shot out of the water beside the ship, and the toddler dropped the rope to run to the railing, clapping and squealing. Sparkling water reflected the brilliant aquamarine blues, valiant goldenrod yellows, and kiss of rose pink of the sunrise as the sun broke the horizon to herald a new dawn. And for Aviama, it wasn't just a new dawn, but a new era. Promise of life anew, filled to the brim with hope, freedom, and the spark of change.

"Sabah. I like it."

Aviama said the name again, once, twice, as if tasting the lovely, pure elegance of it. Chenzira had come up with the name—a name for the toddler girl that Aviama had officially decided to take in as her own. It was a Keketi name that meant "born in the morning," and Aviama couldn't think of anything more perfect.

"Oh!" Aviama slapped the rail with her hand, then wrung it out as the strike stung her palm. "I have a middle name for her. Wait—do Keketi or Radhan people use middle names?"

Chenzira chuckled. "No, but if Jannemari people do, and you have one you like, I think you should go for it."

Aviama took a deep breath. "Okay. I think her middle name should be Bishakha."

"A Radhan name?"

She nodded. "It was her mother's name. I'd like to honor her somehow, and this will be an easy way to explain her history to her as she grows."

The little girl—Sabah—ran to Aviama, and Aviama knelt to receive her with wide-open arms. Sabah jumped into her, and Aviama wrapped her little body close to hers in a bear hug. She stood and whirled the girl around in circles until the little one collapsed in dizzy giggles against her chest. Chenzira plucked her from Aviama's arms and tossed her high into the air against the light of the sunrise, and Aviama thought her chest might explode from the tender joy of the moment.

Nothing was as beautiful as this sight. Not Manan making cheesy heart-shaped water shapes for Sai further down the deck. Not Durga punching Osahar's arm and rolling her eyes at whatever he'd said. Not Zahur waggling his eyebrows at his brother and casting obnoxious sparks this way and that whenever Durga's back was turned.

But this—the family they'd made that felt like home wherever they roamed. The gorgeous man that kissed her good morning before the sun came up and held her close in the evenings until the moon came out. The giggling daughter who called her "Amma"—which Teja had told her was not an attempt at Aviama's given name at all, but the close, familiar Radhan word for "mom."

Even Florian's skulking presence added to the insanity of their new phase of life as he took the wheel for the morning shift. Somehow, the man served as a reminder of all they had been through. Black-market swindlers, pickpocket thieves, legendary ocean passes—they'd survived every single crooked twist and come out the other side all the stronger.

The sea pirate's black hat and red feather bobbed into view, and Chenzira let out an audible groan as he relinquished Sabah to the ship deck and turned to the weasel of a man whom they had permitted to live.

"If it isn't Sutekh's reaver."

Florian gave a dramatic flourish with his hand to announce himself and cleared his throat. "Yes, that's me." He plucked candied ginger from his pocket and popped one in his mouth. "I was wondering if perhaps you'd allow me to keep *Raisa's Revenge* as payment for my services getting the ship seaworthy again in such a short period of time. I see that you left the lady's homeland with only two accompanying ships, and surely you will want to exchange the rabble crew you currently have with a more trustworthy bunch once you reach whatever shores you are headed to."

Chenzira quirked an eyebrow. "Your payment is keeping your head attached to your neck, Florian."

The reaver popped another piece of ginger into his mouth and eyed Chenzira darkly. "Still, you cannot be certain they won't turn on you, and you don't trust ... easily. You don't have the means to crew three vessels."

Aviama leaned into Chenzira and turned to her companions across the ship deck, raising her voice loud enough for the others to hear. "What did I do last time someone threatened my life and the lives of my friends?"

Umed quirked an eyebrow. "Which time?"

Manan and Sai exchanged a glance. "Do you mean the time you took over the *Wraithweaver*?"

"Or when you blew up everything on board?"

"Maybe she means what happened to Abasi." Durga

grinned, and with a flick of her wrist, a sudden waft of air lifted Florian's hat off his head.

Aviama shrugged and turned back to Florian as he leaped after his hat. "I'm not particularly worried."

The pirate snatched his hat out of the air and smashed it back into place with a withering glare in Durga's direction. "Any proper endeavor needs two things: funding and information. I can help. Give me the ship, and I'll provide you with the latter."

"I can help with the former."

All eyes glanced up at the crow's nest, where Rana peered down at them. She leaped down, a gust of wind guiding her descent until she alighted beside Florian and popped an elbow up on his shoulder. "I'm *very* well connected."

Florian shrugged out from under her elbow and brushed the place where Rana had touched him, as if wiping scum from an otherwise pristine jacket. "I doubt you know enough about the circles *I* run in."

"You might be onto something." Aviama glanced at Chenzira, and he gave her a nod. From the twinkle in his eye, he knew where she was going. Aviama turned back to Florian. "Chenzira and I have decided to dismantle the slave trade in Keket. You will be our mouthpiece to all the slavers in the area. When you get back to Keket, tell them they've got a month to head into port and end their business deals. A single day past that, and they're fair game."

Florian's jaw dropped. "You can't be serious. I'll be skinned alive for delivering a message like that."

Flames leaped into Rana's palm, and the bobbing red feather of Florian's hat caught fire. The man yelped, snatching his hat off his head and beating out the flames against his trousers. By the time his hat returned to his head, the feather was half as tall, and the tip of the thing was sadder than a spindly little tree sprout whose leaves had all but withered under a desert sun.

"You're a resourceful man." Chenzira threw his arm around Florian's shoulders. "I'm sure you'll figure it out."

Florian choked on his candied ginger.

Chenzira patted him on the shoulder and paced three paces down and then back. "When Sutekh found out Father planned to split the kingdom up and offer pieces to me, and that he even planned to reserve a portion for Rana, within a week my contacts informed me of a plot on our lives. I knew he'd never stop, and I knew Father would never give up slave labor. Every day became a misery, and I was afraid of what I would become if I didn't do something—what I'd turn to, to escape the pain. I also knew there were others who would die if Sutekh thought I was within reach. With me gone, he'd stop hunting, and I could find a life. A life worth living." Chenzira looked straight at Aviama. "And I found it."

Aviama's insides turned to melted butter, and she smiled.

Chenzira turned to his sister. "I thought you'd be safe to find your own life too. I'm sorry. But I hope now you can find your own way too. For us, with Sutekh out of the way, and the Iolani fending off Radha, there's no better time to go after the slave trade. It's a small way to make up for my failures."

Durga sent a spiral of air up through the rigging and whistling through the sails. "Is the sister coming along on the anti-pirate rampage?"

Rana grimaced and looked out onto the sparkling ocean as the sun spread its rays across the horizon as far as the eye could see.

Chenzira hesitated, then broke the silence. "I'd love the chance to get to know the person you've become. To make things right between us, to mend what was broken. But if you'd like more—if you want to travel with us—I'd love it. I'm sure Aviama would love it too."

Aviama nodded. "You're welcome to join us if you'd like."

Rana gazed far out over the water, but Aviama had a feeling the Keketi princess's mind had taken her someplace else entirely. When Rana spoke again, her expression was set. "I need to sort out what happened to me. Who all were involved in lying to me on Sutekh's dime, and what he did to our mother. If I wait too long, some of those threads may be gone forever. I have to know."

Aviama had watched her mother die and been there when the explosion went off that killed her father. She knew who was responsible, and though seeing justice served could never bring them back, Rana had the answers to mysteries she'd chased all her life that could be right there at the end of her fingertips.

"If there's anything we can do to help, let us know."

Rana dipped her head and drifted further down the deck, and minutes later, Florian had fled to the helm, and the others had returned to their various duties and amusements. Aviama wound her arms around Chenzira's waist and leaned her head on his chest, watching Sabah chase a pebble Teja had thrown down the deck for her.

"Sabah Bishakha. Sabah Bishakha Shamaran doesn't sound so bad. A Keketi name, a Radhan name, and a Jannemari name. Daughter of all the world." Aviama twisted to look up at Chenzira. "What do you think?"

Chenzira gazed down at her as if all the love in the universe was in her eyes and could be obtained if only one looked deep and long enough. "That does sound beautiful. But I thought, maybe, we could add one more to the list."

Aviama arched an eyebrow. "How many names does one kid need?"

Chenzira took her hand, twirled her round in a pristine waltz spin, and when she whirled back toward him, he was on one knee with his free hand holding up a golden ring set with glittering white and sapphire stones. "I'd be honored if you both take mine."

It was impossible not to envision him in her future. She hadn't remembered when it had happened, exactly, but somewhere along the line, he showed up in every hopeful image of the future she could dream up. Whenever she pictured survival, and life, and purpose, he appeared beside her.

But they'd only just escaped death for the thousandth time together. Then again, that made it sort of perfect too.

The ring sparkled up at her, brilliant white gemstones fashioned into the shape of a lily in homage to his mother, surrounded by a halo of sapphires in memory of Aviama's mother. It was too unique, too flawlessly fitting, for him to have picked it up just anywhere.

"How did you do this?"

"My jeweler informant, Bassel, made it. Remember him? I asked him for it when we stepped behind the curtain that day, and when I sent my servant Ozan from the palace to tell the others where we were and that we were captives, I also told him to get the ring for me."

"You're kidding. You asked him to pick up an engagement ring for you while you were about to be tortured?"

Chenzira laughed. "I guess I did, yes. But sand and sea, I knew if I made it out alive, it would only be with you. And I knew that I'd always want to be with you, forever onward, if only you'd have me."

"Biscuits, I think you're the most handsome and romantic person I've ever met in all my life."

He laughed again, and the music of it rivaled the song of the Iolani. "Tally. Focus, gorgeous." He adjusted his position on the ship floorboards and lifted the ring again. "Will you marry me?"

A rush of tingles and butterflies flooded her from head to toe. Aviama squealed like a schoolgirl and threw her arms around him, knocking him to the deck. Chenzira rolled her over and kissed her. Sparks flew from her fingertips and wind rippled over them. The fabric of the ship shook beneath them as his lips moved against hers. He pulled her in like a desert desperate for rain, a warrior claiming victory.

And when at last they parted, both out of breath, and looked up on a ship full of grinning friends pretending not to watch, Sabah stood before them blinking down at the sparkly ring they'd somehow forgotten all about. She giggled and handed it out toward Aviama.

"Amma!"

Aviama pulled her into a group hug with Chenzira and tousled the girl's hair. Aviama plucked the ring from the girl's fingers and slipped it onto her hand. Chenzira's eyes glittered brighter than any gemstone any exotic place in the world could have formed as he took in the sight of her hand in the ring.

"Can I take that as a yes?"

"Did I forget to say yes?"

Chenzira gave her a shove. "You're going to drive me crazy, aren't you?"

"Yes!" Aviama grinned. "To both questions."

Chenzira kissed her soundly on the mouth once more, before Sabah interrupted and planted a kiss of her own on Aviama's cheek.

"Good." Chenzira's voice came as a rumbled murmur against her ear that sent a shiver down her spine. "And while we're on the subject of you saying yes, I have one more suggestion."

Aviama turned to look at him and cocked her head to one side. "I'm listening."

"I think we need to rename the ship, Commander."

"Is that so?"

"It is." Chenzira couldn't help the impish smile that took over his whole face, and Aviama laughed at his excitement.

"Go on, then."

He winked. "I was thinking *Reaverbane.*"

THANK YOU FOR READING!

Thank you so much for reading *Reaverbane,* the 4th and final book of *The Melderblood Chronicles*! I hope you enjoyed reading it as much as I enjoyed writing it.

If you did, would you be willing to leave a review? Reviews help enable authors to continue doing what they do, and help other readers to find books best suited to them.

If you'd like to leave a review on Amazon, scan the QR code.

THE BLOOD & FLAME SAGA

This explosive new dragons and assassins series is about to become your new addiction.

In *The Blood & Flame Saga*, discover how magic returned to the world, meet Aviama and her family, and delve deeper into the secrets that shaped *The Melderblood Chronicles*.

Scan the QR code to start reading.

ABOUT THE AUTHOR

Author of *The Forgotten Stone* and *The Blood and Flame Saga*, E.A. Winters loves pouring a hot chai tea latte and delving into creating epic fantasy worlds for you to enjoy.

Erin lives in Virginia with her husband and two boys. When she's not writing, she sees clients as a Licensed Professional Counselor, and spends time with her family. She loves playing board games and reading, whenever the elusive "free time" opportunity arises.

- Website and newsletter: eawinters.com
- Facebook: facebook.com/eawintersnovels
- TikTok: @eawinters
- Instagram: @e.a.winters

ALSO BY E.A. WINTERS

Blood & Flame Saga

Book 1: Dragon's Kiss

Book 2: Broken Bonds

Book 3: Noble Claims

Book 4: Crimson Queen

The Melderblood Chronicles

Book 1: Melderblood

Book 2: Shadow Caste

Book 3: Wraithweaver

Book 4: Reaverbane

Stand Alones

The Forgotten Stone

Made in the USA
Coppell, TX
08 October 2024